STAR BRIGHT

"Merry Christmas, Kate," Joseph Barsimson said, and handed her a tiny package wrapped in golden paper.

"Oh, Joseph." Smiling, Kate Wendell held it in her hand, then unwrapped it. Lifting the lid, she saw a small golden star, with a tiny diamond glittering at its heart. "The star of your people . . . the star of David . . . it's lovely . . . so delicate."

"It's also your Christmas star." His voice had never sounded so intimate, so gentle. She heard the swift whisper of her own heartbeat answering it as she reached over to touch his strong hand.

And Kate knew then as she would know always that this star was more than a symbol of his heritage or of hers. It was a symbol of the love that would have to light their way across the vast gulf that separated them . . . and guide them in overcoming all the dark forces that so easily could divide them. . . .

THE
CONSTANT
STAR

THE
CONSTANT
STAR

Patricia Strother

A SIGNET BOOK

NEW AMERICAN LIBRARY

PUBLISHER'S NOTE

This novel is a work of fiction. Names, characters, places, and incidents either are the product of the author's imagination or, if real, used fictitiously.

NAL BOOKS ARE AVAILABLE AT QUANTITY DISCOUNTS
WHEN USED TO PROMOTE PRODUCTS OR SERVICES.
FOR INFORMATION PLEASE WRITE TO PREMIUM MARKETING DIVISION.
NEW AMERICAN LIBRARY, 1633 BROADWAY,
NEW YORK, NEW YORK 10019.

Copyright © 1986 by Patricia Strother

SIGNET TRADEMARK REG. U.S. PAT. OFF. AND FOREIGN COUNTRIES
REGISTERED TRADEMARK—MARCA REGISTRADA
HECHO EN CHICAGO, U.S.A.

SIGNET, SIGNET CLASSIC, MENTOR, ONYX, PLUME, MERIDIAN
and NAL BOOKS are published by New American Library,
1633 Broadway, New York, New York 10019

First Printing, December, 1986

1 2 3 4 5 6 7 8 9

PRINTED IN THE UNITED STATES OF AMERICA

*For My Grandfather
Harry White English*

Acknowledgments

I am indebted to Harry and Maureen Baron for the loan of the exciting *ILGWU News-History, 1900–1950*. I also found helpful *The WPA Guide to New York City; New York Panorama* (Pantheon Books, 1984); and *Israel Observed* (Oxford University Press, 1980).

Author's Note

I have tampered with actual chronologies and events, in minor ways, for the sake of this story.

Most of the characters are imaginary, but there was a boy named Harry Gladstone who pulled a strike at the age of twelve, unaided by "Joseph Barsimson"; the "Jewish firebrand," Clara Lemlich, also was once alive and real.

Although I was deeply inspired by the incomparable International Ladies' Garment Workers' Union, this is in no way its actual history. I would not have the temerity to attempt that.

PART I

Kate and Joseph

Chapter 1

Two by two the girls and women formed an orderly line in front of a tall white building on the northern edge of Washington Square. Their skirts brushed booted ankles, but their faces, under broad-brimmed hats, reddened from November cold, were less demure. The women looked rebellious and determined. They pointedly ignored the sullen policemen who lounged below the portico of the bleak white building.

Eight stories over Washington Place a sign on the corner of the building identified the Triangle Shirtwaist Company as the occupant of the top three floors.

Some of the marchers carried cardboard signs tacked to slats, others wore theirs over their bodies—broad paper strips extending from the right shoulder across the bosom to the opposite hip, emblazoned with the legend "Triangle Shirtwaist Makers' Strike."

Most of the women and girls were garment workers, but not all of them worked for Triangle. They had come from sweatshops throughout lower New York, from jammed and airless shops on Allen and Essex and Chrystie streets, from littered, grubby cells on Waverly Place where young and old sewed elbow to elbow for eighteen hours a day, at three to five dollars a week, making the clothes for New York, and America, to wear.

The picket line on that November afternoon in 1909 had been forming, in a sense, for decades—ever since the first

Jewish and Italian immigrants had been crowded into tenement-house shops to sew for a living from early in the morning until late at night. The workers were mostly women; some of them worked with babies on their laps, stopping only to snatch a meager meal. Young children carried heavy bundles of finished clothes to the factories, staggering beneath the weight.

The garment union—born nine years ago—was the true beginning of the workers' hope, the spark of their rebellion. And now a strike of two hundred women employees of Triangle had exploded into a sympathy walkout of thirty thousand factory girls. The conditions in the factories were even worse than in the tenement shops—at least there the workers were among their families, where they could sing once in a while or make a bitter joke. In the factories there were bosses to yell at the girls as if they were black slaves, and talking was considered a waste of time.

On the Monday past, November 22, 1909, thousands of workers had gathered to debate a general strike. The crowd at one of the several great mass meetings, held at Cooper Union, unanimously voted to strike. When the news reached the other gatherings, the workers were fired with desperate zeal. And the first general strike in New York's needle trades began.

Many of those who marched today were not even workers: New York women from every segment of society, incensed over the misery of the workers, angered at their manhandling by police and thugs, had joined the fray. Wellesley College students had collected a thousand dollars for the workers' strike fund; society women such as Mrs. Oliver Belmont were frequent visitors to the Jefferson Market Courthouse, posting bail for the girls who were arrested. College students and professional women marched in the picket lines, coached by Miss Mary Dreier of Brooklyn, president of the Women's Trade Union League.

Two of the young women in the line this afternoon were obviously from that contingent. Their clothes, though dark and austere were subtly different from those of the workers. Their suits were finely tailored; they wore leather gloves and well-made boots; the condition of their fresh skin, their shining hair, testified to generations of good food, spacious, aired rooms, and watchful care.

One of them was very tall. At five feet, seven inches, Kate Wendell resembled the Gibson Girl of a decade before. She had an austere, regal manner, and towered over her companion by half a foot. Her Dutch ancestry was patent in her corn-gold hair, small, straight nose, and startling blue eyes. Narrow from corner to corner, her firm lips seemed about to bud.

In striking contrast, the dark young woman beside Kate looked like a wise and frivolous French doll. Rose Nathan's brown eyes matched the dark luxuriance of her hair; her body was volumptous where the other's was slender, and her features had a piquant sharpness, revealing ironic humor.

One of the workers, the "Jewish firebrand," Clara Lemlich, started to sing. The others took up the song, to the tune of the old familiar "East Side, West Side," until most of the girls and women were singing lustily, "And we shall ring the death knell of the sweatshops of New York."

Over the marchers' singing Kate Wendell heard one of the policemen say, in a high, metallic brogue, "Here comes that troublemaking Hebe."

Kate felt her hackles rise. Afraid that Rose had overheard the remark, Kate glanced at her friend. Rose's large-brimmed hat hid the top half of her face but her generous mouth was visible. Kate saw it tighten.

The two young women had met at Barnard College, where both were students. Rose's family boasted the famous poet Emma Lazarus, whose passionate sonnet to the "huddled masses" adorned the Statue of Liberty; the suffragette Maud Nathan; and the prominent Annie Nathan Meyer, who had founded the women's college Kate and Rose attended.

They were oddly matched companions, Kate a remote

Saxon princess and Rose an intellectual coquette. What could not be seen by the naked eye were their likenesses—their earnest ideals, their stubborn ambition, their fervent sympathy for the oppressed. Rose had visited the sweatshops in the company of settlement-house women. Kate had never set foot in one of the shops, but she had studied sketches of them in *Leslie's Weekly*—drawings of frail women bent under the load of sacks of garments, little boys and girls ironing pieces of jackets or bowed over sewing, toddling infants crying while their desperate parents worked on in resigned and feverish haste to turn out the garments quickly, quickly enough to be paid the few dollars they needed so badly. The drawings had been enough to convince Kate. She was an artist herself; they had fired her with more than compassion. The drawings had inspired her to seek more significant subjects for her own brush and pencil.

And now she smoldered at the policeman's comment. To distract Rose, Kate shivered and said, "It's getting cold."

They had both left their fur coats home in deference to the working girls on the line. Kate's mother had noticed her wearing the dark gray cloth coat and observed, "You look like a worker in one of those dreary settlement houses. I hope you're not turning into a bluestocking, Kate." Kate had replied that furs were a nuisance in the overheated stores, and that she was only going shopping.

"Look, Kate," Rose said abruptly. "There's Joseph Barsimson. He was the one who really started this strike, not Gompers. I wish you could have heard him at the Cooper Union."

Kate saw a tall man in a black overcoat approach from Greene Street. His collar, turned high against the cold, met his rakish cap; his almond-shaped eyes shone like chips of anthracite. He had an arrogant, almost Spanish look. He moved along the line, calling marchers by their first names, lifting his gloveless hand in defiant salute.

Kate felt a peculiar quickening in her body.

She heard the policeman speak again as they paced by him: "Handiest Jew I've ever seen. Knocked my cousin Sean right on his ass, Sean with his head like rock and mitts like great hams. Barsimson's damned dangerous!"

Kate had never thought of Jewish men as "dangerous"; they were rabbis and scholars, delicate poets like Rose's friends or boyish socialists at the Liberal Club. She had never seen *any* man like Joseph Barsimson. He was tough and muscular beyond the power of the Gentile boys in Kate's circle, Yalies and Harvard students with crew awards and boxing prizes. He was nothing like the Wendell relatives, stolid Dutchmen of the Hudson Valley. Yet for all his hardness, Barsimson's features were finely drawn. There was a proud fire in his black eyes.

"He looks like a Spanish grandee," Kate murmured to Rose.

Rose smiled. "He is, in a way. His people are Sephardim, Spanish Jews, like mine. We're distantly related. All the Sephardim are." Kate remembered what Rose had told her about the reticent, tight-knit Spanish Jews. They considered themselves the "royal Jews"; a group of them had arrived in America even before Kate's people had.

Two policemen were abreast of them now, one of them the man who had called Barsimson a "Hebe."

Kate heard his partner say, "Doesn't look like a fighter. Not much heft. Not a mark on him."

That was true enough. Barsimson was slender; his long, aquiline face didn't look like a pugilist's.

The first patrolman retorted, "That's why he's dangerous. Too fast to get marked up."

"We call Joseph the fighting scholar," Rose murmured.

"You know him, then?" Kate tried to sound casual.

"Oh, yes. The family doesn't 'recognize' his family, though. They're the 'poor branch.' " Rose's tone was ironic. "We met at the Liberal Club, on MacDougal Street. You know."

Kate thought: The one time I went to the Liberal Club

with Rose, he wasn't there. Joseph Barsimson came toward them.

Rose smiled. "Hello, Joseph." She introduced Kate.

Glancing up at him, Kate marveled at his unusual height: he was well over six feet tall. Most people with Spanish blood were shorter, like Rose. Kate had to tilt her head back, to the imminent peril of her velvet hat, to look into his eyes.

He did not seem so remote. As soon as their glances met she was conscious of a quick change in his expression, a surprised stillness. Barsimson took a quick, ragged breath.

Staring into his deep black eyes, Kate felt as if she were sinking into their glitter. The eyes no longer reminded her of hard coal.

He still hadn't spoken.

Kate was so dismayed by his silence she nearly broke her step. Her own breath stopped with surprise; she felt strangely exposed and vulnerable.

She swallowed over a pulse in her throat that beat like wings. "Mr. Barsimson."

"How do you do, Miss Wendell. You're very good to come," Barsimson added. He grinned. "Maybe you ladies will give us some extra insurance against trouble . . . like Mary Dreier."

Kate grinned back. "Wasn't that outrageous?" she demanded. By now everyone involved in the garment strike knew the story of a policeman's embarrassment when he arrested the president of the Trade Union League "by mistake," having taken Mary Dreier for a "mere" factory girl.

Suddenly Barsimson bore no resemblance to the stern grandee of moments before. His smile, which uncovered two faintly overlapping front teeth, changed him. The minor flaw relieved the almost awesome perfection of the mobile mouth, those austere features.

"Coming here is the best we can do, Mr. Barsimson. These women have suffered so much, and so long—"

"What's this now? What's all this?" An abrupt, harsh bellow broke into Kate's reply, made her jump. There were loud yells from farther down the line; Kate saw a dozen huge, rough men emerge from Greene Street.

Barsimson frowned, involuntarily moving closer to Kate.

"We've got some gorillas," he muttered. It was a good name for them, Kate judged. They looked subhuman. Her flesh prickled with unease. She remembered what she had read about the gangs and scab protectors who had beaten strikers half to death, hitting the helpless girls, jerking them so hard their arms were almost pulled from their sockets.

Everything began to happen very fast. Two of the thugs rushed on the line and shoved the girls in front of Rose and Kate.

Kate gasped, her throat too tight to scream, horrified that the police were doing nothing to stop them.

Joseph Barsimson cursed and grabbed one of the strike-breakers by his coat collar, jerking him backward with such force the man's thick neck almost snapped on his monstrous shoulders, and Kate saw the sullen policeman moving toward Barsimson with his billy raised.

There were screams, and the line had fallen into chaos: events moved so rapidly and terrifyingly that Kate could hardly register their sequence, but in the roiling mass of people she was dimly aware that the other gorilla was attacking Barsimson. Barsimson's fist smashed into his jaw, and the second man fell, knocking the policeman off his feet.

Then Barsimson yelled to her and Rose, "Are you all right?"

Kate was too afraid to speak; her vocal cords seemed to be paralyzed. A couple of girls behind her had fallen, almost knocking her down, too, in a grotesque domino effect, but before it could happen Joseph Barsimson took Kate's arm and dragged her across the street out of the melee. He pulled Rose, too, until they were out of danger. Barsimson ran back to the line.

Suddenly a dozen policemen appeared from nowhere; in

the wild confusion it was hard to tell exactly who the adversaries were; it seemed to Kate that some of the police were shoving the strikers, not protecting them.

She saw a policeman raise his billy club and smash it down on Barsimson's back as he struggled with one of the thugs. That awful crack of wood on bone was the most sickening sound she had ever heard. She stood rooted to the spot in horror, holding on to Rose, without the slightest idea of what to do. She couldn't take her eyes off the nightmare scene.

A mass of scratching, screaming factory girls were struggling in the grasp of the policemen. Whistles blew. A troop of mounted policemen appeared, cantering in from the west; the strikers began to draw back, intimidated by the enormous horses.

A sinister-looking carriage, solid black, rumbled down Washington Place, and the policemen began to haul the girls into the vehicle's open rear. They were shoved inside with such force that one of the smaller women fell to her knees.

"I can't stand this any longer!" Kate shrieked at Rose, who was staring numbly at the scene. "Where can we go?"

Rose seemed to come out of her trance. She shouted back, "Let's go to the park. I've got to sit down."

Kate realized that her legs were trembling so they could not support her much longer. Yet she peered into the melee more, hoping to get a final glimpse of Joseph Barsimson. He was nowhere to be seen.

Clinging to Rose's arm, she turned and walked with stumbling steps into Washington Square Park, surprised that her legs were able to move. The two women sank down on a bench near the middle of the park, where the noise of the riot was softened a little. Crowds of curious people hurried toward the northeast corner of the square.

Rose shuddered. "It was horrible. I can hardly believe

it. Reading about things and seeing them are very different matters."

Kate nodded. "Like the sweatshops. You saw them firsthand, and I only read about them."

Rose touched her arm. "I didn't mean it that way. It's only natural for me. My whole family is involved in things like that . . . always has been. I know how hard it is for you to get away, Kate."

It certainly was, Kate reflected. Practically impossible. She was running out of excuses to give her mother. But she had to get away, to see what the real world was like.

"I'm freezing," Rose announced. "why don't we go get some tea? There are lots of cafés on MacDougal."

"Why don't we go to Grandfather's?" Kate suggested. "You can see his new paintings. He's not doing portraits anymore, did you know that? The new pictures are . . . well, you'll just have to *see* them."

Infected by Kate's eagerness, Rose grinned. "I'd *love* it. I was just waiting for you to ask."

They rose. Looking back, Kate saw that the sidewalk in front of the Triangle was almost deserted now.

Rose followed her glance. "They've taken most of the women away, I suppose . . . over to the courthouse. Sixth Avenue will be a mess. Why don't we walk up Fifth?"

Kate assented, not deceived by Rose's casual tone. She knew her friend was as shaken as she was by the horrors they had witnessed, but that was Rose's style. Kate noticed with amusement that the stiff-upper-lip manner was not, after all, confined to Gentiles, as her parents seemed to think. The Wendells thought of Jews as highly emotional, almost hysterical people. Despite her outer calm, there was pain in Rose's eyes; her lips were twisted in a sad smile.

"Kate, I was scared to death back there," Rose confessed.

"You weren't the only one," Kate retorted. "I've never fainted in my life, but for a minute, I thought I might." She hesitated, then went on, "We were lucky Mr. Barsimson was there." Once again Kate was assailed by a peculiar tremor. She couldn't forget the first quick meeting of their eyes. She had never seen eyes so glittering, so black, or a man's face that had such strength and power. "Is he really related to you?"

"Yes." Rose nodded. They had reached Tenth Street. "Thank heaven, only one more block."

"Have you known him long?"

"Joseph? Oh, no, just a few months. As I said, he doesn't move in our 'exalted' circles."

Kate could hear the ironic quotation marks in Rose's comment. She decided to drop the subject, because Rose was staring at her.

"At last!" Kate said as they turned onto Eleventh Street. They hurried down the block toward the southwest corner, where they ran up the stoop of a narrow red Georgian house. Kate rang the bell.

An immense black woman with grizzled hair stood at the opened door, her broad face full of welcome.

"I saw you all coming. Lord have mercy, get in this house. You girls look cold as little frogs." She practically pulled them into the warm foyer, her black dress rustling under a pristine apron. "Where in the world have you been?"

"Up to no good, Letha." Kate hugged her.

"It's sure good to see you, child. You, too, Miss Rose. Give me your things, now, and then you run up and see your granddaddy. I'm too fat to climb them stairs again. He's up in his studio. I done climb the stairs already to take him his cake and coffee. There's plenty for you all."

Rose beamed. Both she and Kate were used to Irish servants, and the exotic black represented all that was pleasantly strange in the house of Harry Dryver.

Kate paused in front of the console mirror to smooth her hair. The blue eyes staring back at her seemed twice their usual size; they sparkled. Her mouth looked full and foreign. She wondered how she had looked to Joseph Barsimson. That thought, and the warmth of the hall, combined to cause sudden redness in her cheeks. She caught sight of Letha's curious eyes reflected in the mirror.

"Miss Kate, you up to something," Letha commented.

A prickly dew broke out between Kate's shoulder blades. Embarrassed, she pulled her shirtwaist away from her skin, gave a final shake to the full sleeves flattened by her coat and jacket. "How's your 'mis'ry, Letha?"

"It'll be better when it quits hurtin'." The old woman's laughter ended in a wheeze. "Mr. Harry got me another gal to help me out. But you all, run on now."

"Maybe we should wait," Rose offered. "I don't want to bother him when he's working."

"What you talkin' about?" Letha demanded. "He been up there all the morning, 'cept when he came down to talk to the postman about that ruckus over there. Did you all see it?"

Kate and Rose exchanged glances. "Yes. It was terrible," Kate said, not wanting to go into the rest of it. She could just imagine what Letha would say.

"Mr. Harry'd skin me alive if I didn't send you all right up. You all know you're the apple of his eye."

Relieved that Letha hadn't pursued the subject of the picket line, Kate pressed Rose, "Let's go up."

Rose followed her up the stairs past the first, then the second landing. A bit breathless, they reached the top floor, went down the hall toward the street side of the house, where a door was ajar.

In the studio they blinked under the brilliance from the wide skylight: the sun was out again in all its force.

Kate's grandfather, Harry Dryver, stood before the rough wooden device that served him as an easel, rapidly working with a thick brush on the representation of a tall white building with a Doric facade. On the sidewalk in front of the building was a line of young women walking two by two.

"Why, it's the line!" Kate blurted.

Dryver chuckled. He put the finishing touches on the

building and retorted, without turning around, "I might have known you revolutionaries would know what *this* is. I was there the first day."

Then he sighed, put down his brush, and turned around. "Hello, Kate, Rose. It's wonderful to see you both. I heard your voices."

His dark eyes shone, Mephistophelan in his fine-drawn face. He always looked a bit drunk to Kate when he painted, drunk with excitement, and she felt a quick rush of love, of utter awe in the presence of his creation.

"It's wonderful," she said softly, staring at the painting. Glancing aside at Rose, Kate saw that she, too, was gazing with admiration at the painting of the line. Harry Dryver had captured all the vitality and hope of the marchers, the defiant tilt of female heads, the quickness of their steps; the painted skirts swirled about the girls' ankles as if they were even now in motion. "I can feel the wind," Kate murmured.

"Then I've gotten it, maybe," Dryver remarked with his usual modesty.

"*Maybe!*" Rose repeated. "It's alive. It breathes and moves. It's just the way it *is*."

"Ah-*ha*." Dryver grinned at them. "So that's where you've been today. I might have known. Sit down, both of you, and let me give you some coffee."

Oh, dear, Rose had done it now, Kate thought. She herself might not have told him; she realized she should have discussed it with Rose before they came.

She sat down beside Rose on the Recamier couch that her grandfather used for his models, murmuring thanks when he handed them mugs of coffee.

"Help yourself to cake. And tell me what happened over there. All I have is the postman's version, and he's no *raconteur*. But I gather it wasn't exactly . . . peaceful," he concluded dryly with a glance at Kate.

He looks Jewish, Kate decided suddenly, with his black eyes and hawkish nose, his thick handlebar mustache.

There was a kind of sad gaiety, a raffish confidence about him. And she realized that Joseph Barsimson had reminded her of her grandfather; maybe *that* was why he had affected her so strongly.

"Kate?" Dryver prompted.

She gathered her wandering thoughts and replied slowly, "Well, it certainly wasn't peaceful." She told him exactly what had happened, all of it—the thugs' sudden entrance, the roughing-up of the girls, the arrests, and the unsympathetic attitude of the police toward the strikers.

Dryver shook his head. "It's always the same. You remember that quote in the *Tribune* . . . the policeman's? 'We ain't here to take care of the strikers.' " He smiled a one-sided smile; then he sobered. "It's dangerous, you know, for you girls. It's a miracle you weren't hurt."

Kate felt her cheeks grow warm again. "We were rescued by one of the union men," she mumbled. Her grandfather studied her keenly.

"Joseph Barsimson," Rose supplied. "He's a general organizer for the union."

"I see." Dryver spoke in a noncommittal tone, but Kate sensed he was still observing her. "Well, that was very fortunate." He got up, poured himself another mug of coffee, then resumed his seat on the stool. "I take it that Howard and Elizabeth weren't in on this."

Kate grinned. "You take it exactly right." She knew what her mother would do if she found out—she would faint. She always fainted when anything upset her, more, Kate suspected, to gain attention than from actual weakness. And how her father would rage!

"Good Lord!" They both looked at Rose. "I've got to call Mama. My cousin was on the line earlier and saw me there, so Mama must know by now. She'll think I'm in jail . . . or the hospital."

"By all means," Dryver said.

Rose excused herself and hurried out. They heard her running down the stairs to the first floor.

"Well, well," Dryver commented with a smile, "I see my Black Lamb is living up to her title."

The Black lamb was Dryver's private name for Kate, the Black Sheep her sobriquet for him. Her agnostic grandfather knew he had sown the irreversible seeds of rebellion in Kate. Even though he was a successful portrait painter who had gained an international reputation, Harry Dryver was an *artist*, and therefore suspect to Kate's parents, Howard and Elizabeth Wendell. Her father treated Dryver with courteous respect, but she had the feeling that her father and his associates looked on Dryver the way busy roosters would observe a bird of paradise. And Kate's mother would prefer not to be reminded that Dryver was "one of those artists" rather than something less sensational. Elizabeth Wendell also took her father to task for continuing to live in the house on Eleventh Street after his wife's death. Greenwich Village, Elizabeth maintained, was not what it had been. The nice people were moving out to leave the area to the bohemians.

"But I *am* a bohemian," Dryver protested, to Kate's delight. He seemed to love the Village more than ever, now that so many young artists and rebels were moving in, and he was a regular at the "revolutionaries' " cafés as well as at the stately Salmagundi Club, where the more academic painters looked askance at his new themes and technique.

When Kate had decided to go to Barnard instead of a more conventional girls' college, Elizabeth had given in with ill grace. That had been bad enough; the news that Kate planned to follow in Dryver's footsteps and pursue a career in art upset both her parents. The idea of Kate's sketching unclothed men in life classes nearly sent her mother into hysteria.

"Yes, indeed." Kate grinned. "I'm adding up demerits. Now I'm adopting your politics as well as your profession."

"Never mind the politics, darling. That's all very well, and I admire you for your convictions. But in a hundred years not many people will know what the Triangle was. On the other hand, they'll still be looking at Rembrandt and Renoir. And while we're on the subject, how are you doing with Livermore?" George Livermore was the drawing master at Barnard.

"Better," she admitted. "I've taken your advice, and I'm showing him the 'proper respect.'"

"Good. He *is* your teacher, you know. The fool's an absolute machine and he has no grasp at all of what I'm doing. But he's one of the best draftsmen in the world, Kate, and you can learn from him. When your drawing meets his standards, you'll have the basis for departure from it." Dryver chuckled. "Even *I* had to learn to draw," he added with self-mocking arrogance.

Kate laughed. Her grandfather was such a paradox that no one was ever bored in his presence. Even now his mercurial temper swayed and settled into another mood; his expression grew serious.

"About this business today, Kate . . . I don't—"

They heard Rose's footsteps in the hall, and she came into the studio.

"What's the news?" Dryver asked Rose.

"Not good." She plumped down on the couch, making a sour mouth. "Mama's livid. Even Aunt Maud was upset . . . Maud, of all people. She said it wasn't this dangerous when she was chaining herself to buildings to get the vote." Rose gave them her one-sided smile. "Both of them said Papa will go up in smoke."

"Oh, that's awful." Kate put her arm around the smaller woman's shoulder. "I never thought *your* family would react this way."

"A family's convictions don't always extend to allowing its daughter's involvement," Dryver retorted. "Mine don't extend to your activities today, Kate."

She stared at him, shocked. He was always sympathetic toward causes like the strike.

"Anyway," Rose said dolefully, "they've positively forbidden me to go back to the picket line."

"Oh, *Rose*." Kate stroked her friend's arm, knowing how much the strike meant to her.

"In any case," Dryver consoled her, "there probably won't be any line tomorrow."

"Why on earth not?" Kate asked.

Her grandfather stared at her. "Have you forgotten? Tomorrow's Thanksgiving. You *are* preoccupied, Kate."

Kate flushed, feeling like an idiot. She had been preoccupied, indeed, ever since she had met Joseph Barsimson. Thoughts of him had intruded, again and again, during this visit with her grandfather. First, seeing his resemblance to Harry Dryver . . . then the reminder of him in the painting of the picket line . . .

Rose got up, saying something about the holiday. ". . . cousins from out of town. Mama wants me to be at home to greet them."

Dryver stood, too, and took Rose's hand. "Of course. It was good to see you, child. I hope you'll come more often." He bent to kiss her cheek.

"Thank you, Mr. Dryver. I *love* the painting."

Kate rose, too, and kissed her grandfather. "I should leave with Rose. I told Mother I'd be shopping, and by now I could have bought up Fifth Avenue and Broadway together. Anyway, we'll be seeing each other tomorrow. At the Palace," she added, using their name for the Wendells' stately house uptown.

Dryver chuckled. "Definitely . . . the day when even the blackest sheep are taken into the fold." He hugged Kate. "You're a wicked child, after my own heart."

When the two were outside on Eleventh Street again, Rose suggested they take the el at Eighth Street, saying it would be quicker than a cab.

Kate agreed; the rattle of the el would enclose her in privacy, discourage conversation. She could review to her heart's content this landmark day, this day of peril and excitement, her first glimpse into a real and brutal world. The day she met Joseph Barsimson.

As they walked down Sixth Avenue, Kate glanced across

the street at the Jefferson Market Courthouse, where the strikers had been taken. With its gables and turrets, its belfry and balconies, the old red building had always reminded Kate of a Gothic castle. It looked strangely peaceful now. She wondered if Barsimson was still there. She could not forget that in the midst of all that danger he had concerned himself to see that she, a stranger, would be safe.

Chapter 2

Joseph, walking west on Eighth Street, heard the shriek of the el's departure.

He was achingly tired, sore in every muscle. When he had taken the two society girls across the street and ran back to the line, the battle was at its worst. He had had to take out two more strikebreakers, despite the influx of police. In fact the cops had been more hindrance than help; his back still pained from the blow of that bastard's club. Two of his knuckles were split, his face was cut, and his body throbbed from blows the thugs had gotten in before he could take them. He had butted a couple of them with his shoulder, and that hurt too.

Joseph turned into MacDougal Street—only three more blocks to his apartment, to a hot bath and some food. He hadn't had a chance either to tend his stinging flesh or to eat, what with the courthouse, the lawyers, the trip back to the union hall. It had all gone by so fast.

He trudged wearily past Washington Square, hoping he wouldn't run into any of his friends; he didn't feel talkative. He kept to the east side of MacDougal to avoid the Liberal Club.

All Joseph could think of right now was that girl Kate Wendell. He had never had any traffic with upper-class women, Gentile or Jew. Little Rose was the first rich Jewish girl he had met, and somehow she didn't count. He found her perpetual earnestness tiring.

He thought he had never seen a woman as beautiful as Kate Wendell, not up close. The wings of her pale blond hair, her huge forget-me-not eyes, the mouth that seemed to be . . . newly blooming.

Joseph crossed MacDougal Street and went in the shabby building that housed his apartment. Mounting the stairs, he quickened his step, like one of the police horses, he thought dryly, trotting faster when it neared the stables at day's end.

The fourth-floor hall was warm, and when he let himself into the flat, it was even warmer. Its coziness gratified Joseph. It wasn't much but it was sure as hell warm in the winter. He would never forget the drafty rooms on Essex Street.

Joseph rubbed his hands, threw off his cap and over-coat. His cheek and knuckles hurt like sixty. He shouldn't have neglected them this long. Going into the closetlike bathroom, he took down some salve from a shelf that served as a cabinet, and began to cover his injuries.

Suddenly, the thought of food was repellent. But he had to have something; he hadn't eaten since morning. He went into the kitchen to check his provisions—a bottle of soda water, some coffee, the hardening oblongs of a ko-sher salami, a loaf of pumpernickel. Joseph smiled, recall-ing his mother's perpetual query: "How do you do for yourself there, Joseph? Do you eat, *tateleh*?"

"Occasionally, Mama," he answered her now, aloud. He cut away some of the hard salami with a big, efficient knife; sliced the pumpernickel, bit with difficulty into the tough, dry sandwich. Still, he'd be damned if he'd go to a café. He was in no mood for company tonight. He had too much to think about, and wanted to go over the plans for tomorrow. Besides, he didn't have the money to eat out.

Joseph filled the pot to start coffee, thinking about the girls on the line. Damned good girls, with a lot of heart, plenty of *chutzpah*. Joseph smiled. They learned so fast. And in many ways some of them were better organized than he was; they could talk to women about women's problems.

And he knew that even after today, they would still be ready to go back tomorrow. When he had addressed the meeting at the hall, they had all shouted that they were "sticking to the union," holiday or not. The bosses wouldn't be there, but they would tell the public tomorrow, by God, with a show of strength.

Not that they would miss much at home, anyway. Few of them had enough money to buy a turkey for Thanksgiving. That realization filled Joseph with gloom.

"Dammit," he whispered, "they'll have turkeys for their Christmas . . . they'll have their Hanukkah."

With renewed determination Joseph searched his overcoat pockets for his small notebook. While they were waiting for the judge at the courthouse, he had scribbled down some plans. Now, after the meeting, he had to make some additions and revisions. But when he started reading over his notes, all of a sudden he began to feel a mighty torpor. He went back to the kitchen and turned off the gas under the coffeepot. Then walked on shaky legs to his bedroom and stretched out on the unmade bed. The day had taken more out of him than he had realized. And still, sleep was the last thing he wanted.

He was haunted by the image of that girl, Kate Wendell.

Joseph had literally had no time for women in his twenty-three years, aside from a random encounter with a willing factory girl or one of the talkative, wearisome proponents of this new "Free Love." Even those had been few and far between. He had always been left with gnawing guilt when his partner experienced deeper emotions than his own. He could not often afford the impersonal safety of sporting women and shrank from getting a girl in trouble. His mother, Anzia, always urged him to get married, but that was even worse. It would be years before he could afford to; in any case, no one had inspired in him an urgent desire to marry, so far. He had a feeling it would have to be someone like Kate Wendell.

Besides, after years of eighteen-hour days, Joseph wanted more than anything just to sleep at night. At twenty-three he had already put in eleven years, one way or another, with the union. In 1898 Joseph had joined a fifteen-year-old "basting puller" in at East Side sweat-shop, Harry Gladstone, and helped organize boys and girls of the trade. At twelve, Joseph was the youngest member of the seventy-five-member union. During that time Joseph had been working fourteen to fifteen hours a day with his parents in their tenement flat on Essex Street. The head-quarters of three striking tailors' organizations was just a few doors away from the Barsimsons' flat, and that was where the children's union met.

Harry Gladstone and Joseph Barsimson, the "boy agita-tors" of the East Side, called a strike and won an agree-ment with the bosses in August 1898. That was the beginning of Joseph's union career.

He smiled at himself, reflecting with irony that he put in more hours with the garment union than he ever had in his own parents' shop. Yes, what he wanted most at night was to sleep. He forced himself to close his eyes, but the images of the long day would not let him rest. And he knew tomorrow would be just as long. He would have to be at the union hall to see that things were set up properly, address the workers again, and then join the line.

Kate Wendell would probably never come back. He had never met anyone who made him feel the way she did. He felt as if he could hardly breathe when he was around her; she was so beautiful she hurt his eyes. He was a dreamer, "lusting after a strange woman" from the scornful world of pale-haired, pale-eyed people. She probably hadn't been able to see his brains or pride; likely all she had seen was a shabby, troublesome Jew—just what that hostile cop had called him.

Kate looked like the princess in a fairy tale who could feel a pea under twenty mattresses . . . that was just what she was, Joseph concluded. Someone out of a fairy tale;

someone to look at, like a lovely picture that had nothing to do with life as it really was.

And the Kate Wendells of the world had nothing to do with *him*. His work and life were all mapped out already, and they didn't include a fairy-tale princess.

Thanksgiving afternoon was gray and cold, but it made no difference to Joseph or the other strikers. Even with the factory closed they had to be on the line today, to show the city they were not beaten by what had happened yesterday. Joseph jammed his hands into his pockets; he ought to get himself some gloves. The clock on the outside of an opposite store read four. They would stick it out for another half-hour.

At least the day had been peaceful, which was something. From his vantage point Joseph could check out the whole situation: many of the girls were carrying the signs they had hastily assembled last night at the hall, lettered with such slogans as "HUNGER TAKES NO HOLIDAYS," "WE CAN'T BUY TURKEYS," "THANKFUL TO BE OUT OF JAIL."

There were very few policemen on duty—a good omen—but the few who were present seemed especially resentful about their assignment to this holiday stint.

Although the factory was closed, and there were no conflicts with scabs to worry about, Joseph had instructed the marchers to keep to the usual rules for picketing—don't walk in groups of more than two or three; don't stand in front of the shop, but walk up and down the block; don't shout. There would be no singing today to disturb the peace. They were all too cold, too subdued and grim.

Nevertheless a mild holiday relaxation could be sensed in both the strikers and the police; no one wanted any trouble. Everybody wanted to get the day over with and go home to get a little warmer; they were sure to be back to business as usual tomorrow. The girls moved somewhat wearily this afternoon, and now and then one or two bought pretzels from the vendor who, muffled up to his shovel-shaped beard, his cap pulled down over his eyes, was their roving canteen.

Joseph bought one too, and ate it hungrily, wishing he could get a cup of coffee. Police regulations forbade a coffee stand near the line, and there was very little available at the hall today. On ordinary days the society women brought in food and coffee, but most of them were involved with their families on Thanksgiving, he supposed.

His eyes began to water from the rising wind. When Joseph turned his head away, he blinked with amazement to see Kate Wendell walking quickly toward the factory from Fifth Avenue, carrying a heavy-looking basket. She looked earnest, excited, and incredibly beautiful, dressed in another simple cloth coat of navy blue. In the cold gray light the somber color pointed up her golden fairness, emphasizing her pure white skin, the astonishing blue of her eyes.

Kate Wendell smiled at him. For a minute he couldn't move. Then, seeing her struggle with the basket's weight, he hurried toward her to help.

"Thank you," she gasped, and smiled again. "This is *heavy*."

Joseph said, "I didn't expect to see you . . . not after yesterday."

"I'm so contrary, it just made me more determined."

Joseph thought his heart was going to hammer his chest to pieces but he had to laugh at her pronouncement. "What's in the basket?"

The pink color of her cheeks deepened. He decided her perfect skin looked like a white flower petal with a flush of rosiness. Her golden lashes veiled her eyes for an instant as she looked down. A minute before, she had reminded him of a young queen; now she almost seemed like a child.

She looked up again and answered in an offhand way, "Well, it *is* Thanksgiving, so I thought I should bring something. There's mince pie and some turkey sandwiches."

"That's so kind of you," he said fervently.

"Shall we pass them around?" She giggled nervously. "I don't know how on earth I'll serve the pie, without plates or forks. That just occurred to me."

He looked in the basket. "You have napkins here; we'll just wrap the slices of pie in those. Nobody's going to worry about table manners today, when we've got no tables."

He carried the basket for her along the line while she handed out the sandwiches and pie. To her dismay, there wasn't enough left for Joseph.

"Oh, dear, this is awful," Kate said, looking chagrined.

A sudden impulse made him ask, "Why don't we have dinner together? I can eat then. We'll break up in a half-hour."

"It might be difficult," she said softly.

He cursed himself for being so hasty. After all, the girl hardly knew him. "I guess you think I have a lot of gall."

"Oh, no! It's not that . . . it's not that at *all*." Her disclaimer was quick and earnest. "You see, I'm . . . on French leave." Her eyes sparkled.

"My Lord." She had run off from her family, actually sneaked away, on this of all days, to join the line.

"Oh, well, as my grandfather says—he's a painter— 'in for a sketch, in for a mural,' " she declared. Joseph grinned. "I *would* like to have dinner with you. Very much. Meanwhile I'll join the line."

Joseph made an awkward bow as she walked away and got into the line beside another marcher. He noticed with admiration how naturally she did so, how easily she began to talk to the workers beside her.

And a peculiar apprehension mingled with his elation; what was he getting himself into? This line, this strike, was his whole life, and here he was going out to dinner with a society girl from another universe, a girl who couldn't possibly grasp what it was all about. But if that were true, what was she doing here in the first place, in the cold, on Thanksgiving Day? This girl was such a paradox she fascinated him.

* * *

Joseph led Kate east but he hadn't yet asked her where she wanted to dine. A hollow dread formed in his stomach. He didn't have very much money. "Where would you like to go?" he asked her.

"How about Marie's? We're not far away."

"Marie's?" He couldn't hide his surprised relief. He could cover that. Marie's was a casual artists' café on Broadway and Tenth Street. He would never have imagined that Kate Wendell would know of its existence.

"My grandfather's taken me there many times," she offered in answer to Joseph's unspoken query.

"You said he's a painter."

"He's Harry Dryver. We've gone to a lot of places like that together. He lives right here in the Village on Eleventh Street," she said.

"Good Lord," he said explosively. "Harry Dryver! He's one of the best painters in the *world*. Why, his portraits are . . ."

They were already on Broadway, heading toward Marie's Café.

"I suppose you couldn't know," she broke in, "but he's given up portraiture. He's painting very differently now. He just did a painting of the Triangle line."

"The *line*?" Joseph was delighted. He listened closely to her description of the painting.

"I saw a man in it who looked like you," she blurted.

Joseph looked down at her, observing the flush on her cheeks. A wild idea came to him: had she come downtown today to see him? No, it was too unlikely. And yet . . . she had consented to dine with him.

A thunderous wave of Bach made them glance across the street. The organ music came from Grace Church. That's where she belongs, he thought, not out here with a shabby Jew. The church's stonework was almost like lace, its pinnacles, piers, and crenellations as delicate as a castle from a fairy tale.

She followed his glance and murmured, "My grandfather says that sometimes he thinks even Bach and Michelangelo can't compensate for religion's crimes.''

Joseph was oddly touched and excited. He thought of the other church, whose Inquisitors had driven his people from Spain. He and Kate Wendell—and her grandfather—had something in common. ''Your grandfather sounds like quite a man. I'd like to meet him.''

He was immediately embarrassed, realizing the implications of his statement, but she did not look affronted. Far from it. Kate's astonishing blue eyes, when they locked with his, had a warm expression.

Joseph felt more confused than ever, and not a little weak in the knees. But he was hungry. When they entered the café the smell of food revived him. Once their food arrived he could hardly contain his ravenousness; Kate barely touched her sandwich but drank several cups of coffee. He thought it might be his imagination, but she seemed to observe his hunger with something like tenderness.

They started to talk and he found himself opening up to her as he rarely had to anyone; her interested questions, her sympathetic eyes drew him out. And he told her about himself, from the drab beginnings on Essex Street to his brief boxing career and the early union work.

She marveled, ''You were *twelve* when you started the jacket strike?''

''That's right. I started early,'' he admitted, smiling.

''Good heavens. Twelve.'' She was incredulous.

''How did you get involved in this strike?'' he asked.

She pondered the question with a seriousness that utterly charmed him, then began slowly, ''I think it really started years ago when I heard my grandfather arguing with my father about the sweatshops. I sided with my grandfather; I always do.'' She smiled. ''We're the renegades of the family, you see. We've always been very close. And then . . . one thing led to another. I met Rose at Barnard, and other people who got me interested in trying to do something about all that misery.'' She paused, then added shyly, "Rose told me you're a kind of cousin, and you're both Sephardim . . ."

He stared at her, bemused, and nodded.

She went on in a soft voice, "Your people were scientists and scholars while mine were still scratching around in caves, or wearing horns on their helmets, pillaging and ravaging." She spoke with dramatic emphasis. "Before they became dull upstate Dutchmen, that is."

He had to smile at her solemnity, the melodrama of the her description. She pursed her lips in a comical way, and Joseph wondered what it would be like to kiss them, to run his hand over that satiny face. . . . To find out what her body felt like.

It made him sweat to wonder that. Just to have something to say, he asked suddenly, "How did you manage to get away this afternoon? From the sound of things, your parents are hardly in sympathy with your views."

"You're right about that." She chuckled. "Well, I pretended to have that old standby, a 'dreadful headache,' " she confided. "With any luck, my mother won't look in on me before evening. They were going visiting after lunch."

He registered her fashionable way of referring to Thanksgiving dinner, and waited for her to continue.

"I went out the back way after I heard them leave. The servants were very curious about the pie and sandwiches. But they won't talk." She grinned impishly and Joseph decided that she had probably bribed them. What an alien world she lived in, he reflected. She said, "servants" so matter-of-factly; she had extra money for bribes. How different her life was.

Her glance touched his face and she murmured, "You were hurt yesterday."

"It wasn't much," he said lightly. He looked away from her with an effort: he had to get hold of himself. Her voice stroked him like fingers, her concern reached right inside him. No woman had ever affected him that way. It was one thing to find her lovely and desirable, but this feeling was something else altogether. He had better keep talking. "Really, Miss Wendell, it wasn't much at all. Others had it a lot worse."

She took a quick, deep breath. "Please . . . call me Kate."

"Then you'd better call me Joseph."

She nodded. Her cheeks reddened, and her amazing eyes darkened. The color of her eyes reminded Joseph of vivid Egyptian faience he had seen in a museum, or the rich blue velvet on which the Torah rested in temple. Everything about her brought ancient, holy images to mind. He couldn't understand it.

He was silent for so long that she made a restless motion in her chair. "It's getting dark," she said. He couldn't read her tone. Turning to lift her coat from the back of her chair, she shrugged herself into it before he could help her. She spoke as she put on her gloves. "I must go. They're bound to miss me."

Joseph inclined his head. His throat was too tight for him to speak. He did not want her to go. But he rose and paid the bill, put on his coat and cap, and followed her out into the gathering night.

While they walked he felt a touch of desperation: time was running out. There was so much he burned to say; if he lost his chance now he might not get another.

"Kate . . ."

She slowed her step and looked up at him. With delight, and a strange, paradoxical dread, he saw expectation in her eyes, in the shape of her mouth.

Speak, fool, he told himself. "This has been a wonderful evening for me," he said. It sounded inadequate, banal. But he saw that even that comment made her glow. His very loins felt heavy with a desire.

"And for me, Joseph," she answered softly, in such a low voice he had to bend his head to hear. He realized he had no idea where they were heading. He had been thinking about putting his arm around her, not daring to. Thinking about it so hard that everything else had gone right out of his mind.

"I don't even know where you live," he blurted. "Would you like me to put you in a cab?"

"I'll take the el, or a motorbus," she said quickly. He suspected she was saving him embarrassment, in case he tried to pay for a cab.

"You can't do that at this time of night. I won't let you," he said sternly. "How far is it?"

"Madison between Thirty-sixth and Thirty-seventh."

His heart sank. Madison Avenue in the Thirties was the neighborhood of Italianate mansions, the bastions of the rich. J. P. Morgan himself lived in that area. "That's too far for you to go alone. There are all kinds of . . . mashers and people like that. Let me go with you"—he caught her look of consternation—"at least to your corner."

"I'd like that." She smiled up at him; her impish smile warmed him all over. It was getting cold, too; they quickened their pace and soon were climbing the stairs to the el station at Eighth Street and Sixth Avenue.

Joseph paid their fares and said, "Let's go inside so you can keep warm. No need to stand out here in the wind."

Kate laughed. "No need at all. The train sounds like a small earthquake when it's coming." She walked to the potbellied stove in the middle of the station and stretched out her gloved hands to it. Another woman and an old man were warming themselves on the other side of the stove, and both stared at Kate with admiration.

Joseph thought: She probably affects everybody that way. She's like the sun in a summer sky, all blue and golden. He was mystified at his sudden lyrical turn of mind; he had never been a poet. His feet had always been planted firmly on the ground—at least, until now.

Finally the floor beneath him began to vibrate and the train rumbled in. The brief journey north was all over too soon for Joseph: sitting by Kate's side on the blessedly crowded train, he was ignited by the feel of her warm body next to his. It was hard to talk above the rattle and roar, which was just as well. Joseph would have had a hard time putting two consecutive thoughts together.

If only time could slow down, he reflected, and stretch these minutes into hours and days, moving as slowly as honey from a jar. But for now it was enough to enjoy the accidental contact of her arm, the slender roundness of her as they swayed together from the movement of the train.

When they reached her station, he held out his hand to assist her. Kate's hand, in its thin leather glove, felt incredibly small and very warm. A white-hot, jagged bolt of excitement struck him at the touch. As they descended from the platform, the racket of the departing train filled his ears, and Joseph felt his sense of command deserting him.

He had never ever seen this neighborhood, only read about it in the papers. It was truly another world, with its ordered, stately rows of mansions, and its quiet streets, where you couldn't imagine anything ever *happening*.

In a kind of suspenseful quiet they walked toward Thirty-sixth Street and turned east. Kate's happy, easy manner was gone, Joseph noticed. There was tension in the posture of her neck, in her whole slim form. Maybe she was worried about her parents seeing her with him. From the way she had talked, she was at odds with her family about a lot of things.

"My house is right over there," she said in a muffled voice, indicating a mansion on the avenue's near side. It looked intimidating, with its dark stone facade; oddly, its lights did not make it any brighter. By the lamplight Joseph could make out decorative bands and panels of carving, arched windows and rosettes—features he had seen only in architecture books.

"I'll say good night, then." He was so unwilling to see her go that he had to force the words out. "Do you . . .do you think you might come back to the line tomorrow?" He was instantly dismayed at his choice of words. "I mean, when may I see you again?"

"Tomorrow, Joseph. Tomorrow, absolutely." She held out her hand.

He squeezed it tightly in his. Then he raised it to his mouth and pressed a fervent kiss on her gloved palm. He watched her eyes change until they were as bright as blue tongues of flame.

Slowly Kate withdrew her hand and gave him one long, final look before she hurried off and was swallowed up in the shadows of the entranceway. Joseph stared into the shadows. They embraced her the way he did not dare to. He envied the shadows as Romeo envied Juliet's glove.

Some Romeo—he must be *meshugeh*. The el fare had taken the last of his money. And Kate Wendell lived in a mansion . . . on a block with only two other houses.

A block with three houses, Joseph marveled, thinking of the tenements on Essex Street that were jammed so close together you could hear someone sneeze next door.

He trudged to Fifth Avenue and started the cold hike downtown. All of a sudden Joseph remembered the look in her eyes after he had kissed her hand, and what she had said: "Tomorrow. Absolutely."

Nothing else mattered.

Joseph swept off his cap and threw it high into the air. He caught it as it fell, and oblivious of the stares of elegant, suspicious passersby, basked in the warm borrowed light from stately houses.

Chapter 3

As she crept into the mansion's cellar entranceway, Kate could feel her heart pound. She imagined her fingers were still tingling, warmed by the touch of Joseph Barsimson's lips. She didn't use the street door for fear her parents had returned. But she knew, as soon as she opened the door, that they were not in yet. The door to the big kitchen was ajar and the servants were noisily enjoying themselves. If her mother were upstairs they would never let themselves go like that.

Kate grinned in the semidarkness of the hall, sniffing the strong odors of beer and baking. She unlaced her boots, took them off, and padded up the stairs in her stocking feet. She slipped past the kitchen, catching a blurred glimpse of scrubbed tiles, polished coal scuttles, and the long table covered with white oilcloth with six or seven servants seated around it.

Near the top of the stairs, Kate's heart was almost in her mouth when she heard the cook demand, "Go check the door, Mr. Lynn. I think I heard something."

But to Kate's relief the butler responded, "Nonsense, Miss Wood. You fancied it."

Kate raced up the rest of the stairs, through the Gothic dining room with its imposing family crest, its ornate furniture and profuse gilding, and into the main entrance hall. Running lightly upstairs to the bedroom floor, she reached the shelter of her room at last. Her luck was remarkable.

45

To get her breath, she leaned against the closed door and studied the pastel room with its sky-blue carpet and ornate bed whose *couronne-de-lit* draperies touched the beaded molding along the ceiling; the ivory-colored tables and chairs, the soft *chaise* with her nightgown spread over its foot.

It seemed like a stranger's room tonight: the Kate who had left it was not the same Kate who had returned.

She heard a commotion in the lower hall. Her parents were back.

Like lightning she ran to the closet and snatched off her clothes, throwing them in a heap on the floor, along with her discarded boots. By the time she heard her mother's voice at the door she had already put on her nightgown and was under the covers.

"I'll just look in on Kate a moment."

With her eyes squeezed shut and her face turned toward the windows, Kate heard the door open and her mother's stage whisper, "She's asleep." The door closed again. There was more muffled talk from the hall: "If she's not . . . tomorrow . . . the doctor."

Kate decided she had better look bright in the morning. Otherwise, they would send for the doctor or keep her indoors. She heard her parents go downstairs, and felt a touch of remorse for causing her father to worry. Her mother wasn't really concerned, Kate was sure. Kate detested subterfuge, but she had learned long ago that it was the best way of dealing with her mother.

Lying back in the carved bed, bathed in the light from a silk-shaded lamp, Kate quickly forgot her guilt. Now that she had the leisure, she could relive her evening with Joseph Barsimson.

She recalled every word he had spoken, and each caressing look. At times she had felt his eyes kiss her while he spoke. Kate traced the shape of his face from memory; the black of his eyes, that sudden uncharacteristic smile that made him seem so vulnerable. It had pained her not to be able to invite him to the house, and she hoped he had understood.

The worst pain of all, she realized with utter amazement, had been saying goodnight, having to walk away from him. She had never experienced romantic love; she had always loved Harry Dryver, but that was not the same thing. In all this time, only two of her bland escorts had ever had the temerity to kiss her. Those kisses had had no effect at all. And yet, when Joseph Barsimson had merely kissed her *hand*, her whole self had thrilled and responded. It was a new and alien feeling.

For all the chatter about "Free Love" at school and in Greenwich Village, Kate was still as ignorant as she had ever been of love between men and women. So was Rose, she suspected. They had told each other they would never marry. Rose wanted to be a teacher or a writer; Kate of course was devoted to her art.

At least she always had been, but now she was not so sure. All she was sure of was that she wanted to be with Joseph. She wished he could be with her now, in this very room. She wanted to listen to him, to look at him; to have him kiss her mouth as he had kissed her hand.

I wonder if I'm another Marite, Kate reflected. It drove her mother wild when Harry Dryver called Kate a "latter-day Marite." The painting of Kate's scandalous ancestor had been relegated to the downstairs hall, while the more respectable relatives hung in the drawing room. After more than a century Marite was still unforgiven: for in 1770 she had eloped with a Jew, Dryver had told Kate. Another rebel.

All his life her grandfather had gone against his proud, aristocratic English family's strictures. Dryver came from a long line of scholars and judges and men who had pursued the more "practical" arts of engineering and architecture. But when Harry Dryver had returned from the obligatory Grand Tour of Europe, where he had been sent to study Old World buildings, he was resolved to become a painter. And while the portraits he painted had been acceptable enough as a specialty, there had always been a satirical, Goyaesque quality to his representations of the great; some small feature of each portrait managed to comment on the sitter's emptiness or pomposity.

One of Harry Dryver's favorite devices was a twist on the traditional background behind rigidly posed figures; generally an upper corner of the canvas opened on a landscape of clouds and classical architecture. In Dryver's portraits of great men and ladies that corner frequently opened onto a desolate wintry landscape of vacant, barren trees with limbs like predatory claws. Nevertheless the unsuspecting buyers were enchanted with his portraits, because he had the skill of a Whistler or Sargent when it came to depicting the sheen of pearls, the richness of furs and velvets, the fiery brilliance of gems. If he caught an expression in the sitter's eyes that was revealing, it escaped most viewers' notice; after all, Dryver had captured magnificence, and that was what he was paid to do.

When he was far too young, Harry Dryver had met and married an even younger Southern girl with an unacceptable background, over the protests of his disapproving and violently abolitionist family. He could afford to laugh at the family disapproval. By that time he was an extremely successful portrait painter. Kate's grandmother, Jenny, had had two stillborn children, then finally her mother, Elizabeth. With Elizabeth's birth there was a family reconciliation. Early in her life, Elizabeth fell under the influence of the Dryvers, so much so that by the time she was eighteen she chose to marry the well-connected Howard Wendell, who was already prominent in real estate. Despite the suspect occupation of her father, Elizabeth was welcomed by the ancient Wendell clan; in all other respects the Dryver name was unimpeachable.

Kate knew her beautiful Grandmother Dryver only from pictures; Jenny had died soon after Kate was born. Even though she was very small, Kate had seen her grandfather's loneliness. He visited the Wendells often, or Kate was taken to visit his house on Eleventh Street. Sometimes he would stand with her in the little garden behind his house, and tell her that if they were very quiet, they might be able to see the elves who painted the flowers just before dark. They never caught sight of the elves, but Kate knew they had to be there.

Her grandfather gave her a whole different view of life than that of her parents. Harry Dryver was also the one to lift her from her crib when she cried, the one to bring her special presents and wonderful things to read. He gave her her first paint box, and was overjoyed when she showed a precocious talent for coloring.

When she was old enough, he gave her a book called *The Light of Asia*, the life of Buddah in verse; later, *Progress and Poverty* by Henry George. Her father was furious when he caught her reading the latter. Kate learned early on that her grandfather, whom she adored, and her parents, whom she did not, would always be politely at war. Her grandfather loved her without qualification; her mother seemed to love her when she obeyed. Her father, Kate decided, would never love her no matter what she did. She had overheard something when she was twelve that explained it—her father was terribly jealous of her. When Kate was born her mother had apparently transferred all her affections, all her hopes, to her daughter. And it was still that way, Kate thought.

Elizabeth Wendell, in her turn, was jealous of Kate's love for Harry Dryver. What a burden it was—Kate wished her mother could live her own life, instead of living it through a reluctant daughter.

But I will live my own life, Kate vowed silently, just as Grandfather did. Starting tomorrow.

Thinking of Joseph Barsimson, Kate repeated aloud, and very softly, "Tomorrow."

Chapter 4

Kate's anticipation woke her early. By the time her maid, Eileen, came in with her coffee, the tumbled clothes in the closet already had been properly hung and Kate was at her table sketching. Eileen looked startled to see Kate up at that hour.

Kate grinned at her. "Just put it anywhere," she said. She covered the sketch, which was of Joseph, with a blank sheet when Eileen placed the coffee on a corner of the table. "How did Jerry like the dress?"

"He said I looked like a queen." The girl colored with pleasure. "All I had to do was take up the hem a bit." Eileen picked up Kate's nightgown from the chaise and shook out its creases. "Everything . . . go well for you yesterday, ma'am?"

"Very well indeed. Thanks to you."

"I came up twice." Eileen hung the nightgown in the closet. "Miss Wood sent you one of her special remedies. I poured it in the sink and took the cup back."

Kate chuckled. "I'll be sure to thank her, Eileen. My headache is *so* much better." They gave each other a conspiratorial look and Eileen's blue eyes twinkled.

When she was gone, Kate closed her sketchbook and put on one of the dresses her mother favored. She examined herself in the glass. Good: she looked alert, bright, and well.

Her father and mother were sitting at opposite ends of

the table in the family dining room, immersed in the newspaper.

"Good morning," Kate said cheerfully. They both looked up with surprise. She usually didn't come down for breakfast on holidays.

"Someone's early today," her father commented with a tight, artificial smile. Kate felt a faint pity for him; he did try so hard to like her. She considered kissing him on the cheek, but Kate knew that if she did, her mother, who seemed almost psychic, would know that something had happened to her. So instead Kate answered as warmly as she could, "Yes. I'm feeling *so* much better."

She sat down as Elizabeth rang for another setting.

"You didn't dress warmly enough Wednesday," Elizabeth said triumphantly. "I *told* you, Kate."

"You were right as usual, Mother."

The wry admission mollified Elizabeth, but she grumbled, nevertheless, "Someday you'll learn, I suppose."

Kate let that pass. While the servant set her breakfast before her, she covertly studied her parents, who had progressed to the coffee stage and resumed their reading. Her father and she looked so much alike that it was startling; his large blue eyes, however, had a look of resignation she hoped hers would never show. He was an extraordinarily handsome man, with his noble head, straight nose, and neat mouth.

If opposites attracted, her parents had certainly married well. Elizabeth Wendell was quite dark, with the almost Satanic black eyes of Harry Dryver, and his fine facial bones. But her nose could only be described as "snub." It gave her an impudent, rather naughty look which was far from unattractive—what Kate's grandfather described as the "devil's beauty," which had been so prized during the last century.

"Would you like some of the paper?" Howard asked Kate, belatedly polite.

"Yes, thank you. The front page, if it won't interfere

with you," she said, smiling. Kate was eager to see if there were something in the *Times* about the strike.

Her father detached the business section and handed the rest of the paper to Kate. "The same old nonsense," he declared. "Wars and rumors of wars, disasters and peasant uprisings in Greenwich Village."

Kate restrained herself and glanced eagerly at the front page. Nothing special today, she noticed.

Elizabeth remarked in her high, sharp voice, "It's outrageous. Those . . . barbarians making such a disturbance right next *door* to Papa's house. Maybe this will convince him to move to a more civilized neighborhood." Her dark glance flicked at Kate.

Refusing to take the bait, Kate ate her scrambled eggs and turned to the editorial page.

"Well." Howard Wendell touched his lips to his napkin and rose. "I must be off." He'd said that every weekday morning since Kate could remember. And once again she felt that odd, new pity for him. Why now, all of a sudden? she wondered.

Because her emotions had all been vitalized, newly opened. By Joseph Barsimson.

Kate was glad her mother was still occupied with the society pages; otherwise she was sure Elizabeth would be able to read her thoughts.

"If I live to be a thousand," Elizabeth began the variation of a refrain Kate had also been hearing for years, "I still won't understand why you take that train, Howard, when we have two cars."

"Nonsense, my dear." Howard Wendell kissed his wife on her cheek. "It's the city's most efficient means of travel. Mark my word, there'll soon be a thousand miles of track underground, too, and not this measly two hundred we've got now. And I intend to have a piece of the pie, Elizabeth. Besides, a car's a damned nuisance downtown. You know that. All the best fellows ride the train."

"And I *have* to, Mother," Kate defended her father.

"Otherwise it would take me two days to get to school."
She chuckled. But immediately she realized her mistake.

It was a perfect opening, and Elizabeth took it. "You
wouldn't *have* to, you know," she retorted, "if you went
to Miss Hewitt's or some proper school, where you could
be driven like a young lady."

"Bye-bye, Kate," Howard said hastily, and went out to
the hall for his hat and coat.

Elizabeth sighed and shook her head, leafing back through
the newspaper. "These little purses at Saks are charming.
They'd make splendid Christmas presents. Why don't you
come along with me and have a look at them? And you
need some more evening gowns for the holidays, Kate. I
want to get that out of the way before the stores get too
crowded."

"I can't, Mother, I've got to study. We have some tests
next week," Kate said quickly.

"Right after Thanksgiving? Fiddle-dee-dee. You can study
tomorrow, or Sunday." Elizabeth looked impatient. "Your
clothes are more important . . . and have more to do with
your future . . . than that idiotic school. I won't have you
turning into a bookworm, Kate, not with all your beauty."

"I'm sorry, Mother. I really must study today," Kate
responded firmly. "I'm behind on my assignments for
Professor Livermore."

"Artists!" Elizabeth sniffed. "They're all immoral."

"Even Grandfather?" Kate countered.

"I won't have your insolence, young lady," Elizabeth
snapped. "Certainly not your grandfather. And don't correct your mother." She got up and flounced out of the
room.

Kate regretted her unkind remark. She needed to keep
the peace now more than ever; Elizabeth was at her most
psychic when she was offended. Kate finished her breakfast and went back upstairs to her bedroom. She could hear
Elizabeth giving irritable directions to her maid from the
master bedroom down the hall.

Waiting until she heard her mother go downstairs again,

Kate changed into dark, plain school clothes. Listening at the door, she gave her mother time to come back for a forgotten item, then went to the window to watch the car drive off before she got into her outdoor things and went downstairs.

She rode a double-decker motorbus down Fifth Avenue, sitting on top. From there New York City was a blur, the people's faces less than real. Disembarking at Eighth Street, she caught sight of Joseph, towering over the others, before he noticed her. He looked tense, preoccupied; he was talking to two other men who wore union badges on their coats. Then, in his survey of the picket line, Joseph recognized her.

A sudden brightness sparked his eyes, and yet his expression puzzled her—it was as if she had come into existence at the moment of his seeing her. The men with him looked at her admiringly. Joseph murmured to one of them and started toward her.

She walked toward him, suddenly shy in their first public encounter after the moment of closeness the night before.

"Hello," he said, smiling.

Kate responded immediately to his deep, rhythmic voice—it touched her like his hands.

"You came to walk with us again."

I came to walk with you: the words suddenly shamed her. She knew now with utter certainty that it was for him, and not for the workers, that she had come. Her selfishness in the face of their desperate plight struck her with dismay, leaving her speechless for a moment.

But she contrived to answer, "Of course. I keep my promises."

That dark brilliance lit his eyes again, relieving the tension in his fine-boned face. "I believe you do." The look lasted only an instant before he said quickly, "I've got to get back. Maybe you'll walk with Elvira, the girl back there, at the end of the line. She doesn't have a partner."

"Of course," Kate took her place beside a small, thin girl with frizzy hair, her heart still pounding from the brief contact with Joseph. "Hello, Elvira. I'm Kate."

"Where do you work?"

"I'm a student. I came to help," Kate said.

Elvira shook her head in amazement. "I sure wouldn't be here if I were *you*."

It was not Kate's idea of "workers' dedication," but she kept quiet.

"Damned scabs!" Elvira's sudden outcry made Kate jump. "Keep goin' in, keep breakin' our backs."

Kate saw a group of girls, huddled together like scared rabbits, approaching the factory door. They had an escort of uniformed police and a couple of men in overcoats and bowlers.

"Who are those men with the police?"

"Shop bosses," Elvira hissed. "We don't got enough trouble from the cops, they got to have the bosses, too."

The girls on the line called out, "Please don't go in! We've got to stick together!" Elvira added her voice: "Stick with the union!"

"Stand back! Coming through, coming through!" A policeman raised his billy club and the line parted to let them through.

Kate and Elvira had to stop to make a pathway for the scabs.

One of the bosses shouted at them, "Keep moving!"

The order was so stupid it made Kate's blood boil. "Well, make up your mind! We can either let them pass or keep moving . . . we can't do *both*!"

But she wished she had kept quiet: the boss had a huge neck and mean little eyes like an angered bull. He looked her up and down. "Who asked you? Keep moving. You're obstructing my sidewalk."

Some devil made Kate retort, "It's not your sidewalk. It belongs to the people in this city."

Elvira was tugging at her coat sleeve. Kate saw Joseph coming toward them. An unwilling smile tugged at his mouth, but it didn't extend to his eyes. "Easy, ladies. Keep the line moving."

Kate complied but she was shaking with anger.

"You gotta watch your mouth," Elvira said. "We can get pinched for what we say. Like if we call those bitches scabs, to their face. And we touch even a sleeve, a button on 'em, and the judge'll say it's 'technical assault.' "

"That's not fair!"

"No kiddin'." Elvira's smile was sour. "Oh, they won't hit *you*. They'll take it out on us."

Chagrined, Kate couldn't find a word to say. The line was quiet, though, as the morning stretched toward noon.

The pretzel man appeared. In his long dark overcoat, with his hat pulled down over his eyes, he reminded Kate of a character from a Russian novel. "Would you like a pretzel?" Kate asked Elvira.

"Well, yeah. Thanks." Elvira sounded grudging.

They munched as they walked. When the clock across the street tolled twelve, Elvira said, "I gotta go. My mama's sick and I gotta make her dinner." She walked off abruptly.

Kate saw Joseph approaching out of the corner of her eye. "I can take a few minutes," he said quietly. "Let's walk over to the square."

She consented gladly, relieved at the thought of escaping the dreary line, though she could sense the others watching them leave together.

As they walked into the square, Joseph asked her, "Did everything go all right at home last night?"

She looked up at him. His eyes belied his casual tone, but she kept her voice light. "I stole in like the best of thieves, undetected." When they sat down her arm brushed his. She felt the same astonishing electric crackle from the contact that she'd experienced when he'd kissed her hand. There was a faint tremor in her words when she added, "I managed to invent something else this morning—I'm supposed to be sketching, for a school assignment."

Joseph had smiled when she'd first spoken. Now he

looked somber, thoughtful. "You go back to classes Monday."

"Yes."

"That's just as well, Kate. The strike's getting rough. It's going to get rougher. You're better off in class." He spoke in a rush, like a man who was always pressed for time.

"But I'm not afraid," she protested.

"I know that." His grim face relaxed into a brief grin. "I heard you giving the shop boss what-for. But it's dangerous, Kate."

"Elvira told me they'd take it out on the girls. It's not fair," she cried out. "We're all human beings."

The anthracite darkness of his eyes softened. "We know that. They don't. Anyway, you're not the same as the girls, Kate. If you want to help the strike, why don't you help at the union hall? You could do more for us there. You're an artist; you could help with the signs. You're a reader, so you could think up slogans. There are a dozen things you can do better than walk in the line. That's like assigning a skilled tailor to carry bundles."

His sudden smile was infectious. He made good sense; Kate realized how persuasive he could be.

"No wonder you stirred up the strike." She grinned at him. "There's no way to argue with you at all. I think I'd like that. When do I start . . . and where is it?"

"We're open every day, from seven in the morning until midnight." There was delight in his voice, and relief. She was warmed by his concern for her safety, and her heart thudded.

He gave her the address. The hall was just off Union Square.

"I'll come tomorrow," she promised.

Joseph started to speak, when they heard a commotion from the direction of the factory. He got up and blurted, "I've got to go." He grabbed her hand and squeezed it hard. "I'm sorry, Kate."

After one long look he strode off toward the northeastern border of the park, his loping stride as quick and purposeful as a greyhound's on the run. Kate watched him until he disappeared from view.

She sat in the tree-dappled sun for another few moments, thinking how strange and different Joseph was from all the other men she had known—except Harry Dryver, of course. Only he and Joseph had that single-minded fire, that noble preoccupation that set them apart.

She thought of Joseph all the way uptown, smiling at her own naiveté. Expecting him to take up just where they had left off last night. Another man would. Joseph wasn't that kind of man; he had no time for luxuries. She couldn't picture him flirting or acting on impulse, either. Joseph would always hold something back, and that very quality fascinated her.

He was nothing like that Southern boy who had proposed to her the second time they met. Mounting her front stairs, Kate remembered how outraged her parents had been. Harry Dryver, who was used to Southerners, had been amused and called the boy "very dashing."

As Lynn opened the door for her, Kate heard her mother call out irritably, "Is that you, Kate? Where *have* you been?"

Elizabeth came into the hall, giving Kate's austere clothes her usual disapproving survey.

"I went for a walk," Kate answered calmly, starting up the stairs.

"Just one moment, Kate." She paused on the stairs.

"I should get back to work, Mother."

"Very well, but you've got to promise me you'll get fitted for your dresses tomorrow."

Kate's heart sank. There was probably no way out of it; she had been putting it off for two weeks. "All right, Mother."

The fittings ate up Saturday, and Sunday was just as bad—mandatory church, visits afterward. The Wendells didn't get home until four. Resigned, Kate went to her room to finish Livermore's assignment: capturing figures in motion.

She sketched the strikers, and Joseph. The exercise brought her even closer to him. But she worried that Joseph would conclude that she had only been gratifying a whim, that the whim was over now. She had indicated she would be at the union hall on Saturday morning. On Monday, Livermore raised his brows over her choice of subject, but he was obliged to compliment her drawing. She was determined to go to the union hall on Tuesday.

Union Square was at its most depressed. Where fine theaters and hotels had once stood, there was a row of burlesque houses, shooting galleries, and shoddy stores. The old Union Square houses had been converted into tenements, housing thousands of needle-trade workers.

The union hall was in a small, grimy building. Kate climbed three flights of rickety stairs and found herself in a noisy, chaotic room thick with cigar smoke. Her entrance went unnoticed. She approached a dowdy woman sitting at a table by herself, speaking into a telephone. The woman hung up and looked at Kate. "Yes?"

Kate explained her business.

"Joseph? You want the Waistmakers' office. Over there. Ask for Martin." She nodded toward a cramped corner where a young man with glasses and a frizz of curly hair was seated at a table with four girls. They were working on posters.

"Ready, Ruth," the dowdy woman called out to a thin, younger woman, who elbowed Kate aside to pick up piles of leaflets.

Kate went over to the table. She waited until the young man lettered the final E of "HOME, SWEAT HOME" and stated her business again. Martin ran paint-stained fingers through his great froth of hair. He looked quite revolutionary.

"We can use you. Got to do all those by six." Martin pointed to a stack of blank cardboard rectangles leaning against the wall. "Are you fast?"

Kate's face felt hot.

He laughed. "Sorry. Can you letter fast?" She nodded. "Fine. Get started." He went back to work. She located a wall hook for her coat and hat and picked up a poster cardboard. He hadn't said a word about *what* to letter.

Kate dragged a stool to the table and began to work. She patterned her first sign on one of the others—"WE'RE STICKING"—and lettered it neatly and fast. Watching what the others did, she leaned it against the wall to dry.

What next? Then she found herself listening to an exchange between a well-dressed young man and a group of girls—he must be a reporter, she decided—and heard him ask, "You mean to hold out?"

There was a clamor from the girls. One voice rose over the others. "Hold *out*? You just look. You'll see."

Kate's next sign read "LOOK! WE'RE HOLDING OUT."

She heard another girl say, "I got no kick. The girls what got a kick made three and four a week."

Kate lettered "I GOT A KICK—THREE A WEEK."

By five o'clock she had finished twenty signs. She ached all over from working on the backless stool, but her heart was high. She was helping with the struggle. She couldn't wait for Joseph to see what she had done. He had to show up soon; he always checked in at the end of the day.

Kate glowed when Martin said, "You do good work," but she was getting nervous now about being so late getting home. Nonetheless, she wasn't going to leave until she saw Joseph.

It was six o'clock when he arrived. Kate spotted him at once in the group of men; he looked weary, harried, and grim, and he didn't even see her for some minutes. He spoke words of encouragement to several of the girls, conferred with the dowdy lady, and then started toward her corner.

A quick brightness lit the sad darkness of his eyes, and he smiled broadly. "Kate. You came," he said. "I'm glad to see you."

He greeted the others.

The sight of Joseph gave Kate the same quick lift of the heart that she always felt when she saw her grandfather. But this emotion was a thousand times more powerful; it was shot through with a bright ache that was alien to her.

"This girl gets things done," Martin told Joseph, indicating the row of signs along the wall.

"You did all that?" Joseph marveled. "That's amazing."

She nodded and flushed, feeling absurdly proud. "Yes. But I . . . must go now." She retrieved her hat and coat from the hook and put them on."

"I'll walk with you," Joseph murmured. "It's getting dark."

Self-conscious, she said good night to Martin and walked out with Joseph. They were silent until they reached the teeming street. "Will you take the el?" he asked her rather awkwardly.

"Yes." As they walked west she was sharply conscious of his lean height beside her, the way he moderated his long stride to better match her step. For the first time in their acquaintance, Joseph seemed at a loss for words.

They were almost at the el station before he spoke. "I owe you an apology, Kate."

"What for?" She was bewildered.

"For thinking you had . . . changed your mind," he admitted. He stared down at her earnestly, his fine face troubled.

They walked on again, and she murmured, "I will never change my mind, Joseph." The crack of rifles from a nearby shooting gallery drowned out her words, and he bent, asking her to repeat them.

He took her arm; his fingers closed around it. She felt a dart of lightning-heat along her flesh and their gazes locked once more.

"You must never walk on this street alone in the evening," he said firmly. The protective tenderness in the words made her heart leap.

When he put her on the train, his eyes still spoke for

him. All he said aloud was, "Thank you, Kate. Thank you."

She knew he was thanking her for more than the neatly lettered picket signs.

From that evening on Kate was grimly resolved that nothing would keep her from being with Joseph. He had not mentioned another meeting, but Kate knew it was because he was unwilling to take her for granted, to presume that his concerns would intrude into her daily life. If only he knew, she thought, how much of her life was already bound up in him.

What her grandfather had once told her was true: caring must happen in a moment, or it never happened at all. All her life she had deeply believed in this romantic notion; it was more than a notion now. For Kate it was unalterable law.

Eagerly she caught the downtown bus on Saturday morning. If only there weren't so many people involved in her affairs. First, there was her grandfather. On Tuesday night she had told Elizabeth that she had dropped in on Harry Dryver. Her mother had been incensed about his not telephoning to let her know; Kate's lie made her grandfather seem irresponsible.

And Rose, who was worried about her absences from school, warned her not to let the strike interfere with her studies.

Worst of all was her inquisitive mother. Last night Kate had told Elizabeth she was going Christmas shopping today. Kate detested lying. But it would be so wonderful to have a whole free day with Joseph.

At the union Kate was surprised to see a huge crowd of workers and learned there would be no picket line that day. "You musta seen it in the papers," one of the girls said to Kate. "It was real bad yesterday. We had a rally here last night and we're marching to City Hall," Joseph was nowhere to be found; Kate was terrified that he had been hurt. And she hadn't read the newspaper that morning. She had been too eager to get away.

"Was . . . anyone injured?" she asked the girl, with her heart in her mouth.

"Some o' the girls got roughed up, like always. Are you comin'? Joseph's getting the parade together, down to Lipzin's Theater on Rivin'ton Street."

Kate felt relieved: she was sorry about the girls, but Joseph was all right.

"Yes," she said firmly. "Yes, I am." She took a streetcar with some of the workers to the Bowery and Rivington Street. Joseph was there, surrounded by workers. When he saw her, his face showed surprise and consternation. It was some time before he had a chance to talk to her.

This was still another Joseph—excited, preoccupied, treating her just like the others. He told her where to march—"Right behind me"; for an instant his look was warm and reassuring—and then he was gone again. Kate looked around her. There were surely more than a thousand workers. With pride she recognized some of her signs. Her breath quickened and her heart beat in her throat as the march began to move down the Bowery toward City Hall.

Kate linked arms with the girls in her row, watching Joseph's tall body ahead of her. From somewhere above the clamor she heard the biblical words "Whither thou goest I will go; thy people shall be my people."

She felt, at last, that she belonged.

"Well, Elizabeth! What's this?" Howard Wendell demanded at the breakfast table, gesturing at the December 16th *Times*. "Is this club of yours turning into a Fabian society?"

Kate had been trying to decide whether to buy Joseph a Christmas or Hanukkah present, and was only half-listening. When she heard her father say "Fabian," she was suddenly all ears.

"What on earth do you mean?" Elizabeth looked up from her perusal of the advertisements. "Don't tell me you're reading the *society* pages, Howard."

"No, indeed. The Colony Club made the front page this time. Weren't you there yesterday?"

Now they had Kate's complete attention.

"No," Elizabeth declared. "At this time of year? I have too much to do to go to some silly lecture. Let me see."

Kate's father passed her mother the front page, remarking with a twinkle, "It sounds quite racy. Shame on the ladies."

"*Racy*?" Elizabeth could not contain her amazement, nor could Kate. The Colony Club was the most exclusive club in the city, whose membership roster included names like Morgan and Harriman. The membership represented some of the richest women in the world.

Reading avidly, Elizabeth exclaimed, "This is positively disgusting. Mrs. Edgerton *did* call me, as a matter of fact, to tell me there would be an especially 'interesting' program, but I was not going to miss the fashion show for *that*. And now I'm glad I didn't. Why, they were addressed by those bomb-throwing *radicals* . . . those shirtwaistmakers. Good heavens, one of those creatures actually referred to 'immoral girls.' "

Kate wanted to read the article desperately, but she managed to look only mildly interested.

"Well," Howard Wendell interjected, "she said the factory owners *hired* . . . er, immoral girls to mingle with the others, to give the police clear grounds for arrest. You are absolutely right, my dear. They are radicals, of course, and highly disruptive to our economy. But bomb-throwing seems a little strong."

"Surely, Howard, you are not defending these . . . guttersnipes!" Elizabeth cried out.

Kate broke in before her mother could finish. ". . . Guttersnipes who earn less in one week than you spend for a hat, Mother."

Her parents were startled—Kate had been so quiet

throughout the meal—but E....abeth said triumphantly, "I told you so, Howard. I told you no good would come of sending Kate to that college with these 'New Women,' where she's caught all these radical ideas. And to think that the perfectly nice women in my own club—"

"I wasn't 'defending' the strikers, for God's sake." Howard's face was flushed with vexation. "Don't you ever listen to a word I say?"

Kate almost laughed at her mother's look of shock. Her father rarely took such a tone with Elizabeth.

"I'm going downtown," he growled, and getting up with a scrape of his chair, stormed out.

"Well, they haven't heard the end of this," Elizabeth vowed. "I'm going to give that club a piece of my mind."

There was nothing Kate could say that wouldn't start a battle, so she was silent, studying her mother. She felt an almost planetary distance separating them.

Chapter 5

Emerging from Arnold Constable on Friday afternoon, the seventeenth of December, Kate hunched under her big fur collar and pulled her hat over her face against the driving snow. She almost collided with another young woman on the way in and stepped aside without looking at her.

"Kate!"

It was Rose.

"Where have you *been*?" Rose demanded. "I've hardly seen you for the last three *weeks*." She strained upward to kiss Kate on the cheek. "I thought you'd been avoiding me or something. Let's go somewhere and have a cup of tea."

Kate was uneasy and chagrined. Three weeks without contacting a friend like Rose Nathan would have seemed incredible before; they usually saw or spoke to each other almost daily. But in these last weeks Kate had hardly given a thought to anything but Joseph and her work. She had even been neglecting her grandfather.

"I'd love to, Rose, but I was going home." That was untrue. She was on her way to Brooks Brothers to buy a sweater and gloves for Joseph.

Rose's huge dark eyes, brilliant and curious in the shadow of her stylish hat—like Kate's, it resembled a coal scuttle upside down—revealed her hurt. "What's the matter, Kate? Have I done something to . . . offend you?"

"Oh, Rose, of course not. It's just that I've been so . . . busy." She hugged her small friend.

"Kate, I'm so *relieved*. When I've phoned you, you've been all—I don't know—distant. And every time I've run into you at school, you've hardly said hello."

The snow was thickening on their hats.

"Good heavens, I don't want to get stuck in *this*," Rose commented. "I'll do my errands some other time. Look, why don't we both go uptown? We can share a cab—if we can find one—and then we can talk."

"I'd like that," Kate said sincerely. She had to make it up to Rose, make her understand how her absence had nothing to do with their friendship. It was time to tell Rose the truth. "Maybe we'll have better luck on Fifth."

They waited for a long time in the swirling snow; all the bright-red motor cabs were occupied. At last they were successful, and climbed in with sighs of relief.

After Rose had given the driver their addresses, she began to chatter, "I tried to find you yesterday, to invite you to Esther Weber's tea party in her room; you know, Esther Weber, who comes from Pennsylvania. She was giving a little fete to celebrate exams being over, and . . . How did you do on your exams, Kate? You said something on the phone about a problem with art history. Why art history, of all things? I thought that would be your easiest one."

Feeling shy now about telling Rose her secret, Kate grasped eagerly at the last question. She went into the matter of her art-history course in great detail.

The snow and the heavy traffic slowed their progress: the red Darracq was motionless. When at last it moved, it fairly crawled.

"We won't get there for hours." Rose chuckled. "That's good. It'll give us a chance to talk. Isn't it marvelous that we'll have two whole weeks of holiday?"

"It certainly is," Kate agreed with fervor. She intended to spend every moment she could with Joseph. Suddenly she thought of their recent conversation on Wednesday night, when they had snatched a half-hour together in a small café. Joseph had not spoken a word of love. Their talk had been about her work, and his, their words merely circling and skimming off their unexpressed emotion. And yet, even though he had not spoken his feelings, or kissed her mouth, Kate had felt Joseph's longing for her.

". . . at the Trade Union League?" Rose was saying.

"I beg your pardon?"

"Kate? You were a million miles away," Rose remarked ruefully. "What on earth has happened to you?"

"I think I'm falling in love with Joseph Barsimson," Kate blurted out. Flushing, she turned to confront Rose.

"What? What did you say?" An uncertain smile twitched at the corners of Rose's rich mouth. "My cousin Joseph? Kate, you're joking."

"No, Rose. I'm not joking at all."

The seriousness of her answer erased Rose's incipient smile. "But . . . how could it happen? You told me you only went back to the line once, after that first day."

"That wasn't true. I just couldn't tell you then. It was too soon to even think of such a thing," Kate said miserably.

"And *this* isn't soon?" Rose countered. "Good heavens, Kate, you've known him . . . how long? A magnificent three weeks?"

Kate smiled. "You sound like my mother."

Ignoring her remark, Rose demanded, "Have you been seeing him all this time, then?"

"Of course." And Kate told her about all of it—her maneuvers with her parents, the hurried meetings with Joseph, her work at the union hall. She felt immensely light, suddenly unburdened. It was so good to tell someone about it at last. Gathering her courage, she concluded, "I care for him, Rose. And I . . . think he cares for me. Although he hasn't said so yet, not in so many words."

"And he won't, Kate, in few or many words," Rose asserted.

"What do you mean?"

"I know something about Joseph. He's too honorable for that."

"Too *honorable*!" Kate gasped.

"Yes. Too honorable to ask you to live in a . . . tenement, to give up everything. He's in no position to marry you, Kate."

"I don't know how you can talk like that," Kate retorted. "I've always admired you so for having ideals . . . for not thinking about things the way other people do— average, narrow people." She stared at Rose.

"This is not art or politics, Kate. This is life we're talking about. Good Lord, I imagine his whole flat is no bigger than your dressing room at home. What would you live on, Kate? I can picture you cooking on a gas ring." Rose giggled. "Neither one of us has ever even made a cup of tea."

"That has nothing to do with it," Kate maintained.

"It has everything to do with it. My grandfather says, 'I've been poor and I've been rich, and believe me, rich is better.' " Rose reached out and took Kate's hand. "Darling, it's one thing to have ideals, but this idea is madness. You couldn't stand Joseph's life, not even for a week. And as lovely as you are, you'd drive him crazy, he'd feel so guilty. I can tell you about Jewish guilt, Kate." Rose grinned. "It makes Christian guilt look like ecstasy."

The cab was approaching the Wendell mansion.

"You don't understand, Rose. You just don't understand. I wish you would."

"I wish I *could*. Oh, please, Kate, come home with me and we'll talk some more. You may be making such a terrible mistake," Rose pleaded. "I'm sorry if I said anything to make you mad, but I just . . . "

"You didn't, Rose." Kate leaned toward her, brushing her smooth cheek with a quick kiss. The cab came to a stop. Kate quickly pressed her portion of the fare into Rose's hand and said, "I'll phone you soon."

But Kate knew she wouldn't. She couldn't count on Rose

either. They would have to avoid the one subject that was closest to Kate's heart.

Polly's restaurant on West Fourth Street in Greenwich Village was a favored gathering place for artists and anarchists, social protesters and bohemians. The famous anarchist Hyppolyte Havel—dubbed "Hyp" by Joseph and his friends—was cook and waiter. Unconventional patrons streamed in and out, among them Jack London and Theodore Dreiser, who came from their apartments on the south side of Washington Square.

But even Polly Holliday's was not immune to Christmas Eve: there was a special glow, a new bonhomie. Candles gleamed in miniature from the many-colored mirrors of globes on a tall fir tree. Dressed in vivid green velvet, Kate sat framed against the tree, her spirits high.

There was something in the air tonight, a certain difference in Joseph's manner; the light in his eyes, she thought, was not just a reflection of the candles. And Kate felt a quiver of excitement, a nibble of expectation along her every nerve.

For several moments they sat in contented silence, smiling at each other, part of the scene and yet separate from it. People they knew greeted them but did not approach the little table, and Kate was glad; she and Joseph never had enough time together.

Suddenly Joseph shifted in his chair, reaching deep in his jacket pocket for something. The inclination of his proud head on his strong, lean neck, the lines of his torso that revealed such power and grace, dragged at Kate's heart like a sweet burden. She longed to sketch him, just as he was at that instant. Her breath caught in her throat.

"Merry Christmas, Kate." He handed her a tiny package wrapped in golden paper.

"Oh, Joseph." Smiling, she held it in her hand, then gently unwrapped it to find a dark-blue velvet box. Lifting the lid, she saw a small golden star with a microscopic diamond glittering at its heart. "It's lovely . . . it's so delicate."

Kate detached the frail golden chain from its nest and clasped it around her neck. She saw his eyes glitter at the sight of the fragile gold ornament against her green dress.

"You gave me the Mogen David, Joseph," she said softly. "Thank you." The solemn symbolism of the gift moved her profoundly. He had honored her with the mark of his pride—the star of his ancient people.

"It is also your Christmas star." His voice had never sounded quite so intimate, so gentle.

She heard the swift whisper of her own heartbeat like the sound of a small sea in her ears as she reached over to touch his hand.

Then she remembered the big box on the floor by her chair. "Happy Hanukkah, Joseph," she said as she handed it to him.

He opened the package and carefully set its wrappings aside. Kate looked at his hands and his fine-boned face. She watched his black brows lift at the sight of the prestigious store name.

"Kate, this is wonderful." He ran his hands over the fine leather of the fur-lined gloves, then parted the scarlet tissue below them to find the heavy, luxurious sweater. It was the rich color of red wine. "I've never owned anything so fine."

The admission touched her.

"I'll wear the gloves tonight." He slipped one of them on his long hand; it was a perfect fit. "It feels wonderful."

"Would you like to go to Grandfather's now?"

"That's a good idea." He paid the bill and they walked out into the lightly drifting snow. Joseph flexed his hands in the fine new gloves, smiling at her, and Kate felt inordinately happy. She couldn't wait for her grandfather to meet Joseph. In another hour, her presence uptown would be absolutely mandatory, a requirement on family Christmas Eve. Christmas Day itself was devoted to an open house for the more distant relatives, her father's business associates, and friends of the family. Kate had longed to ask Joseph to the Christmas celebration, but something in his expression deterred her when she told him about it.

As they walked up Sixth Avenue toward Eleventh Street, she thought: I am not the only one with secrets to keep. Joseph had never suggested visiting his parents. She recalled his frequent and mysterious silences, sensing some kind of inner conflict. He might be thinking of their respective families now; he was so silent.

Kate matched his silence, but when they reached the small Sephardic burial ground near Harry Dryver's house, Joseph stopped, exclaiming, "Good Lord, I'd almost forgotten."

Kate had passed the little cemetery hundreds of times, and Rose had often remarked on it, but now she felt as if she were seeing it for the first time. Joseph touched the bronze plaque naming its consecration date, 1805.

"There's a Barsimson buried here," he murmured, looking down at Kate. His dark eyes glittered in the golden lamplight misted by the snow.

"And my grandfather's house," she said in amazement, "is right next door." She added, "It's like a . . . sign from fate."

"Yes, Kate. Yes, it is." His face was regal and somber in the mica-light of the swirling flakes.

"I love you, Kate." Joseph set his package down and abruptly pulled her close. With a moan he lowered his mouth to hers. She could taste the snow, melting on the hotness of their mouths, as her whole being flowed into his.

They stood alone in the dazzled half-dark and Kate felt her old, known self turn vaporous; she was like a phoenix rising from its fire.

When he let her go, she breathed, "I love you, Joseph. I've loved you all along, from the first, from the very first time I saw your face."

He held her close again; she sensed an overpowering

need in him. "Kate, oh, Kate." His breath was short and ragged. "We'd better go in. I feel quite . . . mad."

"So do I!" All of a sudden she was feverish with joy. Her whole body glowed. Joseph kept his arm around her as they matched each other's steps walking toward her grandfather's house.

Letha opened the door, grinning broadly. "Christmas gif', Miss Kate!" Seeing Joseph, she added warmly, "And to you, sir."

"Merry Christmas, Letha." Kate hugged her and reached into her coat pocket for Letha's package, which contained a handsome little brooch. "Why, thank you, sweet child. Bless your heart."

During the flurry of introductions and the disposal of coats and hats, Harry Dryver emerged from the parlor, smiling. He kissed Kate and extended his hand to Joseph. "Happy Hanukkah."

Kate watched Joseph beam. More than ever she was struck by the amazing resemblance between the two men.

"You both look cold," Dryver said. "Come in and have a toddy."

The followed him into the firelit parlor. "Take that chair, Joseph." Dryver indicated a comfortable wing chair next to the brick-faced hearth.

As Kate settled on the divan with its many cushions in the "Baghdad corner," and Dryver dropped into an easy chair, Joseph looked around him.

The picket-line painting had recently been hung on the white wall. Dryver saw Joseph studying it.

Joseph said with a slight laugh, "Forgive me. I come right into your house . . . a perfect stranger . . . and sit here staring like an idiot, not saying a word. But that's a wonderful painting." He accepted a toddy from Letha with absent thanks.

"You're no stranger than my other visitors," Dryver retorted. This time Joseph let out a hearty laugh. "And besides, a compliment like that is not something to forgive."

Kate could tell they were utterly at ease with each other.

There was an instant and obvious rapport between her grandfather and Joseph; her delight knew no bounds. To have the two people she cared for most on earth enjoy each other's company seemed the greatest gift she had ever been given.

Joseph began to talk easily, and Kate was pleased with her grandfather's wide-ranging conversation, his skill at drawing Joseph out. Almost at once, their talk touched on the strike. Dryver turned to Kate and teased her, "As for you, missy, I'm glad you've stopped harassing the policemen and decided to help elsewhere. I understand that was your idea." He looked at Joseph. "You are a very sensible man."

Kate repeated what Joseph had said when comparing her picket duty to a tailor carrying bundles. Dryver guffawed.

"Better and better," he observed, shooting a respectful glance at Joseph.

My grandfather likes him, she exulted in silence.

They were having such a good time that Kate was startled by the sudden gong of the tall clock in the corner, reminding them all of the hour.

Joseph looked at Kate and got to his feet. "I'm afraid I'd better be going." The reluctance in his voice was matched by her grandfather's reply.

"We were just getting started," he said wistfully. "I hope, Joseph, that you will come to see me again. You are always welcome."

Joseph's thank-you, and his strong clasp of Dryver's hand represented more, Kate felt, than simple courtesy.

"I'll walk you to the door," she said, aware that Dryver's keen look was upon her.

Letha helped Joseph with his coat; he seemed pleased but somewhat bewildered by the unaccustomed attention. Then the old woman tactfully withdrew.

"Oh, Joseph," Kate whispered as he glanced around swiftly, then took her in his arms. "I'm going to miss you tomorrow." They had agreed it would be best to spend the day with their respective parents.

"I know, Kate. I know. And I'll miss you. Awfully." His mouth looked tender and regretful.

She whispered his name again and lifted her face for his kiss. He held her as if he could not bear to let her go. Then quite abruptly he loosened his hold, looking down hungrily into her eyes. "Good night, Kate. Sweet Kate."

And he was gone.

She stood at the narrow hall-window for a long moment, watching him go. Willing herself to move, she went back to rejoin her grandfather.

He was standing with his back to the doorway, peering into the orange fire.

"We must leave soon," she murmured.

He sighed. "I know." She thought: He dreads it as much as I do.

Dryver turned around then and said more cheerfully, "I like Joseph Barsimson."

"Oh, Grandfather, I'm glad. I'm so glad."

He held out his arms to her and she went into them with the sense of homecoming his embrace had always given her . . . that Joseph's embrace had given her a short while ago, out on Eleventh Street by the little cemetery in the drifting snow.

The memory of that moment brought a sudden rush of heat to her face. Dryver stepped back, observing her.

"You care for this young fellow, don't you, darling?"

"Yes." She nodded solemnly. "Yes, Grandfather. I love him. And he loves me." Her voice thickened with excitement as her heart thudded rapidly, recalling Joseph's declaration.

"Kate." Dryver's tone was coaxing and gentle. "Sit down a moment. We still have a little time. I want to talk to you."

She sat down in the wing chair, her grandfather in the one on the opposite side of the hearth.

"I ran into George Livermore," Dryver began casually, "at the Salmagundi. We had quite a talk."

Kate hadn't been to Livermore's classes for the last three times.

"He happened to mention that you've been absent lately. I was sorry to hear you're neglecting your work."

"I don't care!" she cried out passionately. "I have to be with Joseph."

"From what you've told me of that young man," Dryver commented, "I'll wager he asked you not to disrupt your life."

"He did," Kate admitted. There was a brief silence.

Then Dryver said, "If you are serious about each other— and I think you are; I can see it in both your faces—it won't be easy, Kate. Neither his family nor yours will accept it."

"Haven't you told me a hundred times that nothing worthwhile is easy?" she countered.

"Indeed I have. I wasn't talking about this, however. You may be making a difficult commitment. I've never been on the side of the Grundys, Kate. But my liberalism doesn't extend to you. Every man wants an easy life for those he loves."

"I can't believe you're talking like this," she cried.

"I know. I know." He smiled. "I caused a furor myself when I married your grandmother. Nothing could have kept me from doing it—nothing. But I was in a different position, Kate. I had money."

"How can you mention money, you of all people?"

"It pains me to, in the light of what you must be feeling . . . the tragic glory, or the glorious tragedy"—his mouth twisted—"that I experienced myself. Joseph is a splendid young man. But if you plan to share a life with him, it may be very hard. I can't bear the thought of that. How can you be so sure, my dear?"

"I am sure. That's all I know. And nothing can ever make me change my mind." She answered him so quietly that she knew she had convinced him of her determination.

He sighed. "Very well, Kate. Once more I'm your confederate. I'll keep your secret."

"Oh, thank you!" She got up and went to his chair, bending over him to kiss the top of his head. "That's the best gift you've ever given me."

When she released him, he patted her shoulder. "We'd better be off to the Palace. And, Kate"—he glanced at the little Mogen David—"I wouldn't forget to hide that lovely ornament."

She slipped the small star inside the neckline of her dress, thinking how symbolic the gesture was. She would be obliged to hide her newly created happiness, like the candle behind the bushel. But it didn't matter. Nothing on earth now could ever put out that star, shining beneath her dress as her joy shone hidden within her heart.

Joseph found his mother sitting on the bottom steps when he entered his building.

"You are late, Joseph." Anzia regarded him with reproachful eyes. She looked so tired and old that remorse tinged his irritation. Anzia was only forty-one, yet she seemed at least ten years older.

"Mama, why didn't you ask the superintendent to let you in?" Joseph bent to give her a dutiful kiss, then helped her up.

"I would no more go into your rooms than I would pick your pocket." She pulled her faded shawl around her shoulders.

"Come on, Mama." They began to climb the stairs. On his floor at last, Anzia leaned against the wall, gasping. Joseph wondered at the martyrdom that impelled her to climb so many stairs to visit him. Or the love, he amended shamefully. He unlocked his door, waited for Anzia to get her breath, and stood aside for her to enter.

When they were inside, she frowned. "I don't see your menorah, Joseph."

"Hanukkah's over, Mama." He threw off his coat and cap, put his hands on her shoulders to take her shawl.

"So does a menorah disappear when Hanukkah's over?" she asked.

"I don't have one."

She flung his hands away, repeating, "Don't have one? Don't *have* one? Joseph, what's happened to you? Are you turning into a Christian? You don't come to see your parents every week anymore . . . you didn't come when I lit the first candle for Hanukkah. What is it, you have no time anymore for anything, except your strikes and revolutions?"

"Mamaleh, sit down," he coaxed her. "Take off your shawl. I'll make you a cup of tea."

Anzia sat abruptly on a straight chair but clutched her shawl to her. "A cup *tea*? A cup tea you offer me instead of my son?"

He went into the minuscule kitchen to put the kettle on, calling back over his shoulder, "I've been busy. I'm sorry."

"Busy," she called out. "do you have enough coal? Do you have what to eat, in that broom closet?"

Joseph was more amused than annoyed. Her kitchen was hardly much larger than his. And she always asked about coal, although he had told her time and again that the coal was in the cellar; the heat came up through pipes and radiators.

He made two cups of tea and took them into the other room.

"Thank you, Joseph." Anzia's voice was wearied into gentleness. "Forgive me. I keep on forgetting you're not a little boy in knickers anymore. All I want is that things should be better for you. But I guess they're not." She broke off; a mottled flush crept over her cheeks.

Joseph was guilt-stricken. He had sent her less money last week because he had used it for Kate's star. "Things are all right. Next week I'll do better."

Anzia seemed deeply embarrassed. She sipped the scalding tea and joked, trying to change the subject, "This is a terrible cup tea. You ought to get married, Joseph."

He could not hide his expression.

"What is it, son?" She stroked his hand. The feel of her

work-roughened skin filled Joseph with a terrible pity. He could not possibly tell her about Kate Wendell now.

"Nothing, Mama. I'm tired, that's all. The strike takes up all my time."

"It goes on still, Solomon told me." Anzia could not read very much in Hebrew or English, but Joseph's father read to her from the *Forward.* "And will it be different when it's over . . . aside from some more cracked heads?"

He had to smile at her dark humor. "Of course it will. It'll mean the end of sweatshops, Mama. There will come a time when men and women won't have to sew from morning till night to make a living. Little boys won't have to *schlepp* bundles, and people won't die young." Speaking the words brought back Joseph's enthusiasm and for an instant he forgot his private dilemma.

Anzia sighed. "From your mouth to God's ear. And in the meantime," she added sourly, "when your papa and I don't hear from you we don't know whether you're dead or alive . . . or if the cossacks have carried you away to prison."

Joseph smiled. He had told his mother that the police were mostly Irish and Italian, but to Anzia they would always be the czar's troops who had trampled the Jews in Kiev.

"And your papa still doesn't like what you're doing," Anzia said after a moment.

"Doesn't he listen to what they say at the tailors' union, Mama?" Joseph felt the familiar exasperation.

"Solomon is old, Joseph. He's not a young man full of courage anymore, like the Solomon who took me to his father." Her intonation was wistful.

"Old! Good God, he's only forty-seven."

"Forty-seven is old on Essex Street, Joseph."

His heart sank. It was true. Noticing his expression, Anzia said, "I must go soon." She heaved herself to her feet and went into the kitchen. Joseph heard the icebox open. "Oy," she cried out, "is this the same salami you had in September? It looks like the same salami."

He laughed and followed her into the kitchen. "No, it's a whole new salami, I swear."

She shook her head, closed the icebox door, and brushed past him back to the living room. She picked up her shawl and wrapped it around her.

"Look, how are you going home?"

"How should I be going?" Anzia retorted. "In my shiny new motorcar like a Seligman. On a streetcar, that's how I'm going."

"No, you're not," he asserted. "Not this time. I'm going to send you home in a cab." If he had to skip a meal tomorrow she was going to ride in comfort, Joseph decided.

Her brows shot up into her babushka. She smiled. "You're a good son, Joseph. A sweet boy."

Once Joseph had put Anzia in a cab and given the driver money for the fare, he trudged back toward the flat, feeling very alone. He could have gone to any one of three New Year's Eve parties, but he didn't want to go without Kate.

Before Thanksgiving Kate had committed herself to one of the society balls; her only excuse for missing it, she said, could have been illness, which would have only complicated their lives further.

Joseph was tempted to stop in at the Liberal Club, where there was a small celebration, just to talk to someone. But that was no good. This was no evening for a man alone; it wouldn't help. All he could think of was Kate.

He gave it up and climbed back to the flat. As he let himself in he saw the place with new eyes: he had never paid attention before to how bare, how ugly it really was. The grimy curtains, left by a previous tenant, had once been white. Now there was no name for the color they were, he thought sardonically. The only cheerful notes were his treasured books and a few scarlet cushions he'd picked up on Orchard Street. Even those looked garish, not bright.

Joseph lay down on his bed in his stocking feet. He knew that to picture Kate Wendell here was unrealistic to the point of fantasy. Yet that was exactly what he wanted right now—to have her here beside him in this bed.

And that could never happen with a girl like Kate, not before marriage. To people like the Wendells marriage meant a cathedral wedding with a rich groom and a European honeymoon.

Joseph reviewed the crowded weeks since their first meeting, remembering his early reluctance to succumb to her appeal. But even that afternoon at Marie's, when he had first taken her out, his body had already began to demand what his rational mind resisted.

Joseph almost hoped that her enthusiasm for the cause would wane as the days went on. He had told himself there was no time for anything but the movement. He was no romantic kid; he was a man with a commitment.

But the day after they met, when she appeared again on the line, the simple magnetism of her presence had become so strong, so damned powerful. And after that, when he began to realize just how patient and determined she was, Kate's appeal became a hundred times more dangerous. In no time at all she involved his mind, his deeper emotions.

Joseph could not remember when it had happened, but he knew that she cared for him, truly cared. And that he had come to love her. He could no more have stopped himself from telling her that, on Christmas Eve, than he could have prevented the beating of his heart, the very rhythm of his breath.

Joseph stretched out, sighing, and allowing himself the luxury of recalling their first kiss: the taste of her sweet mouth with a snowflake melting on it; the sight of the little star glittering on the bosom of her bright green dress. Her feeling for that symbol had such deep significance; he knew she loved him for what he was, not in spite of it. Her image of Jews, poetic and naive, was incredibly touching to him.

He had also been very moved by the visit to her grandfather. Harry Dryver's unusual personality and gifts, and his easy, warm acceptance of Joseph made him a real *mensch*—an unquestioned genius. It wasn't hard to see where Kate had gotten her original and rosy view of the world.

There was the rub, Joseph thought darkly. The very qualities that glorified the world for him made her unattainable and alien to his part of it. His glowing recollections faded, suddenly tarnished by banal questions, as Joseph's dreams and hopes collided with the brick wall of the real. If only Kate could see the reality behind the poetic symbol of the Mogen David, Joseph thought. Yet he doubted that she would ever fully understand the strange awareness of hardship and pride that he had inherited from his Sephardic ancestors.

The first of Joseph's ancestors to arrive in America was Jacob Barsimson. Jacob sailed from Brazil for Amsterdam in 1654. Blown off course, he landed instead in New Amsterdam, one of the first two Jews in the young world, hundreds of years ahead of the Italian and Irish immigrants.

Joseph's father, Solomon, alienated his proud Sephardic family by marrying Anzia Letski, a Russian Jew. Her family hadn't arrived until 1880. Examined and tagged at Ellis Island, the Letskis were given an American approximation of their name and herded onto a Manhattan-bound ferry. They walked to the Lower East Side from the Battery. The "Jewish Pilgrims" who had come on the heels of the Plymouth Rock settlers said that "uncouth strangers" like the Letskis gave settled Jews a bad name. So when Solomon presented Anzia to his family, the patriarch, Benjamin, was devastated. "For your wedding I give you a father's curse," he shouted.

Solomon apprenticed himself to a tailor and moved with his wife to New York's Lower East Side. When the children came, Anzia took in piecework to make ends meet, sewing by hand until her fingers blistered. Their home sweatshop was born.

Joseph's older brother died at birth, his sister from tuberculosis. The family constantly breathed the dust and lint from cut fabric in the ill-aired, crowded flat. Life in the flat on Essex Street was mean and bare; the family scrimped for a year to pay for leased sewing machines so Solomon and Anzia could turn out more jackets, that lifeblood of their existence. Joseph helped at home and delivered the bundles of jackets to factories for refinishing.

Despite the curse of Benjamin, Joseph's Uncle Rafael offered him help. The obstinate Solomon refused. "Begged bread is made bitter by shame," he said. Solomon also declined his brother's invitations to visit. Rafael had married an elegant German Jew who was related to the famous banking Seligmans; the couple had only one child and called him Lionel. They changed their name to "Simson" because it sounded more American. When Rafael put his false name on a large sign, "SIMSON COMPANY," Solomon Barsimson declared he would have nothing to do with such a brother.

When Lionel was bar-mitzvahed two years after Joseph's own paltry celebration, Solomon tore Rafael's invitation in half. Joseph smoldered with resentment. For years he had looked forward to being invited, just to taste the splendid food, see the magnificent house.

Joseph recalled how sore he had been over that—he had resolved to go. His only decent suit was the one his father had made for his own bar mitzvah. Joseph knew enough to lengthen the jacket sleeves and trouser hems but he couldn't cope with the loose waist or the jacket's tight shoulders. At fifteen he had an unusual breadth of shoulder, leanness of waist and haunch. He had already been boxing for a year. He lied about his age so he could box for money against the lighter fellows at the gym, sometimes even welterweights. Joseph was already lethal, valuable to the unions whose members' physical strength had been sapped by years of poor food and living conditions.

Joseph occasionally stole extra food; he knew a strong body needed fuel. But it wasn't only the extra food that powered him. He had a relentless drive most other boys lacked. And if life in the flat was drab and constricting, the streets were not. They formed a harsher, wider world where street fighting put Joseph on a par with older boxers, making him look like a man when he was still a kid.

When Solomon learned about the boxing, he beat Joseph. Jews didn't do such a thing. Solomon's attitude contrasted oddly with that of Rafael Simson, who often came to the gym to watch Joseph fight and urge him on. Sometimes Rafael gave Joseph a few dollars and told him he wished his own son were such a *mensch*. Joseph didn't dare tell Solomon that, but sometimes he felt as if Rafael were more his father than Solomon was. He went on boxing, heartened by his uncle's interest, bringing the extra money to Anzia. She asked no questions, just as she had not queried him about the extra food. The money was a godsend, and she couldn't prove it came from boxing, because Joseph never got marked up much. Even then he had such a long reach and was so fast on his feet, he was hard to hit.

On that landmark day nine years ago, Joseph crammed himself into his old bar-mitzvah suit, feeling like a greenhorn but determined to attend Lionel's fete. Rafael had been good to him; besides, Joseph couldn't wait to see how rich people did things. He had never forgotten the well-dressed congregation, Lionel in his beautiful new suit, getting into his parents' limousine. Joseph walked into the Simson house empty-handed among the gift-bearing guests, shabby but proud as David the King.

The occasion was still vivid in his memory. Rafael received him amiably but Lionel was stiff and resentful. Joseph was introduced to his grandfather, the fearsome Benjamin, with his long white beard and burning eyes, like a vengeful god. Rafael brought Joseph to the patriarch's thronelike chair, saying, "This is your grandson Joseph Barsimson, the son of Solomon. See what a man he is already, and only fifteen." Lionel, who was standing by, scowled at Joseph as if that were an insult to himself.

The old man's eyes looked through Joseph. "I have no son named Solomon. I cut *kriah* for him nearly twenty years ago. This boy is a dead man's son."

Joseph was too proud to flinch. Cutting *kriah* was enact-
ing the ceremony of grief for the dead by cutting off a
piece of your own clothes, like the old rending of mourners' garments. Rafael led Joseph away, whispering, "My
father's an old man. Never mind. You are a fine young
man, don't forget it. Go, enjoy yourself. Talk to the young
people. Eat something."

Lionel wouldn't talk to Joseph at all, and the other boys
and girls looked at him strangely. But there was an incredible display of rich, wonderful-smelling food. Joseph consoled himself with *pasteles*, the meat pies of the Sephardim;
thinly sliced oranges sprinkled with cinnamon, tasting of
rosewater; hearty meat stew made with fruit and melons and
fresh ripening apricots. He tasted the *calsones*, small pasta
squares filled with cheeses and nutmeg, and took a sam-
pling from the sweet-and-sour Persian dishes.

His stomach hurt when he got back to the flat, which
suddenly looked even dingier than before. Joseph marveled at his father's weak acceptance of their lot. Solomon
wanted him to be a tailor; he scoffed at Joseph's longing
for an education.

"A good tailor," Solomon used to declare, "learns his
trade by doing. What do you need with college? Already
you know *Ladino*, you learned Hebrew at *schul*. You
learned to be a good Jew. I've taught you to be a good
tailor. These are the main things in life."

The main thing in life, Joseph always retorted in silence, was to receive just pay for one's work, not to be
treated like a serf, the way his mother's people had been
treated by the cossacks. True, his father had a tailoring
shop downstairs; in that respect he was well ahead of most
other poor Jews. But they all had to work in their own
home-shop as well, backbreaking work, he and Anzia and
Solomon, done for too few dollars. His brother and sister
had died because the Barsimsons were too poor to afford
the medical attention to keep them alive.

The unions could change all that. The unions needed
men with education. Joseph read hungrily from every book

he could find, studying until he got an education that was almost as good as what he could have gotten at City College; he studied when he was almost too tired to hold his books, too sleepy to understand them.

After he had gotten his feet wet in the children's jacket union, Joseph attracted the attention of some men in the United Brotherhood of Cloakmakers. Then, when Joseph was only fourteen, the International Ladies' Garment Workers' Union was formed, combining the cloakmakers and pressers of Philadelphia with cloak-and-shirtmakers of Baltimore and New York. Joseph was hired as an organizer for one of the locals when he was just fifteen. He served at first for very little pay, and still had to continue his other activities—his studies, an occasional boxing match, helping Solomon and Anzia.

He was tough and unafraid, blessed with the gift of persuasion—qualities that stood him in good stead. Solomon was an unwilling member of the tailors' local; he had bowed to the pressure of his peers, declaring that he didn't want "any trouble" from the bosses. He was afraid they would give the piecework to nonunion workers and cost the Barsimsons part of their income.

Joseph was saddened by this evidence of shilly-shallying on his father's part; Solomon had been brave enough, Joseph thought, when he married against Benjamin's will. But something had happened to his father in the intervening years—he had lost his fight. When Joe Zeinfeld, a striker against the Triangle, was punched and kicked by scabs and lay in bed bandaged for weeks, Solomon lectured Joseph. "That could happen to you," he warned. "Is it worth it?"

Joseph hadn't answered. The argument was typical of the debates he had been having with his father for the last four years, ever since Joseph moved out on his own and visited Essex Street only once a week. At first he had rented a small furnished room; then when he could afford it, his present flat on MacDougal Street.

The four years in Greenwich Village had been wonder-

fully exciting, he had to admit; Joseph had met socialists
and artists, poets and revolutionaries. For the first time in
his life he had people really to *talk* to.

Joseph rose and went to the window. At the moment,
MacDougal Street was fairly quiet. Above the ragged sky-
line only a few stars disturbed the blue-black silence.
Suddenly an image of Kate's face—her bright eyes and
sensuous mouth, framed by yellow hair—flooded Joseph's
thoughts. He realized then that he missed her terribly.

But thinking about his family reminded Joseph that he
had little to offer Kate Wendell. Soon, he knew, Kate's
passionate kisses would become more of a torment than a
joy. Yet marriage was out of the question. Even if he
could somehow manage to scrape together enough money
to support them both, their different backgrounds would
make marriage plans virtually impossible.

Frustrated and weary, Joseph returned to his narrow bed
and lay down. A soft tapping sound brought him out of his
reverie.

He sat up abruptly; someone was knocking at his door.

"Just a minute," he called hoarsely.

Joseph rose cautiously and went to answer it.

Chapter 6

Joseph opened the door only slightly and looked down. His breath was almost knocked out of him.

Kate stood there, staring up into his eyes.

He found his voice, saying her name again and again as he pulled her to his body, until her name sounded like a small, constantly beaten bell in his whirring ears. Now her bright head rested on his chest; he smelled her scent of strange lilies and pressed his lips against her snow-wet hair.

Dimly he realized they were embracing in the cold public hall and he urged her into the room, slamming the door. Then he held her close to him again and planted kisses on her burnished head, her upturned face, leaning to bury his mouth in the white, delicious hollow of her neck.

With half-closed eyes he glimpsed the gilt crescents of her lashes that fanned against the delicate skin of her cheeks. He heard her cry out when he covered her mouth with his.

Joy lit him like a flare.

Kate raised her lids as Joseph's mouth released hers; his face was so near that all she could see were his black, glittering eyes. They had never looked quite like that before—all the sadness and distance in them were gone. She moved closer to lean against his strong, wiry body, and was immediately aware of its magnificent hardness.

There was a sense of rightness and shelter in his strength that quieted her every fear.

She was too full of him to say a word, and felt that all the years of her life her body had been asleep, and now she was waking. It must have been like this to be born, she decided, feeling the light on my skin for the first time.

Joseph moved back slightly, staring down at her, and she sensed that he was as dazed as she. He, too, found it impossible to speak, to move from where they stood.

She was first to find her voice again. "Oh, Joseph, I had to come. I couldn't bear it. I couldn't be . . . away from you."

His arms folded around her hard and he held her so tightly that she could feel his urgent need; he lowered his head to kiss her mouth. The caress was so savage and so gentle all at once that she was astounded by the paradox of him—this stranger who was so familiar, this man who was fiercely proud and yet beseeching.

"You're trembling, Kate. Come, let's sit down." Joseph began to remove her cloak. He took it off and laid it over a chair. "There's only one place we can sit together," he said wryly. He put his arm around her waist and led her into the bedroom. They sat down together on his narrow bed.

"Oh, Kate, right now I'm not much stronger than you," he admitted, urging her with his hand to lean against his shoulder. "I still can't quite believe it. I can't believe that you're here."

For the first time she noticed that he was not wearing any shoes. When she looked up again he flushed.

She felt her own face heat and hid herself against his chest, inhaling the scent of his body. With her mouth against his shirt, she spoke softly. "Joseph, I feel so shy."

He kissed the top of her head. Then he turned her face upward. "I want to look at you. I've dreamed your face so many nights, and now I want to look and look at it . . . here in this awful room."

She smiled. "It's not awful at all. As a matter of fact, I

can't see anything but you." Obediently she raised her face for his inspection, transfixed by his profound black eyes. What power they have over me, she thought. Her pulse quickened; a swift, racing fire flooded her whole body.

His eyes alone filled her with desire. As they looked at each other in the enchanted silence, broken only by the loud breath of the hissing steam and the minute rustle of their clothes as they moved toward each other again, Kate felt as if he already possessed her with those eyes. She drowned in them.

All of a sudden that awakened thing—the force she had never truly known before—was wholly alive in her astonished flesh. She whispered in a voice that hardly sounded like her own, "Joseph, Joseph, turn out the light."

Elated and daring, she almost laughed at his expression of disbelief. Then he seemed to shake himself from sleep; he reached out and turned off the room's single lamp. The reflections of the streetlights, the lamps still shining from other windows, gave the room a silvery glow.

His features were dimmed and dreamlike, but when he knelt before her the pale light caught the glitter of his dark, excited eyes and she was still bemused by their power. Breathing quickly, he lifted one of her small, slippered feet with a slow, ceremonious motion, divesting it of its covering. Then he removed the other shoe. She felt his warm hands upon her feet, and she trembled throughout her frame.

Crying out, she leaned over and put her hands on his head, caressing the thick, vital hair. Then he rose, sat beside her again, and unfastened the back of her dress. He buried his face in her neck, kissing her vibrant skin with many small nibbling kisses, and she could feel the warm tip of his tongue. All of her now was only a great, warm need and a vast forgetting.

All her hesitation was gone, all her shyness might never have existed. Nothing remained but the longing to be near to him and ever nearer. With the hazy, timeless perception of someone in high fever, Kate was aware that they were undressing each other swiftly, and felt the kiss of skin. His body was as warm as the sun. Marveling, Kate traced its lithe and muscular proportions, from the strong neck and broad shoulders down the mighty biceps to the leanness of his waist. He seemed so slender when clothed; she had never fully realized his power.

Now, under his eager, wild caressing she felt herself becoming fire and vapor and there was no more holding back from that ultimate meeting. The strange and unimagined kisses of his mouth upon her secret flesh caused her to give herself with utter joy. Waiting for the pain this strange new converse had to bring, she puzzled at the height of their fulfillment to sense only one quick dart, a minute sting, before she felt a long and aching fire of such sweetness that all her senses drowned.

Their skin still kissed where he held her. His heart seemed to thud in her own astonished breast as she caught his quick, gasped, inchoate gutturals, exhaled with the heat of his breath on her hair.

Later, Joseph muttered something into Kate's hair.

She whispered against his throbbing neck, "What are you saying, Joseph? What are you saying, darling?" She put her fingers on his lips, feeling his smile.

Joseph lay down beside her, drawing her toward him. He stroked her loosened hair, ran an exploratory finger down the bones of her face. "A poem in Ladino, by Judah al-Harizi. 'She brought me in the house of love, her light shone in the dark; the night sounded like a lute, and the hills began to dance like rams.' "

Kate looked up at him. His face was in shadow, his proud head only a dark silhouette against the window curtains that framed the thick-falling snow. She was too moved to speak, and fearful that no words would be adequate to meet his words. She could speak only with her touch, eloquent and soft on his face and chest.

At last she said, "The snow is dancing; it looks like mica in the light." He turned his head to look, and she caught a glimpse of his face again; the beauty and pride of it aroused her to an ache of tenderness. "Oh, Joseph, I love you. I love you."

"Kate, Kate." He turned back to her, kissing her with a slow sweetness, running his hand down her naked body. "I love you, Kate. Love you in a way that transfigures everything . . . makes everything else inconsequential." He gathered her to him; she gloried in their bodies' close warmth, sliding her arms around him. "Compared to this," he whispered, "nothing else makes sense. I'm never going to let you go."

"Oh, Joseph, Joseph." She kissed his neck and chest, stroking his lean, muscular sides. "I would die if you ever let me go again."

"I told you." She felt his warm breath on the top of her head. "That will never happen. I would feel like half a person without you now." His fingers stroked her skin, pressed her closer to his body. "I just can't get you close enough." His voice was soft and shaky.

She burrowed closer, tightening her hold, and they lay in a dazed silence.

Suddenly she started to laugh and he drew back a little. "What is it?"

Kate looked up, observing his puzzled smile. She traced his mouth delicately with one finger. "I was thinking of that ball, imagining everyone's surprise when I went away to fix my hair and disappeared in a puff of smoke. Oh, Joseph, it was torture; it was so *dull*. All I could think of was being with you. Then I just decided that I *would* be with you; I had to be. I couldn't have stood it another minute." She spoke against his chest and felt the slight shudder of his smooth skin at the movement of her lips.

He squeezed her arm, resting his chin lightly for an instant on the top of her head. "I was thinking about you," he said, "thinking about all the times we've been together, at the very minute you knocked on the door. That's why I was so speechless. I couldn't take it in. It was like waking up from a dream, and still dreaming." He paused, then added, "Your escort is going to be one unhappy man. Who was he?"

Kate heard the jealous, possessive note in his voice. It was very exciting. "No one, Joseph. No one at all."

His tone thrilled her in every nerve; her whole body reacted to it. She found herself stroking his naked flesh with a new boldness, heard him make deep, inchoate sounds of longing. Before she could speak, his mouth was over hers, he was pulling her to him roughly, and they were moving against each other, into each other, with a sweet and savage impatience. Incredulous, she let go of all thought, climbing, drowning at once in a wild, unknown sensation, as she found in their bodies' meeting almost unendurable delight.

Gasping, they lay side by side, her head resting on his arm. With one languid hand she gently stroked his hair-roughened chest, the hard length of his upper leg, and the flatness of his stomach. His skin was vibrant underneath her fingers.

The silence was so deep she could hear the rasp of his hand as it caressed her arm.

Then out of the snowy distance the factory whistles began to blow, joined by the deep, honking basso of the ships' horns in the harbor and the soprano toot of whistles on the tugs. The great clock from the church tower started to toll.

When it had tolled twelve strokes, Joseph said jubilantly, "Happy New Year, Kate."

"Happy New Year, Joseph." They kissed each other, and the kiss was different from all the others. It was a pledge, a vow.

"I think we have a lot to celebrate." He grinned at her and got out of bed; he seemed a bit self-conscious now about his nakedness, and put on a bathrobe. "I'm afraid this establishment doesn't run to imported wine, but I have some Italian red from down the street."

Kate watched him light a candle. "Italian red would be just wonderful."

"But first things first," he said, bringing her an old flannel shirt. "The heat's gone down. Put this on, my darling."

She took the shirt from him and put it on; it was soft and cozy from many washings and felt very good—as good as hearing him say "my darling." It was the first time he'd ever used such an endearment.

She heard him fumbling around in a kitchen drawer, muttering, "Corkscrew, corkscrew," and smiled to herself. Finally she heard the drawn cork's resounding pop, and Joseph emerged with a water glass of wine in each hand, a straw-covered bottle clamped awkwardly between his side and his arm.

Laughing, Kate got up and hurried to him to relieve him of the bottle, enjoying the feel of the flannel shirttails that covered her almost to the knees.

He set the glasses of wine down on the table, staring at her in the candlelight. She thought: I must look like a wild woman, with my hair all fallen down.

But he said, with awe, "You are so beautiful, Kate. So . . . blue and gold and white. So gold with your hair like that, down on your shoulders." He came to her and clasped her to his body. "And you feel so soft, so soft."

When they drew apart again, she retorted, "Thank you kindly. I was afraid I looked like something 'scared out of the woods,' as Letha puts it." She sat down on one of the hard, straight chairs at the table and he took the one opposite.

"Letha?"

"My grandfather's housekeeper. I introduced you to her on Christmas Eve." She nodded her thanks as he handed her a glass of wine.

"I couldn't remember my own name on Christmas Eve," he admitted with a smile, and Kate was sharply aware, all over again, of how much his smile changed the sad look of his face. "Not after I'd kissed you."

"Happy New Year, Joseph. The happiest new year I've ever had. *Mazel tov!*" She lifted her glass.

His eyes glinted when she made the Jewish toast, and he raised his glass to hers before they drank. "To 1910, Kate, the best year of my life."

They drifted into happy talk, so eager to tell each other everything about themselves that the church clock struck one before they realized it. Chilled, they got back in bed to continue their conversation.

When the great clock near the park tolled twice, Kate said dolefully, "Oh, Joseph, I've got to go."

"No, no," he blurted, gathering her close to him again. "I don't want to let you go, not just yet."

"Don't you know it's the same for me?" she protested tenderly, planting quick, small kisses on his neck and face. Trying to lighten the moment's ache, she said, "I can't be delivered with the milk, not in that dress!" She waved at the splendid evening gown thrown over one of the small straight chairs.

"Let me hold you, then, just one more time," he pleaded. She moved very close, putting her arms around him, squeezing him with all her strength while he ran a wondering hand down the shining length of her hair and gave her a long, dizzying kiss.

With terrible reluctance she rose, retrieved her underthings and her dress, and went to the little bathroom to put them on. When she emerged, with her hair pinned up again on her head, she found Joseph sitting on the bed, dressed for the street.

"Good Lord, you look like a queen," he whispered. "I couldn't even see what you were wearing before," he admitted with a self-mocking grin.

"I'm glad. Believe me, I liked the shirt much better," she said softly, and laid the shirt over the back of a chair. It was hard to read Joseph's expression; there was something uncertain in his eyes as he gazed at the dress. And then, when he took her in his arms to kiss her again, somehow everything was all right.

They were happily silent in the motor cab, Kate leaning her

head against his shoulder. But as it neared the Wendell house, she murmured, "I wish this ride would never end."

"So do I." Joseph's grasp tightened. "But tomorrow, there's a whole wonderful holiday, and we can spend it together."

"Oh, yes. Yes. There's a tradition that whatever you do on New Year's Day you'll be doing all year long. Isn't that nice?" She looked at him.

He beamed at her. "That's very nice indeed. I've never heard of it. It's a fine tradition, and we'll honor it to the letter."

His remark was so mischievously weighted that she giggled, feeling an overpowering happiness. They were not smiling, however, when the cab drew to a stop. She felt she could not bear to say good night; her reluctance was a physical ache.

"I know now," she whispered, "what Shakespeare meant by 'sweet sorrow.' "

He held her in a bruising grip. His voice shook a little when he answered, "I know. But it rhymed with 'tomorrow.' " Joseph gave her one last kiss.

"Tomorrow," she repeated, feeling tears gather in her eyes. Then she made herself smile as he helped her from the cab and stood beside it to watch her cross the sidewalk and mount the stairs. She looked back to see him get in and waited until the motor cab drove away before she entered the house.

The house was still. Kate slipped out of her shoes, crept up the stairs and down the hall. She was opening her door when her father's head emerged from behind the door to his room. "Good. You're home." He smiled at her sleepily. "How was your evening?"

"Wonderful." Kate felt guilty when his face brightened; she knew he had misinterpreted her elated answer as a rare compliment to her "proper" escort. "Good night."

"Good night, my dear."

He closed his door and Kate went into her bedroom, letting out a sigh of relief. It was lucky that her father had been the one to see her; even half-asleep, Elizabeth would have noticed the careless rearrangement of her hair and read her dreamy look in quite another way.

Kate tossed off her cloak and dropped her slippers onto the carpet. She sat down at her sketching table and opened her portfolio. Hidden in the center was the sketch of Joseph. She sat there for a long time, staring at his image.

Chapter 7

"*Mazel tov*, my children." Harry Dryver raised his champagne glass in a bar of early-April sun that slanted through the restaurant window. Joseph and Kate Barsimson touched their crystal glasses to Dryver's and they drank to their marriage. It is like a benediction, Joseph thought. He looked into the glowing blue of Kate's eyes.

"You should be stamping on this glass, of course." Dryver smiled at Joseph. "But I don't know how that would go over in the Lafayette."

Joseph laughed. "Mr. Dryver, you have a Jewish soul."

Kate's fingers pressed against his. "He always has had." Kate had never looked so happy. And Joseph had never *felt* happier. It was still hard to believe that she was actually his wife—they had taken the solemn step he had hardly dared to think of taking before.

"Shall we order?" Dryver suggested. "Kate?"

"Order for me, Joseph," she said gaily. "I won't know what I'm eating anyway."

Joseph let go of her hand reluctantly and picked up the big gilt menu. He wouldn't know what he was eating, either, even though this was the best restaurant he had ever been to. He gazed at the menu through a kind of fog.

While Dryver ordered, Joseph took Kate's hand again. Tonight we can actually fall asleep, he thought incredulously, and wake up together in the morning. Kate had never looked so beautiful; everything about her shone—her

99

hair and eyes, her small, full lips. His star on her dress, the golden band on her finger, the pearls like moonlight against her dress, the color of spring leaves. They were her grandmother's pearls; Dryver had given them to Kate this morning for a wedding present before they all went to City Hall.

Dryver's check crackled in Joseph's pocket now, impelling him to say, "I want you to know, sir, that our . . . situation isn't always going to be like this. I mean to change it. I have a reason now"—he glanced at Kate—"to turn the world upside down if I have to."

"I *do* know, Joseph. I could see that from the first." Dryver's eyes shone with kindness. "Ah," he sighed, "you know, this takes me back. Kate can tell you—her grandmother and I had just this kind of wedding. And wonderful years together. And I believe that wonderful years can *only* come from this kind of union. If people don't love each other right away, they never love each other at all." Dryver grinned at Kate. "And my granddaughter shares my shocking beliefs."

Joseph grinned back. "Thank God for that." He looked at Kate for a long moment. Then he said slowly, "I think it's time, don't you?"

They would have to tell the Wendells of their marriage. And Solomon and Anzia. He could read Kate's expression of dread, but Joseph anticipated the confrontation with her father almost eagerly. He welcomed the challenge, the chance to stand up to Wendell. And Solomon.

"Shall I go uptown with you?" Dryver offered. "After all, I'm a co-conspirator."

Dryver had been just that, from the very beginning. Kate had dressed for the wedding at his house; he had bought flowers and taken care of all the details. Warm with gratitude, Joseph protested, "You've done too much already, sir. Besides, I think I should tell Kate's parents myself."

"I like that." Dryver gave him a look of respect.

Outside, the thin city trees were unfurling; there was a

faint hint of summer in the gentle air. The light had reddened toward sunset, but as Joseph looked at Kate, he thought: She looks like the morning of the world. Kate had looked like this in the el station on that first winter afternoon; Joseph recalled how strangers had stared at her—as if she gladdened and refreshed their eyes too. He knew this was the morning of his life.

Joseph's heart hammered against his ribs. He came to himself with a start: Dryver was holding out his hand, and a scarlet cab had already pulled up beside them. Joseph shook Dryver's hand in silence.

Then he and Kate, alone at last, got into the cab. Sitting close, he put his arm around her, and drawing her to him, pressed his lips to the satiny skin of her brow.

As the cab headed north, they sat in blissful silence. Kneading Kate's arm with his hand, Joseph reviewed the months that had led to this dreamlike day. He smiled against Kate's fragrant hair. Who would have thought that his rotten cousin Lionel Simson could have had a part in this glorious happening? And that had happened only two weeks ago.

This winter had been the most remarkable time of Joseph's life: ever since New Year's Eve he had felt as though he were walking on air. He hardly knew himself: from the time he was twelve years old, he had dreamed and breathed little else but the unions. But this year, after the holidays, all he could think about was Kate, and their plots and plans to be together.

As January became February and the winter moved toward spring, his days had alternated between glory and despair. The glory was the time spent with Kate; the despair came when, after their brief moments together, he and Kate had to endure the long nights alone. Joseph had thought marriage would be impossible—at least for a long, long time. It tormented him that their love had to find expression in the dingy surroundings of his flat. Although Kate, bless her, hardly seemed to notice or care.

He drew her closer to him now, and looking down at her, saw that she had closed her eyes and was smiling.

What a treasure she was, he marveled; another woman would have asked him why he was so silent, what he was thinking. But Kate asked for nothing more than his caresses, his nearness.

Joseph remembered those many nights—nearly a hundred of them—when parting from her had been so painful it was like tearing away the scab from a wound. But what had hurt even more was the expression in Kate's eyes—a kind of wistful sadness whose origin he now understood. She had been waiting for him to ask her to marry him. And he had truly believed he couldn't . . . until the night they ran into Lionel Simson.

That windy night in March was rife with spring: early daffodils and blazing tulips had begun to appear in the flower stalls. Kate wore her bright green dress, the dress she'd worn on Christmas Eve, and his star glittered against it. Joseph was utterly happy. The strike had ended, too: nearly four hundred employers had signed the union contract for a closed shop, fewer hours, and wage raises. The union had grown so much that Joseph hardly recognized it, and it would continue to grow. It had gained new public respect; now there was real solidarity among the workers. Of course the fight was just beginning; many shops and factories were still unorganized. But they had won the first decisive battle.

And it was spring . . . and he was with Kate.

They were approaching Joseph's building when he heard his name called in a drunken voice. Turning, he recognized his cousin Lionel Simson. Joseph smothered a curse.

He hadn't spoken to Lionel for nearly ten years, not since the awkward occasion of his cousin's bar mitzvah. Once in a while, over the years, Joseph had glimpsed Lionel in a tavern or café, usually with a brightly painted woman. This evening he was with two of them.

"Let's go," Joseph urged the surprised Kate.

But Lionel was determined to be acknowledged. "Where are you rushing off to, cousin?" he demanded. He lurched toward Kate and Joseph, dragging his two companions by their hands. "I want my friends to meet the savior of the masses."

Lionel was practically shouting, and people were beginning to stare at them. Lionel grabbed Joseph's arm, mumbling, "My cousin's got a Polack *shiksa*, too, just like little Wanda here." He leered at the blond girl by his side. She was a travesty of Kate, reminding Joseph of a painted pug dog, with blunt features and protruding eyes.

An icy rage took hold of Joseph, making him dangerously calm. He knew this feeling; he always got it just before entering the ring. With one smooth motion he shook off his cousin's hand and his fist shot out, catching Lionel on the point of his jaw. With a look of glazed surprise, Lionel crumpled onto the pavement.

"Whadja do that for, ya bastid?" the blond shrieked at Joseph. She and the other girl, a brunette with a ferretlike face, were bending over the befuddled Lionel.

Joseph took Kate by the arm. "Come on, darling." He shouldered a curious man aside and led Kate into the building, pulling her by the hand.

They climbed the stairs in silence. When they reached his flat, Kate went in slowly. She still looked shocked. Joseph closed the door softly and gathered her in his arms.

"I'm sorry you had to hear that, Kate." He felt her body shake. "I'm sorry you had to see me acting like a lowlife . . . but I just . . . Oh, darling, please don't cry."

Joseph stepped back and looked down at her. Kate wasn't crying at all; her body had been trembling with incipient laughter. She burst into giggles.

"You're *laughing*," he said, sounding so fatuous that she giggled more wildly."

"Oh, Joseph," she gasped. She took his face in her hands. "You were *wonderful*. I never saw anything so *fast*—I didn't even see you hit him, and there he was, on the sidewalk, looking so ridiculous. Who *is* he? Is he really your cousin?"

Joseph stared at her, speechless. He thought he had never loved her so much. She could always surprise him.

Another woman might have screamed, or fainted, or called him a barbarian. And here she was, saying he was "wonderful."

He hugged her, kissing her face, her hair, her upturned mouth. Now there was no more laughter, only a sweet gravity between them. She was moving close to him, into him, and he could smell her faint, arousing scent of lilies that always moved him to a madness of desire. She was touching him with a new boldness, and Joseph realized that the primitive scene had excited her. Now he was past all thinking.

Afterward, Joseph stroked her white naked body with a gentle hand and murmured, "You don't know how it hurts me, Kate . . . that I've exposed you to a thing like that."

"What do you mean?"

"I mean our situation." He pulled her close, speaking against her tousled hair. "No matter how much our friends rattle on about 'Free Love' and the free life, and all that nonsense, this is not the way I want to live with you."

She was very still.

"There's another world beyond ours, outside the Village," he went on.

"If this Lionel represents it," she retorted, "I don't think much of it." He hugged her closer. "Who is he, exactly? You've never mentioned him."

Joseph told her then about Rafael and his son, describing the day of the long-ago bar mitzvah, when Rafael had proclaimed Joseph a *mensch* before the jealous Lionel; how Rafael had come to the gym to see Joseph fight, telling Joseph he wished his own son were as much a man. "You see," Joseph said, "my uncle's always been partial to me, in spite of my job"—he grinned wryly—"and the fact that he's a garment manufacturer. I think he's always wanted his son to be like me. And he's made the mistake of telling him that. I'm sure that Lionel must hate me. He couldn't give up an opportunity to get at me . . . through you."

"How horrible. But, Joseph, why does it matter? Who is this . . . awful man to us?"

"It's not just him, Kate." Joseph sat up abruptly. "It's the whole . . . furtiveness of our being together like this that I can't stand anymore. I don't want us to live like two sneaky children. I don't want to say good night to you. Oh, Kate, I want you to belong to me before the whole world. I want to marry you." He held out his arms.

"Oh, Joseph, Joseph." She buried her head against his chest. "I've been waiting so long for you to ask me."

"I thought I couldn't, darling. I have so little to offer you."

"So *little*?" She raised her head; her beautiful eyes looked enormous. "Joseph, you are offering me everything."

Now, next to her in the taxi on their wedding day, Joseph could hear her words again. He was surprised to see that the cab had already drawn up outside the Wendell house.

"You look as if you were dreaming," Kate whispered with a smile.

"I was." He raised her hand to his lips and kissed it. "Dreaming about that day I asked you to marry me . . . and about tonight. But now it's time for me to wake up."

Kate looked up at the gloomy chocolate-brown mansion. "Yes. Let's get it over with."

As they climbed the stoop to the ornate entrance door, he asked, "Are you all right?"

"I'm always all right when I'm with you." The look she gave him made him feel as strong as Samson, ready for anything.

An impassive butler opened the door. "Good afternoon, Miss Kate." Joseph saw a ripple on his blank face when the man took in Kate's festive clothes and the stranger standing behind her.

"Good afternoon, Lynn. Is my father home yet?"

"He is, miss. He has just come in. He is with your mother in the small drawing room." Lynn was taking their wraps.

The *small* drawing room, Joseph thought silently. My God.

"Lynn, this is . . . Kate stopped abruptly, giving Joseph a twinkling look. He realized she could hardly announce her marriage to a servant before she told her parents. ". . . Mr. Barsimson," she said finally.

"How do you do, sir."

"How do you do, Lynn." Joseph had almost called him "Mister." He had never even seen a butler before, much less been introduced to one.

Kate led Joseph to a set of double doors, and he admired the straightening of her shoulders, the quick defiant lift of her lovely head. He pulled the doors back for her and followed her into a glistening flower-filled room. A dark, irritable-looking woman who resembled Harry Dryver sat on a brocade sofa before a tea table that gleamed with heavy silver. She wore a magnificent gown and held a thin china cup halfway to her lips.

When she saw Kate and Joseph, she continued to hold the cup in midair, like a statue of a woman drinking tea. She frowned with puzzled surprise.

"Well, Kate." Her voice was sharp and unpleasant. So unlike Kate's, Joseph could not help thinking. She lowered the cup, staring at Kate's dress, at the pearls, with bewilderment. "What on earth is the meaning of this? What are you doing in your grandmother's pearls?"

"Elizabeth." A deep, reproachful voice came from a corner of the room. A tall, handsome middle-aged man who looked like Kate moved toward the center of the room. He held a glass of wine in his hand. He smiled at Kate and looked interrogatively at Joseph.

"Mother . . . Father." Kate took Joseph's hand. "I have come to present my husband, Joseph Barsimson."

For a long instant the Wendells were utterly still; they just kept staring. Then her mother shrieked, "Your *husband*!" The convulsive movement of her hand tilted the cup of tea: it splashed onto her silken lap and an ugly brown stain spread over the pale-yellow skirt of the voluminous gown.

Kate's father continued to stand there like a graven idol, his face expressionless. His weary blue-gray eyes, a faded copy of Kate's own, took in Joseph's features, skimming over his body down to his rather worn shoes. A movement like a tic twitched at the corner of his austere mouth.

"My God, my God!" Kate's mother cried out, dropping the empty teacup onto the carpet. She burst into tears. Then she ran blindly out of the room, holding up the skirt of her ruined dress and slamming the double doors behind her.

"Please, Father," Kate said calmly. "Can't we all sit down?"

At her poise, Joseph's heart swelled with love. He felt sorry for her father. The man looked as if he might have a stroke. Mr. Wendell nodded numbly and sank into a chair. Kate sat down on the sofa where her hysterical mother had sat. Joseph remained standing.

He still had a strange feeling of compassion for Mr. Wendell; the man seemed to be struggling for speech. At last he said flatly, "You are married," as though he needed to voice the fact to believe it. "When . . . when did this happen, Kate?"

"Today, at City Hall. Grandfather went with us."

"Mr. *Dryver* . . . ?" Wendell's eyes widened, then a quick redness suffused his whole face. "How . . . how long have you known each other? Who *are* you, Mr. Barsimson?"

"We've known each other since last November, sir. I am a general organizer for the Garment Union. We met on the picket line, through my cousin, Rose Nathan." Better let him have it all at once, Joseph thought dryly.

Again Wendell spoke with a dazed flatness. "The Garment Union . . . Rose Nathan." He swallowed and looked at the wineglass in his hand as if it were a strange object. He set it down. "I take it, then, that you are a . . . Jew, Barsimson."

"Joseph," Kate corrected, but her father ignored her.

"And you have never bothered to present yourself in

this house?'' Wendell demanded. He was more in command of himself now, and his rising anger was patent.

"How could I, sir,'' Joseph asked him quietly, "when you would have given me just this reception?''

"Don't be insolent, boy!'' Wendell said sharply. "My daughter is not of age, and I can have this marriage annulled in a snap of my fingers.''

"Father!'' Kate was no longer calm; her voice trembled. "If you do that, I will never speak to you, never let you see my face again!'' She leapt up from the sofa.

"Be quite, Kate.'' Wendell's voice was steely. He rose from his chair, facing Joseph. They were almost the same height and they stared into each other's eyes. "If you had hoped to enrich yourself by this marriage, Barsimson,'' Wendell said coldly, "you are going to be bitterly disappointed. You will never see a penny of my money.'' Kate cried out.

Joseph balled his hands into fists; it took every ounce of his control not to hit the older man. "That was never my intention, sir,'' he said quietly. "I will provide for my wife. We came here to do you the courtesy of telling you we're married.''

"The *courtesy!*'' Wendell laughed softly.

"We're going, Father. I won't be back . . . until you can accept my husband.'' She held out her hand to Joseph. "Please, let's go.''

Joseph nodded to Wendell and followed Kate out of the room, pulling the great doors shut behind them. The butler was nowhere to be seen. They took their coats from a closet in the hall and made their way to the street.

On the long ride downtown, Kate clung to his hand in miserable silence. At last she said, "Oh, Joseph, I'm so ashamed.''

"It's all right, darling. It wasn't even as bad as I expected.'' In fact, it hadn't been what he expected at all. Her father's reaction was exactly what he might have predicted, but her mother's . . . That instant, cold withdrawal was incredible. The woman had abandoned Kate without a word. No wonder Kate was so strangely distant from her parents, so hungry for warmth. She always curled up against him when they were alone, like a newly adopted kitten. Tenderness choked his throat, and he pulled her close.

She spoke against his chest. "I will never, never speak to either one of them again."

Joseph patted her shoulder, knowing that any debate would be pointless now. The cab was turning into the narrow chaos of Essex Street, impeded by pushcarts and drays; the sidewalks in front of the small shops and huddled tenements overflowed with after-work crowds, chattering peddlers, and shrill children.

"This is it," Joseph called out to the driver when they reached his father's shop. He glanced at Kate as he paid the fare; she looked inordinately frightened.

"Don't worry," he said as they got out. "They'll love you." He smiled at her. "You are so sweet, so beautiful." But she did not seem reassured.

Joseph's father was in the shop talking to a customer. Joseph took a deep breath and stood aside for Kate to enter. The customer came out as they went in; he started to brush past them. Then, getting a better look at Kate, he touched his hat and held the door for them, admiring her with his eyes. Joseph thought the shop had never looked so poky or so sad. Solomon stared at them. To Joseph he looked older than the last time.

"Hello, Papa."

"So, Joseph, you finally decided to pay us a visit. Your mother's upstairs." Solomon hadn't acknowledged Kate's presence, aside from a curious and rather hostile glance. But finally he asked, "And who is this young lady?"

"Papa, this is Kate, my wife."

At first Solomon didn't seem to take it in. Then he stiffened. His tired eyes noted Kate's brief, tilted nose, her blue eyes and golden hair. "Your wife?"

"Hello, Mr. Barsimson." Kate smiled shakily.

"Your wife? She is not Jewish, my son." Solomon

spoke as if Kate were not present. Joseph felt his anger building slowly.

"My name was Wendell," Kate said quietly. "But I love your son. I'll do everything in my power to make him happy."

"Ah, God. Ah, God." Solomon sank down on a stool and began to rock back and forth, the picture of agony. Kate stood very still, watching Solomon uneasily. Joseph put his arm around her.

"Solomon! Solomon? What is the matter?"

Anzia appeared at the foot of the stairs that led to the flat above.

"This is my mother, Kate. Mama, I want you to know my wife." He gestured with his free hand toward Anzia.

"Joseph." Anzia came toward them, smiling. "My daughter-in-law." She held out her arms to Kate. "My daughter-in-law is such a beautiful girl."

Solomon jumped up from his stool. "Are you *meshugeh*, woman? You call this girl our daughter-in-law, when you can see she is not one of us?"

Joseph could no longer contain himself. "Will you cut *kriah* for me, then, the way Benjamin did for you? Come on, Kate. We're leaving."

Kate hesitated, glancing from Joseph to his mother, and Anzia cried, "No, Joseph, no, son. Stay awhile. Don't go."

But Joseph was already urging Kate through the door; he was shaking all over, sickened by the scene, shamed by the insult to Kate. At least her father had not stated his prejudice so crudely. Now, in the tumult of the street, Joseph was deafened by the clatter of the carts and shrill voices. He felt almost sorry he was a Jew.

He realized that the beautiful woman by his side was the one who made him feel like an alien. People were staring at her; he practically had to pull her along, to get her past the habitual assembly of gossipy old Jewish women on the stoops. They had known him all his life and always stopped him to ask pointed and embarrassing questions. The women's eyes were nearly popping out today at the sight of the lovely blond woman.

"Joseph." He came back to his senses, aware of his hasty touch, horrified by his disloyal thoughts. "Darling, please." He looked down into her face. It was frightened.

"Oh, Kate, forgive me. I was just so . . ."

"I know, Joseph. I know. Now it's my turn to say it's all right. It is, my love. We have each other."

"Yes. Oh, yes." He saw the joy in her eyes, and knew nothing else was real. "Come on, darling. Let's walk over to Broadway. We'll have a better chance of getting a cab there. And we'll go back to the Village . . . where we belong."

When Joseph unlocked the door of the flat, he stopped and said to her softly, "Wait. Don't cross the threshold yet." He scooped her up and carried her in.

He set her down gently and she came into his arms. "Oh, Joseph, Joseph. We're home." She looked around the flat.

Its ugliness was softened by the twilight, and it was shining clean. Joseph had bought a lot of daffodils, and had jammed them awkwardly into some vases from a secondhand store. He had bought glass candlesticks at the same place, and had put yellow candles in them.

"How beautiful." Kate touched one of the blossoms delicately with her finger; her eyes shown in the dimness. "And candles. Let's light them."

When she touched the wicks to flame, Kate murmured, "The winter is over . . . the voice of the turtle is heard in the land." To Joseph, her beautiful face and the golden glow of her hair in the candlelight were like flowers of the spring, growing from the calyx of her leaf-colored dress.

And he knew, with a deep, ecstatic certainty, that Kate would be all the family he would ever need.

Chapter 8

That first weekend, it seemed their long hunger would never be appeased. They didn't leave the flat at all until Sunday morning. Kate was dazzled by the wonder of falling asleep in Joseph's arms, and waking up to see him lying beside her. After all the months of nights alone, of endless yearning for his presence, the luxury of his nearness overwhelmed her.

Joseph felt the same; they couldn't pass each other without touching. His dark eyes had lost their starved look; already the lines of tension had begun to disappear from his face.

At last, on Sunday afternoon, they emerged from the flat into the sunshine of an almost summery day. They sat for several lazy hours on a bench in Washington Square Park, then ate supper at Polly's. They had been picnicking, to Kate's delight, on the funny food that Joseph had in the flat. She had never eaten salami, which made him laugh; she enjoyed its strange spicy taste. Joseph had been the one to scramble eggs for them both mornings.

"I'll cook dinner for you tomorrow night," Kate said impulsively.

"You know how to cook?" Joseph asked, amazed.

"Oh, no. But I'm going to Grandfather's tomorrow and watch Letha," she said blithely. "Then by tomorrow night I'll know how."

"Admirable," Joseph teased her, kissing her in front of

everyone at Polly's. It was a festive evening, with friends stopping by frequently to offer congratulations. Kate thought Joseph's face had an odd expression when he paid the bill, but she quickly forgot it in the joy of their return to the little flat.

On Monday morning she awoke to find him gone. She had an absurd sensation of panic until she found the note Joseph had left on the table, explaining that he hadn't had the heart to wake her. It was still early—only nine o'clock— and Kate faced the day's plans with zest.

After dressing in the simple shirtwaist and skirt she had brought from her grandfather's, Kate tried to scramble some eggs. They were awful—part burned and part runny— but she ate them anyway, taking an inventory of the flat. She hadn't really looked at it before. It was clean and neat; the walls must have been freshly painted not long ago: they were a bright, cheerful white. But the table was scratched and ugly, the chairs nondescript, and the curtains and bedspread were completely colorless.

Today, she decided, she would do the whole thing over. She still had her whole allowance from last week. But first, she must go to Letha for cooking lessons. She would also call her maid, Eileen, from her grandfather's house and ask her to bring some more clothes, her drawing materials, to the flat.

Letha received Kate with open arms. "Well, child, this is so nice! Your granddaddy'll be sorry he missed you. He went all the way up there on the train to those Bo . . . Bote . . ."

"Botanical Gardens," Kate supplied.

"That's right . . . to paint some flowers. Come on in the kitchen, let me give you a cup of coffee."

Seated at the big table in the basement kitchen overlooking the garden, Kate studied Letha's gleaming implements. "Letha, I've got to learn how to cook today."

The old woman whooped. "Today? Lord, honey, you can't learn all that in a day." Kate's heart sank. Her disappointment must have been plain, because Letha said quickly, "I didn't mean to make fun of you, child. It's not your fault. You were raised not to know a skillet from a pot, which is just the way it should be."

"Not anymore," Kate said firmly. "I want to cook Joseph's dinner tonight."

"All right, then, I guess I can help you do that." She gave Kate a few rudimentary directions and told her where to go for the best vegetables and cuts of meat. Kate wrote it all down conscientiously in a small notebook.

"Now, steak is easy," Letha suggested. "I wouldn't start right out with fried chicken. There's not a man in shoe leather doesn't like steak. What I do is pan-fry it for your granddaddy; he likes the Southern style. These Yankees, though . . . they generally want it b'oiled, in the oven."

Kate, without allowing for Letha's accent, scribbled, "boiled in the oven." There was nothing to that; all she had to do was put some steaks in a pot of water, put the pot in the oven. She was elated.

After calling Eileen, she hurried off to a hardware store on Sixth Avenue for paints and brushes. They were a heavy burden to carry up the stairs to the flat, but she was filled with eager anticipation. Any kind of paint was something she really understood. Changing into one of her older dresses, Kate spread out some newspapers she had found in a corner and painted the scarred table and ugly chairs a spanking white.

Then she painted the little table by Joseph's side of the bed, and a small cabinet in the living room, a cheerful apple red. Now it would all be dry by the time he came home. She was delighted with the result.

She was picking up the newspapers and balling them into her hands for the trash when she heard a soft rap at the door. She disposed of the papers, rubbed her grimy hands on her dress, and went to open the door.

Eileen was standing in the hall. "Miss Kate?"

The girl's face was so incredulous that Kate almost laughed out loud. Eileen took in her tousled, paint-stained appearance with wide eyes. On either side of Eileen were heavy-looking grips and the big chest in which Kate kept her art supplies. Now she noticed that the Wendell chauffeur was standing diffidently behind Eileen.

"Jerry . . . Eileen. Please, come in." The dark, neatly dressed girl brought in one of the bags; the big redheaded man hauled in the others, then indicated the chest.

"Where do you want this, ma'am?"

Kate pointed to an empty space near the door and Jerry placed the heavy chest there. "The bedroom's in there, Jerry. If you'll just put the grips there, please . . . "

While he was doing so, Kate could hardly contain her amusement. Eileen was staring around the room, obviously groping for something to say. It occurred to Kate that her maid's room in the Wendell mansion was far more elegantly furnished. At last Eileen murmured, "It's a nice place, ma'am. Very . . . cozy."

Jerry came back into the small living room. Touching his cap to Kate, he said, "Well, if that's all, then . . ."

"Yes. Thank you so much. But just a moment." She picked up her purse from the cot that served as a couch.

"No, Miss Kate," Jerry said hastily. He seemed embarrassed. He touched his cap again and, muttering to Eileen, "I'll wait for you in the car," hurried out.

Eileen's cheeks reddened. "I'd better go soon, Miss Kate. The Madam didn't . . . I mean . . . "

"It's all right, Eileen. I think I understand. My mother didn't know about this errand. Is that what you mean? And you have to get back before you're missed."

"Yes." The girl nodded, chagrined. "I'm sorry, Miss Kate. But you see, Jerry mustn't lose his job, not now. *We're* going to be married too." Eileen's smile broke out.

"I'm so glad," Kate said warmly. "I hope you'll be very, very happy. Oh, I wish I could give you a wonderful wedding present." She thought a moment. "The ivory dress! You packed that, didn't you?"

"Oh, yes, but you can't give me *that*." Eileen looked shocked.

"Why on earth not? It will make a perfect wedding

dress, and I won't have much use for it now," Kate protested gaily. She was about to explain to Eileen about the bohemians of Greenwich Village, but looking into her naive eyes, realized it would be incomprehensible to her. "Come, let's get it right now."

Over Eileen's weak protests Kate led her into the bedroom, and they found the lovely dress of ivory lace and satin. The girl held it tenderly over both arms.

"Oh, Miss Kate, how can I thank you?"

"Please don't. I have a lot to thank you for, remember, since we've been together. Just be happy. Like me." Kate grinned at her.

When they had gone, Kate realized that it was nearly noon; there was still so much to do. She hung her clothes hurriedly in the curtained alcove that Joseph called the closet, noticing how even the few garments crowded the space, and shoved the empty grips under the bed.

Washing up hastily and changing her paint-stained old dress, she ran down the long flights of stairs and headed for Fourteenth Street. She remembered seeing a shop there, when she had gone to the union hall, that sold cushions, fabrics, and inexpensive curtains. Everything was so cheap that she was able to buy a cheerful yellow bedspread and harmonizing curtains for the bedroom's one window.

Inspired, she realized her art chest could double as another seat for the living room; she bought some red and blue-green cushions for it; a solid red covering for the cot; and to her joy, found some remnants of fabric in a wonderful stripe of white, blue-green, and red. After a solemn consultation with the clerk, she learned that the fabric would be enough to curtain two windows. With its finished ends, all she would have to do was hem the tops.

She struggled along Fourteenth Street with her huge bundles, and had to stop for another purchase—a frame in the window of a secondhand shop that ought to fit the sketch of Joseph. By the time she was back in the flat her arms ached and she was breathless; she had completely forgotten about lunch. Standing up impatiently, she wolfed down a sandwich and drank some milk, then set to work on hemming the curtains. It was terribly difficult; she'd never sewn anything in her life, but finally she was finished. Triumphant, she slipped the ugly old curtains from their rods and hung the new ones.

The room was transformed after everything was in place; she had never dreamed it could look so nice. The charcoal portrait of Joseph, in its silver-colored frame, was striking over the red-painted chest, and the other touches of brightness brought a whole new light and cheer to the room.

She hurried to replace the bedspread and the dun-colored bedroom curtains with the sunny new ones, then consulted the clock. She couldn't believe it was almost four, and she still hadn't bought anything for dinner. Joseph's note had said "Home at six."

But the final errands—groceries, more candles, and fresh red-and-yellow-striped tulips to replace the withered daffodils—were completed by five, and Kate was inordinately proud of all she had accomplished in one short day. She put potatoes on to boil and slipped the steak into the oven, immersed in water, in the other pot. Then she bathed and changed her dress again. Everything was ready, everything as perfect as she could make it. She was buoyant.

Setting the table with Joseph's plain white dishes, Kate added the flair of the two red-and-white-checked napkins she'd bought at the fabric store; with the vase of striped tulips in the center, the effect was charming, even better than she had hoped. It gave the feeling of a French café, transforming the whole room into a real artist's garret.

When she tested the potatoes with a fork, as Letha had directed, they felt just right. She managed to devise a salad, too. However, when she peeked at the boiling steak, it didn't look at all like the steaks she'd had in restaurants, or at home. Kate took the pot out and examined the meat with dismay; it was a horrible color, and looked like nothing so much as the dreadful specimens she had glimpsed once in the biology lab at Barnard. What on earth was she going to do? Dinner was ruined.

There was a sharp click at the front door and she heard Joseph come in. "Darling?"

"In here," she quavered, near tears.

"Kate . . . what's the matter?" Joseph stood in the arched entranceway to the kitchen, his face mirroring anxiety. "What is it?" He came to her in two long strides and took her in his arms.

She collapsed against his chest. "Oh, Joseph," she sobbed, "I worked so hard . . . I did so many things. I wanted dinner to be nice, and now it's . . . Oh, my God, *look*."

She held out the pot with the offensive hunk of meat.

"Darling, what *is* it?" Joseph asked gently, trying not to smile.

"It's not funny!" she cried out. "It's supposed to be steak. Letha told me to boil it in the oven."

Joseph could no longer contain himself. He burst out laughing and hugged Kate to him. "She must have meant 'broil' it, sweetheart. There's nothing to cry about, really there isn't." He held her close and tilted up her face, wiping her tears away. "The living room looks all different. Come, let me see it. I haven't really had a chance. When I heard you sobbing, all I could think of was to come in here." He put his arm around her waist, persuading her with the pressure of his fingers.

Consoled, she walked with him into the little living room and watched him as he looked around. His eyes gleamed with pleasure. "Kate, it's beautiful! You did all this, in just one day?"

"Not only this," she said proudly. "Come here." Excited as a child, she took him by the hand and led him into the bedroom enjoying his expression when he saw the bright yellow additions, the second vase of red-and-yellow tulips. "This is lovely, Kate," he said softly. He turned to her and cupped her face in his hands. "Why should you worry about being a cook?" His voice was very gentle. "You're an artist. And, I see now, an interior decorator."

She felt a quick, warm rush of love and raised her mouth to his.

"Besides," he whispered, "who's hungry now, anyway?"

Later, as Kate lay with half-closed eyes, languorous in the fading light of yellow candles, Joseph got up and wandered back into the living room.

"Kate! I didn't see this before. The picture. It's very fine," he called out. She got up, slipped on a wrapper, and padded in to join him. "Come here," he ordered tenderly. He put his arm around her, still staring at the drawing of himself. "*That's* what you were meant to do, Kate. That's what you must do."

She felt a deep sense of gratification. But she responded in a teasing voice, "Thanks. However, there's still a dinner to cope with."

"Nothing to it. I'll help you." Joseph fried the steak in the pan for a few minutes and after they had gotten dinner on the table, Kate declared the steak "almost edible."

Joseph grinned at her in the candlelight. Then he sobered. "Kate, how did you manage? I mean, buying all these things? You know, I'm so damned happy I'm crazy. I didn't remember until almost five o'clock that I hadn't even left you any money. I'll never do that again, I promise."

"It didn't occur to me," Kate said brightly. "I still had all my allowance from last week." A strange expression crossed his face: she realized she hadn't been very tactful, referring to her own money. But the moment was brief; he smiled at her again.

"You're wonderful, to do so much. You've made this place look lovely, Kate, the way you've always made everything for me. I love you so much, so much."

"I love you, Joseph."

Later, when they dressed again and went out to take a walk in the green twilight of Washington Square, they moved slowly, their arms around each other's waists. For Kate, all life seemed to breathe through Joseph, close by her side.

*   *   *

That dazzling April, most of Kate's waking hours were like a dream. The flat was so small and bright that she felt as if she were living in a playhouse. But she soon learned that playhouses had to be cleaned. She had lived her whole life without ever making a bed, or even washing her own hair. A nurse, and then Eileen, had done that for her. In the middle of the first week she realized there were things that had to be done. She had gotten up early with Joseph and tried to make his breakfast, but observing her struggles with kindly eyes, he had offered to do it for her. As soon as he was gone, Kate sat down at the table and drank another cup of the rather bitter coffee, considering the tasks that faced her. Well, she would master them if it killed her. She got up and began to put things away busily—the small rooms seemed to get cluttered all the time—and washed the breakfast dishes.

The kitchen floor had gotten very dirty. She looked in the tall, ugly metal cabinet and found a broom, two mops, and a bucket. She chose the softer, cleaner mop and wet it in the sink; it was very frustrating. The mop seemed to resist moisture altogether. Determined, however, she added soap powder to the water and kept soaking the mop until it was finally wet. Lifting it out of the sink, she splashed herself from head to toe; soap stung her eyes.

She slammed the mop down to the tiny floor and began to pull it back and forth. The dirt clotted and kept resurfacing. Kate was almost ready to weep. She gave up on the mop and put it back in the cabinet, but dirty water gushed out on the floor. She took the mop out again, wrung it out with her hands over the sudsy water, and replaced it. The water was dark gray. She ran a new sinkful of soap and water and, despairingly, dipped the dish rag in it. Then she knelt down and washed the floor with the dishrag. At least it was clean now, but she was in the far corner and now she'd have to walk on it. She backed out of the kitchen on her knees, realizing that she'd planned to wash the tablecloth and napkins in the kitchen sink, and now she couldn't, until the floor was dry. Even when it was, she would surely splash it again. All this seemed such a wretched mystery, she decided she would never solve it.

And her dress was ruined. Despondently she took it off and hung it outside the closet to dry. There was no point in putting on another dress now until she'd washed her lingerie—most of it was soiled—and her hair. Kate was dismayed at the effect of the soap on her first piece of delicate underwear; some of the tiny threads seemed almost to dissolve. She washed her hair, and then the bathroom was flooded. Kate cleaned up as best she could, then padded back to the kitchen. The little floor was clean and bright, but now there was the sink to be scoured, and the dishrag had to be thrown away.

Overwhelmed, Kate washed the napkins and tablecloth and with difficulty managed to run them out in the sun on the washline strung from the kitchen window; she hadn't yet mastered the pulley. Her eyes stung and her back and haunches hurt. She still had to take Joseph's shirts to the Chinese laundry—he didn't have many; if she didn't get them back on time, he would be without—and buy food for dinner. Now the morning was nearly gone. She had planned to go out and do some sketching and visit her grandfather. And Joseph had invited her to come over to the union hall that afternoon to see the new improvements they had made. Her hair wouldn't dry for two more hours. It would make sense to cut it. A lot of women were getting bobs. Kate envied them their light, carefree air.

But she could imagine what Joseph would say. He was positively lyrical about her long, heavy hair and always complimented her on it. She couldn't displease him, not ever.

She decided there was one thing she could do while she was trapped here with her hair. Still in her underclothes, with the strands of wet hair streaming down her back and over her shoulders, Kate took a roll of canvas from her supply chest, along with slats, nails, and a small hammer. Quick and sure, she put together the frame where she would stretch her canvas, then set up her colors and brushes near one of the back windows.

Looking out, she saw the bright motley of washing, strung like merry flags, vivid in the sun, dancing in the spring breeze; the somber brick buildings on Minetta Lane formed a stark background. With swift certainty, and a thrill of pleasure, Kate began to paint the dancing garments, only the bright ones—red and pink and yellow, orange and blue and green.

When she paused, her eyes were blurred, her neck and arms had a satisfying ache. She got up, stretching, and stepped back to judge the canvas. It was good.

It was really good. The breeze seemed to be blowing, still, in the picture itself, and the bright wet clothes had a merry life. It moved. It actually moved, Kate thought with astonishment. Her pleasure was so hot and whole it was almost like the experience of love.

She sank down on the stool and stared at the canvas. Suddenly, then, she wondered what time it was: the clock's hands were pointing toward five.

She jumped up and put her paints away, hastily set up some cans in the kitchen to soak her brushes in, leaving the canvas propped against the wall to dry. As she was replacing the small hammer and minute nails, she made a sudden decision, and tapped several nails into the blank wall between the two windows. Then she hung the canvas on the nails, moving back to survey her handiwork.

It was perfect, heart-lifting: the simple gaiety of the canvas, between the striped curtains, made a merry circus of the entire wall.

But now she had to hurry. In minutes she flung on a dress, tied back her hair with a ribbon, grabbed up Joseph's shirts and her purse, and raced down the stairs.

When Joseph got home, Kate's hair was brushed, loose and shining, and she was dressed in her dark-green "artistic" dress with its flowing comfort. The chops were sizzling in the pan—Kate found she could cope with them—and their appetizing smell mingled with the acrid scent of turpentine.

Joseph kissed her soundly and grinned, sniffing. "What's all this?" Then he saw the canvas on the wall. "Kate. Oh, Kate."

He stood there staring at the painting for a long while. Then he held her close, squeezing her hard with his lean, muscular arms. "It's beautiful, Kate. It's so . . . happy. And, do you know,"—he leaned back, looking earnestly down into her eyes— "it has something that even your grandfather's work doesn't have."

"What's that?" she asked eagerly.

"The washing's very real, and yet it's not. I don't express these things very well, I'm afraid. But it's as if you've painted a world that's happier than this one, a world that *should* be."

Kate was wild with delight as they stood together looking at the canvas. It was a while before she realized the chops were smoking, but it didn't matter. They were both laughing when they raced into the murky kitchen.

That night was a kind of turning point for both of them. She had never doubted Joseph's love; now it seemed he also felt a new respect for her work. Kate had pictured her days as adjuncts to Joseph's; she had vaguely assumed she would work with him in the union. Her fervor for the cause was undiminished. But she hadn't counted on the time-consuming housework, the bargain-shopping. Least of all this new passion for her art—what she had felt before was lukewarm compared to this new sensation. Rather than constricting her, marriage seemed to have freed her to be herself.

When she told Joseph that, he beamed.

It was true: she had never felt so free before, or been so deeply happy. Her world had telescoped to Joseph and the flat, her growing number of canvases and the small perimeter of certain streets in Greenwich Village. And although Joseph told her in great detail each night about his day, and the union, he seemed to take for granted that his work was his, Kate's hers; he no longer suggested that she help out at the union. On occasion he would bring someone home with him for a glass of wine, obviously proud of her, their small home, and her paintings.

It was still very difficult for her to manage the tiny allowance Joseph gave her; Kate was often irritated to find that there was no money left for flowers or candles after she had bought the groceries and paid the Chinese laundry. Now when she dropped in on her grandfather, or invited him to the flat to look at her latest painting, she stopped protesting about his invariable gifts.

"I've always given you something every time we've been together," he reminded her, "since you were a baby. Why should it be different now?"

Sometimes the gift was as small as a bunch of flowers from his garden; on her birthday, it was a generous money gift and a Victrola. Dryver pressed art supplies on Kate and various small household items that he said "came from Letha—I don't know what they're for." At first Dryver refused to visit Joseph and Kate in the evenings, not wanting to intrude on the honeymoon. But by summer he consented to drop in occasionally. Not only did he delight their contemporaries; he was family to Kate and Joseph.

Neither the Wendells nor the Barsimsons were mentioned often, although Dryver had hinted to Kate in the early days that he wasn't "going uptown anymore." She had been his reason for doing so, and that reason no longer existed. At times Kate was still fearful that her father would make good his threat to have the marriage annulled, but Joseph and her grandfather reassured her. If he had not taken steps by now, it was unlikely that he would. Kate was appalled at how little she missed her parents, although she still felt faintly sorry for her father.

She longed to visit Joseph's mother, who had been so kind on that one occasion. But when she told Joseph that, he responded curtly, "My mother knows where we live. I won't have you insulted by my father again. Let it rest, Kate." And she did, reluctantly, to avoid a quarrel with Joseph.

She had completely lost touch with Rose Nathan. When she had phoned Rose to tell her about their marriage, her friend had been shocked and cool, offering the most perfunctory congratulations. Kate was too hurt and angry to call again. Besides, there was no time to miss anyone—Kate's world was full, and utterly perfect.

Until that day near the end of June.

"The trouble for me is—" Joseph smiled at Kate—"my wife's too charming. Once people get here, they won't go home." He brandished an empty Chianti bottle at her. "Do you want to burn candles in this?" He started to empty the ashtrays.

"Yes." Her answer was tense and absent.

Joseph put the bottle and the ashtrays down. "What is it, darling? You were strange all evening. when Abe and Meyer were talking to you about your paintings, you were hardly paying attention."

"I'm sorry, Joseph." Kate carried a stack of plates into the kitchen and began to fill the sink.

"That's not exactly an answer," he said gently. He came up behind her and put his arms around her waist.

Automatically she began to scatter soap powder into the water.

"Stop that, darling. Please, talk to me. What's the matter?" Joseph's strong hands pressed her, pulling her around.

She looked up at him. His dark, glittering eyes were anxious. "Oh, Joseph," she moaned, and buried her face against his chest. "I'm . . . going to have a baby."

"Kate." He tilted her face upward. "Oh, my God, you look so *unhappy*."

"It's just so soon. And everything's been so good, so lovely. There's just been us, and now . . ." She burst into tears. "What will I *do*, Joseph? What will I do with a baby? How will we manage?"

"Darling, darling, don't cry." He gathered her into his arms again and held her tightly to his body. "Don't cry.

We'll be fine." Joseph stroked her hair. He let her cry it out for a little, then, loosening his hold, reached into his pocket for a handkerchief. "Now, blow your nose," he said as if she were a child. She blew; there was an awful honking noise that made her laugh. Then she wiped her face.

"There, you see? It's better already." Joseph smiled at her. "Come on, now. Come and sit down with me," he cajoled her.

She dried her hands and followed him into the living room. They sat down on the cot and he held out one arm invitingly. She leaned against him as he wrapped his muscular arm around her shoulder.

"Now," he said briskly, "are you sure? You've been to a doctor?"

She nodded, wordless, and exhaled a sobbing breath. Then she said shakily, "It will be next spring, near the beginning of April, he said."

Joseph's hand pressed her shoulder. "I know it's soon," he said quietly, "but, Kate, think how wonderful it will be. We might have a baby that will look like you. That would make me so happy."

She looked up at his face; he was smiling again.

"But, Joseph, how can we *afford* it?"

His jaw tightened; he looked very determined. "We'll manage, Kate. Don't worry. We still have your grandfather's wedding present, and believe it or not, I've saved a little money. I've hated it, having to be so . . . ungenerous with you." He flushed. "But now, at least, it will be all right."

"Oh, Joseph, I'm sorry. I'm sorry I brought that up, but—"

"These things have to be brought up," he said matter-of-factly. "I only wish you . . . weren't so unhappy."

"I'm frightened!" She started to cry again.

"I know, I know. Of course you are." Joseph took the wet handkerchief from her hand and gently touched it to her face. "And I'll be big and ugly," she sobbed, "and you'll begin to hate me. You'll love the baby more than me!''

"Oh, Kate, Kate.'' He held her close, tossing the handkerchief on the floor. ''You could never be anything but beautiful to me. And I could never love anyone, or anything, more than you. Without you, the whole world would just be . . . dark. Don't you know that?''

She nodded against him, ashamed, and her arms crept around his neck, drawing his face down to hers. He kissed her with a wild and hungry longing, and then they moved nearer, nearer to each other, and his hands stroked her down her sides; he made pleading sounds deep in his throat. His hands were on hers now, urging her upward, and he picked her up in his arms and took her into the bedroom, laying her gently on the bed.

The meeting of their bodies shook her with its cataclysm.

When they could speak again, he whispered, ''There is nothing in the world but you, Kate. Nothing on earth can ever change this between us.''

She buried her face in the hollow of his arm and kissed the naked skin of his side, feeling him shudder pleasurably under her touch.

"Without you, without this,'' he murmured, ''I told you . . . the whole world is one dark night, without a star. So how could I ever love another human being, even our child, more than you . . . or think you're anything but beautiful? You're my star, Kate. My constant star. Like the one I gave you.''

She touched the small glittering star on the chain around her neck. "I love you, Joseph. I love you so much.''

"I love *you*, Kate. And you'll see. It won't be so long before the baby's here. It won't be that long at all.''

Chapter 9
1911

Joseph was excited as he strode down Greene Street on a windy afternoon in late March. It wouldn't be long until the baby came. He could tell Kate was weary of the heaviness of her body, uncertain of her own attractiveness. He couldn't quite make her believe that she was more beautiful to him than ever; her face had a glow and softness, her eyes a new depth. All of her beauty now was centered in her face and hair, and she was constantly surprising him with little changes. Sometimes she would wear a black ribbon around her throat, above a flowing housedress, with her hair up like the Empress Josephine; another time he might find her painting in an old shirt of his that reached below her knees, like a short dress, with her hair in wild tendrils, brushed so that from the front it looked like a boy's. She had made his life a continual amazement.

When they were first married, there had been nights, heading home, that Joseph had almost been afraid he wouldn't find her there, that he had dreamed the whole thing. Even now sometimes during the small hours he would wake in a cold sweat and reach out for her to reassure himself that she was beside him. Kate had brought him into an unknown world, a place that was sheltered and full of peace. He knew that being born in a moneyed family had helped make her that way, but that wasn't all of it—there was something deep in her, as there was in Harry

Dryver, that urged her to glorify the world around her. When Joseph shut the door at night, he had a feeling that they lived together in an imaginary place, serene as a little house in the woods or on the shore of the sea.

He itched to get his business over and go back to her. The baby wasn't due until next week, but you never knew. It must be awful for her—the heaviness and unease, the fear of her body's final rending. A bad arrangement, he thought drily. There must be something wrong with him, feeling this way about his own child's birth. But there was no way he could wax poetic. On Essex Street another baby meant less room, the necessity of more food and clothes.

At least their child would never carry bundles. And Kate would be all right. Joseph had gotten together enough money for a semi-private hospital room; he couldn't stand the idea of Kate jammed into a ward. Then, too, they were staying at Dryver's for the last few weeks of her pregnancy, which was the greatest relief of all. Someone would be with her all the time, and she didn't have to drag herself up and down all those stairs.

It had been typical of Harry Dryver—that diffident invitation. He was always reluctant to "intrude." But Joseph had never imagined staying in such a place. It was comfortable beyond anything in his experience.

He was so deep in thought that the heavy smell of smoke, the clamor of fire bells, took him completely by surprise. Joseph saw a fire wagon rattle by and pull into Washington Place; and another right behind it. A mob of people milled around the Asch Building. He could hear shouts and women screaming.

Good God. The Asch building, where the Triangle Shirtwaist Factory was.

Joseph quickened his pace, his long stride bringing him to the corner.

There was pandemonium.

Looking up in horror, Joseph saw billows of black smoke, tongues of orange fire darting from the three top floors. Four fire wagons were parked in front of the building; firemen were raising their ladders toward the upper floors.

Dodging a police sawhorse, Joseph stepped on something soft that gave beneath his weight. He jerked his foot back: it was a woman's body, one of a dozen charred bodies lying on the pavement. And he recognized the woman. She was Rhoda Klein, one of the union's stewards. Joseph felt a strangled cry deep in his throat.

"Out of the way!" A wild-eyed fireman shouldered Joseph, feeding the hose to another fireman. Joseph edged past them toward the Washington Place entrance.

"Are you crazy?" A cop lunged at Joseph. "You can't go in there!" Joseph threw out his arms abruptly, dislodging the policeman's hold, and ran into the building. He raced up the stairs. Screaming girls clattered down: Joseph pressed himself against the wall to let them pass, and ran up three more flights. He paused for a second to get his breath; on the sixth-floor landing he could already feel the heat from above. The railing was like the top of a stove.

A knot of hysterical girls crouched on the floor, some of them bleeding from cuts and abrasions. They must have had to break the glass to get out, he figured. And they were either too weakened by loss of blood or too paralyzed with fear to move. One of them was Elvira.

"Come on!" he shouted at them. "Elvira . . . all of you, come on!"

Elvira was so dazed he had to slap her face. The blow revived her. She struggled to her feet and pulled at another girl, but her companion fainted. The others began to scramble madly down the stairs. Joseph hauled the senseless girl onto his back and grabbed Elvira roughly, dragging her down the stairs with him and his burden.

When they were on the street, Elvira gasped to Joseph, "Washington Place door . . . locked. To keep . . . union out." Her knees buckled. Joseph grabbed her by the waist and dragged her along with him, grunting under the weight of the girl on his back. Elvira was bleeding profusely; he had to get her to an ambulance. An attendant took the girl from Joseph's back and slid her into the ambulance next to a staring corpse. There were a dozen mangled corpses in the ambulance already. Elvira saw them and began to scream. Then mercifully she, too, crumpled and fell unconscious against Joseph. He laid her gently in the ambulance beside a dead worker. Joseph felt a sharp, quick nausea.

His head was ringing with the screams, and he could hear his own soundless bellow—the bastards, the bastards. Two of the union's demands, which had not yet been met, were adequate fire escapes for the building, unlocked doors so the workers could get out in case of fire. The goddamned wind must have fed the fire in seconds. The south and east windows were always open in the spring so the girls could get a little air. For a second Joseph was too numb to move. He looked up again.

Three girls were standing on a ninth-story ledge, holding hands. They were waiting for the firemen to raise the ladders. When the ladders finally rose, they only reached the seventh floor.

Joseph swore wildly; his throat, his belly, his whole body ached and flamed with frustrated anger. Good God, good God in heaven, this was New York, and the damned fools were equipped with ladders that wouldn't reach above the seventh floor. Life was a black farce, a nightmare comedy.

Nets were being spread. Girls were jumping right onto the roofs of ambulances. Two dived headfirst into the street. One struck the ghastly carpet of burned bodies spread out along Washington Place. Shuddering, Joseph knew he would never forget that sound; he heard a terrible sobbing breath and knew it was his own.

He had to to something, even if he died trying. He ran across the street, and shoving through the crazed mob and the desperate cops and firemen, sought out the Greene Street entrance. He shouldered his way in. The open elevator stood useless, idle.

Joseph got in and pulled the lever. He had never run one

of these things, but he would now. The car began to rise. He narrowed his eyes against the all-pervasive smoke, inhaling shallowly; the billows were so thick they hid the numbers of the floors, so he just had to guess . . . and hope, opening the doors at random. The first time he opened them he saw a scene from hell: more shrieking girls, and more and more, their faces turned to gargoyle masks of fear, were trampling others to scramble onto the car. There were so many Joseph was afraid the cables would break, but even if he had had the heart he couldn't have kept them from coming—streams of them, like maddened runaway cattle, so many of them, shrilling and screaming, herding in. The car jerked and wobbled; others were jumping on the roof.

Joseph made the first hellish descent, and then went back again and once again. Finally, after he had made too many trips to count, the car refused to move at all.

He stumbled out of the car, spent, and leaned against the lobby wall, taking grateful gulps of the clearer air. He was shaking all over his body and his arms and legs felt leaden, yet horribly light, as if they were composed of water or of air. His head pounded, and the nausea, the overpowering nausea, would not let him go.

A black man staggered from the cellar door and gasped, "That boy, that boy just run away and left the car!" He was crying, and his eyes were huge in his face, and dazed. "Circuit breakers blowing out," he sobbed to Joseph. "It's stuck now for good. We been putting in switch cables, putting 'em in and putting 'em in. They been drowned in the water."

Joseph saw bodies wedged between the shaft and the elevator car. Stumbling out onto the street, he turned his back and vomited against the building.

Kate heard the fire bells clanging to the east. It sounded like a terrible fire. The thought oppressed her. It was so windy today. She shifted awkwardly on the couch in the Baghdad corner of the living room and stared morosely out the window. The sun had disappeared and the wind bent the small city trees on Eleventh Street. Why did she keep recalling that poem, the one that always chilled her, about a "crying of the wind"?

A swift, shooting pain assailed her lower body, then another. So close together. The baby was asking to be born. Kate hoped that Joseph would come home soon.

There was another series of swift, darting pains.

"Letha!" Where was she? Down in the kitchen, probably, where it was hard to hear. Kate yelled, "Letha!"

She heard a distant rattle from below, then a heavy, lumbering tread on the lower stairs and across the hall. Kate thought: this is supposed to be a "natural thing," but I don't feel natural.

She saw Letha at the door, concern on her face.

"The pains . . ." Kate gasped. "*Close.*"

"Oh, Lord have mercy." Letha disappeared and Kate could hear her talking on the phone. "Oh, my Lord, miss, can't they . . . Not any? Yes, ma'am, I reckon so. I reckon we'll *have* to."

What was the matter at the hospital? Kate fought the need to cry. Letha had helped at births herself—Kate knew that—but she wanted a doctor, an ambulance.

She heard Letha replace the receiver, mumble something, and come into the room.

"Honey," she said softly, stroking Kate's head, "the hospital got no more ambulances. None of the other ones got them neither. They're all at that terrible fire, over to the Tria . . ." Letha stopped short.

"The Triangle! Is it the Triangle, Letha?" Kate shrieked. "Oh, my God, Joseph's there . . . he said he was going by there this afternoon!" Kate's tears come, and she sobbed wildly.

"Now, child, you hush," Letha soothed her, gathering Kate into her arms. "You do that or that baby's going to come right here. You listen to me, now."

Kate fought for control, trying to be quiet. Letha was

right. She had to hold on just a little longer. "Oh, Letha, I'm worried about Joseph . . ."

Letha rocked her gently. "Mr. Joseph'll be here any minute. You'll see. Right now, though, old Letha's got to go out and see if I can find us a taxi."

"Don't leave me!" Kate begged her, grasping her big, soft arms.

Kate was suddenly embarrassed. "I'm sorry. I sound like an infant."

"Shh, shh. Now, honey, you just lie back and be still. I'll be back before you know it."

Kate let go of her and lay back watching through the window as the old woman lumbered down the stoop and ran heavily toward the curb. The traffic was almost at a standstill; Kate couldn't see a taxi anywhere. Some cars and a truck pulled over to let another fire wagon go by.

God, God, she prayed, don't let Joseph be there.

Letha had rushed off toward Sixth Avenue, and Kate couldn't see her any longer.

It seemed an eternity before a scarlet taxi drew up in front of the house and Kate saw Letha emerge. The traffic on that usually quiet street was still extremely heavy; Kate heard the honking of horns, the yells of indignant drivers. Letha was gesturing to the driver of the cab, but even through the half-open window Kate could not hear what she was saying. The din of horns and the yelling were too loud.

Finally, to Kate's surprise, the driver got out, leaving the taxi just where it was, blocking all the other traffic. She heard a policeman's whistle from somewhere. But none of it mattered now: the pains had sharpened and increased, blotting out everything else.

Letha and the driver came rushing in and Kate struggled to rise. "Wait a minute, sweetheart! Take it easy," Letha blurted. There were heavy footsteps in the hall. A policeman was standing behind the driver and Letha.

"What's going on here?" he demanded. "You move

that cab, buddy, or I'm gonna run you in. The traffic's got to get through.''

Letha hurried to Kate, and bracing her, yelled at the taxi driver, "Please, mister! Help me with this lady."

The abashed policeman understood. "Mother of God! I'll try to get those others out of your way, buddy. But hurry, will you, for pity's sake?" He rushed out of the room.

The nervous driver tried his best to assist them; Kate could feel him shaking as they traversed the endless distance from the corner to the door.

Slowly, slowly, Kate hobbled down the stoop, then made it at a tortoise pace across the sidewalk to the back seat of the taxi. With a moan of relief, Letha got in, and Kate collapsed against her, dimly aware of the policeman's whistle, sharp cries of "Make way here! Lady going to the hospital!" and, as before, the loudly honking horns. Farther east, Kate perceived, on the edge of her consciousness, the clang of fire bells, piercing, relentless; the ghost of desperate voices, hundreds of them, raised in horror and protest.

"Joseph . . . Joseph," she began to sob again.

"Hush, now, sweet child," Letha soothed her. "Your Joseph is all right. He'll come right along to the hospital, when he sees we're gone. Don't you worry about your Joseph, honey. He's a smart man, a strong man. He won't come to no harm." Letha let out a shaky laugh. "We got to worry about *you* right now, child."

In the crawling traffic they had only reached Fifth Avenue. The driver swore nervously and began to shoot in and out among the trucks and vans and cars, taking the Eighth Street corner on what felt like two wheels.

Kate kept her eyes closed, feeling the lurch of the taxi as it negotiated the tangle of the short Village cross streets; a huge weight seemed to be pulling her body down and then almost apart.

"Jesus, we're here!" Kate heard the driver shouting. His relief was so enormous that she would have laughed if she hadn't been so frightened; besides, laughing would bring the baby, right then and there.

They drove slowly into the ambulance tunnel of St. Vincent's; the door opened and Kate was helped onto a stretcher. The drafty tunnel was full of noise and confusion, and more ambulances. Kate felt a hand on her stomach.

She heard a woman say, "Get her out of here fast . . . a corner of Emergency. We've got a baby coming. Right now."

Kate glimpsed the inside of one of the ambulances—there were stacks of bodies in it. Young women's bodies but they didn't look like women anymore—only burned, mangled lumps of flesh in tatters of clothes.

"Doctor!" The woman's voice was shrill in Kate's ears. A man in white bent over her and something jabbed her arm.

Kate saw inky waves of blackness. Then she was aware of nothing.

The first thing Kate saw when she opened her eyes was Joseph's face. His face was so *dirty*; his onyx eyes looked very shiny against the grime, and his teeth were incredibly white when he gave her a shaky smile.

Kate's body felt so light she could hardly believe it, and there was a soreness in her lower quarters, a very sharp ache. But it didn't matter. Nothing mattered except that Joseph was there.

"You're *alive*," she said. Her lips were stiff and her voice was hardly more than a whisper.

"Of course I am." He stopped smiling, but his eyes were bright, full of tenderness as he stared at her, staring as if he could never get enough of the sight of her. He tried to smile again but his face was drawn and tense.

"Oh, Joseph. Joseph, you were in the fire."

He nodded and his bright black eyes assumed a strange expression.

"I saw them," she mumbled. "I saw them in the ambulance." She started to cry.

"Kate. Oh, my darling, don't cry, please don't cry." Joseph bent to her and kissed her brow and cheeks and mouth. "Don't think about it now. Not now. Please, darling, get some rest."

She clung to his hand. "Is the baby . . . all right?"

There it was again—that strange, tight, sad smile that was so unlike the one she loved—his broad, clownish smile that always transformed his fine face and crinkled around his eyes.

"The baby's fine, Kate. Just fine. We have a daughter."

Maybe that's why he seemed so strange, she thought. Maybe he had wanted his firstborn to be a son. "Did you . . . did you want a boy?"

"No, darling, *no*. How could I want a boy when I can have a little girl who will look like you?" She loved him for his reassurance, but there was something so different about him, as if all his vitality had oozed away.

The fire.

"Joseph, you look so *tired*," she murmured. She felt her own energy dissipating; it took all her strength just to say that, and there was so much more she wanted to say to him. "I want to talk to you, Joseph, but I'm so . . ."

She felt an overwhelming drowsiness and her eyelids wouldn't stay open. With eyes closed, she mumbled, ". . . love you, Joseph. So much. Please . . . rest."

As she fell asleep, she was aware of his hand holding hers very tightly.

Joseph sat by her bedside for a long time, still holding on to her limp hand, staring at her sleeping face.

Her peaceful breath, the quiet room, even the baby's birth, seemed no more substantial to him than a dream. He had left reality out there, with the appalling horror of the fire.

Joseph heard a soft step and looked up. A smiling aide, holding a vase of yellow roses, crept past him and set the vase gently on Kate's bedside table. As she left, Joseph looked back at Kate, thinking: I didn't even bring her flowers.

There was a tapping sound of leather as Harry Dryver tiptoed into the room. He came to Joseph and put his hand on his shoulder.

"Good. She's sleeping," Dryver whispered. "Come out in the hall a minute, will you, son?"

Joseph hesitated. Then he kissed Kate and rose. Dryver touched his granddaughter's hair lightly and followed Joseph out into the corridor.

By now Joseph was so exhausted he was swaying on his feet. Letha was standing in the corridor. She smiled at Joseph, but her eyes, taking in his grimy appearance, were full of compassion. "You sure look tuckered out."

"You look awful, Joseph," Dryver added. "Come on, let's sit down. I want to talk to you. Letha's going in now to sit with Kate."

"I don't want to go too far." Joseph shook his head wearily. "It's bad enough that I wasn't even here when she needed me."

"It's obvious where you were, boy. What else could you do, Joseph? How could you know the baby was coming today? Come on, now, I mean it. If you don't sit down, you're going to fall down. Just over there."

Dryver indicated an area a few feet away where there were couches and chairs. It looked incredibly inviting.

Joseph almost staggered after Dryver and flung himself into a chair. "Good God, I wasn't even here. I didn't bring her anything. I've put her second again, even on the day our child was born."

"Nonsense, son." Dryver sat down in the chair next to Joseph's and patted him on the arm. "The doctor says Kate, and the baby, are doing fine. Letha was with her, and brought her here in a taxi."

"A taxi . . . my God." Joseph put his head in his hands.

"I wasn't here either, you know. Kate insisted I go out, and not 'hover' over her." Dryver smiled crookedly. "Joseph, I know what happened at the fire," he added in a low, gentle voice. "I heard what you did . . . you saved many lives, son. Don't you think Kate will understand that, that we all do?"

Joseph nodded. His stomach rumbled loudly.

"I think you ought to have something to eat, get a little rest," Dryver suggested, "before you go back."

Joseph raised his head, staring at Harry Dryver. "How did you know I have to go back?"

Dryver grinned. "Because I know the kind of man you are, Joseph. Look here, they told me the sedative will make Kate sleep for several hours. And either Letha or I will be here, if she should wake up. So why don't you go back to the house and lie down awhile, get some food, and come back here later?"

Joseph got up. His legs were still trembling. "All right, Mr. Dryver. Maybe I'll get something to eat, but I can't rest. Not right now."

"At least wash your face, or they'll pick you up for vagrancy."

For the first time in hours, Joseph felt like laughing. "I'll do that." He smiled, put his hand on Dryver's shoulder, and pressed it hard. "Thank you, Mr. Dryver."

As he sought out a bathroom for a hasty wash, Joseph thought: I know now more that ever, why Kate loves him.

Making his way back to the street and heading east again, Joseph knew he could neither eat nor rest until he'd been back to the scene of the fire. Everything was overshadowed by the outrage he had seen; the birth of one small baby, even his own, shrank by comparison. He cursed himself for thinking that, but he couldn't help it. He hadn't even looked at his daughter yet. He couldn't, not until he'd done everything he could do at the fire.

It was after seven o'clock, and the crowd of people had grown to twenty thousand, spilling onto the streets adjacent to the Asch Building—people who had marched up from the Lower East Side to see if their loved ones were dead or alive. In the darkness the bodies being lifted into coffins could hardly be recognized.

Joseph tried to gather what information he could. Moving from group to group, he saw familiar faces contorted into unfamiliarity by stares of unbelieving horror, spasms of tearing grief. Their mourning cries cut into him, like knives into his skin. He spoke to the parents of girls who had survived, able to tell a few that their children might be alive, that he had seen them put into ambulances.

He was overjoyed to encounter Elvira's sister, to give her the news. The worst part was telling the parents of the dead.

After a while he gave up trying to find people he knew, and helped the overwhelmed police wrap bodies in blankets, attach tags, and carry individual coffins from a great hill of them to be lifted to patrol wagons. By eight there were no more coffins.

Again and again the very horror of the task would overcome another policeman or morgue attendant; Joseph saw husky men break out into hysterical sobbing. His own face was wet with tears. His legs felt more watery than ever, and he tasted an overwhelming nausea. He realized he had eaten nothing for nearly fourteen hours.

But he took a deep breath and returned to the nightmare task of moving the rest of the bodies. Placing the burned body of a young woman on top of the last coffin, he began to sob uncontrollably. A human being, he thought, without even the dignity of a blanket to cover her, to be carted away with hundreds of others, like so many sticks of wood.

He felt a heavy hand on his shoulder. "You've done enough, boy. Get out of here. I saw you this afternoon. I know what you did."

Looking up, Joseph recognized with amazement the same policeman who had tried to keep him from going into the building. That one man, out of all these thousands . . . and they had encountered each other again. It was strange, and wonderful. Joseph was overcome with a feeling of fellowship: the police, who had so often been his enemies on the picket line, were human beings now, helping them in this disaster.

"It's all right." Joseph's reply came out in a croak. "There's still plenty left to do." And he returned to the monstrous hill of bodies.

It was nearly eleven before he lurched away, moving blindly through the thick mob of crazed, shoving people, stumbling to the west. When he saw Dryver's house, he was suddenly almost insane with hunger; his stomach pained him sharply, and he doubled over for a moment at the door.

He let himself in and went on unsteady feet down the stairs to the kitchen, where he wolfed some food, standing, like an animal. Then he dragged himself upstairs again to the first-floor bedroom they had devised for him and Kate. He washed and changed into fresh clothes. He looked at the bed, and it drew him like a siren's song; he longed for sleep with an almost erotic need.

But he couldn't lie down. He had to be at the hospital if Kate woke up again. On leaden feet Joseph walked slowly back to the hospital. When he went in the front entrance he realized he still hadn't left the scene of the fire—stretchers lined the hall in the admitting area, and when the stretchers had apparently been depleted, the injured and the burned had simply been placed on sheets or blankets.

No one questioned Joseph's business; he might have been invisible. In any case, he already knew there were no set visiting hours in Obstetrics. He would probably be able to sleep there all night, on a couch, without even being noticed. The whole hospital was frantically trying to save the lives of the women who hadn't perished in the fire.

He waited for two elevators to ascend with their terrible burdens. Finally, giving up, he took the stairs, walking the five flights to Kate's floor.

There, blessedly, Joseph saw less evidence of the fire. The area was relatively quiet and empty. There seemed to be only one nurse on duty for the whole floor; apparently all the others had been detailed to the emergency. The nurse barely looked up from her desk when Joseph passed—a simple thing like childbirth didn't cut much ice tonight, Joseph thought wryly.

He stole into Kate's room, relieved to find her still asleep. The faithful Letha was nodding in a chair by the bed. Joseph went to her softly and touched her plump shoulder.

Letha jerked awake. "Oh, Mr. Joseph. I'm glad to see you."

"You go home now, Letha. I'll stay here the rest of the night."

The woman studied him. "You ought to be in bed, Mr. Joseph."

Joseph smiled at her. "Not on your life. I can bunk on a couch in the hall later on." He sobered. "I want to thank you for what you did today."

"Lord, Mr. Joseph." Letha grinned back at him. She rose and almost pushed him down onto the chair. "I been nursing Dryvers for three generations. Now we got a fourth one." She twinkled at him and they both looked at Kate. Kate smiled in her sleep, undisturbed by their whispers.

"All the same, I'm eternally grateful." He took her gnarled hand and lifted it to his lips.

She stared at him, beaming: then another slow smile split her dark face. "Nobody ever did that to me in my life. Mr. Joseph, you are the finest gentleman I ever met in all my days . . . save Mr. Dryver." He realized what an accolade that was, and a knot formed in his throat. "Well," Letha added, embarrassed, "I will get on now. That chair's no good for my miz'ry. I know you'll take care of my child."

Joseph looked at Kate, at her yellow hair spread out on the pillow, and her peaceful, lovely face. Her hair was almost the color of the roses. Joseph reached out and touched a strand of the gleaming tress with trembling fingers. He ached with love for her, for the fear and pain she must have endured in his absence on this landmark day. He would always feel that he had somehow betrayed her. She was the light of his world, and yet he had had no thought for anyone but the workers.

If he had died in the fire, what would Kate have done? She had made him see, with every look and touch, with every small gesture of consideration, that he was also the center of her life.

And he had hardly spared an instant's thought for the baby. Thank God all the babies were asleep now; he felt emptied of all emotion. To see his child, for the first time, in this half-dead state, would be so sad.

Half-asleep now, Joseph wondered whether he would ever be able to celebrate the baby's birthday with a carefree heart, recalling that she had entered the world on this day of obscene horror. But it was not his daughter's fault that fate decreed her entrance on this day. He must try to think of her now.

Quite suddenly, tormented by love and guilt, confusion and sorrow, Joseph fell asleep, sitting stiffly upright in the chair.

When he woke to weak sunlight, sore in every muscle, Kate had not yet stirred.

He heard his name called softly.

Anzia, his mother, poked her head timidly around the opening door.

Chapter 10

*I*t was so dark for May, Kate thought, watching the driving rain through a rear window of the flat. She had always loved rain before, but now it meant confinement—neither Letha nor Anzia would come out in this. And she certainly couldn't take the baby out in a downpour.

Poor Joseph. He would have to trudge around all day, from factory to factory, getting soaked.

But, Kate consoled herself, soon she would have something new, something lovely to show him. She got up and stood back from her easel, studying the new painting. It was different from anything she had done before—a dreamlike jungle clearing with a glimpse of gentle hills behind, full of bright, unlikely vegetation and populated with strange, vivid birds and deerlike creatures whose horns were shaped as no deer's have ever been shaped. Their bodies were colored as no deer's had ever been. She wondered where this fantastic scene had come from. Probably from her need and longing to escape.

The baby made a fretful sound from the huge laundry basket that Kate had converted into a bassinet. Kate put down her brush and went to the basket to examine the baby and touch her tiny face. The skin was quite cool. There was nothing the matter with her. Kate smiled crookedly at her daughter, imagining reproach in the dark, fixed gaze that was Joseph's and yet was so different. Marite always fussed when Kate was painting, apparently annoyed at the lack of attention.

Kate picked Marite up and patted her on the back, trying to summon up the proper emotions. It was wrong to associate her birth with the fire, with fear and tragedy and separateness from Joseph. But the shadow remained.

Kate put her down again and began to move around the flat, tidying up while she reflected.

The baby never seemed so happy as when Joseph held her.

Joseph. The thought of him had once given Kate unalloyed delight, but now the feeling was mingled with anxiety.

He was invariably gentle and tender with her and with Marite. If anything, Kate knew that Joseph loved her more than ever; she was ashamed of the earlier fear that the baby might have come between them. But Joseph seemed so tired these days. If he had been dedicated to the union before, he was like a man obsessed with it now; he worked longer hours, came home exhausted. And even if Kate felt weak and despondent herself at times, she felt obligated to show him a cheerful face.

No one could forget the fire. No one had talked about anything but the fire for weeks and weeks, and Kate almost regretted reading the reports of it—firemen discovering the burned bodies of workers still sitting in position at the sewing machines on the morning after the fire . . . and a thousand other sickening details. Kate had had nightmares for two weeks afterward and that had physically weakened her. But something stolid and obdurate in her, perhaps the rooted strength she had inherited from her Dutch ancestors, made her purposefully blot those dread pictures out. She had to, to survive and regain her body's power. Besides herself, Joseph must be sustained. And the baby.

Still the preoccupation, the rather absent tenderness persisted in Joseph. A grand jury had indicted the Triangle proprietors for manslaughter, but there were, even now, sixty-three shops with no fire escapes at all. The workers still labored in unhealthy squalor. It was like trying to clean the Augean stables, Joseph had told her bitterly.

But she knew this painting would cheer him—it had done wonders for her. After the flat was tidy, Kate removed another painting from between the two back windows and hung the new one there to dry. She squinted: the striped curtains looked garish, too primary, framing the subtler brightness of the "enchanted jungle." Tomorrow, *if* it stopped raining, and *if* she could take the baby to her grandfather's, she would make some new curtains.

Letha adored the baby and was delighted to care for her. So did Anzia.

The baby began to whimper again and then she howled. It was time to nurse her, a task that Kate knew she would never learn to like. The sensation of the baby's tugging mouth at her breast made Kate want to scream. But she unbuttoned her dress determinedly and offered her breast to Marite.

She would not have survived these weeks, she thought, if it hadn't been for Anzia and Letha. Only other women could understand, she decided. She loved Anzia for her encouragement—"You were just learning to be a wife when you had to learn to be a mother too. I am proud of my beautiful daughter-in-law."

Anzia visited and sat with the baby regularly, freeing Kate for a brief, guilty ramble alone in the square or to do a little shopping.

Kate felt guilty these days about a number of things—her first reaction to the cramped flat, after the luxurious weeks at her grandfather's; the feeling that the baby's presence crowded it more.

Joseph was always glad to see his mother, but Kate knew he held a silent, unchanging resentment against Solomon, who remained aloof. That saddened Kate, but she usually dismissed the thought; they had enough to think about.

At last, Marite, evidently sated, stopped feeding and her

tiny head with its fuzz of golden hair drooped sleepily against Kate, who put her down in the basket.

As Kate was buttoning her dress, the doorbell sounded. Surely it wouldn't be Anzia on such a day. But Kate was hopeful. It would be wonderful to take a walk and just get drenched, for sheer refreshment.

The knock that sounded a little later was heavier than Anzia's. Puzzled, Kate went to the door.

Her father, Howard Wendell, was standing there in his costly raincoat and dripping hat.

Kate was too shocked to utter a word.

Her father took off his hat and slapped it against his coat. He hadn't smiled at all but his weary eyes pleaded with her. "Kate . . . may I come in?"

"Of . . . course." She faltered. "Come in, Father." She stood back to let him in, watching his face as he looked around the flat. He appeared to be as scandalized, as unbelieving as Jerry and Eileen had been when they came to bring her things last year. "Let me take your coat," she said in a steadier voice.

He relinquished it and she hung it in the bathroom. "Kate," he called out, and she could hear his hesitant steps behind her. In his shock he'd forgotten his sopping hat. He held it out to her apologetically and she tried to reshape it a little before she hung it on a hook.

"Never mind that," he said gruffly, and she looked at his face again. There was painful embarrassment in its lines—doubtless because he had observed her automatic habit of economy. He had probably planned just to throw the hat away.

She thought: He must be under great stress. Otherwise he would have carried an umbrella; he always did.

"Please," she said, feeling naked and exposed as her father's glance flicked over the narrow, pathetic bathroom, "go back and sit down, Father. Make yourself comfortable. I'll warm up some coffee."

"Thank you," he said stiffly, and retraced his steps. But he did not sit down as she followed him into the living

room. "But I don't want you to *serve* me, Kate. I came
here to . . . apologize. To see how you are. You look
thin." He examined her with anxious eyes. "Are you
getting enough to . . . ?" He reddened.

"To eat?" she concluded with a wry smile. "Oh, yes,
Father. My husband doesn't starve me, or even beat me.
Or the baby."

"Oh, Kate. Please." Her father's smooth-shaven cheeks
were mottled with the color of his chagrin. "We're getting
off to a very bad start."

He still hasn't even touched me, she thought sadly. It had
always been so hard for him to express physical affection.
But he was trying to reach her now, and she must meet
him halfway. Kate looked at Howard Wendell through
strangely mature, compassionate eyes; her tutored senses,
her whole body that had been aroused to the easy expression of passion and tenderness by Joseph, or warm affection by her grandfather and Letha and Anzia, pitied his
tethered feeling.

"Can you forgive me, Kate?" He looked as if he might
cry; his gaze was pleading, his lips grimaced. Good God,
she thought, what a tradition has nourished me. Once
again she envied Joseph's emotional people; if it hadn't
been for Harry Dryver, she might have married a repressed
man just like her father.

"Yes. Yes, I can," she said gently, reflecting that she
must also forgive the cool blood that coursed so sluggishly
in his veins, making him what he was. She went to him
and took him awkwardly in her arms—it was difficult to
encompass his big body. He kissed her almost furtively on
the edge of her brow, and then she let him go, knowing
the embrace was painfully embarrassing to him.

He was still flushed, uncertain. "Well," he said inade-
quately, clearing his throat, and looked around for a diversion. "Where is . . . the baby?"

"In the bedroom. Would you like to see her?"

"Certainly."

He followed her in a touchingly obedient way as she led

him into the little bedroom with its sunny yellow spread and curtains, to Marite's basket on the rug by the bed.

"My, my. Isn't she . . . small?" he murmured. He sat down gingerly on the bed and peered down at the baby. "What . . . what do you call her, Kate?"

"Marite." She had to smile at her father's expression. Marite for her rebellious ancestor, the beautiful Marite Wendell, who had eloped with a Jew.

"Well." For the first time he smiled at her. "I suppose that's appropriate, under the circumstances." His wry comment was so human, so resigned, that Kate felt affection well up in her. He seemed a bit more comfortable now. "We mustn't disturb her sleep," he whispered.

"Let's go in the other room," she whispered back. "I just got her to sleep a little while ago, and the breather," she admitted, "is marvelous."

They stole out of the bedroom and finally Howard Wendell made a move to sit down. He tested the couch with his glance, as if uncertain it would bear his weight.

Kate grinned. "It's all right. It holds Joseph."

He smiled at her sheepishly, then looked around the room again. "This is very . . . bohemian," he remarked, apparently at a loss for something positive to say. Then he saw her paintings. "Did you do those, Kate?"

She nodded with pride.

"You know I am not versed much in these things," he conceded, "but they appear to be very . . . fine."

"Thank you, Father." She noticed that his trouser hems were darkened with moisture, his shoes were wet. "Please let me give you some coffee."

"All right. Thank you." He sat forward on the cot that served as a couch, his hands splayed over his knees. She went to warm up the coffee and brought back cups for them both.

"Kate, it is very gracious of you to receive me," he began with his stiff, almost painful courtesy. Taking a sip of his coffee, he leaned over and put the cup on the dining table. "I came here to . . . say how sorry I am for the things I said when you sprang your marriage . . . when you advised us of your marriage. You must know that my, er . . . anger was really concern. Your mother and I—''

"How is Mother?" Kate asked calmly.

"As well as can be expected." Her father reddened again, realizing he hadn't been too tactful. But neither was I, Kate thought, to bring the subject up at all. It was obvious that her mother wanted nothing to do with her errant daughter.

"But as I was saying," Howard Wendell rushed on, "it was only our . . . my concern for your welfare that made me say such things. Mr. Dryver called us the day the baby was born. I was hesitant to come to the hospital, Kate. I didn't know what my reception would be. But today, somehow, I had to come. It's wrong for us to be at odds. You are my daughter, after all. I wanted to give you this.'' He reached in his breast pocket and handed her a check.

She was startled by the amount, and stared at it for a moment, ready to refuse it.

"Please don't give it back to me, Kate. It's all that I can . . . do.''

Kate hesitated. Then she remembered something she had read, something a philosopher had written—that giving was a need, and receiving a form of pity. This was the only way her father had ever been able to show love; if she rejected his check, she rejected him.

"Thank you, Father. It's very sweet of you.'' she reached over and touched his hand.

"I hope you can use it," he said. Involuntarily his glance flicked over the room, with its makeshift curtains, its flimsy furniture, and over her rather shabby dress. "Well''—he slapped his knees with his hands—"I've got to get back to the office.''

She did not protest, bringing him his damp coat and misshapen hat.

"Good-bye, Kate. Thank you for letting me see the baby. And for . . . receiving me," he said carefully as they stood at the parted door.

"Thank you for coming, Father."

He put on his hat and, nodding, walked down the hall. Kate shut the door slowly and walked around the living room, seeing it with new eyes. Her poor father, with all his money and position, possessed nothing as splendid as this little room, this house of happiness. All of a sudden she was wild with impatience for Joseph to come home.

Chapter 11

"Mr. Simson will be right with you," the blond typist simpered at Joseph. He thought there was something familiar about her, although he hadn't looked at her for long. She had unnaturally red cheeks and spoke with a rough New York accent. She was chewing gum.

An odd secretary for his Uncle Rafael, Joseph thought. "Thank you."

He sat down in the stuffy reception area and tugged at his collar.

The pug-faced blond girl noticed. "Warm today," she commented, eyeing Joseph. She pronounced it "wohm."

"Very," Joseph agreed, wondering how he knew her. "Very warm for June."

The woman returned to her typing, and Joseph looked up at the calendar over her desk: June 1913. He couldn't believe how much time had passed, and how swiftly, since Marite's birth and the Triangle fire. Everything was different, so much better now. He had risen from general organizer to secretary-treasurer of the union; there was a little more money, and he thought with satisfaction of their new, larger apartment on the second floor.

And of David.

When Kate found out she was pregnant again, late last summer, it had been nothing like the first time. She had been happy, eager, to Joseph's delight. "This time," she said, "we'll have a son."

And she had, just last month. They named him David, at her suggestion, Hebrew for "beloved." Already he promised to have Joseph's pitch-black hair, Kate's bright-blue eyes. Everyone agreed that it was going to do Marite good to have a brother; she was as spoiled and demanding as a little princess.

A buzzer sounded on the blonde's desk. Continuing to chew her gum, she pushed down a key. "Yeah?"

An angry squawk came from the box. "Oh," she said, "okay. I'm sorry." She said to Joseph, "Go on in."

It wasn't his imagination. She was staring at him now, fascinated. But he had no time to think about that. He was still wondering what this meeting was all about, why he had been summoned to Simson's. Rafael hadn't caught up with the improved conditions in other factories. And if his uncle thought Joseph was going to make some kind of unilateral deal, he had another think coming.

Joseph opened the door and walked in.

"Well, Mr. Secretary." His uncle got up from behind his wide desk, extending his hand. "It's been a long time since the gym."

So that's the way it was going to be, Joseph thought. His uncle was taking the lateral approach. Joseph smiled warily and shook Rafael's hand. This was the first time they had been alone in years; otherwise they had met as adversaries, across the bargaining table, or on the picket line. It was hard to remember the old days now.

"Take a load off your feet, boy. Sit down. Have a cigar." Rafael sank down in his leather chair and proffered a handsome tooled case, its lid open, to Joseph.

"No, thanks." Joseph had no patience at all with the process of cigar-smoking—the unwrapping, smelling, cutting, lighting, drawing. And he disliked the grim look of fat, rich lips grasping expensive cigars. He waited for Rafael to go through the ceremony of preparing his.

He studied his uncle's face—so much like Solomon's, yet so unrelated. The thin, sagging, defeated features of

Solomon had translated themselves into hard, pouchy prosperity on Rafael's genial face.

"So you married a beautiful Gentile girl, I hear, and now you have two children already." Rafael blew out a cloud of smoke, twinkling at Joseph.

The way he said it emphasized Joseph's status as a psychological exile. The man with the Gentile wife, the one who had deserted the institutions which nourished him, just as his father had, by marrying out of his class.

"How does she take this union business, Joseph?"

Joseph felt his hackles rise. "She's behind me a hundred percent," he said calmly. "As a matter of fact, we met on a picket line."

"Well, how about that?" Rafael's heavy brows shot up. "That's pretty broad-minded, for a rich girl."

Rafael made it sound as if Joseph were some kind of gigolo, but he let it pass. He wished his uncle would get to the point.

"Well, boy, I hope you have better luck with your children than I've had with my son." Rafael sighed. "Lionel's had the world handed to him on a platter, but he's not worth two-cents-plain. A bohemian, he calls himself. For every hour he puts in working for me, he puts in eight with his drinking and his women. He even hired that *shiksa* tramp out there to be his secretary . . . *secretary*, please." Rafael threw up his hands. "She wouldn't be sitting outside my office now if my own girl wasn't sick. One of those Poles, Wanda Something." Rafael made a face.

Wanda. Now Joseph remembered. One of the girls who had been with Lionel the time Joseph had flattened him on MacDougal Street. A girl with bulging eyes and a flat face like a pug dog's. Joseph's mouth twitched.

"Did I say something funny?" Rafael grumbled.

"No." So Lionel had been on French leave that day with a typist from Simson's. Joseph was having a hell of a time keeping a straight face. "She's not exactly your style."

"Always the gentleman." Rafael studied him. " And

still as tough as nails. *You* should have been my son, Joseph. I've been thinking that all these years, ever since I watched you take those palookas in the ring, back when you were just a boy. You could have gone professional. I bet you could have made a bundle.''

When Joseph didn't answer, Rafael asked him, "What kind of money can you make with this red outfit of yours, Joseph? *Bubkes* is what.''

Joseph felt his temper slip. "The union isn't red, and I'm not in it for money, Rafael.''

"Not in it for money? What else does a man work for, Joseph?''

"So other kids won't have to grow up the way I did . . . or burn to death in a factory fire.'' Rafael looked impatient. "What did you call me here for?'' Joseph asked coldly.

Rafael's brows shot up. "Don't get so high and mighty, boy. I'm going to tell you. The doctors tell me with my blood pressure I've got to slow down. I should slow down, with nobody but Lionel to count on? I'm making you an offer, Joseph. It's madness for you to keep on with this union garbage; they'll never get anywhere. The unions won't last . . . and there'll never be any money in them. All you'll get is maybe a broken head, or go to jail with all those reds.'' Rafael's face was flushed in his earnest excitement.

Joseph was too flabbergasted to interrupt.

"What do you say, Joseph?''

Say? He could say plenty. Did this crazy old man actually believe he could throw away everything he had fought and bled for, everything he'd always believed in, to run this sweatshop operation?

As he struggled for a reply, Joseph noticed that the office door was slightly ajar. Wanda's giggle drifted in and Joseph thought he recognized Lionel's voice.

But Rafael was too intent on the subject at hand to notice. He was staring at Joseph. "What do you say, son?'' he repeated. "Do you really understand me? I'm offering you a place in my business, and eventually you'll take over instead of my son." Joseph could see beads of moisture on his uncle's upper lip, and in spite of himself he felt sorry for this man who had been so good to him long ago.

The door was shoved open abruptly and Lionel Simson stood on the threshold. "I heard that, Dad. I heard you tell this bastard that you were offering him my place. Just where in hell does that leave *me*?"

Rafael, without looking at him, said calmly, "Shut up, Lionel. Well, Joseph? You didn't give me any answer."

"I'm sorry, Uncle Rafael. The answer's no." Joseph got up and held out his hand to Rafael.

Rafael took it. "Think about it, Joseph."

Joseph shook his head, turned and walked out of the office without looking at Lionel, brushing past him as if he were not there.

" 'Bye, Joseph," the incorrigible Wanda called out.

Joseph nodded, hearing the door to his uncle's office slam, the shouts of his uncle and his cousin. He still couldn't get over Rafael's offer; it was incredible.

All the way down in the elevator, and out on Twenty-third Street, Joseph kept thinking about it. Who in the hell did Rafael Simson think he *was*, assuming a union man would break his neck to get into the boss category? Joseph's long stride took him to Sixth Avenue in record time. Almost time to go home, and he was glad. He couldn't wait to tell Kate. He looked forward to the coolness and quiet of the flat after the hot tumult of the streets.

Still, as Joseph walked downtown he couldn't help pitying Rafael Simson. An aging, ailing man with only one son to pin everything on . . . a son like Lionel.

Bubkes, he'd called Joseph's salary. That's exactly what it was. Ever since he had met Kate, his lack of money had haunted Joseph. What Joseph had told Rafael was the plain truth—he wasn't in the union business for that. Kate never seemed to think about it at all, taking their life-style for granted—one of the many qualities Joseph loved her for. But he couldn't forget the checks from Wendell—another had been presented after David's birth. Joseph wished that all their money could come from his salary. And plenty would, if he accepted Rafael's offer.

Maybe he owed it to Kate and the children to accept, no matter what he himself wanted. They were his responsibility. But how could he stand to give up the union?

What the hell was he thinking about? It was like giving up breath.

Joseph stripped off his jacket and rolled up his shirt-sleeves. By the time he was on MacDougal his head was pounding and he was wretched in his confusion.

As soon as Kate opened the door, Joseph began to feel calmer. "Don't get too close," he warned her. "I'm as sweaty as a pig."

Ignoring him, she put her arms around his neck and kissed him.

"You look so cool," he commented when she let go of him, stepping back. She was wearing a thin, low-cut dress the color of limes and her golden hair was gathered on top of her shapely head.

"Get out of those awful clothes," she commanded, "and go take a bath. I'll bring you something cold to drink."

He couldn't believe how glowing and healthy she looked, so soon after David's birth. She had been so weak and dragged out after Marite came. But then, that had been after the fire.

It occurred to him that he hadn't said a word to Rafael about more fire escapes. But for the moment he forced the worrisome thought from his mind and asked Kate, "How are the children?"

"Fine. David's fast asleep and the Princess is still on Eleventh Street. Letha will be bringing her back soon. You're early . . . and I'm *glad*. But go on, darling, take your bath." Kate began to unbutton his shirt. He finished the job, smiling, and let her take it from him.

Coming out of the bath, he felt like a whole new man.

He found Kate in the dining space she'd set up in their living room, putting cold meats and salad on the table.

"If this is June," she said lightly, "I'm going to *love* July."

"Well, that looks good. Can I eat like this?" He indicated his bathrobe.

"Absolutely."

He hugged her to him and then sat down. "King Solomon couldn't ask for better."

Kate's smile disappeared and they looked at each other. They hadn't seen his father, Solomon, since their wedding day.

Then Kate smiled at him again and said, "You're a little short on wives for a Solomon."

"I love you, Kate. Whenever I've been on the edge of something . . . dark, and looked over the precipice, you've shone your light on it, kept me from going over."

"Oh, Joseph." Kate's eyes were shining. She put down the dish she was holding and came to him, taking his head in her hands and drawing it against her fragrant neck. She stroked his hair and kissed the top of his head.

More than ever he wondered whether he should accept Rafael's offer, if he didn't owe it to her. She had always given him so much. He put his arms around her soft, slender body. "I saw Rafael Simson today."

Kate moved gently out of his grasp, cued to the change of mood, and poured lemonade for them. "About the fire escapes."

"No. About me."

She sat down and looked at him questioningly.

He told her about Rafael's offer.

"Of all the *chutzpah*," she exploded.

Joseph laughed. Her pronunciation never failed to charm him; she could not cope with the gutturals.

"What on earth makes him think you want to line up with the bosses?" she demanded. "How did he react when you turned him down?"

He felt another wave of loving gratitude. She had taken

it for granted that he would refuse. "What in the hell did I ever do to deserve you?"

"What are you talking about?" She seemed sincerely puzzled.

"I'm talking about you. You sound as if there's only one answer I *could* have given him, Kate."

"Well, isn't there?"

"Right now I'm not too sure."

"Joseph, I can't believe I'm hearing this. How could you consider it?"

He told her how he had felt after leaving Rafael's office. When he finished, she looked steadily into his eyes.

"What you 'owe' us," she said quietly, "is to do what you were meant to do, Joseph. To keep on doing the work that makes you the man you are. Think how you would be cheating us otherwise."

"Cheating you?"

"Of course. Wouldn't you rather have the children say 'My father's part of history' than 'My daddy runs a factory'?" She was smiling but her eyes were serious.

He reached across the table and grabbed her hand, wishing he knew just how to answer her.

Right at that moment he was the man who had everything.

Chapter 12

"*I hate* him!"

Three-year-old Marite pummeled her brother's playpen, shattering the peace of Harry Dryver's garden; her shrill cry pierced the quiet April evening, making Kate jump.

"No, you don't," Joseph said calmly. He was sprawled on the grass, holding the small rubber ball he had been using to teach David to throw to Marite. David began to cry.

"Damn," Kate muttered to Dryver. She got up from her place at his side and went over to the playpen. Marite became more of a handful every day, jealous of everyone Joseph paid the slightest attention to. Kate picked David up and hugged him to her, reaching out her hand to tousle Marite's short blond hair.

Her daughter pulled away from Kate and clung to Joseph. Dandling the year-old boy, Kate smiled at Marite's mutinous expression. The small, sullen face was a carbon copy of her own, except for the black, obliquely set eyes. "You know you don't hate your brother," Kate said softly.

"Yes, I do! Daddy likes him better then me."

"I do not like him better than you, sweetheart." Joseph sat Marite on his knees and cuddled her. "You're my girl."

"Mama's your girl. I heard you tell her."

"You're *both* my girls." Joseph kissed Marite's head, his dark, exasperated eyes meeting Kate's.

161

Kate went back to her chair beside Harry Dryver, thinking how tired her grandfather looked this evening. She leaned back and sighed. Somehow her daughter always seemed to be the one to disturb the peace. And it had been so pleasant, here in the garden, with the familiar sounds of dinner being prepared in the adjoining kitchen, the glass doors open to the summery air, and music from the Victrola.

She was relieved to see that Joseph had coaxed the children back to their game.

"Do you realize," she murmured to Dryver, "how long it's been since we've had a private visit?" Kate studied Harry Dryver's beloved face; his eyes looked heavy-lidded with fatigue, with dark circles underneath.

"I certainly do. Since the Armory show last year." He gave her a crooked smile. Kate would always remember that show as one of the high points of her life—the most memorable event in the American world of art. Its aim had been to bring under one roof everything that was vital in contemporary art, both American and foreign. Harry Dryver had exhibited his latest work along with people like Childe Hassam and John Sloan and there had been Gaston Lachaise's stunning *Figure of a Woman* and the startling examples of cubism. "And that's about the last time you showed me anything new of yours, Kate."

His comment was so gentle it was hardly a reproach, but she couldn't help taking it as one. "I have a few other things to do," she said a bit sharply.

"I know." Dryver sounded sad. "I'm an unnatural old man, Kate, but I've never believed a woman with talent should be . . . consumed by her children. No matter how dear and lovely they are." He added that, she thought, perfunctorily. "I refuse to see nature as anything but chaos; art is the only order in the world . . . or rather the attempt to make order from chaotic materials," he amended in a dry tone. "Every civilized activity of man is a form of art, a protest against nature. Joseph's work, for one— attempting to curb the runaway greed of men who are as primal as any prehistoric creature. But I'm rambling. What I started to say was that some women are meant to be mothers, some women are not."

"And you think I'm not?" Kate was aghast.

"Probably not," Dryver said with an uncharacteristic bluntness. "However, you are, my dear, and we have to deal with that. I've seen your guilt, Kate. It's so plain to me. I wish you'd try to put it away from you. Instead of guilt you have a right to feel great pride."

"Pride for being impatient with my children?"

"No. For meeting responsibilities, very *well*, that go against your deepest character." He took her hand.

"I've never heard you talk like this," she said.

"The older I get, the clearer things become. I realize now that I loved you inordinately because I always had such a hard time loving your mother. That probably shocks you."

"No . . . no," she responded slowly. "*Astonishes* me." Something about his brutal frankness made her uneasy. Kate was suddenly terrified. "Grandfather . . . is there something you're not telling me? Something about . . . yourself? Oh, my God, you're not ill, are you?"

Dryver laughed. "Good Lord, no," he said. "I'm just a grouchy old man, getting older, more acidulous by the hour."

Kate's touch on his hand was a disclaimer. "Was I as . . . difficult as Marite when I was her age?"

"*You*? Never. You were such a quiet, solemn little thing, it was like having a fairy in my garden, from some mysterious place," Dryver said dreamily. "I was always afraid that you were going to fly away to your own people. You were so good it almost worried me. You can imagine what a relief it was when your rebellion popped out at last." He grinned. Kate reflected, as she had so many times before, on her grandfather's utter uniqueness. There had never been anyone like him; there never would be again.

"I am a rotten egotist," he remarked after a moment. "I always valued you because I saw myself in you, Kate."

She knew he was trying to joke her out of a somber mood, to dismiss the rather awkward comments he had made; the tenderness in his eyes belied his statement.

Kate was about to retort when she was interrupted by the shrill ring of the phone from the upper hall.

Kate heard Letha grumble loudly, "Lord have mercy." She leaned forward and looked into the kitchen. The old woman was peering into the oven; apparently she was at a critical point with the dinner, and her young helper hadn't come in today.

"I'll go," Kate called out. She jumped up to forestall Joseph, who was relaxing for the first time in days, and hurried through the kitchen and up the stairs. The phone still clamored.

"Oh, Kate." It was Anzia. Kate knew something had happened; her mother-in-law's voice was so stricken, so faraway. "Kate, my Solomon's . . . dead."

"No, Anzia. Oh, my God." Kate's hand, squeezing the telephone, turned slippery with sweat. "I will . . . get Joseph."

Kate felt he knew, as soon as he saw her face. She followed him into the house and up the stairs again, put her arm around his body as he picked up the phone. Kate leaned against him, feeling his strong, wiry body go slack, hearing the almost imperceptible murmur of Anzia's words.

"Of course, Mama. I will say *kaddish* for him. How can you even ask?" Joseph sounded shaky. There was another long murmur from the telephone. Then he said heavily, "All that is past now. I will say *kaddish*."

The Hebrew word for the mourner's prayer sounded dark and ponderous from Joseph's mouth. "And we will come to see you now."

Joseph hung up and turned to Kate, his body encircled by her arms, his face resting against her hair. She could feel a tremor in his big frame. "Joseph, oh, Joseph." She pressed him to her.

"Kate, I was wrong not to go to him before." His voice was muffled in her hair. "You told me I should forgive him, try to make it up, but I wouldn't listen. We'll go to him now."

Emerging from the tiny synagogue on Rivington Street at Joseph's side, Kate could feel her husband's tension in his rigid arm. His face was inordinately pale below his black hair that made his black *yarmulke*, the small skullcap, almost invisible.

Kate had never felt so alien. Even if it shamed her to think of herself while Joseph was so stricken, she could not help fearing that she might seem alien to Joseph too. Yet, as if he knew what she was thinking, he gave her one long tender look that dispelled the notion. He was hardly more at home in the synagogue than she, having long ago moved away from the religion of his fathers.

Still, she felt uneasy observing Joseph's almost unnatural control, reflecting on the ardors and the burdens of the time before the funeral. It had been a relief to learn that the obnoxious Lionel would not be sitting *shivah* with Joseph. Joseph had explained to Kate that the closest relatives of the dead sat on low stools in the survivor's home to receive condolences during the first days of mourning. Rafael, Anzia, and Joseph sat together.

Rafael was upset by Anzia's plans for the funeral and the burial, and he turned to Joseph for support. "A Barsimson," Rafael protested, "should not be buried out of Rivington Street and laid in Chatham Square. It's not right. I can have the service in a proper temple, Joseph, and bury Solomon out on Long Island."

Joseph retorted that his mother's wishes must be respected, that Solomon must lie among his friends. Joseph and Rafael had had sharp words, but Joseph had won.

Lionel, Joseph told Kate, had not appeared at all. "Rafael was very ashamed," Joseph said, "but his son still hates me."

The unpleasant Lionel attended the funeral, however, since that was obligatory. Kate carefully kept her eyes away from his, aware of his intrusive, insolent stare.

Now, as they waited to get into one of the cars, Rafael approached Joseph and embraced him. The tears were coursing down Rafael's face. "My brother is gone," he said, "but he has left a fine son, a fine son to say *kaddish* for him."

Kate happened to glance beyond Rafael, and caught sight of Lionel. His face was dark red with anger. It gave Kate a cold and fearful sense of impending trouble.

"You make me sick," Lionel called out to Rafael. "Slobbering over the great Joseph, the savior of the masses, Joseph with his *shiksa*." The shocked mourners turned to look at Lionel. Someone said, "Be quiet. Have you no respect?"

Kate could feel Joseph's muscles tense until they were as hard as rocks.

Then the incredible happened. Lionel reached into his pocket and brought out a gun, pointed it at his father. Joseph flung Kate away from him, shouting, "Get down!" Then he shoved Rafael, who stumbled backward in his surprise.

There was an explosion like a loud firecracker. Aghast, unbelieving, crouched on her hands and knees on the pavement, Kate saw Joseph crumple and fall.

A woman screamed. A man knelt over Joseph, doing something with a handkerchief; the kneeling man shouted something and two other men came to lift Joseph into a car. Galvanized into motion, Kate scrambled to her feet and ran after them, screaming, "Wait! Wait! Let me come!"

Someone pushed her gently into the front seat of the car.

Stupefied, Rafael Simson got up from the pavement, swaying. The fall must have hurt his head, but he had hardly noticed, and was unaware that the sleeve of his jacket has almost been ripped off the shoulder from the force of Joseph's hand.

All he knew was that Joseph had saved his life and might lose his own. Lionel, his hateful son, stood before him now, crying like a girl. Two men took the gun from Lionel and pinioned his arms behind him. Rafael heard them mutter about the police, then look at him uncertainly.

Wide-eyed with shock, Anzia struggled with those who were trying to keep her from getting out of the car. Rafael realized she still didn't know what had happened. "What is it?" she shrieked. "What was that?" Then she saw Lionel between the two men. "Where is Joseph? Where is my son?"

She looked so frail that Rafael was instantly seared with pity. He went to her and took both of her arms. "Joseph has had . . . an accident, Anzia. They have taken him to the hospital. We will go there as soon as the service is over. Come now. Get in the car. Please."

Rafael hated himself for the implied lie. But what else could he say? They must go on with the funeral, for Anzia's and for Joseph's sake. Numbly, like someone walking in her sleep, Anzia obeyed. It was the shock, he thought. She hadn't taken it in.

Rafael turned to the two husky young men guarding Lionel. "No police," he muttered. "No police at my brother's funeral. I'll be responsible. Take him ho . . . to my house," Rafael amended bitterly. He took out a card and scribbled something on it. "Show this to the butler, and lock my son in his room. And please, take my wife with you. No matter what she says, do what I have told you. I must go now with . . . my brother."

A woman helped the weeping Bertha into the front seat of the Simsons' car, to sit by the chauffeur; the two young men got in the back with the unprotesting Lionel.

"What can we do to help?" One of the Seligman nephews, the son of Bertha Simson's sister, addressed Rafael.

"You can say *kaddish* for my brother," Rafael said, swallowing over the great lump of pain in his throat. "Right now, help me get everyone together again."

Rafael and his nephews went from group to group, speaking to them quietly; at last the little procession set out for the cemetery at Chatham Square. Supporting Anzia at the grave, Rafael realized she was too dazed even to weep any longer. She looked as if her legs could not support her. When the service was over, Rafael murmured to one of his nephews, "Take her home, send some of the women with her. Call a doctor and have him give her something to make her sleep. And please, don't tell her what happened to Joseph until she has rested."

When Rafael reached his mansion, the two young men without names were waiting in the downstairs hall. He shook their hands. "I can't thank you enough for what you've done. Will you have a drink?"

Both declined. Rafael reached into his pocket and took out a fat pocketbook. One of the stalwart youths held up his hand, shaking his head. "We work with Joseph for the union. We've got to get to the hospital now."

"So do I. We'll take my car. If you'll just give me a minute to look in on my wife . . . "

The young men went out to wait in the car.

Rafael found Bertha lying on the sofa in the drawing room, with her maid in attendance. He said curtly, "That will be all, Hilda."

When the woman had gone, Bertha asked him weakly, "How could you lock up our son like a wild animal? Our very own son, Rafael."

"And I am your very own *husband,* Bertha. Our son tried to kill me. Does that mean nothing to you?" Rafael's head was pounding; he was sick with grief for Solomon, and for Joseph. The scrapes on his face stung; he was dizzy with exhaustion. "I'm going down to the hospital now to see if Joseph is still alive. That boy saved my life. I am leaving word with Ross that if Lionel tries to get out of his room, to call the police and turn him over to them. So see to it, Bertha. We will decide what to do when I get back."

Rafael turned on his heel and left her weeping.

"Kate, you've been standing here for hours, darling. Please . . . please come and sit down." Her grandfather tugged at her arm.

She shook her head. "I will stay here until they let me see him." She closed her eyes, pressing her head back against the wall, hearing her grandfather walk away.

"Kate."

She started, having no idea of how much time had elapsed between her grandfather's departing step and this gentle voice in her ear. She opened her eyes again to meet the dark, compassionate stare of their friend, Jake Lapidus.

"He's dead," she said dully.

"No, no, Kate. The operation's over now."

"Is he going to live?" she demanded.

"I've got to tell you the truth—they don't know yet." Jake touched her arm.

Her head reeled. If he dies, I will die. If he dies, I want no more life.

"Kate, you've got to sit down at least. Mr. Dryver says you've been standing here in the same position all the afternoon."

"I will stay here until they let me see him," she repeated in a tired, dead voice. Jake studied her; then, shaking his head, he went off in the direction her grandfather had taken.

She continued to stand there, unmoving, stiff with pain, as the evening lights went on in the echoing corridors. Waiting, waiting for someone to tell her something about Joseph. Suddenly all the lights went out and she felt a hard blow on the back of her head.

Kate woke to find herself on a narrow bed in a little room; her head ached abominably. Letha was bending over her; when she opened her eyes, Letha began to smile. Kate saw her grandfather standing on the other side of the bed.

"Joseph . . . how is Joseph?" Kate demanded, sitting up, putting her feet on the floor.

"You can see him now, Kate. But not for long," Dryver warned her. "You took an awful crack on the head."

Ignoring him, Kate cried out, "Where are my shoes? Give me my shoes, Letha. I can't find them."

"Child, child." Letha brought her the shoes from a closet and slipped them on her feet. "Honey, you look as wild as something scared right out of the woods. Let me fix your hair."

With frantic impatience, Kate submitted as Letha smoothed her hair, and before she was done, rushed out of the room and ran up the stairs to intensive care. She knew if she waited for an elevator she would go quite mad. When she reached the room where Joseph lay, they told her she could not go in, but that she could look at him through the glass. He looked so white and still that she was terrified he was dying.

She felt Jake's presence beside her. Joseph had still not opened his eyes.

"Jake," Kate said hoarsely, turning to him. "Tell me. Tell me the truth."

His glance swept her face and hair, her disheveled appearance. He hesitated. At last he said, "The truth is, Kate, we won't know for another day. Now, please get back to your room."

"I will sit outside." She sat in the waiting room for the rest of the day, refusing to listen when Letha or her grandfather advised her to eat something. The thought of food was abhorrent, but at Jake's insistence she drank water.

"I wish you would go home for a little while, Kate," Dryver said.

"My home is here." She realized at last that she hadn't even asked about the children, had not inquired about Anzia. The only thing that mattered now was Joseph, lying pale and motionless, his eyes closed.

"All right, then, my dear. I will be back a little later." Harry Dryver kissed her cheek and walked off down the hall.

Unable to settle anywhere, she paced between the waiting room and the hall; that night she slept for a few fitful hours on the couch. When the first light entered the grimy windows, Kate sat up, light-headed with weariness and hunger. Some food, congealing in its gravy, lay on a table in the waiting room. Kate's stomach heaved when she smelled it, and she pushed it away. With astonishment she saw that her hands were dirty. She stood up and looked at her reflection in the window. Her hair was a mess and her face looked gaunt, unclean. Good God, Joseph must not see her like this.

On rubbery legs Kate hurried to a washroom, sketchily bathed her face, hands, and body; fumbling in her bag, she found her comb and righted her hair. Then she sought out the nurses' station near Joseph, where she was told she could not see him for another hour. Now her stomach was racked with hunger pains. She knew she had to eat something, so she took the elevator to the hospital cafeteria, telling one of the nurses where she was going.

Kate had been without food for so long now that she feared her stomach would rebel, so she drank a little milk, ate a forkful of scrambled egg.

Looking up, amazed, she saw her mother enter the dining room.

Elizabeth Wendell glanced around the room with disapproval—this was a "poor persons' hospital," the nearest one to the scene of the shooting, and Kate was sure her mother had never seen anything like it. She was flabbergasted. Why had Elizabeth come here now, when they hadn't exchanged a word for four whole years?

Elizabeth was dressed with almost painful smartness in the spring's latest ensemble—a dark fitted jacket over a narrow cream-colored skirt; a broad-brimmed straw hat, like a big fedora, was set rakishly on her dark puffed hair. She saw Kate and came to her table.

"May I sit down?" she asked coolly, eyeing Kate's haggard face and wrinkled clothes.

"I can't stop you. But I'm about to leave. I have to get back upstairs." Kate could not hide her bitterness; Elizabeth had shown no interest in her grandchildren, had not come near them for all this time. "Have you come to gloat, Mother? If so, you'll be disappointed. I know Joseph will live'' Her voice broke with the last word.

Elizabeth's narrow mouth stiffened. ''I can see that living among working people has not improved your manners. And you have begun to resemble a slattern.''

Kate pushed back her chair, starting too rise. ''Excuse me, Mother. but I've had other things on my mind than fashion.''

''Please, Kate. Sit down. Surely you can give me a moment.''

Deterred by this half-apology, Kate lowered her body into the chair. ''Was it you who discouraged Father from coming back to see me? Or did he tell you?''

''Of course he told me,'' Elizabeth said huffily. ''He did not come back because he couldn't bear to see you in such squalor.''

''I don't have time for this,'' Kate snapped. ''I've got to see my husband.'' She trembled all over, feeling powerless. This confrontation was unbearable, especially now. She pushed back her chair with a harsh scrape and stood up, supporting herself on the table. ''How did you find out?''

''Your grandfather told me, of course. He also told me his servants are having a difficult time with your little daughter. I consider it my duty to take the child to our house until you can met your responsibilities as a mother. That is why I came.'' Elizabeth's voice shook with indignation. ''Your grandfather insisted that I speak to you first.''

''Why is it your duty, Mother, all of a sudden?'' Kate demanded.

''Because I don't want my granddaughter . . .'' Elizabeth paused, flushing. ''I don't want to see her neglected while you . . . have other matters on your mind.''

''And David?''

Elizabeth looked down at her gloved hands, then up again at Kate with dark, opaque eyes. ''He is too young to be taken from his mother. Anyway, boys are not so . . . delicate.''

Kate fought her rising hysteria. Her mother was in for a rude surprise if she expected the obstinate, bumptious Marite to be "delicate." This whole encounter was so upsetting that Kate was afraid she couldn't bear much more. Her mother had never once expressed concern for Joseph or asked how Kate felt; she had spoken only of her "duty"—not her desire—to help her daughter. It was as if Elizabeth had chosen to confront Kate at her weakest moment.

"I must go, Mother," she said shakily. "If you wish to take care of Marite for a little while, then by all means do so."

"Very well, Kate. Thank you."

Kate was incredulous. Even now her mother sounded cold, grudging. Tears gathered in her eyes as she hurried toward the elevator and took the slow, excruciating ascent to Joseph's floor.

She found Jake Lapidus and Joseph's attending physician outside his room. At the sight of them her heart almost choked her, fluttering and hammering in her throat. But both men were smiling.

"Kate." Jake came toward her and squeezed her shoulder. "He's out of the woods. He's asking for you."

She sobbed with relief and ran into the room where Joseph lay. He was awake, and smiling at her. The smile was like a benediction. Her throat was so constricted that she could barely say his name.

She knelt down on the floor beside his bed, all her pent-up tears releasing in a sudden flood. She held on to his hand, hiding her face on the bed close to his beloved body, and gave herself up to the convulsive weeping that she had held in for too long. His fingers stroked her head.

When she raised her face, she knew it must look swollen and ugly. But Joseph said softly, "I have never seen you look so beautiful. I never thought I'd see your face again."

She rose and bent over him, giving him the lightest

possible kiss on his mouth. The whole world was suddenly singing inside her. She sat down in the chair beside him and just kept looking at him. Her heart was so full she couldn't speak.

Finally she was able to whisper, "This is the second time you have given me my life."

When the news of Lionel Simson's act swept the Sephardic community, everyone agreed that there hadn't been such a scandal for nearly half a century. Not since the summer of 1870, when a son of the prominent Benjamin Seixas Nathan was suspected of patricide.

But Lionel, like the notorious Nathan son, was never charged. For weeks the Sephardic, socialist, and artistic circles of Greenwich village talked and speculated, burning with indignation. Lionel Simson had disappeared. Some said he had been sent to a hospital for dipsomaniacs, others that he had left the country.

Joseph was not allowed to leave the hospital for three weeks after his operation, but he scoffed at the statement that he must recuperate at home for four months more. During his second week of confinement he decided he had to get up; he had too much work to do. Kate knew this was not the only reason for his restlessness; this confinement gave him too much time to brood about the desecration of his father's last rites, his mother's look of frailty, the fact that he had not been there to say *kaddish* for Solomon Barsimson.

Kate did everything in her power to cheer and distract him. When he asked about the children, she gave him a revised version of her mother's visit. It was the first lie she had ever told him, and she hated that. But it was too early in his convalescence for the truth. So when he said, "It is kind of your mother to help out," Kate let it go.

She tried to make it up to the others for her savagely selfish preoccupation during those first terrifying days; she had hardly given a thought to Anzia or Rafael, or even to her grandfather. Now that she had come back to her senses, Kate dimly recalled the early visits of her mother-in-law and Rafael. There had been a constant stream of

gifts from Rafael Simson—fruit and flowers, newly published novels, a handsome dressing gown and Moroccan
slippers. There was also an awkward, touchingly worded
letter: "It will do you no good to see my face now. All the
same, I will keep up the installments of my debt to you,
which can never be repaid." Joseph handed the letter to
Kate to read; she saw tears in his eyes.

One of the ways Rafael "kept up his installments" was
by persuading Anzia to move into the Simson house.
Joseph was surprised that she would be willing to leave the
Lower East Side, where she had spent most of her life. But
when he saw her regaining some of her old strength,
looking rested and smart in a handsome new dress Bertha
had given her, Joseph was very pleased. And Kate breathed
a sigh of relief: at least one worry could be eliminated.

But there was still the problem of Marite, a problem she
felt she could not yet share with Joseph. When she had
gone to her parents' house to bring the child back home,
her daughter had rebelled. "I want to stay with Nana,"
she shouted. Kate observed Marite's fairy-tale room with
its walls papered in pastel scenes from stories of the
Brothers Grimm, the closet full of pretty dresses, and the
shelves crowded with dolls and toys. She felt an odd
apprehension. Marite would not be able to adapt so easily
to MacDougal Street after all this. But Kate decided not to
borrow trouble; there was already more than enough to
concern her. Her father's strangely cold reception, for one.
Kate could not comprehend his sudden reversal. On that
one long-ago visit he had seemed so eager for a reconciliation.

This time when Joseph asked her about the visit, she
was less successful in hiding her dismay.

"What's the matter, Kate? You're not telling me
everything."

Uneasily she met his dark, penetrating stare. "I'm just a
little . . . uneasy about my mother's influence over Marite."

"She's hardly more than a baby," Joseph consoled her.
"I wouldn't worry about it, darling. I do miss them,

though. I wish they could visit." The hospital rules forbade visits from children under twelve. "I can't wait to get
out of this damned place, Kate . . . to be back home,
where I belong, with you and the children."

"Just a few more days," she said cheerfully, and kissed
him, trying to dismiss her worries about Marite.

The next morning, when Kate was buying copies of the
newspapers for Joseph, she saw the headline on a sensational weekly: "*REAL STORY OF SIMSON HEIR.*"

She bought that paper, too, and skimmed it while standing there. The article, supposedly written by a former
Simson servant, purported to tell the "whole shocking
truth" about Lionel Simson. It revealed the fact that Lionel had tried to shoot his own father, injuring instead the
"notorious rabble-rouser" Joseph Barsimson. The writer
claimed that he had overheard a "terrible scene" between
Rafael Simson and his son during which the former had
said, "Here's some money. Take it and get out of the
house; never let me see your face again. I don't care where
you go—the farther away, the better."

It was alleged that Lionel had gone to Europe. There
were other distasteful disclosures, including the "fact"
that Lionel's heartbroken mother was going insane from
grief; that the mother of the injured man had blackmailed
Rafael Simson into admitting her into his home and was
even trying to influence Rafael into making her son his
heir.

The horrible piece ended with speculation—why had the
injured nephew failed to bring charges against his cousin?
Was Joseph Barsimson indeed trying to blackmail his uncle? And why had the witnesses failed to report the crime
to police? There was even a malicious reference to Kate
Wendell Barsimson, "socialite socialist, daughter of the
prominent Howard Wendell."

Kate was so upset the paper shook in her grasp. Good
God, they hadn't spared *anyone* . . . not even the innocent
Anzia or Kate's poor father. The "rabble-rouser" and
"socialite socialist" ran off her like water from a duck's

oiled feathers; both she and Joseph were used to comments like that. But Kate could not bear the shame to Anzia.

Kate crumpled the offending paper in her hands. She was certainly not going to show it to Joseph.

But if she didn't . . . and he learned of this from someone else . . .

She smoothed out the paper, folded it, and put it underneath the other daily newspapers. It was foolish to try to keep anything from him. Rafael, for one, would be raving, bringing suit no doubt against that awful publication.

But in another month the whole matter faded into obscurity. Local scandals no longer seemed very significant.

Europe had gone to war.

Chapter 13

On a Sunday afternoon in May 1917, Kate walked into Harry Dryver's studio.

"Kate!" He turned from his easel; his aquiline face beamed. A rain-grayed light poured through the skylight. That sunny autumn afternoon eight years ago, when she had first met Joseph, flashed into her mind. She had had a secret to keep then. Today she had secrets to tell, feelings she could share only with her grandfather.

But his unvarying welcome, their pleasure in each other, had no season.

"I thought I recognized your step, but I put it down to delirium, I was in such a fury." He grinned, lowered his brush, and kissed her gingerly. "I mustn't ruin your 'court dress.' "

She laughed. They would never cease to refer to the Wendell house as the Palace.

Dryver forestalled her next question. "Just winding up. You came at a perfect time. I'm aching like a stevedore." He stretched his arms and moved his shoulders.

Kate stook back and squinted at his oil. It was a departure for him; a semiabstract representation of a threatening storm at sea. Yet the breakers managed to convey flying banners and falling men, the smoke of weaponry through the rolling clouds. Harry Dryver's comment on America at war.

"The deluge," she murmured. "This is the most powerful thing you've ever done." She sat down on the Recamier couch, still staring.

"Thank you. It's part and parcel of my Angry Period." He cocked an eye at the satirical paintings and drawings lining the walls—dark-humored horrors showing the grim inanities of patriotism, the "glories" of war.

Dryver went to his hot plate, questioning Kate with a lifted coffeepot.

She nodded yes absently. "Even the light today is perfect for those. And this." Kate waved her hand at the works on the wall, the painting on the easel. "Do you remember how sunny it was that afternoon I came here with Rose from the picket line? And you were painting the picketers. They had such motion and life—such hope. The whole world was shinier then."

Sitting on his stool against the background of the ominous painting, Dryver smiled in recollection. "And so innocent, in contrast to this battle. Today, I take it, you've been brooding about the war, and you come here to find me painting it."

"*Yes.* No one has ever understood me the way you do."

"We're like the bright and dark sides of a planet, Kate. You're the bright side, of course. Sticking to your colors, like Childe Hassam. I should emulate both of you, and find what beauty there is in all this horror—the flags flying, the brasses of the bands. You know, you're a better colorist than I will ever be." He smiled at her fondly.

"That's hard to swallow, but it thrills me to hear you say it."

"It's true, Kate. It shows even in the clothes you wear. That dress, for instance. It's the most remarkable shade of blue I've even seen." Dryver narrowed his dark eyes as if he were choosing a tube of blue for painting. "Neither periwinkle nor hyacinth. More purple."

"A royal shade for the Palace," she retorted. "You haven't said a word about that yet."

He sighed. "I was trying not to. I'm in no mood to get rigged out today. Good Lord, it's like a presidential inauguration! I couldn't believe it when Elizabeth said you and Joseph were dining. What induced you to accept?''

"Joseph said there should be some peace somewhere," Kate said darkly.

Dryver's mouth narrowed from its smile. "But what about this détente between MacDougal Street and Madison Avenue? What's gotten into Elizabeth, after all these years?''

"Marite," Kate said curtly. "I'm a witch to say it, but I think Mother wants to sweeten us, for fear we'll cut down on Marite's visits uptown." Dryver nodded quickly several times in agreement. "And Joseph said if I can put up with Rafael, he can put up with Madison Avenue."

"Poor old Rafael." It amused Kate to hear her grandfather say that. Rafael Simson was young enough to be his son, but Harry Dryver said Rafael had always been old in his attitudes. Dryver poured himself another cup of the strong, dark coffee and refilled Kate's cup. "What's he done now?''

"You know what a raving patriot he is," Kate began. "Well, just the other day he dropped in with more toys for David—tanks and guns and soldiers. And he said when the factory starts making uniforms, he's going to have a little uniform made for David. Naturally David was thrilled. He couldn't know what it means. Of course, if we don't let him have it, he'll be devastated."

Dryver threw up his hands. "My God. The poor man must have lost his mind over Lionel. A four-year-old 'soldier.' There hasn't been a pccp out of Lionel, has there?''

"Not a one. There was a rumor he was in France. But I can't picture him in the Lafayette Escadrille," Kate commented dryly.

"Like the fervent Wendells and Dryvers." As early as 1914 three of the Wendell cousins and a Dryver boy had joined the British Army, the Lafayette arm of the French Air Force and even the French Foreign Legion.

"Marite's already come home with glowing tales of her

heroic cousins. *And* Mother's genealogical nonsense about the Vikings and the Battle of Hastings, all that.''

"A noble lineage," Dryver mocked, raising his brows.

"I begged off from Rafael's today so I could spend a little time with you. Poor Joseph will have had the war at both houses by the time this day's over. But it's been too long since I've seen you alone. That sounds selfish as hell. And I don't care." Kate grinned. "Joseph's strong."

"Bravo!" Harry Dryver started cleaning his brushes. "I told you years ago you deserve a decoration for coping at *all*. Besides, there's a positive aspect: your work's better than ever, with your enlightened self-interest." His smile was faintly demonic, and made her chuckle.

She was gratified. Despite all her duties as a parent and her work with Joseph in the pacifist movement the past three years, she had painted an impressive number of canvasses. Good ones. And what her grandfather had said had some truth; she was growing as a colorist.

"The same old greedy Kate" she said, smiling. "I'm ashamed to tell you—with so many men dying over there every hour—but I can't consider anyone but Joseph. If he had to go to war . . . I nearly passed out Friday when I heard the news about Selective Service. The first thing I thought was: Thank God he's too old." By just one year. She shuddered.

"Why should you be ashamed?" Dryver demanded. Now he was holding a hammer, searching through a box of nails. He chose one, drove it into the wall, and hung the new canvas to dry. Squinting at it, he said, "You're a natural woman, Kate. And Joseph is blessed to have you. You're head and shoulders above those idiots who are ashamed of a man *not* in uniform."

Kate was reassured. "You help me so much. Some of these things, I couldn't even say to Joseph. You know how he is—never concerned with his personal safety, looking at everything from the Olympian heights, at the wide picture through a telescope. If you'll excuse the anachronism."

Dryver laughed. "The old gods were bad enough without having telescopes. Yes, that's Joseph, the savior of the masses.'' He spoke as fondly as she had, with loving tolerance. Kate recalled that Lionel had also called Joseph that, but then it had sounded like a curse. The way her grandfather said it, it sounded like an endearment. ''That's another thing, darling. The wide picture may be splendid, but you lose too many fine details. Good old Michelangelo, 'trifles make perfection.' ''

''Yes, yes! We're individuals, for God's sake. I'm so fed up with groups and movements. Another seditious thing I can't say to Joseph,'' Kate rushed on. ''I'm damned tired of conflict. And war is the worst mass movement of all, the ultimate waste. Why, why are we *in* it?''

Dryver sat on the couch beside her and leaned back against a pillow. ''For the very reasons the socialists advance: to fatten munitions makers and bankers.''

''Why won't people accept that? Besides the lives, think of the other damage. The art, the homes, the cathedrals. The very thought of cleaning up after a war leaves me exhausted. No woman would ever allow such a mess to be made.''

''That's because women have more sense than men. Always have had, always will have. Don Quixote could never have been portrayed as a woman; only men enjoy fighting absurdities, abstractions. Even the economic bases for war are myths. Wall Street deals in fairy gold.''

Dryver gestured at his drawings. ''Those are all about money. I would probably be hauled away if I showed them in public. You know what might relieve your anger?''

''Putting it on canvas, where it belongs.''

''Bulls eye.'' Dryver clapped his long-fingered hands together. ''You know, darling, the older I get, the more I'm sure there's nothing but work and love. Don't be political too long. Life's too short. And the only art that's long is timeless, not didactic.'' Dryver laughed. ''Like me,'' he added, mocking himself. ''End of lecture.''

There was a sudden shrill ringing from the corner, and Kate jumped. ''What was *that*?''

"My alarm clock. To 'wake' me in time to change my overalls for the Palace Guard uniform. I finished painting sooner than I expected." He laughed. "It should have rung during the lecture."

"Never." Kate kissed him. "I've always treasured your advice."

He looked at her fondly, then got up with reluctance. "I don't know where the time goes. I'd better go get myself cleaned up."

Kate left him on the second floor and headed for the kitchen to visit Letha. Soon Kate would be refreshed enough to handle the upcoming visit at Elizabeth's.

When the Wendells' door was opened by the butler, Lynn, Joseph was amazed. He thought that after eight year's of alienation one of Kate's parents would surely greet them. He would never understand these people.

Lynn's face was impassive but his slate-gray eyes were warmer than Joseph remembered from last time. "Miss Kate! Mr. Harry . . . Mr. Barsimson."

"Hello, Lynn." Kate sounded as casual as if they dined there every night. "This is our son, David."

"Master David." Lynn beamed down at the little boy, who was holding Joseph's hand. "Welcome, Miss Kate. Your parents are in the big drawing room."

While Lynn disposed of their hats, Joseph glanced around. The place had been a blur when they had come here on their wedding day; this was the first time he had really looked at the entrance hall. It was rich and somber, with a riot of patterns that made the eyes dance—carved walls, furniture, and doors; Oriental carpets even on the stairs, which warred, to his taste, with other patterns of fringed brocade and screens. A costly horror, making his and Kate's apartment and Dryver's simple house seem even lovelier by contrast.

Kate and Dryver followed Lynn over the rare Persian carpet toward the double doors directly ahead, with Joseph and David in their wake.

Lynn opened the doors. "Thank you, Lynn." Kate's voice was firm and decisive. Joseph realized the butler had been at a loss about how to announce them. *Announce* them, to her own parents! The situation was grotesque. Even so, it had seemed wrong to him for Kate to remain alienated from her flesh and blood.

In some ways it was like the last visit: Elizabeth Wendell, ornately dressed, was seated on a brocade sofa. A heavy silver tea service rested on the table in front of her.

And the stately Howard Wendell stood in the center of the room. He came toward them to give Kate a brief kiss on her cheek and shake the men's hands. Elizabeth stayed where she was, as if she were posing for a portrait, waiting to be approached.

"Hello, Mother," Kate said coolly, and leaned over to kiss her mother. Elizabeth only smiled, and Joseph observed how different the smile was from Dryver's, although they had the same look around the eyes. In Elizabeth Dryver's face, independence translated itself into arrogance.

Elizabeth greeted her father then held out her hand to Joseph. When he took it, it was very cold.

"And this is David," Kate said without inflection. Once again Joseph was struck by the awkwardness of it—Elizabeth had made no attempt to see her grandson in four years.

Elizabeth examined David with her predator's eyes; he stepped back a little, involuntarily, sheltering himself against Joseph's trousers. His grandmother made no move to touch or caress him. "What a handsome young man," she said in a tinkling voice. She seemed to be trying to trace a resemblance to Kate: she glanced back and forth from him to her daughter. Elizabeth brightened. "He has Kate's eyes."

Harry Dryver gave her a mischievous smile. "Just exactly. Otherwise I think he's going to be the image of Joseph."

There was an uneasy little silence.

Kate sat down in one of the more comfortable chairs. "Where's Marite, Mother?"

Dryver and Joseph sat down too, on a love seat, with David between them. Wendell stayed on his feet, looking tense and somewhat at a loss.

Elizabeth's harsh face was transformed. "She'll be down in a moment. She had a little nap and now she's being dressed. But excuse me." She smiled artificially at Dryver and Joseph. "Do let me ring for Lynn so serve you something."

"Never mind, Elizabeth." Wendell intervened with a slight frown. "May I offer you something?" he asked the men. He seemed eager for some kind of informality to ease the visit, and Joseph suddenly felt sorry for him. "I know you'll want some tea or coffee, Kate. And Mr. Dryver's a sherry drinker. How about you, Joseph?"

"Sherry would be fine, sir," Joseph said.

"As a matter of fact, I'd like some too." Kate smiled at her father. "Mother, perhaps Lynn could bring David a glass of milk."

Joseph accepted a glass of sherry from Wendell, marveling at Kate's composure. She had spoken with the same careful lack of inflection, but Elizabeth flushed slightly. It was apparent she had totally forgotten David. "Of course. Would you ring, Howard?"

Lynn was dispatched with the order.

Joseph sipped. "This is excellent wine, sir."

Wendell's gloomy face lightened as he sat down in a high-backed brocade chair. "Amontillado."

The wine was delicious, with a nutty flavor to it. Dryver started chatting easily with Elizabeth and Kate about Sarah Bernhardt's American tour, and Wendell, though silent, seemed more at ease. Joseph caressed David's hair and glanced around the lavish drawing room.

Suddenly the double doors opened and, flinging off the nurse's hand, Marite cried out, "Daddy! Daddy!" and ran straight to Joseph. But she almost fell over David in her eagerness to get to Joseph.

"Hello, there!" Joseph righted David, holding on to him with one hand while he kissed his six-year-old daughter. "I'm so glad to see you! Be careful of David," he added gently. "You look very pretty."

Marite preened herself for her father; she was wearing an elaborate dress, all lace and ruffles, which Joseph had never seen. Anything that well-made had to be a gift from Elizabeth.

"There's my wicked angel!" Elizabeth was practically cooing at Marite. "Aren't you going to give your poor old grandmother a kiss . . . and say hello to your mother and Great-Grandfather Dryver?"

Marite went to Elizabeth to be hugged and submitted to Kate's and Dryver's kisses, but she came quickly back to Joseph.

Marite was about to climb onto Joseph's lap when Lynn announced dinner. "Kate, perhaps you want to consult with the nurse about David's dinner. The nurse can feed him in a small dining room."

"Please don't go to the trouble, Mother. David always eats with us. I'm afraid it's not a good idea to have him eat alone."

Joseph repressed a smile. Kate sounded perfectly amiable, but there was steel under the velvet.

"I'll have Lynn bring in my little chair," Kate added, trying to be helpful, "since Marite uses a regular one now." Elizabeth was miffed, but when Wendell intervened with: "That's smart of you, Kate; we should have thought of it," she withdrew from the discussion.

After a minor flurry they were seated at the baronial table. Wendell sat at the head, flanked by Kate and Elizabeth, with Marite on Elizabeth's left and David in a fancy elevated chair on Kate's right. Joseph was glad to find himself assigned to the chair next to David, with Harry Dryver, at the table's foot, his neighbor.

Joseph's place gave him a view of the Wendell family crest, emblazoned opposite above the marble fireplace, now empty for the summer. The Wendell crest was repeated on a semicircular wooden panel above the enclosed mantel, six times more in gilded carving. The entire room was as dark and ornamented and intimidating as a temple.

He was aware of Dryver's ironic glance. When he met the painter's eyes, they were gleaming with wicked humor. Joseph felt his appetite return.

The dinner itself was superb, and he was able to enjoy it, as Wendell and Elizabeth were seated too far away to require constant replies from him.

Kate divided her attention between the table conversation and helping David enjoy his dinner. Joseph noticed with annoyance that Marite had been furnished with a little set of children's silver, while David had not. The embarrassed Lynn soon righted that omission.

Marite began to monopolize the conversation until Kate adroitly brought David and her father into the talk. After that, Marite talked only to Elizabeth, but at least Joseph was able to relax more. He could see that Kate was taking it all in stride, and he loved having the chance to talk to Dryver.

There was a sticky moment when David said proudly to Wendell, "My Unca Raff'l's going to make me a so-jur."

"A soldier?" Howard Wendell repeated interestedly, smiling. "How's that, David?"

"Make me a yoon . . . a yooni . . ."

"A uniform?" prompted Wendell. "Why, that's splendid, isn't it, Elizabeth?" Elizabeth ignored them, instructing Marite how to use her napkin. "And who is 'Unca Raffle?' " Wendell genially demanded of Kate.

"Joseph's uncle, Rafael Simson, of Simson Company," Kate answered, again without inflection.

Wendell said, "Of *course*. The . . ." He stopped abruptly, turning beet-red. Joseph thought: He's remembered. The whole damned mess about Rafael and Lionel. Another subject to be avoided.

Wendell said quickly, "Of course. The noted manufacturer." And he hastened to change the subject.

Whatever else he was, Joseph decided, Wendell was not

deliberately unkind. And he had the most perfect manners of any man Joseph had ever met.

Kate was struggling to keep up the conversation with her father while she fed David his pudding.

"My turn," Joseph murmured to her, and took over the task.

All this was apparently too much for the neglected Marite. "Mother!" she said peremptorily. "Mother!"

Kate finished what she was saying to Wendell. "Yes? What is it, darling?"

"I want you to come upstairs *right now* and see my new dolls and dresses!"

"I will, just as soon as we've finished dinner," Kate said with kind firmness. Marite subsided.

As soon as they rose from the dinner table, Kate went upstairs with Marite. Elizabeth directed Lynn to serve coffee in the small drawing room and Wendell invited Joseph and Dryver to his library. Joseph was holding David in his arms now; the boy's eyes were at half-mast, as it was nearly his bedtime. Joseph caught Dryver's eye again and saw him twinkle at the absurd formality of it all.

After the somber ritual of port and brandy, Wendell ushered them into the small drawing room, where Kate and Elizabeth were drinking coffee. Joseph saw his daughter pirouetting, holding out the skirt of her elaborate dress. Her long golden hair, her neat little features, and her pursed, prim mouth were very like Kate's—and yet a travesty of them somehow. Joseph felt a stab of compassion and tenderness; the child lived in the midst of such conflict and confusion. Riches on the weekend, a plain working-class home with subversive parents all week.

"This has been perfectly lovely, Mother," Kate said in a social tone. "But we should go. It's long past David's bedtime."

"No!" Marite startled them all by stamping her small foot on the Oriental carpet. "I want to stay!"

Joseph saw a triumphant glint in Elizabeth's dark eyes. He held out his arms to his daughter. "Now, that's a fine thing to say. Your daddy hasn't seen you for two whole days. Don't you want to come home with me?''

Marite hesitated an instant, looking at him. Then she said, "Oh, yes, Daddy! I do, I do!" And Marite ran to Joseph to be hugged.

In a few moments the good-byes were over and their big Checker taxi was taking them back to the apartment on MacDougal Street.

Chapter 14

"Marite?"

Kate stopped short at the door of the children's brightly decorated room. Marite was still in bed with her face to the wall of white toy shelves, the striped cover drawn up to her nose. "You're going to be late for school, darling. Are you sick?"

Walking to the bed, Kate put her hand to her daughter's forehead. It was perfectly cool. "What's the matter?" she asked Marite gently.

The child did not turn over. "I'm not going." Her answer was muffled by bedclothes.

Kate thought she had misheard. "What, honey?"

"I'm not going back to school anymore." Marite turned and sat up in bed. Her rebellious eyes were startlingly like Joseph's, her small mouth stubbornly pursed.

Kate fought the impulse to retort: That's what you think. But she had to get to the bottom of this; it must be carefully handled. When Marite took this tone it was so much like Elizabeth's that Kate had to remind herself Marite was a nine-year-old child. *Her child*. Not her mother.

Kate reached out slowly and stroked her daughter's golden hair, combing her bangs gently with her fingers. The hair was so straight and fine it hardly tangled. "Now, why do you say that?"

"I hate that school." Marite moved her head away.

Kate dropped her hand. "My goodness," she said mildly, "this is your third year. You never said that before."

It's different now. It's full of Bolsheek Jews.'' Marite lay down again, turning her face back to the gaily laden shelves below the small circus painting Kate had done for her.

Kate felt a chill run through her. The war had been over for nearly two years, but talk of the ''Red Menace'' was sweeping America, fueled by the Bolsheviks' success in Russia and their growing influence over the socialists. Marite must have picked up the mispronounced word from Elizabeth.

Kate decided to try humor. ''If you're going to be against something, she teased, you'd better learn how to say it. It's *Bole*-shee-veek. And Jews aren't necessarily Bolsheviks, Marite. You daddy stood up against the Bolsheviks last summer in Chicago, remember?''

She realized she had made a tactical error when Marite said, ''I remember. You and Daddy left me.'' Last August Kate had accompanied Joseph to the Socialist party convention.

''But you said you wanted to stay with Granma, Marite.''

Her daughter was silent.

''Marite,'' Kate cajoled her.

''Granma said Daddy's a Bole . . . a *Bole*-shee-veek, and that all Jews are. She said I'm not a Jew.''

Kate struggled to control her temper. Marite had spent the day uptown yesterday, and yesterday must have been something special. ''Well, she's right about that. You're *not* a Jew.''

Marite turned over and sat up in bed. She looked flabbergasted. ''You never say Granma's right. You always say she's mistaken.''

''Well, she's not mistaken this time. Your mother's a Gentile, so you can't be a Jew, even if your daddy is. And I don't see what this has to do with school, Marite.'' Kate thought: I should be firmer. This has gone on long enough. But she was careful to keep her impatience from her voice.

''It's not a real school.'' Marite threw the covers from her shoulders, color staining her cheeks. She was so pretty:

her yellow nightgown was the color of her hair, contrasting with the blackness of her eyes against the orange-and-
gold-striped spread.

Kate resisted the distraction. "What do you mean?"

"It's not as good as the schools uptown. Granma said I
should go to school up there. I want to, too. You can't
make me go to that awful school." Now the dark almond
eyes looked like a stranger's.

How dare her mother try to alienate their child from
them? Kate's first reaction was fury, but she knew she
couldn't give in to it. Suddenly she had an inspiration.

"I won't make you go. As a matter of fact, you can
help me a lot today, while I do some painting." Kate
smiled at her. "I'll make a list right now, if you'll hand
me your notebook and one of your pencils."

Puzzled, Marite obeyed.

"Now, let's see." Kate pretended to be thinking deeply.
"After you have breakfast, you can wash the dishes for
me. The next thing will be to make up the beds, and dust
. . . and then I'll show you how to mop the kitchen floor.
That'll do for a start." Still simulating enthusiasm, she
tore off the page and handed the pencil and notebook back.

Marite replaced them on her shelf, looking uncertain.

"And of course you'll have to wear one of your old
dresses, so you won't ruin a pretty one."

Now Marite frowned: she hated wearing old dresses.
Her greatest pleasure was putting on a different dress for
school. "Why do I have to do these things?"

"Well, everybody has to do something, darling. David's
going to school and your daddy's going to work and so am
I. There won't be anyone for you to play with, so you'll
have to find some way to pass the time, won't you?"

Marite considered what she had said, then threw back
the covers all the way and jumped out of bed.

"Are you getting your old dress?"

"No, Mother." Marite was at the closet now, taking out
her new green dress. "I decided I will go to school, after
all."

"You're sure now?" Kate played up. "I don't want to *make* you go, Marite."

"Oh, yes, Mother! I'm really sure." Kate watched her daughter brush her long golden hair and quickly put her books in her satchel.

"Good. Let's get your breakfast, then. It's all ready. Come on."

Kate turned and saw Joseph standing by the door, grinning at her. Marite dashed by him and headed for the dining area.

Joseph chuckled, hugging Kate. "You're a twister. I could use you in the union."

She wiped away imaginary sweat from her brow. "Did you walk David to school already?"

He nodded. "Can you take care of the second shift? I've got to get over to the parade. I dropped back here to see what was up with our daughter."

"Now you know. Of course I'll take her. Joseph . . . please be careful today." She put her hand on his arm.

"There's not a thing to worry about. Nothing will happen."

"If it's all that peaceful, why can't I go too?" she asked him skeptically. "I've marched in every May Day parade with you."

He looked caught out. "Not today. Darling, I'm sorry, but I've got to go." He kissed her hard.

Kate stood where she was for a moment, hearing the door close and his quick footsteps descending the stairs. She went into the living room and hurried to the window, watching him stride quickly to the corner and head northeast below the square.

"Mother?" Marite was regarding her curiously, wiping her milk mustache away with a napkin. "I'm ready."

Trying to shake off her anxiety, Kate smiled at her daughter. "Fine. Let's go."

After she left Marite at the door of the school, Kate retraced her steps, unwilling to go directly home. She decided to stop at Eighth Street and buy another *Times*.

There had been no time to read the one delivered to their apartment. She bought the paper and went to sit in Washington Square. Its greenness was inviting, but the fine May morning seemed to mock her dark mood. Not a merry month this year.

Today, the first of May 1920, the insanity brought on by the Sacco and Vanzetti case had reached its height. The anti-Communists claimed, that the "revolution" would start with the May Day parade, that the U.S. government would be overthrown. New York had called out the National Guard, and the city's police force had been put on twenty-four-hour duty.

Joseph had gone to march in the parade, where a bomb or bullet could put an end to his life—an end to Kate's world.

She felt more frantic by the second. To quell her anxiety she got up and walked briskly back to the apartment. It wouldn't help her or Joseph or the children to come home to a disordered house. She rushed into activity as soon as she walked in the door: clearing the breakfast table, washing the dishes, wiping all the cabinets and counters, mopping the floor. After that she attacked the living room and left it shining, then made the childrens' beds. She was making hers and Joseph's when she was abruptly overcome with exhaustion.

Sitting down in a chair, she gazed around the bedroom, the scene of so much love and happiness. Two of Kate's own paintings hung there—the old "mythical jungle" and a powerful seascape she had painted at Coney Island. That had been such a happy day. She remembered Joseph saying, as he had when he saw the old oil of the washing, "This is what you should be doing, Kate."

Inspired, she went to the "studio corner" of the living room and quickly prepared a canvas. With sure, passionate strokes she began to outline the head and torso of her husband. She could paint his every eyelash and every small line on his face from memory. And she envisioned the finished work: Joseph Barsimson, as he had looked this very morning, against a vivid, multicolored ground of strife and splendor, the baroque of the Sephardim blending into the struggle of today.

Soon she was so intent that she forgot almost everything but the canvas before her. She was so startled by the sudden ringing of the telephone that, leaning forward to use her brush again, she almost toppled against the painting. She jerked back.

The phone. Joseph! With her brush still in her hand she ran to answer. "Darling?"

It was his voice, sounding jubilant and whole. "Oh, Joseph!"

"Calm down, darling. Calm down. The demonstration was as quiet as six o'clock Sunday morning. Couldn't be better. Our Anti-Communist friends really look foolish." He laughed.

"Nothing?" she asked weakly, trying not to cry with relief.

"Nothing whatsoever. The poor bored cops had to amuse themselves with pickpockets."

She was finally able to join his laughter.

"I saw your grandfather," he added.

"I might have known." She could hear the shakiness in her own voice, but now her overpowering relief was making her feel quite dizzy. She realized she hadn't eaten lunch. "Joseph, I'm so . . . happy."

"I know, I know." He sounded tender. "I'm going back to work now. Get yourself dressed up, and we'll all go out to dinner and take your grandfather along. About seven. All right? Could you call him?"

"Right now I can do *anything*. I love you, Joseph. I love you so much."

"I love you, Kate."

She hung up in a glow. Returning to her easel, she stood back from the painting. On the canvas, Joseph lived and breathed . . . just as he blessedly still lived and breathed in their chaotic life.

His mature features were even more magnificent than

his face had been eleven years ago, when she first saw it. And the dark eyes still gleamed in the fine face with their unchanging fire.

Late that night Kate emerged from ber bath in a jade-green nightgown, her newly short hair a gleaming drift around her ears. "What a wonderful night."

Joseph was lying under the golden spread; it made his dark eyes look even deeper. "What a wonderful *picture*," he said, looking at her face and hair, her body through the thinness of the gown. His eyes still had that distracted glow she knew so well, reflecting tension and desire. His buoyance had carried them all along, throughout their celebration dinner and the rest of the evening.

Now Kate saw his transparent need. It was the same as hers: the need to ease the long, high tension that had stretched their nerves in expectation of this day.

She turned out the lights and lay down beside him, nestling close. He gathered her into his arms and with one hand stroked the brief softness of her hair.

Then his hand was on her side, caressing her from her breast to her narrow waist, following the curve of her slender hip. "I can't believe you're even lovelier, after eleven whole years," he whispered.

"Oh, Joseph, it's like the first time, all over again. After . . . today, I feel that I know what it really is to love you."

She moved into him, began to caress the bare skin of his chest with the tip of her tongue, bringing from him a deep sound of arousal.

He said her name, and his voice was congested with excitement, the same dazzled voice of the early days. That intonation was so dear to her memory she had never stopped hearing it, not in all this time. And now his vibrant response was also the same, the same as on that first snowy night.

Her own flesh tingled and warmed when he stroked her back with urgent strokes. His long fingers met at her waist, parted again to trace her hips' gentle arc, the shape of her trembling legs. There was no need or reason to say more: they could speak now with their mouths, their touches.

His hard hands ascended again to her bare arms that encircled his neck, as if to learn the form of them all over, and the motion made her shudder, made her want him with a new ferocity. She moved ever closer to him, feeling her body become weightless.

Now he was sliding downward, caressing her skin with his lips as he moved, caressing her most secret flesh. Hot waves of pleasure spread from the center of her being throughout her quaking body. She moaned and cried out, abandoning all sensation beyond the circumference of pleasure: she rode its breakers, alive in every nerve, crying out.

And then she, too, was stroking his naked torso and his loins, aware of his instant reaction, the deep quiver of his powerful frame. He made a questioning motion, trying to raise her with his hands, but with a teasing murmur she put the hands away. Moving her head from side to side, she began to caress him wildly.

Joseph said her name hoarsely, again and again. He drew her naked, resounding body upward against his, kissing her head and her brow, her cheeks, the beating space below her ear; he tilted her face upward so that his lips could find the softness of her neck, before covering her mouth at last with his.

She was holding him so tightly now that it was hard to tell his heartbeat from her own, and they were utterly together. Astounded, she felt another long, sweet invasion of unsated lust; incredulous, she rose to a newer frenzy with the very tempo of his own, and their low outcries blended.

They lay near and warm, with slackening breath.

Finally Kate spoke against his chest. "Time turned back then, Joseph. Turned back and stayed still. Do you remember how it was in summer, when you used to get home before dark?" She raised her hand to his lips and felt his smile.

"How could I not remember?" He squeezed her arm. "We had so little time alone. And before we knew it, there were two babies."

"Joseph," she asked abruptly, "was I cruel to Marite this morning?" She leaned back to look up at him; the darkness was gray, now that her eyes had gotten used to it, and she could see him shaking his head, smiling.

"Cruel! Sweetheart, you wouldn't know how to be. I thought it was excellent psychology. But you should have let me help; maybe it was time for Daddy to put his foot down."

"I didn't want to bother you with anything today. And frankly, I was in no mood for another problem, either." She added, "Now that it's all over, I feel free to tell you how hysterical I felt today." And she did, in detail.

When she had finished describing her day, Joseph leaned over and kissed her head. "This is crazy as hell, but I'm wide-awake. And hungry."

"After that dinner?" She was always amazed at his appetite.

"Are you sleepy?" She shook her head. "Come on, then, dear, I'll cook us some eggs."

"You'll cook *you* some eggs. I'll watch and have some coffee." Kate got up and belted herself into a thin ivory robe. Joseph put on a robe and, with their arms around each other, they walked on bare, soundless feet past the children's room and into the kitchen.

Kate sat down on one of the wooden chairs and watched Joseph heat the coffee and break eggs into a pan. She rubbed her hand affectionately over the old wooden table which had been their first dining table in the old flat. She loved this little room. They had put down new ivory linoleum themselves, which added even more light. With the ivory walls and floor, and the neutral wood of chairs and table, Kate had felt free to add riots of color.

Kate smiled. She had done so many paintings that they had even spilled over into this room and the bathroom.

"What's that Cheshire-cat smile for?" Joseph sat down

with his scrambled eggs and toast, his dark eyes gazing at her as he bit into his food.

"No one else in New York has oil paintings in a kitchen." She giggled as she looked around. The early painting of the bright washday hung over the refrigerator; Kate's version of a parade was on the wall over their table, and one of children on swings in the park brightened a small space by the door.

"No one else in the world is like us," Joseph retorted. "Like you." He put down his fork and reached for her hand. "Now, this reminds me of the early days, too. When we used to sit up half the night, and stumble through the next day." He smiled and returned to his food.

"You're going to be stumbling tomorrow if you don't get some sleep." She sipped her coffee.

Joseph swallowed the last of his eggs and said ruefully, "I know. You're right. But today was such a great day I hate to see it end. Besides I can't go to sleep until I look at your new painting again. There was so much going on before, I could hardly study it."

She was enormously touched by that. "Go on. I'll be right there." He went off to the living room. After she had put the dishes into soapy water, Kate followed.

There was only one light in the pretty, serene room—the lamp that illuminated the painting. Kate stood in the doorway looking at her work with fresh perspective: it was good. Very good. She had been able to convey the ancient Spanish pride of Joseph's people as well as his passionate dedication to the workers. The background was gold and scarlet, with overtones of blue-gray, a unique city whose spires hinted at the shape of Moorish minarets; below the spires there was an assembly of darkhaired people, the position of their heads indicating burning hope, adamant determination.

And in the foreground was the torso and head of Joseph; his fine head, too, was lifted up, his eyes blazed. Again, in the slight fullness of his white shirt's sleeves and its low-buttoned front, there was a Spanish suggestion—the garment of a hero of high romance. She let her eyes caress Joseph, who stood in half-profile, gazing at the painting.

"You've never done anything quite like this," he said softly. "It's magnificent." He turned and smiled at her.

"I prefer the original." Kate came to him and put her arms around his waist.

He murmured against her hair, "You've made me so heroic." She loved the feeling of his warm breath on the top of her head, and moved closer. "You've always glorified everything for me, Kate. You still do. I suppose you always will."

She raised her head, kissing his neck and chin, drawing his head down so that she could run her fingers through his hair. "I didn't glorify you at all." She let go of him and he smiled down at her. "I was only expressing you as baroque. 'Spectacle, splendor, tension, and contradiction.' That's you, to the life." Joseph stared at her.

He led her to the couch and they sat down very close together. He invited her to lean against him. "I like it when we take our little time. You still let my heart dance like the rams."

She leaned her head back and he played with the thin golden chain around her neck, holding the little star she never ceased to wear.

"You know, Kate, this star is just like you." Joseph looked at it. "The one constant, through all the good times and the bad. My constant star."

Kate raised her hand and stroked his lean, hard neck, rapt in their closeness, soothed by the late-night silence. Neither of them spoke, but let the quiet and their touches speak. There was a whole long night before they had to face the world again.

PART II

Marite

Chapter 15

"Now it's *really* my birthday," Marite confided to Elizabeth Wendell. The twenty-fifth, two weeks ago, had not been like a birthday at all. She fingered the long strand of pearls around her neck; they felt like warm satin and gleamed in the gentle light of the Plaza's Palm Court, where the two were having tea. "I feel like a princess . . . like the girl who married the prince in the operetta."

"You look like one today, my dear." Her grandmother studied her admiringly. Marite was glad now that she hadn't cut her hair; her grandmother said it was her "crowning glory," that she must never cut it, no matter what vulgar girls did. Even if the girls at school teased her and called her "Alice in Wonderland."

"Oh, Grandmother, I never expected *this*"—she stroked the pearls—"not after you'd already given me this wonderful dress and taken me to the operetta."

"Thirteen is a very important birthday." Elizabeth took a minute bite from her pastry and delicately touched the corners of her mouth with the linen napkin. Marite thought how different her other celebration had been, at the Lafayette with all the racket from David and her disgusting Uncle Rafael, who was so Jewish-looking with his cigars and his swarthy skin. Her parents had been upset when Marite had told them she didn't want a party with her friends—she didn't have that many friends in the Village—but they had agreed and had a family-only party at the Lafayette.

Her Great-Grandfather Dryver had come along too. Of course he was so old he didn't count, and the whole thing had hardly seemed like a birthday at all—not hers anyway. Her father and David and Rafael had talked about the most boring things; her mother and great-grandfather just talked about paintings. Marite had felt as if she were hardly there.

"Besides," her grandmother added now, "I felt that you needed a more . . . noticeable necklace. Your other little necklace is quite . . . sweet, but that dress just cried out for pearls." Elizabeth twinkled at her. "Why don't you just slip the other one under your dress, so it won't interfere with the pearls' effect?"

At once Marite obeyed. She always listened to her grandmother when it came to matters of dress, because she was so stylish. It was hard to believe she was fifty-four years old, which seemed such an enormous age to Marite. Today Elizabeth was wearing a magnificent ensemble by a French designer named Lanvin, a simple slip of a dress in a kind of sea-green with a wonderful gray coat with huge sleeves made of black and white and gray velvet, and a high collar lined with the green of the dress. It looked like something out of the movies. Her grandmother's hair wasn't gray at all, but still very black. She wore it short to just below her ears, with pearl earrings hanging down, and a beautiful pearl collar around her throat.

Marite's own pearls made the little necklace her mother had given her seem so dinky, although her mother said the tiny star had been her "treasure" for nearly fifteen years. Of course that was because her father had given the star to her mother, so Marite could understand in a way; her father was the only one besides her grandmother Marite loved at all. And her mother had only given her the small star, anyway, because she had gotten a bigger one on their wedding anniversary this month, Marite decided with resentment. She had missed her father horribly when they went away for a week; David hadn't minded, of course, because he loved to stay at Uncle Rafael's. And Marite *had* been able to stay a whole week with Elizabeth—it was the best time she had ever had in her life.

And yet ever since then, up to and including her birthday, Marite had felt strange, sad. It troubled her when her grandmother had told her that she couldn't come to the Lafayette, even though she had been invited, because Joseph's family "didn't like her."

However, Marite had learned a lot about getting along, and she had learned it all from Elizabeth. The best way to cope at home was not to talk too much about her visits with her grandmother. Elizabeth said there were a lot of "problems" that Marite would understand when she was older; her parents had kept Marite away from her grandmother for years after she had been born because they were jealous. They still tried to keep Marite from seeing Elizabeth often, especially during the last four years. So today was really a red-letter day, this rare and magical visit—the big chauffeured car coming for Marite on poky MacDougal Street, then driving them uptown to the theater to see *The Student Prince*. And now they sat in the Palm Court listening to the soft string quartet instead of David's horrible noisy "jazz," which was really for black people.

David was really awful; all he could talk about was airplanes and taking science in school. When Marite had told him they were going to see *The Student Prince* he had scoffed at her that it was a silly fairy tale, all about damned Germans in silly clothes. Someday she would learn to keep her mouth shut with David, the way her grandmother had taught her to do with her parents.

And she had learned that, all right; learned that it worked two ways. If she didn't repeat what her parents said, she got along better with her grandmother, too. The only thing that bothered Marite was not telling her father the truth. No matter what Elizabeth said, he was still the handsomest man in the world; if he had yellow hair, he would almost look like the prince in the operetta.

"Oh, Grandmother," she blurted, "I wish there was someplace like Heidelberg . . . I mean the one in the story. I know there's a real one from my geography."

"There *is*, Marite." Elizabeth patted her hand. "There's a whole lovely world, in Europe, that you've never dreamed of, where young ladies like you are valued. Our poor country, these days, is sadly changing. There doesn't seem to be any room for tradition, ideals . . . the kind of family you came from, Marite."

Marite knew she was referring to the genealogies, the interesting old maps of the family Elizabeth had shown her many times. She nodded agreeably. Her grandmother liked to be agreed with, and it was a small price to pay for the total attention, the unconditional love, the wonderful presents showered on Marite.

She knew better than to repeat, just now, the things she heard at home, about all the good things in America: the "progress and prosperity" her father talked about. There were certainly enough bad things, too: women drinking and smoking and cutting their hair. Some of the girls at school used bad words among themselves and even said "sex" sometimes.

Her mother's and her grandmother's definitions of that word were totally different: her mother had told her, when she first got the curse in February, that she was becoming a woman now and was capable of having a baby. The idea horrified Marite, even though her mother had said when she grew up and fell in love she would discover that sex was "beautiful" when you really loved someone. And she had added that menstruation shouldn't be called a "curse." Elizabeth, on the other hand, maintained that it was the perfect word; women were burdened with difficulties in life, and now, more than ever, Marite must guard her virtue. Virtue, Elizabeth said, was the quality most prized by men who were like princes. If Marite wanted to marry a nice man, she much bring him her virtue. Most of all, she must be especially careful now of the nasty, common boys at school.

It was certainly easier to take Elizabeth's advice than to understand what her mother meant; Marite had never felt she belonged with the boys and girls at school, anyway.

And it was so pleasant, so lovely, to read the love stories in the books her grandmother gave her, books like *Graustark* and *The Little Colonel*. Those stories were like dreams; they took her far away from the crowded apartment, where even her room was secondhand. Her mother had moved everything out of her painting room and made it into a room for Marite three years ago. Marite was relieved to be away from David, but the room still wasn't *hers*, the way her room was uptown. Elizabeth had made that into a "young lady's" room now, all fluffy and pink and beautiful, and it was heavenly to stay there.

She sipped her lemonade and smiled at Elizabeth. "I wish we could live in a castle together."

"We could, Marite," Her grandmother looked perfectly serious. She wasn't teasing.

"But how?" Marite demanded, incredulous.

"We could, if we went to Europe together. Many Americans live in castles there. You see, American money is often worth more than foreign money."

"Ohhh . . ." Marite let out her breath, dazzled. But then she realized she couldn't. "Mother and Daddy wouldn't let me," she said dolefully. It was hard enough to get permission to see her grandmother once every few weeks, much less be permitted to go away with her for a long time.

"Perhaps they will, Marite. Why don't we wait and see? Perhaps they'll let me take you this summer." Her grandmother's voice sounded funny, and she had an odd, shiny look in her eyes. It gave Marite a wild hope.

"I'd love it, Grandmother! I'd love it more than anything in the world! Do you know what you are? You're my 'fairy grandmother,' instead of a fairy godmother!" Marite giggled.

"My dear, that's *very* clever." The way her grandmother said that was different from the way her parents talked. At home she always had to share their attention with her horrible brother. But her grandmother acted as if there were no one else in the world but Marite. "I *promise* you I'll do something about—" Elizabeth looked up.

Marite's grandfather, Howard Wendell, was standing by the table. Her heart sank. He was always polite and kind to her, but she knew he didn't love her the way her grandmother did; she could just tell. And there were certain matters, Elizabeth always said, that couldn't be discussed "before men." Marite wondered if living in a castle was one of those matters.

"May I join you ladies?" Wendell asked with his stiff, sad smile.

'Of course." Elizabeth's smile was tight, her voice impatient. She glanced at her diamond watch. "Good heavens, look at the time. I quite forgot we were supposed to meet you outside, Howard."

"That's all right." But Marite knew it *wasn't* all right; her grandfather looked annoyed. "Are you ladies ready to go?"

"Not ready, Howard, but I suppose we must. I promised to have Marite home for dinner."

It was all over, then, Marite thought, the lovely afternoon that was all the more delightful with its flavor of the forbidden. Obediently she followed her grandparents out of the Court and through the Plaza hotel lobby to the entrance, where the long dark car was waiting to return her to the reality of MacDougal Street.

"*God,* these Village streets are like a maze," Howard Wendell grumbled as the chauffeur maneuvered the limousine along the narrow thoroughfares.

"*You're* in a jolly mood, I must say," Elizabeth responded tartly.

"I don't take kindly to being insulted, that's all."

"What on earth do you mean?" she demanded.

"The least you can do is not to forget an appointment

with your own husband," Howard snapped. "It's always like this when you're queening it with that child."

Outraged, Elizabeth leaned forward and closed the glass panel behind the chauffeur, Jerry. "*Must* you advertise our private business to the servants?"

"Damn the servants. They are *our* employees; we are not theirs."

Elizabeth peered at her husband in the dim interior. "What *is* the matter with you?" she asked shrilly. "Have you been drinking? You know the doctor forbade it!"

Howard emitted a hard, brief laugh. "No, Elizabeth. Not drinking. *Thinking*. I'm sick and tired of playing second fiddle for more than thirty-four years."

Aghast, Elizabeth protested, "You *have* been drinking. I know it, Howard. Otherwise how could you use such . . . common language?"

"Shut up, Elizabeth."

She was so amazed that she could not speak; she took a quick, sharp breath. He hadn't ever talked to her like this.

"I am going to talk, for once, and you are going to listen."

She was still too taken aback to utter a word. Stealing a glance at his face, she saw that his color was dangerously high; he had been told time and again not to get overexcited. But he looked so . . . savage now that she was almost afraid to open her mouth. If only she could get out of this wretched car, if only the drive could be over. But the heavy traffic had slowed them to a crawl.

"For thirty-four years," he growled, "you have shut me out, Elizabeth. In the year 1890, when Kate was born, you closed your room to me . . . but worse you closed your heart."

Elizabeth could not prevent a sharp retort: "I'm sure you must have found your consolations."

"That is none of your business . . . under the circumstances. And I told you to be quiet."

She bit her lip to keep from screaming at him: he looked quite wild.

"I watched you transfer all your affections—in a way that seemed positively unnatural"—

Unnatural! The word shrieked in her mind. How *dare* he?

"—and then, in an even more unnatural way, abandon your daughter when she married. Yes, yes, I know, don't say it. I opposed the marriage too, but not for the same reasons you did. I was concerned about the economics of the thing."

To Elizabeth's deep relief the limousine had picked up speed and they were approaching midtown Manhattan. Thank heaven. It wouldn't be much longer now. She was frantic to be released from the cage of the car where she was confined with a husband who had abruptly turned into a madman.

Relentless, Howard went on: "You've gone too far with the child, Elizabeth. You are positively rabid on the subject of Jews! You've done everything possible to turn her against her father. And you continue to fill her mind with outrageous notions. Surely you must realize it's a dubious kindness—teaching her about a life that her parents oppose, that she can never have?"

"I will not discuss it now," Elizabeth snapped.

"You *will* discuss it with me, tonight, when we are back at the house," he said in a warning tone. His color was still dangerously high and a sudden tiredness seemed to overtake him. Howard leaned back in the seat, glaring straight ahead.

Elizabeth thought resentfully: He always says "the house," not "home." She was shaking with rage. He was not going to intimidate her. For years he had been so courteous, so mild-mannered and detached, almost indifferent to her concerns. One evening's aberration could not be allowed to undo her long ascendancy.

They rode the rest of the way in bitter silence. When Jerry stopped in front of the mansion and got out to open her door, Elizabeth glanced at his face. It was blank, utterly impassive, just as it had been in her presence for the last twenty years. Forcing herself to sound calm, she thanked him and preceded her husband at an even pace into the house.

The bland mask had slipped back over Howard's face as he greeted Lynn and waited for him to dispose of their coats.

"Elizabeth?" Howard gestured toward the drawing room.

She hesitated. If she did not go with him he might make a scene.

"Madam? Will you require anything?"

"No, thank you, Lynn. If we do we will serve ourselves." She was proud of the steadiness of her voice; she felt more in command as they entered the drawing room and Howard closed the doors.

Without asking her if she wanted a drink, he strode to the sideboard and poured himself a tumbler of whiskey. Elizabeth started to protest. Then she decided spitefully; He knows he mustn't drink. Let it be on his head.

Howard swallowed half the tumbler. "Now, Elizabeth, we are going to have this thing out. What was it you were 'promising' Marite? Diamonds from Cartier next time, instead of costly pearls?"

She plopped into a deep chair and glared at him. "The *newspapers* say"—she emphasized the word sarcastically: he never told her anything—"that you are doing very well. Have we suddenly become so poor I can't buy my granddaughter a birthday present?"

"Matched pearls from Cartier are hardly the proper present for a thirteen-year-old child who lives among the bohemians of Greenwich Village. And much as I myself look askance at those people, they are Marite's friends . . . or could be, if you hadn't set out to alienate her from them." His breath had quickened, and his face was becoming flushed again. "What were you promising her, Elizabeth . . . what are you plotting?"

She leaned forward, grasping the arms of her chair. "I am *plotting* to save her, Howard, as I could not save Kate. If she must marry—and she must—if she must endure the humiliation of some man's bestial desires, and the filthy agony of bearing children, then it will be a titled man, at least, a man with money. Her children will not have to live in some tenement, as Marite has.''

"Bestial . . . filthy,'' Howard repeated softly. His skin was purplish now, his breathing labored. He swallowed the rest of the whiskey and poured more into his tumbler. The inevitable warning died on Elizabeth's mouth as he rushed on, his voice rising, "Good God, how can you speak so? What kind of hideous thoughts have you put in that child's mind? And what do you mean, 'save' her? What do you think you can do, Elizabeth—kidnap her from her own parents?''

The tumbler quivered in his grasp and he swayed on his feet, as if his equilibrium were suddenly gone.

"Yes!'' she hissed at him. "Yes, Howard. That's exactly what I intend to do.''

"You must be crazy!'' He was almost shouting now, and the sound of his voice enraged her. "Have you no feeling for Kate . . . for your own daughter, who was your idol?''

"What do you care about Kate? She's hardly spoken to you in years! She sent back all the checks you sent her!''

His glass stopped halfway to his mouth; she saw his fingers tighten around it. "How do you know that, Elizabeth? Tell me . . . how do you know? All those envelopes had the return address of my office.'' He stared at her. "Oh, I see. I begin to see now. The first ones were mailed from here. *You* returned those checks to my office, Elizabeth. You. Why in the name of heaven did you do such a malicious thing?''

"Because she spat in my face when she married that disgusting Jew!'' Elizabeth shrieked. "She trampled on me, laughed at me, mocked me by that marriage . . . she threw away all my years of care and devotion . . . all my hope that she would become someone, live the kind of life she should have lived. It was the end of my whole life. Now I have hope again, with Marite. Why are you reproaching *me*? Why have you all of a sudden become such a devoted father and grandfather?''

''It's not all of a sudden,'' he retorted. He began to pace with a strange, lopsided motion that she had never seen before. Something was wrong with him. Very wrong. ''Ever since those damned doctors began to nag me, I've been looking at my will. Just this past week, more and more, I've been feeling that I must do more for Kate and her children. Now I'm certain . . . after what's happened tonight.'' He studied her with a mixture of contempt and compassion that was infuriating.

''I'm going to change my will. Whatever else has happened, Kate is my child, our only heir. I am putting your money in trusts, Elizabeth, because I don't think you are capable of handling a fortune. And I am making over a certain amount to Kate, putting other funds in trusts for her children.'' His voice had weakened.

''You are going to deprive me . . . and Marite, and benefit an ungrateful daughter and that horrible little boy who's never given Marite an instant's peace?'' Elizabeth leapt to her feet and confronted him angrily, face-to-face.

Howard's face was purplish-red; a horrible, harsh sound was coming from his throat, as if he were trying to vomit and could not; he seemed to be gasping for air. His lips were turning blue; quite abruptly he was ghost-pale, his eyes swiveling grotesquely upward, to the right.

He fell to the carpet, where he lay on his right side, staring up at Elizabeth with twisted lips. She knelt down to examine him. His chest did not move. There was no breath from his mouth.

Elizabeth was stunned. She could not move.

But she must.

He might be dying.

She scrambled to her feet and stumbled toward the telephone.

Marite had gone to Grace Church with Elizabeth many times, but on the day of her grandfather's funeral it hardly looked like the same place. Easter had been glorious with white silk and lilies; at Christmas, blazing with red poinsettias and vivid green hangings, then after Christmas at the Feast of the Candles, the small cathedral had been brilliant with the golden, dancing flames of hundreds and hundreds of tapers.

But on the day of the funeral, the first one Marite had ever been to, the church looked gray and ugly. The only color came from the feeble light of the overcast afternoon struggling through the stained-glass windows. Even the scarlet and purple, the peacock blue and gold of the one her grandmother called the *Te Deum* window had lost their glow. Everything was draped in gloomy black, like her mother's and father's clothes. All the people there were dressed in white or gray, black or other dreary colors.

Marite's mother looked pale and cold; her father held her mother's hand. Elizabeth's clothes were black, too, but beautiful and shiny; there was a long black shiny feather on her small close hat, and she was not as pale as Marite's mother. She had bought Marite a lovely white dress to wear, and a white hat. Ordinarily when her grandmother gave her something new, her parents exchanged mysterious glances. But this time Marite's mother had hardly noticed.

Elizabeth had told her white was proper for young girls at funerals, and Marite was relieved she would not have to wear the ugly black. All she had to do was sit there quietly, then drive to the cemetery afterward. Her parents were going to let her spend the afternoon with Elizabeth; she had heard her father tell her mother it was a "special dispensation"—something to do with her grandmother's loneliness. Marite couldn't help feeling that her grandfather's death was connected in some strange way with a wonderful new time in her own life, and she didn't feel like crying at all. She wasn't very sad, although she realized it might be wrong not to be.

When they had first entered the church, Marite's mother had kissed her grandmother; Elizabeth had not kissed her back. And when her mother started to take the seat beside Elizabeth, her grandmother had whispered, "Marite," so she had slipped in first to sit next to Elizabeth.

Marite's mother finally began to cry very softly, but Elizabeth hadn't cried at all. She just sat there with a solemn face, her handsome head held high. At the end of the service Marite's mother leaned against her father as they walked out of the church; Elizabeth walked proudly on the arm of one of the cousins. You could hardly see her face behind her heavy veil.

The funeral seemed to go on for hours, and Marite became terribly tired and hungry. At last the long ride there, the burial, and the long ride back were over. Marite had been allowed to ride back with Elizabeth and she was glad when they reached the uptown house.

As soon as Marite was alone with her grandmother, she knew she had been right about things being better now. Elizabeth embraced her, saying, "It's all ours now, Marite. Everything is ours—this whole great house. We are going to have a delicious tea . . . and then I am going to show you the wonderful things I've bought you."

Marite's heart pounded with joy and anticipation. Best of all, her grandmother didn't seem sad in the least; she was just as happy as Marite was. She said what her father had said—Marite was young and while it was a very sad thing that her grandfather was dead, he had been very ill and now he was at peace. Marite's life was just starting out and she shouldn't think about it too much.

And she began to forget it all completely, eating the fluffy pastries, drinking lemonade. She noticed her grandmother would stop laughing when the servants came in; as soon as they had gone out, she looked brighter.

After tea, Elizabeth took her upstairs and opened the closet door in her pretty pink bedroom. Marite gasped with delight: there were dozens of new summer dresses in pale, flowerlike colors, and shoes and hats to go with them. On the dresser were new combs and brushes with silver backs. Marite also saw new bottles of cologne. "You're not old enough for scent, my darling, but it's perfectly proper for you to use this light cologne."

Dazzled, Marite lifted the stopper from one of the intricately shaped bottles; the cologne was the sweetest thing she had ever smelled.

"Oh, Grandmother," she cried, hugging Elizabeth, "I love you, I love you so much. I wish I could stay with you forever."

"I promise you that you will, Marite. Soon. As soon as I can arrange it."

"Do you mean it? Do you mean it, Grandmother? And we'll live in a castle?" It seemed too good to be true. She hated to think of leaving her father; she would miss him so much. Yet she wondered if he would really care; he didn't seem to care for anyone as much as he did for her mother.

And all this splendor . . . all these beautiful things . . . and her grandmother letting her do anything she wanted, giving her everything she wanted.

"They won't let me, though, will they?"

"We'll see, Marite. Just be patient. Until the end of the summer." Elizabeth hugged her hard again. "Now, we must both change for dinner. And I am going to call your mother and ask her if you can't spend a few days with me. I think she'll let you. And, sweetheart, ring your bell for Eileen. She'll dress you and brush your hair."

After her grandmother went out, Marite pondered the treasure trove in the closet, whispering, "She'll dress you and brush your hair." Downtown, of course—Marite didn't think of it as "home" anymore—she had taken care of herself since she was seven years old. She must really be grown up now, to have the guests' maid assigned to her. Elizabeth's maid was a Frenchwoman named Celeste.

With a sense of intoxicating power, Marite rang the bell. "I'll wear the lavender *crêpe de chine*," she said peremptorily to the maid.

"Your grandmother might like you to wear white, miss. For the mourning, you know."

"Please lay out the lavender," Marite said sharply, as

she had heard Elizabeth do, "and don't forget my shoes. One other thing—I'll want my breakfast in bed tomorrow."

The woman's eyes had an unreadable expression as she studied Marite. "Very well, miss." She slipped the dress over Marite's head and then began to brush her long golden hair. Marite was filled with fresh pleasure as she watched the reflected woman, expressionless, serving her.

The months that followed were the happiest in Marite's life. She was living in a fairy tale now; she was a deposed princess who was banished from time to time from her rightful home on Madison Avenue. "In thrall," as the books said, to a peasant faction which had taken power at her school; she hadn't quite worked out her parents' and her brother's roles. Her father looked so princely himself that it was hard to fit him into the fantasy—perhaps he was also deposed from another kingdom. In any case, Marite hugged these secret thoughts to herself, not even telling her grandmother about them.

She felt strange and sad, returning to MacDougal Street on the Sunday night after that first weekend, but the atmosphere was different this time. Her mother's face looked paler and thinner, even after a few days. She spoke very gently to Marite and didn't question her at all, saying that Great-Grandfather Dryver wasn't feeling well. David was his usual stolid, indifferent self, and Marite's father was very affectionate. By the time Marite went back to school on Monday in her ordinary clothes she almost thought that she had imagined the whole weekend; to comfort herself she slipped into her fantasy.

But as the weeks dragged by, and the day of her release from the horrible school approached, Marite was heartened to discover that she was going to be allowed to spend more time with her grandmother this summer. A kind of pattern emerged: her grandmother would sometimes telephone after dinner. After Marite had gone to bed, she would hear her parents' murmuring voices from the living room, catching words like "influence" and "too often." The murmuring went on until late into the night and then the next morning Marite would be given permission to visit Elizabeth again.

One night Marite opened her door a little and stood beside it to listen.

"Mother's closing the house early this year, Joseph. She wants to take Marite to the Long Island house with her. For the whole summer . . . that's so *long*."

"I know, darling. But we won't be able to get away until August at least, you know that. I may have to go back to Chicago to advise them in that dressmakers' strike, and then the Democratic convention's coming up in July."

There was a murmured response from her mother; then her father went on. "Look, darling, I don't like Elizabeth's ideas any better than you do, but you must admit there's been a distinct improvement. It's been a long time since we've heard a quote from Henry Ford." Marite could hear the smile in her father's voice. She wanted to go out to him, ask him to hug her. But if she did that they would ask her why she couldn't sleep; they would stop talking, and she wanted to find out what they were about to say.

"Besides," her father was talking again, "you could use the vacation. That's one reason I gave David permission to stay at Rafael's in June and July. You've got your outdoor art show coming up, and I know you want to spend time with your grandfather. You don't have to say anything, Kate. I ve known all along what you've been feeling."

There was a rustling sound and a silence, then her mother's voice, very soft, with words missing: ". . . died without my ever really knowing him, or him knowing me . . . Grandfather . . . couldn't *take* it." Another silence followed.

"Kate, it wouldn't be fair to forbid Marite to go when we're letting David go . . . tennis, horseback riding . . . away from the heat." Now there were missing words in her father's conversation. ". . . besides, it's been so long since . . . honeymoon . . . all my family, Kate."

"Oh, Joseph, Joseph." Marite had heard her mother's voice sound like that before: whispery and solemn. Then she heard them close the door, shutting Marite and everything else out.

She closed her own door very softly, thinking: They really don't care about anybody but themselves. They're happy to get rid of us this summer. Marite hoped they would let her go to Long Island. She wouldn't even miss her father very much.

She was overjoyed the next day when they told her she could go. The house in Long Island was much smaller than the one on Madison Avenue, but it was cool and pretty and white, right on the ocean. There was a shady veranda, and handsome, well-dressed people came and went almost all the time. Marite learned to ride a horse and play badminton and tennis; she perfected her dancing. Elizabeth was very gay, especially when they were alone; she had suggested that they play a little game of their own, pretending that Marite was Elizabeth's great-niece Marite Wendell.

That seemed a bit strange until Marite remembered her own fantasies, and the idea appealed to her—having another name, just for the summer. It made her feel like the heroine of a novel. The whole summer seemed to be composed of sweet scents and lovely dresses, music, and flowers—exactly like a dream.

The only times her grandmother seemed ill-humored were when she was talking on the telephone to Mr. Burgess, her attorney. Once, as Marite was rushing in to change from her riding things to a dress for a tea dance, she heard Elizabeth speaking sharply into the phone about something called "probate," telling Mr. Burgess that "November is out of the question." Intent on choosing which dress to wear, Marite promptly forgot about it.

Boring things like lawyers and business had no effect on her reality, no more than the conversations she sometimes had with her parents on the phone. They seemed so far away now that for days at a time she thought of Elizabeth as her mother.

One afternoon when it was even too hot to swim, Marite, who was reading on the veranda, overheard her grandmother talking on the phone to Mr. Burgess again. Elizabeth's voice grew very loud, and at last she said, "Very well, then. That's more reasonable," and slammed down the phone.

Elizabeth emerged onto the veranda, fanning herself. "These lawyers act as if they are employing *us*," she grumbled. Then she brightened. "I have some wonderful news for you. Do you remember what I promised you?"

Marite tossed her book onto the wicker table. "That we would live in a castle? Oh, Grand . . . Aunt Elizabeth! We're *going* to?"

"Yes," Elizabeth said triumphantly.

Marite jumped up and embraced her. Her dream was coming true.

On the very first cool day, they went into the city to get everything done. There were suitcases and trunks to be purchased for Marite, and another quantity of clothes. Elizabeth explained that it would be cooler in England and France, requiring heavier-weight things. And later on, there was a puzzling episode at the bank. Marite waited in an anteroom outside while her grandmother conferred for a long time with one of the officers. She could hear their raised, contentious voices through the door. After an even longer interval, Elizabeth emerged at last with a triumphant expression, carrying a heavy-looking briefcase. The officer stood at his open door, staring at them and shaking his head.

From there they went to the passport agency and then to another building, where they received their inoculations. After a final stop at the steamship office, Elizabeth ordered Jerry to drive them back to Long Island.

They were all ready by late that night; the ship would sail the next morning. Marite suddenly realized that she didn't have much time to say goodbye to her parents, and suggested she return to the city to see them.

"Oh, my dear, don't do that!" Elizabeth said quickly.

Marite was puzzled. "Why not?"

"I am so sorry, darling. In all the haste I completely forgot to tell you. I called them today and your mother and father are both out of town."

"Oh . . . in Chicago."

Elizabeth nodded with a strange eagerness. "*Yes*. Chicago. You can write them when we land, Marite. It'll be better that way."

Marite wasn't sure, but it didn't seem to make much difference. Her mother and father had been glad enough to ship her off to Long Island for the summer. And they might try to stop her from going abroad.

She could hardly sleep that night for excitement, and in the rush of departure the next morning, everything else but the imminent sailing was crowded from her mind.

When they arrived at the pier, Marite was dazzled by her first sight of the *Aquitania*: it was immense, like a floating island. She longed to stay on deck, among the crowds of people, but Elizabeth insisted that they must "examine their accommodations."

A respectful purser led them to the first-class stairway; Marite gasped when she saw its splendor. The ship itself was like a castle, she reflected.

"Good heavens, I hardly know it!" Elizabeth exclaimed.

"Madam has sailed on the *Aquitania* before?"

"Many years ago, before the war. It was very different then. I see that it has been modernized." She sounded disapproving.

"I hope that you and the young lady will not be disappointed, madam. The owners seemed to think that the passengers might enjoy the new . . . simplicity, the color."

Marite thought it was quite perfect as it was; the deep, thick rugs were of a modern design, the use of color lavish but restrained to pleasant pastels.

She could hardly believe the size of their private suite. Their sitting room led on through an open archway to a narrower, carpeted corridor. The purser opened a door on the right with a flourish. "One of the bedrooms, madam.

And this"—he stepped across the hall, opening another—"is the second."

"These will do very well," Elizabeth said briskly, and asked Marite which bedroom she would prefer.

"The blue one," Marite answered rather breathlessly.

Elizabeth directed the purser to dispose of their luggage, and he advised them that a maid would be sent to them at once to unpack.

"After I've given the maid her orders, darling, we can go back on deck again, if it will please you." Elizabeth smiled. "We can stand there while the ship sails, and say good-bye to New York."

"Oh, yes, I'd love that."

Elizabeth conferred for a good while with the maid. Then Marite put on her hat again, and they left the woman to her task.

Elizabeth said gaily, "Tonight you will enjoy your first dinner at sea. And remember, it is the custom not to dress in evening dress on the first night out."

Marite absorbed that esoteric information with great seriousness. From now on, she decided, she would always want to do the proper thing. Not only did it please her grandmother, who loved her more than anyone else ever had, but it also seemed right for someone who was going to stay in a castle.

Standing on the deck a little later, though, looking down at the people waving from the pier, Marite was surprised by a quick feeling of sadness. No one had come to see them off; she almost wished she could see her parents waving. But they weren't even in New York. And her grandmother had hinted so many times, very gently, that they didn't really care.

Nevertheless the sound of the great ship's horn sounded sad to Marite for a moment—hollow, like the sensation in her stomach—as she watched the city slide away.

And that evening in her stateroom, when she opened her small jewel box to get her pearls, she noticed the tiny star on its golden chain. She hadn't worn it all summer, and had hardly realized she had brought it with her. But seeing it reminded her sharply of her father; his strong arms and great height, his kind, absentminded words and the dark eyes that were like her own. As much as she had hated the life on MacDougal Street, she began to miss her father sorely.

Chapter 16

Kate felt more like nineteen than thirty-four that wet afternoon in late July; dripping, gasping, and buoyant as she let herself into the flat. One reason was the downpour. It had caught her halfway home from her grandfather's house and promised an end, at least tonight, to the weighty, grasping heat.

She always reacted to rain like a parched plant; it made her wildly creative. As she fled to the bathroom to dry her hair and take off her sopping clothes, she envisioned another new painting. It would be more ambitious than the ones she had done before: a wholly modern theme painted with the careful brushwork, the almost photographic realism of the nineteenth century, that era of her first decade of life. She was a child of the twentieth century, and yet she felt it had not really arrived until after the war; there were aspects of the new world that had always seemed abhorrent and pathetic—the "flappers" with their shrill gaiety, equating mental freedom with rouged knees and drunkenness and a string of sex partners who had no faces.

On the surface, she supposed, Kate could pass for a flapper herself—with her slim body, her brief dresses and briefer hair, except that she painted canvas instead of her face. She could even do a wicked Charleston. Yet it amused her to remember how she had looked at school, how little a demure appearance had to do with an iconoclastic temper.

While Kate hung up her wet clothes, toweled her hair, and got into a robe, the painting formed itself before her inner eye. It almost had the form of an old Dryver portrait of some high-and-mighty posed against a background of desolation. But her figure would be a drunken, laughing flapper emerging from a nightclub against a somber backdrop of tenements. An idea that would be anathema to the current crop of abstract artists, but one she very much wanted to achieve on canvas.

She wandered into the living room, regarding it with new satisfaction. The apartment was a comfortable and attractive blend of the old and new, and they had used every inch of space to its full extent. Kate still didn't know how she'd managed to get all she had into the largest room without crowding—a dining space near the kitchen, Joseph's little "office" in a corner, her miniature studio in another, with room left over for the "living" room proper: couch, chairs, and radio.

Most of the space was created through the effective use of shelves; Joseph had told her they had to "build up," on the skyscraper principle. The cream-painted walls were lined with shelves, accommodating their many books, the telephone, her painting supplies, and Joseph's papers.

She had done a lot with very little money. Most of their furniture had come from secondhand stores, renewed with slipcovers made by a local seamstress. Here and there were pieces of *art nouveau*—some ashtrays, a chair given them by her grandfather and an old lamp base converted to a candleholder. Kate and Joseph loved the naturalistic grace of those pieces, with their air of mystery, of forgotten fantasies.

One could *sit* on the couch and chairs. Kate smiled when she recalled Anzia's comment. "I like to come here, Kate. It's like coming to a *house*, the way it is at Mr. Dryver's." Anzia confided to them that Bertha Simson was "throwing practically everything out," getting "all modern." She described a new skyscraper bookcase that had made Kate and Joseph laugh and shudder. Joseph retorted

that he was glad his mother approved of their style—
"Salvation Army *nouveau*."

Kate went to one of the windows and drew aside the
creamy summer curtains. lifting the pane to breathe in the
silvery moisture. How wonderful. When the rain slackened
she would open all the windows wide again. They would
be able to have dinner at home tonight; it had been so hot
recently that cooking heated up the whole apartment. Joseph loved dinner at home.

She shut the window and looked around the room again,
thinking how different it was from the old flat upstairs,
with its dear, shabby bohemian look, its circus-bright colors. The colors were rich now, not livid—creams and earth
tones, with touches of leaf green and peacock blue and
yellow. Her grandfather's Triangle painting, which he had
presented to them for their last anniversary, held a place of
honor above the mantel. Some of Kate's paintings hung in
other spots; Joseph's corner featured framed photographs
of historic union events from the past fifteen years, all the
way back to a memorial procession for the workers who
had died in the fire. Kate had collected the photographs in
secret for a long time, then framed them herself as a
surprise for one of Joseph's birthdays.

A whole new sense of joy, of gratitude for what she
had, overcame her. She had felt desolate for a few weeks
after her father's death, but slowly she had come to accept
the dark fact that her father had died without ever knowing
her, or her knowing him; that he had still been so unforgiving
that she and her children were not mentioned in his will.
That aspect of his death had not occurred to her until last
month, when she realized that if she or the children had
been beneficiaries they would have been notified.

Right on the heels of her father's funeral, her grandfather seemed to fail. She remembered telling Joseph one
night, in the midst of their anxieties about Marite, that she
couldn't face losing Harry Dryver. But in the last few
weeks, he had mysteriously rallied; he seemed himself
again.

Kate went to the broom closet in the kitchen, where she kept rolled-up canvases, and took one out to stretch. Back in her corner, she began to tack the canvas to a frame that she slid out from behind a section of the bookcase. Joseph had been right, as usual: she had really benefitted from this "vacation" from the children.

She missed them, of course, at some hour almost every day, and the apartment sometimes seemed almost too still without their racket. Joseph did, too. Now and then he remarked that it seemed strange without the "princess" and the "flying Jew," fighting over occupation of the bathroom.

David always laughed at his father's nickname for him, born of his double preoccupation—his Jewishness encouraged by the stubborn Rafael and his new passion for flying machines. He was forever asking them when he would be old enough for a pilot's license.

Still, the children's absence had been a glory in other ways. Joseph told Kate that it was just like the old days, but better. They had a blissful, almost wicked sense of freedom, able to walk around again *déshabillé,* spending long, lazy weekend mornings in bed. And dining *à deux,* Kate reflected. The little dining area looked so cozy with only two chairs and a leaf of the table removed. Kate knew she could ascribe her happy spirits, even the restored glow of her skin, to this blessed privacy.

Besides, David had been in excellent spirits when Kate and Joseph had visited the Simsons' summer house on two occasions, and he had been genuinely glad to see them. Elizabeth, on the other hand, had been perfunctory in her vague invitations that they come to Long Island.

Kate paused in her initial outline strokes on the canvas and put down her brush, aware that she was suddenly warm. Something prickled at her skin. The rain had slackened. She got up and opened the windows wide. A vague feeling of guilt nibbled at her consciousness. She hadn't called Long Island for two days. She went to the phone.

Eileen answered, sounding strangely far away. There

was a roll of thunder in the background, and some other nearer noise—a household racket. "Eileen? How are you? Is it storming there?"

"Oh, Miss Kate, it's horrible. I'm afraid to stay on the telephone."

"I won't keep you. May I speak with Marite?"

There was a strange silence on the line.

"But, Miss *Kate* . . . surely you know!"

"Know *what*?" Kate demanded sharply, feeling her skin prickle again.

"They've gone. I thought you knew. On the ship."

"The ship!" Kate shrieked. There was a crackle on the line.

"On, Lord, Miss Kate, there's such lightning!" Eileen sounded terrified. "Day before yesterday," she rushed on, "Jerry drove them into town, to the *Aquitania*. The Madam said they'd be gone all summer. We're closing the house now, you see."

"All *summer*! Listen to me, Eileen! Did my mother tell you where they were going . . . to what country? Did she leave any forwarding address? Are you sure there's no message for me, Eileen?" The desperate questions tumbled out.

"No, Miss Kate, she didn't say. She didn't tell us anything, except that she'd write us about the New York house." There was another loud crackle on the line. "Miss Kate," Eileen pleaded. The connection was weakening.

"Think, Eileen!" Kate shouted. "Please ! I knew nothing about this. Nothing."

"You didn't *know*?"

"No, Eileen." Kate was trying her utmost to keep from screaming. She *must* make the woman remember. "Please," she said again a little more calmly, as the line cleared. "Any little thing you can remember might help me. What time did Jerry drive them into the city?"

"I'm not sure. I know it was in the morning. I'm sorry, Miss Kate, there just isn't anything else *to* remember."

"All right, Eileen. Thank you," Kate said numbly, and

hung up. What in the name of God should she do now? Call Joseph? Call Harry Dryver?

No. She couldn't expose her grandfather to this kind of anxiety while he was recuperating. And she should have all the facts before she called Joseph. He would be home in less than an hour.

She decided to call the steamship line first and find out everything she could.

As soon as Joseph saw her face, his happy expression faded. Kate blurted the news to him, then collapsed against him, sobbing.

He walked her to the couch and gently sat her down, giving her his handkerchief. "I called the steamship line," she said thickly. "The ship was bound for Southampton, England. They wouldn't give me any other information over the phone. I don't think I handled it very well."

Joseph's face was grim but his eyes gleamed. "I think you handled it damned well, Kate. My God, what an insane thing to do! Take our child away, without a word!" He got up and started pacing.

"Joseph, I wonder if it's only for the summer."

"Do you think she's kidnaped Marite?" Joseph looked stupefied. "Oh, Kate . . ."

Kate nodded slowly, her eyes wide with terror.

"It can't be. That's so crazy I can hardly believe it." He resumed his nervous pacing. Then he stopped and looked down at her. "But, Kate, I'm afraid you could be right."

Now she could see her own fear reflected in his eyes.

"Oh, my God, Joseph . . . if she has, what are we going to do?"

He stared at her; she'd never seen him look so determined. "Everything humanly possible. Starting now."

"After dinner," she said firmly. "You look so tired, and you must be starving."

In a feeble attempt to raise their spirits, he said, "You sound like a Jewish mother."

They both gave up on dinner after a few mouthfuls, too agitated to have an appetite. Joseph swallowed his small glass of wine. "The worst part of it is not knowing what Elizabeth intends to do. We can't start coping until we're sure what we're coping with. No, that's not the worst."

Kate met his eyes. "It's knowing that Marite left without even saying good-bye." He nodded. "I can't believe she'd do that."

His mouth dropped at the corners.

She took his hand. "Maybe there was some kind of . . . deception, darling."

"Maybe." He didn't sound convinced. "But it's hard to deceive someone about things like getting passport pictures, inoculations."

That was true. And Marite had gone very willingly to Long Island, Kate recalled. Joseph noticed her pained expression and hastened to console her. "There must be some explanation. I'll make some calls tonight, get things started. And we can decide what we want to say in a radio message to the ship."

He added confidently. "We'll hear something soon, sweetheart. Marite's bound to write us."

Kate wished she could feel as sure as he sounded.

That night as she tried to fall asleep, she kept thinking: My carelessness may have cost us our daughter.

The next morning when their research began, they learned with consternation that two Wendells appeared on the passenger list.

"She's even taken our *name* from Marite," Kate said, frantic.

Joseph looked anxious. "That's not a good sign. It sounds as if Elizabeth is cutting Marite off from her life with us."

They sent a wireless message to Elizabeth on the ship, pleading with her to wire back her plans, to let them know her address for the summer. Even now they could not entertain the possibility that she would stay in Europe. Joseph reminded Kate it would take a while for a response;

meanwhile they should make other inquiries. A caretaker at the Long Island house told them that all the servants were gone; Lynn answered at the Madison Avenue house, obviously surprised that it was necessary for them to question him. He "assumed, of course," that they knew about the journey; he, Mrs. Wood, and a maid would be the only ones there until he received further word from Mrs. Wendell.

"Further word" gave Kate new hope; apparently she intended to stay in touch. And it was inconceivable that her mother would abandon the great house, with all its treasures.

Her bank, however, was not forthcoming; it was obvious the officer who handled the Wendell personal account feared to become involved in any family squabble and referred them to Mrs. Wendell's attorney, Seldon Burgess. Mr. Burgess was reluctant to discuss the matter on the phone; when Kate and Joseph visited his downtown office and told him what had happened, he expressed chagrin and dismay.

"Frankly, I thought you wanted to discuss a contesting of the will." After a sharp disclaimer from Kate, and learning what the situation was, Burgess confided, "I was extremely surprised by your mother's insistence on rushing the will through probate. It seemed to be a matter of some urgency that the will be probated before the customary six-month period."

He looked shocked and disapproving. "However, she was so . . . extraordinarily determined that I took steps to rush it through. And I need not say how difficult that is. Nevertheless, against my better judgment, I complied. Furthermore, I learned from her bank that she withdrew an outrageous sum of money in cash, converting a great deal of it to traveler's checks."

"Then the numbers of the checks can be traced," Joseph interjected, "and the places of cashing."

Burgess peered at him. "Of course. All these acts were,

in my opinion, the acts of someone whose judgment was
. . . impaired.''

He gave Kate a paternal smile. He had known her since
she was a child. "And although I am technically your
mother's representative, and therefore have no business
advising you, I must say I never approved of your father's
will. You may have firm grounds now for contesting it.
Through another attorney, of course," he said hastily.

"I have no interest in the will!" Kate protested. "I only
want to find out what my mother intends to do about our
daughter.''

"This is an extremely awkward situation," Burgess said
slowly. "You see, unless you intend to bring kidnapping
charges against your mother . . .''

Kate exclaimed, near tears, "Bring charges! That's so
. . . horrible. I could never do that.''

"Besides," Joseph commented, "there's your grandfather to consider.''

"Oh, my God." Kate's tears were flowing freely now.
"It would kill him. He would be so upset . . . he would
feel somehow responsible.''

"Your grandfather is not well?" Burgess asked gently.

"Not at all. He's in his eighties now, and his heart is
not sound.''

The attorney sighed. "This is a problem. If no criminal
charge is filed, the International Police Bureau cannot
intervene, you understand. The only alternative would be
to employ private operatives, which would be a very costly
proceeding"—involuntarily, Burgess' eyes took in Kate's
and Joseph's clothes—"even if you knew where to look.
Mrs. Wendell may not stay in England. Europe is a small
continent. She may go anywhere.''

"We'll find the money somewhere," Joseph said grimly,
and Kate's heart sank. Something like this could wipe out
their meager savings; her grandfather didn't have much
money. Even if he did, how could they tell him what they
needed it for? She thought of Rafael Simson. But Joseph
would hate asking him.

"It is a hopeful sign," Burgess conceded, "that the butler will be waiting to hear from your mother. Perhaps, at that time . . . ."

"But we don't know how long that will be!" Kate cried.

"No. But let me advise you again. If the matter goes beyond a certain period of time—I would have to check that to give you the exact period—it may well be that the property will revert to you, Kate, by default. You might become empowered to sell the properties, if you wish, to help defray any extraordinary expenses."

Kate's head was whirling when they left the attorney's office. "You don't look well," Joseph said. "We'll get a cab. I'll drop you off at home, then I'll go up to see Rafael. He knows an amazing variety of people." Joseph smiled at her, trying to cheer her up. She loved him for it, because it was obvious he didn't feel like smiling.

"I know this must be so hard on *you*, darling."

"I'm all right, Kate. I want you to rest. You tossed and turned half the night. If we don't get an answer to our cable soon, there are other ways to trace their movements."

But the next morning, and the one after, they had still received no reply from Elizabeth. Kate was devastated. However, Joseph was not going to stop there, he told her. If Elizabeth was keeping their message from Marite, he knew a way to get one to their daughter; at least they could try. He had found a friend in the seamen's union who had a mate aboard, a purser in second class. The man could get a message to his first-class mates. Joseph sent a wireless to the purser in question, asking him to have it delivered personally to Miss Marite Wendell.

After several anxious days, they still heard nothing. Soon Elizabeth and Marite would be landing in Southampton, and where they would go from there was anybody's guess. Kate was in despair. "I can't believe she would ignore us like this."

Joseph consoled her. "We'll damned well send another. Maybe Elizabeth intercepted the first one somehow."

"She may do the same with the next one," Kate said despondently. "Then what, Joseph? What can we do then?"

"Take Rafael up on his offer . . . to finance an investigation. In fact I think we'd better start it now, put it in motion while there's still time. I've told Rafael to consider it a loan, which he wouldn't do." Joseph carefully omitted Rafael's fervent answer: "Loan? It's no loan, Joseph. It's a pleasure. I'd do a lot more to keep your child out of that witch's hands."

Kate felt a little better and yet she wondered what good an "investigation" would do them; they could be aware of Elizabeth's every movement, but it wouldn't bring Marite back.

That night she dreamed about her daughter, not as she had seen Marite last—a cool, unreachable adolescent—but as the little girl she used to be. In the dream Marite looked at Kate with three-year-old eyes—Joseph's eyes—and Kate caressed her daughter's hair, cut like a Dutch child's in straight bangs across her brow, golden hair the color of Kate's own.

They had not been at sea for two days before Marite began to notice their peculiar isolation. They had taken most of their meals in the suite and her grandmother hardly spoke to anyone. Marite couldn't understand it: things had been so different on Madison Avenue, and on Long Island, where people were always visiting. And Marite longed to show off her beautiful dresses, her pearls and the bracelets her grandmother had given her. They went on deck sometimes, wrapped against the wind, but Elizabeth discouraged Marite from joining in the games or talking to people. "There is a great deal of new money these days," she said sternly, "and many people who are not even nice have it."

Some of the people looked awfully nice to Marite. They were courteous, well-dressed, and elegant. She watched a dark-haired, laughing family. Their son was very handsome, and they even spoke French. The father reminded

Marite of her own father. But Elizabeth warned her against them. "They're Jews."

"Will people hold it against me?" she asked Elizabeth. "That my father's a Jew?"

"There's no need for anyone to know, my dear. Your name is Wendell now," Elizabeth assured her.

"But will we always live alone?"

"Certainly not. Good heavens, are you bored with your poor old grandmother, Marite?"

"Oh, no." Marite was afraid she might hurt Elizabeth's feelings.

She decided she wouldn't say anything more right now, or mention writing her father. She decided to write him without letting her grandmother know and give the letter to the purser, as she had seen someone else do. She would just write to her father to tell him good-bye and ask him not to stop them from living in a castle. Surely there couldn't be anything wrong in that.

One afternoon the purser came to their suite while Marite was in her bedroom writing the letter. She heard her grandmother talking to him; she could have sworn she heard him say her name. Elizabeth said, "I'll see that she gets it."

There was something else from the purser; then her grandmother, sounding annoyed: "I told you that I would see that she gets it." The door slammed. When Marite came out of her bedroom, her grandmother was reading a yellow piece of paper. She balled it up in her hand.

"What's that?"

"Nothing, darling. An annoying wireless from the lawyers." The rouge stood out on her grandmother's cheeks like two little red powder puffs; the rest of her face was white. "What are you doing with yourself, my dear?"

"Oh, just reading." Her grandmother was staring at her, and Marite realized she had an ink spot on her hand.

"Marite, there's no point in writing to your father now. Do you want him to make you come back home?" Marite shook her head. "Now, how would you like that necklace from the gift shop?"

Momentarily distracted, Marite said, "I'd love it!"

"Then put on your prettiest dress, my dear, and after we buy you something, we'll have dinner in the big salon and listen to the music."

Marite obeyed eagerly. Maybe something in the lawyers' wireless had put Elizabeth in a buying mood. They might even start talking to people.

When the wireless messages to the ship failed to bring them any answer, Joseph admitted to Rafael that they could now use his help. Their hands were tied in so many ways; they could hardly bring in Immigration or the State Department, since Elizabeth could well be in trouble for taking undeclared cash out of the country, and the idea of charging her with kidnapping was abhorrent to all of them as well as positively dangerous for Dryver in his fragile state of health.

And now they couldn't even be sure of where Elizabeth would be heading, had no way of investigating the traveler's checks until they were cashed in Europe. Private operatives were the only solution; Kate and Joseph gave the agency every possible crumb of information, including the names of Wendell relatives in England and France, and their hopes rose again.

"I feel as though one of us should *go* to Europe, Joseph."

"Oh, Kate, even if we could afford it, what good would that do? Where would we *go*? Burgess was right, you know. Europe's a tight little continent. Wait until we know something definite. They could be *anywhere*."

She had to acknowledge the logic of that, and yet she longed to be doing something, to take some action on her own. On the other hand, Harry Dryver's condition was not improving, and she was torn between the desire to be near him and the yearning to follow her daughter.

She had to content herself with writing to the Wendells

in London and to her father's cousin, Felicia Boerum, in France. These were artificial, rather coy letters—she could not face telling them the truth—advising that Elizabeth and Marite were on the way to Europe, asking the relatives to remind her mother that Kate and Joseph wanted to hear from her, that she had been a "rather poor" correspondent. The tone of her letters nauseated Kate but she felt it was the best way to handle the situation for the time being.

Meanwhile they had been fortunate in keeping the whole thing from her grandfather. When he asked about Marite, Kate told him that she was having such a grand time on Long Island that she might not come back to the city until September. "Well, give her my love when you see her," he said. Kate was frightened by the weakness of his voice.

David, of course, knew everything. He was back with them now, looking forward to their short vacation at Brighton Beach. "We might not stay the whole two weeks," Joseph told him. "Your mother wants to be near your great-grandfather, and we're waiting every day to hear something about your sister."

David took his disappointment with a manliness that touched Kate. Her son seemed older than eleven; he was already developing a sturdiness, a reedy height that made him look more than ever like Joseph. He had been in junior boxing and martial-arts groups since he was eight years old. "You know, Mother," he said matter-of-factly, "Marite probably wanted to go. She always liked to be with Grandmother Wendell."

Kate and Joseph looked at each other in silence. If what David said was true, their quest was going to be even more difficult.

"Oh, darling, I'm so glad you're here!" Kate greeted Joseph in a whisper at the front door of Harry Dryver's house.

"Where's your grandfather?" Joseph kissed her, following her into the living room.

"Lying down. He's tired today but he seems a little

better. Darling, look. When I got this it was too late to reach you at the union. He's *seen* them!"

Joseph scanned the report Kate held out to him. The English agent, supplied with detailed descriptions, had spotted the runaways as the Wendells, and followed them from Customs. They registered at the Ritz-Carlton Hotel, where they stayed only one night before taking a Channel boat to France. The "older subject" had not gotten in touch with either English or French relatives; they were now registered at a Paris hotel. The operative gave the address. He said the "younger subject" appeared to be in "excellent health and spirits."

"I've sent a cable to Marite at that hotel," Kate said. "At least we know she's all right."

"I hope they're there long enough to get the cable." Joseph sighed. "And that Elizabeth doesn't keep it from Marite."

"What are you talking about, Joseph?"

Their heads swiveled in surprise; Harry Dryver was standing at the door. They hadn't heard him. His felt slippers were soundless on the polished floor. "Am I to be let in on this mystery?"

His pallid face, the reproach in his weak voice, squeezed Kate's heart like a giant fist.

"Grandfather, please. You must sit down." She got up and started toward him.

"Not until you tell me what's going on in this family. What's all this about cables . . . and Elizabeth keeping them from Marite?"

Kate knew that stony look, that mulish tone. He meant it. "And you can unhand me, Joseph." Dryver grinned crookedly; Joseph was already beside him, steadying his arm. "I'm not a complete wreck, son."

Joseph ignored him and gently pushed the old man into an easy chair. Kate had never seen her grandfather look so feeble, even during this last illness.

"Now," he demanded, "why were you saying that about Marite, Joseph?"

Joseph was standing behind Dryver's chair. His anxious
eyes met Kate's.

"It was only a private joke, Grandfather," Kate blurted.
"It seems so long since she went away that . . ."

"Kate, Kate." Dryver shook his head, giving her a
pitying, weary glance. "You know I won't swallow that.
You've got to tell me. What's happened? Is it . . .
Elizabeth?"

He looked so distraught that now Kate wondered whether
it would do more harm than good to keep lying to him.
Eerily he picked up her thought.

"You've never lied to me before, either of you."

"No, Mr. Dryver, we haven't." Joseph put his hand on
Dryver's shoulder. "Elizabeth has taken Marite to Europe,
without . . . notifying us."

"She's kidnapped her, in other words." Harry Dryver
sounded miserable, but unsurprised. "I should have warned
you, Kate. Warned both of you. I didn't even like it when
Marite went away to stay on Long Island." He stopped,
breathless, and his voice died away on the last word.

"Please, Grandfather. Please, let us—"

"Don't stop me, Kate," Dryver broke in. "I know my
daughter. My God, ever since she was a small child, I
thought there was something not quite . . . right about
Elizabeth. She was such a cold child, so detached from me
and your grandmother. And every time she visited the
Dryvers, she'd come back more distant than ever. I thought
I could see the same thing happening to Marite. Then I
would tell myself it was my vivid and fertile imagination." He gave them a small, sad, mocking smile.

"When Marite went to the Island, I started thinking
about it again. But I couldn't tell you, somehow; I was
inhibited by a foolish shame about my daughter, your own
mother."

"When I was little," Kate said softly, "you always
wanted me to spend as much time with you as I could."

"Yes. But not only because of your mother. I love you,
Kate. I always have. You know that."

"Oh, Grandfather. Of course I do." Kate got up and went to his chair, kneeling down beside it. "And I love *you*. Why else do you think we've been trying to keep this from you?"

He touched her head. "I appreciate that, my darling, but I had to know. Do you think I could let you and Joseph carry this alone . . . do you think I can bear to be shut out of your heart?"

Kate shook her head, and tears began to slip down her face.

"Who's footing the bill for this fancy operative?" Dryver demanded. "Have you dipped into your reserves, son?"

He was too close to them for the question to be offensive, although he had never brought up the subject of their finances before.

"Rafael." Joseph made a restless motion.

"Poor Rafael is paying my debt," Dryver muttered. "It's not right, Joseph. I'm the one responsible. You've got to let me help."

"*You* responsible, sir?" Joseph countered. "You're not responsible in any way. "I'm the one who is, I'm the one who should have seen this coming long ago."

Kate found his bitter self-reproach unbearable. "Stop it, darling! So am *I* . . . you can't take all this on yourself. Anyway, it's fruitless now to place blame, to talk like this."

"You're absolutely right. Guilt is the worst form of self-indulgence." Kate thought her grandfather sounded brighter; there was a little more strength in his assertion. But listening closely, she could tell it was a false strength, a facade assumed for their benefit.

She knew, too, what a strain it would be on his modest fortune to help finance the search. They must try to dissuade him.

"Mr. Dryver, I wish you'd go back to bed for a while," Joseph said mildly.

"Not until I read that report." Knowing it was futile to argue when he sounded like that, Kate passed the report to

Dryver. He skimmed it rapidly and handed it back to her. "I'm sorry to have to say this, but we all have to face it," he began, and Kate felt her skin turn cold with new apprehension. "I doubt that Elizabeth will stay in any one place for long. She'll give the investigator a merry chase. I fear it's going to be a long and costly enterprise."

Joseph looked stricken. "You may be right."

"Elizabeth has always had a special feeling for Germany. One I never shared. Especially now," Dryver said.

Kate's skin prickled; she saw Joseph's gloomy expression. Even in this year of peace, Germany was not that peaceful—since January of last year French and Belgian troops had begun to occupy the Ruhr.

Harry Dryver seemed to regret having mentioned the threat of war abroad. He smiled weakly, trying to make light of his fears. Joseph glanced uneasily at Kate and cleared his throat. "We'll discuss all this later," he said. "Come, sweetheart, let's get your grandfather back to bed." He smiled grimly at Dryver.

Nevertheless, during the flurry of getting her grandfather to his room—which had been moved to the street floor to accommodate his weak heart—Kate could not forget what Dryver had said. Or how ill he appeared.

Now her anxiety, in the flash of an eye, had turned to dread, not only for Marite but also for her grandfather.

Chapter 17

As the last weeks of the oppressive summer crawled by, Kate felt more and more despondent. There had been no reply to her correspondence to Paris, and recently the European operative hired by Rafael had totally lost track of Marite and Elizabeth. Her mother must have realized they were being observed. She had given the man the slip at the Gare du Nord station. Kate was amazed that her mother would be capable of evading the man; Rafael had told them that he was the "best." To continue the search would require additional operatives and a wider field and would be, he said frankly, an "extremely costly" operation. Rafael insisted that they continue the search for at least six more months; Kate became a mass of ambivalent emotions.

On the one hand it was unthinkable to abandon the search for her child; on the other, Marite was obviously well and cared-for. She had never even written to her mother and father; a girl of thirteen was surely responsible enough to at least do that, Kate realized sorely, even if Elizabeth had kept their stream of letters from her.

Worst of all, Harry Dryver was now deeply involved in the matter, and his anxiety over the whole thing was draining his frail resources. Kate was shaken when she learned from Letha that "Mr. Harry is getting the doctor all het up" by holding conferences with Rafael Simson and his lawyer and "all kinds of people."

Kate felt anxious on a sultry afternoon in August when she climbed the stoop on Eleventh Street. As soon as Letha opened the door, she knew that something terrible had happened. Letha's aging face was wet with tears, her eyes shot with blood.

"What is it?" Kate gasped.

"Oh, Miss Kate, he's very bad. The doctor's in there now. I thank the Lord you came. I was just about to call you." Letha's voice broke up, and she started sobbing. She lifted her apron to wipe her face.

"Oh, God." Kate embraced Letha, then brushed past her into Dryver's room.

He was lying propped on pillows in the big four-poster bed, his face almost as white as the linen cases. His eyes were closed.

The doctor was bending over him with an intent face, listening through his stethoscope. There was a nurse there, too. She touched the doctor's arm. Dr. O'Connell looked up and saw Kate.

They had known each other since she was a little girl. He did not smile at her now; his thin, sensitive face was drawn down in lines of grieving anger. She recalled something her grandfather had said about O'Connell: "Death makes him furious. It is the one enemy he cannot withstand."

And, frozen, Kate knew the meaning of O'Connell's expression.

Harry Dryver was dying.

O'Connell's face relaxed a trifle; he summoned up a grimace that passed for a smile, and gestured to her. She stumbled into the room and moved toward the bed.

"Kate," O'Connell whispered. He grasped her upper arm with a painful grip. "He doesn't have much time left."

Her body was stiff with shock. She took a sobbing breath. She felt as if she'd taken a stunning blow that rocked her whole body. Trembling, she sank down on her knees by the bed and brought her face close to Dryver's. His eyelids fluttered.

"Kate." His whisper was so faraway that she hardly recognized her name, but there was the faintest curve on his lips. He was trying hard to smile. The effort was so pitiful that her eyes blurred, dimming his face.

She rubbed at her eyes and leaned closer, with her mouth to his ear. "Grandfather, I love you, I have always loved you so." It was an effort to speak; her mouth felt numb. But there was so much to say in so little time. "You gave me everything."

"You . . . my sun and moon, Kate. Listen . . . listen now. House . . . don't let others . . . live in house. *You* . . . Joseph. House yours. I . . . be in house, too. Paintings. Yours. Live . . . this house . . . be happy. Peace for me then."

"Oh, Grandfather, we will. I promise. But don't talk so much now. Please."

"No . . . time. Must. You . . . paint. Kate . . . black lamb." He was making a mighty effort to say the words. She kept holding his hand tightly, and kissed his face.

There was a great light in his failing eyes and his lips curved again in that enormous pathetic effort to smile. "So happy . . . you came . . . say good-bye," he breathed. His eyes closed again, slowly, and he expelled one long, placid sigh.

The hand in her grasp was still.

His eyes opened again, staring without sight.

A deep sob racked her body. She laid her head down on her grandfather's immobile arm. A dreadful coldness began to creep over her, as if she herself were dying. She could neither move nor cry. The only thing she could feel was an excruciating pain that clawed at her throat, scraped at her chest and vitals with its talons, until she thought her body would be torn to pieces.

Dimly she was aware of O'Connell's hand on her back. He was saying her name, telling her to get up.

She screamed at him, "Leave me alone! Do you think I'm going to leave him now?" The pain was still clawing at her.

She felt hard hands on her shoulders, under her arms, pulling her to her feet. O'Connell slapped her face.

Someone thrust a glass toward her mouth, and she moved her head; the rim of the glass struck her cheek. Then two people grabbed her; someone was clutching her face, and she saw Letha, her old eyes swollen slits from weeping, holding out the glass to her, saying, "Now, honey, now, honey," and Kate was drinking from the glass. The liquid burned, and the glass rattled against her teeth, and then the nurse was trying to make her sit down in a chair.

But Kate broke away from them all, crying out again, "Leave me alone! Leave me alone!"

Her head felt strangely light now, and she could barely see ahead of her as she half-ran, half-stumbled from the room and began to climb the stairs. Staggering, she bumped into the stair walls as she climbed drunkenly upward toward the studio.

She sank down on the stool, in front of his easel, staring at the last painting Harry Dryver had begun.

"What will I *do*? What will I *do*?" she cried out to the silent walls, hung with the last great testament of Harry Dryver. She sat there like a statue, mocked by the invading sun, for a measureless interval until her bones began to ache with motionlessness.

At some time when the light in the studio began to darken and change, she came to a form of awareness. Voices, voices came from the downstairs hall, soft and faraway. And one was Joseph's.

He had never sounded so strong, so kind. Kate began to tremble, she longed for his presence now.

She heard his footsteps climb the stairs, and then he was there with her, engulfing her in his embrace as a father would a child. He didn't say a word.

Kate leaned against him and a miraculous feeling of comfort stole over her, streaming from his warm nearness and his gentle touch. Her numbness melted.

Like a torrential fall of rain after the unbearable pressure of heavy air before a storm, her tears broke, running down her face. Joseph just stood there holding her, stroking her hair. Now and then he wiped her sodden face with his handkerchief.

She put her arms around his body and murmured against his dampened shirt, "You are my rock, Joseph. My rock and my salvation." She looked up at him. His face was blurred to her tear-blinded eyes; she blinked. His cheeks were wet too.

"I loved him too, Kate," Joseph said. He released one of his hands to wipe his face.

"I know." She got up dizzily from the stool and stood beside him, putting her arm around his waist. "He said . . . he said that he wanted us to live here now, in this house. That he would be here with us."

"He will be, Kate. He will be."

In the first days after her grandfather's death, it seemed to Joseph that Kate was showing almost unnatural control; underneath, he sensed a grief so awesome, so potentially destructive that she was afraid to release it. He waited from hour to hour for her to break down.

He offered to relieve her of the practical arrangements, despite his hectic schedule with the union—there was talk of a special convention, of his being eyed for the vice-presidency.

More as a matter of form than in the hope she would receive it, Joseph cabled the news of Dryver's death to Elizabeth at the last address they had. When he tried to take care of other matters, Kate objected. He felt she dreaded the prospect of unoccupied time; as if aloneness or silence, any empty moment, might break her; that if she so much as paused, she would stop, drown in her despondency.

Within two days Kate had made all the funeral arrangements, almost before Joseph knew it. Harry Dryver had requested a nonreligious rite and cremation, with a memorial service rather than a funeral, at which Joseph, Kate, and certain of his friends would speak. His last instructions involved a typically worded request: "If Kate and Joseph would not consider it morbid, it would bring my ashes peace to be enclosed in an urn, the urn to be placed in the garden behind the house, so I may enjoy the company of the flowers and the cats."

" 'Morbid,' " Joseph repeated softly. "Even in death he was considerate of our wishes. I like the idea very much."

He knew that after the ceremony Kate might experience an awful crash, especially with the continuing silence from Europe. The first thing Joseph did was to hustle Kate and David away for an abbreviated vacation at Brighton Beach. Even a brief rest by the ocean would perk Kate up. Besides, Joseph decided slyly, there was no way she could deny the beach to David. The boy hadn't fully grasped the profound fact of his great-grandfather's death.

Only a few days after they had come to Brighton, Joseph could see Kate beginning to unwind. While he and David swam or played ball in the sand, Kate spent a lot of time reading in a beach chair, gazing out over the ocean. Her usual energy seemed to have deserted her, at least during the days, and she complained to Joseph that she felt lazy. He laughed at her, pointing out that she was always ready to prepare their meals, and go to a movie or some boardwalk entertainment in the evening.

"You've never been lazy in your life," he said. "You just don't recognize a little peace when you feel it." Joseph was grateful to notice that she seemed to have calmed down slightly.

With each day she started to regain some of her former nervous energy—the same force that had pushed her through Dryver's funeral. By the second week she was positively restless.

One afternoon near the end of their holiday, Kate and Joseph were lying on the beach at sunset, holding hands. David had gone fishing—a sport that Joseph abhorred— and they watched him trudge toward them along the sand, with a new friend at his side. David was carrying a heavy-looking pail, like the other boy's, and he waved to Kate and Joseph. There was a triumphant expression on his face. The other boy waved too, and went off.

"I have a feeling I'm going to be cooking fish tonight," Kate murmured. She sat up and returned her son's wave.

As she watched him come closer, some of Kate's oppression lifted: with his tanned, sturdy body, his dark, unruly hair and handsome features, their son looked like a younger Joseph. The sight of him warmed her heart.

Her grandfather was gone, and they didn't know when they would see Marite again. But she still had Joseph . . . and they both had David.

Joseph got up and went to meet him, relieving him of the heavy pail. When they came back to her, both of them were smiling like peers, eager to show her the wonderful catch.

Repressing her distaste, she said to David, "You're terrific! You've brought our dinner!"

David grinned from ear to ear. "Already cleaned, too!" he boasted. "Arny's father did it for us."

"Arny's father's terrific too," Joseph said with a mischievous glance at Kate. "Take 'em in the cabin, son, and put 'em in the icebox. Okay?"

"Sure." David went off with his prize.

Kate put her arm around Joseph, watching David go.

"We have a lot to be grateful for," she said.

"We certainly do." He put his arm around her waist as they walked back toward the cabin. "I had a great idea a little while ago."

"Yes?"

"Why don't we move right into Eleventh Street as soon as we go back?"

"I'd love to." She knew why he had suggested it, and her heart warmed all over again: there was nothing like a new project to bring her back to life.

When the lawyer approved, Kate plunged into the task, accomplishing everything in an amazingly short time. Joseph marveled at her energy, though he worried about her appearance; Kate had grown thinner, and there was often a hectic flush on her cheeks. He knew better, though, than to ask her to slow down; he was also finding great solace in long hours' work, to keep himself from missing Dryver and his daughter. And to keep from thinking of his impotence in regard to finding Marite.

He burned with frustration: maybe he had been wrong, all those years ago, not to accept Rafael's job offer. If he had, they would have enough money and he would have the leisure to go to Europe and follow them all over the continent if he had to. It was also a sore point that Rafael was the one financing the search.

Joseph felt another emotion he hardly dared acknowledge, even to himself—an emotion akin to resentment against Marite. She had not written them a single letter, nor told them good-bye. She seemed to have allied herself with a woman who had caused nothing but suffering—for Kate, for himself, for Anzia and Rafael—and who might have been the actual cause of Dryver's and Howard Wendell's deaths.

But now it might be feasible, he realized, for them to take a short trip to Europe—Rafael's money could be used for that instead of the apparently futile search. Kate had hinted that she could ask for an advance on Dryver's estate; his paintings now had enormous value. Joseph decided he would broach the matter to Kate.

Neither of them had brought up the matter of Marite's bedroom. David had been overjoyed by the sunny bedroom Kate had set up for him on the second floor. Then after they moved in, Joseph discovered that Kate had already set aside an upstairs bedroom for Marite's furniture and belongings. He stood in the hall, watching Kate hang new curtains and spread a matching bedspread over the bed. Then she even tacked a pennant on the wall over Marite's desk—a pennant with the colors of the high school Marite was to have entered in the autumn.

The whole operation was so sad that Joseph's eyes stung: it was the room of a thirteen-year-old girl who might be years older before she occupied it again . . . if she ever did. He wanted to cry out in protest, but he held his tongue. Instead he wandered in and said calmly, "This is very pretty, Kate."

She turned and looked at him, and he saw the knowledge of her own futile gesture entered plainly on her face.

He took her in his arms. "You want to go to Europe, don't you, darling?"

Silent, she nodded against him.

"So do I. As soon as we have word that they have settled *anywhere*, Kate, we will go. I will arrange it."

She looked up at him with shining eyes. Then her face fell. "Will we ever find them?"

"Yes, Kate. We will. You've got to believe that."

Four days later, they did. The "subject" had bought a large house thirty miles outside Paris. Joseph exulted, "We're halfway there."

After spending almost a month in Paris looking for Marite and her mother, Kate realized how overoptimistic Joseph had been.

The city's pavements sizzled in the summer heat the afternoon that she and Joseph came back to their pension after a futile visit to the American embassy.

Their room was hardly cooler than the streets.

"Phew!" Joseph snatched off his jacket and his hat.

Kate went to get them both a glass of tepid water; the pension had never heard of ice. But they weren't able to stay in a proper hotel; they had to economize.

She got rid of her hat and shoes. "It's damned discouraging."

Joseph gulped down his water. "That Van Cleve's a typical embassy type," he said sourly. "Did you see the way he looked at Burgess's letter?" He sprawled in a chair.

"Oh, yes. As if it were a forgery." Kate was running a comb through her hair in front of the gray-spotted mirror. She unbuttoned the top of her dress for coolness. "He acted like we'd come to steal the spoons."

"Well, Burgess warned us. And Van Cleve said exactly what Burgess predicted: 'The embassy is hesitant to intervene in a family matter.' " Joseph mimicked the stiff embassy employee, Van Cleve, with a pseudo-English accent. "The pompous idiot. All they want to do is to pass the buck to Interpol if we *charge* Elizabeth with kidnapping. And how the hell can we do that?"

"We can't," she said gloomily. "I don't know why Burgess assumed Van Cleve could be swayed, now that we've met him. He's conveniently forgotten that my father and Burgess got him his appointment in the first place."

"Maybe he thought we were impostors." Joseph gave her an ironic smile. "We should have invested in elegant clothes. Van Cleve looked at me as if he couldn't believe I was Howard Wendell's son-in-law."

"I'd like to strangle that stuffed shirt. But right now I think I'll take another bath instead. If you don't mind being last."

"No, darling, go ahead." Joseph leaned back in the chair, the only comfortable feature in the room.

Kate touched the top of his head affectionately and went down the hall to the antique bathroom. As she bathed she reviewed the last frustrating weeks.

They had visited the enormous country house, where they were received by a gimlet-eyed housekeeper who informed them coldly that "Madame" and the *jeune fille* had left for a journey out of the country.

"I am Madame's daughter and Marite's mother," Kate said. The woman, who had not invited them in, seemed surprised and suspicious of Kate's Parisian French.

As it turned out, she was even more astonished at Kate's claim, because she answered, "There must be some error. She is one child of Madame's son. Her granddaughter is an orphan."

Kate heard Joseph exclaim angrily, from behind her, and she pleaded with the woman to believe her. "Please, at least let us come in and leave a letter. Or tell us where Madame Wendell has gone."

"Either course is impossible," the woman snapped. "Madame Wendell is not here. And I was not advised when they will return." She placed her heavy arm across the door, as if to forbid them to enter. Shortly afterward a rough-looking man stepped up behind them. He was carrying an old-fashioned rifle. "I suggest," he growled, "that you leave the grounds at once." Kate was terrified that Joseph would try to fight with him, but to her relief he didn't. They had no alternative but to go away, to give up for the time being.

"She was 'advised' all right," Joseph said angrily when their hired car was taking them back to Paris. "Good God, what a suspicious tartar. A blind woman could see you're Marite's mother, just looking at you."

"That's a wonderful mixed metaphor," Kate retorted with the first flash of humor in days. "France hasn't changed," she added dryly. "After he took the Tour my grandfather said the average French provincial was so cagey he'd make a New Yorker seem credulous. Speaking of New York suspicion, I'm not too sure they *have* gone."

Neither was Joseph. They came back every day for a solid week and, hidden, observed the house, but saw no sign of Elizabeth or their child. They *were* gone, then. But where? Not to Spain or Italy in this weather. Maybe England. Kate suggested Switzerland, that cool summer haven. Without much hope they had wired many of the prominent hotels. After three days there was still no answer.

Kate's head ached when she recalled their efforts. It was possible they might not even return to the country house before spring. Kate recalled that rich Parisians often stayed in the city until November and wintered on the Riviera.

When she came in from the bathroom, Joseph turned to her with a sweet smile.

She moved into his arms and said slowly, "I'm afraid it's hopeless, Joseph. We've spent a small fortune already, we've run ourselves to exhaustion, for nothing. I think it's useless."

"So do I, Kate, but I wanted you to be the one to say

it,'' Joseph admitted. ''It's time to go home. We have our
lives, too. And it's time we got on with them. At least
now they have a permanent base, of sorts, and we won't
stop trying.''

Kate felt a little surge of hope again. No, they wouldn't
stop trying.

And it would be so good, so good to go home.

They had moved into the country house before Marite
remembered that she had not yet written to her father. At
first, the kaleidoscope of London and the Channel cross-
ing, their arrival in Paris, had crowded all thoughts of
America from her dazzled mind. She was astounded that
they could move from one country to another almost as
easily as one traveled from Manhattan to Long Island, and
their first night in Paris left her so exhausted that all she
wanted was to sleep.

The next morning, exposed to the Gothic beauties of the
City of Light, and the splendors of the shops on the Rue de
la Paix, Marite began to feel that she was living on a
jeweled carousel; her head whirled. In no time at all,
Elizabeth was whisking her away again, to the huge stone
house in the country that was indeed like a miniature
castle.

Marite was glad that they were settled somewhere at
last; as thrilling as their travels had been, it was nice to be
somewhere quiet and cool and green for a while, not loud
and hot, like London and Paris.

She was pleased with the attention of the respectful
servants, who made her feel like a princess again, as the
servants had at the Madison Avenue house. And there was
a pond with ducks, even a pony to ride. Her grandmother
said that when the weather was a little cooler, they would
go back to Paris to see the plays, dine in fine restaurants,
and shop for winter clothes.

After a few weeks, Elizabeth asked Marite how she
would like to go to Switzerland. Marite, who was tired of
their solitude and full of energy, excitedly agreed. Zurich

looked like a place from a fairy tale; Marite was enchanted. But she still felt strange about not writing to her father.

One morning she decided that she must do so. Seeking out the writing room of the hotel, she began a letter. But she had hardly gotten beyond the salutation when her grandmother found her.

"Whom are you writing to, my darling?"

"Father. It's been so long . . . and I've got to tell him where we are."

"Oh, my dear child." Gently Elizabeth took the pen from Marite's fingers and put it back in its well. She took both of Marite's hands in hers, pulling her gently upward from her chair.

"Come here, darling. It's time I told you." Her grandmother's voice was soft and sad.

"Told me what?" Marite demanded.

"Come, dear. Sit down with me here, on the sofa."

Marite obeyed. Her grandmother enclosed Marite in her arm; Marite could smell her sweet, fine scent.

"I have something very terrible to tell you." Elizabeth's words were practically a whisper. "Your parents are . . . gone."

"Gone?"

"They were . . . killed in an accident, Marite. It happened only a few days ago."

Marite stared at Elizabeth, uncomprehending. "Killed?" she whispered. Then her voice rose, and she was shrieking, "Killed! My father is *dead*?" Marite was shaking all over, crying now.

"Hush, dear child, hush. Come, let us go up to our room," Elizabeth said with great gentleness, leading Marite to the stairs. Up in their room, she made Marite lie down and put a cold cloth on her head.

"I don't believe it," Marite sobbed. "My father can't be dead." It didn't seem possible that she would never see him again. He had always been so strong and so alive, the only one at home who had been unfailingly kind to her.

She had been jealous, ever since she was little, of his attention to her mother and David, but she knew that her father *had* loved her; maybe he hadn't been able to find her because she and Elizabeth had moved around so much.

Marite remembered the mysterious message on the ship, the one that had made Elizabeth so angry. That could have been from her father and mother.

Her mother.

Marite had thought she had stopped loving her a long time ago, but suddenly she was overwhelmed by pleasant images of her mother. There had been one Christmas, when Marite was very little, and they must have been awfully poor. But her mother had made her a wonderful doll's hotel from painted orange crates, a marvelous little hotel with many rooms, actually papered in wallpaper; her mother had built all the furniture for it, and sewn lovely dresses for the doll-"guests."

All that must have been done with love . . . every bit as much love as Elizabeth had shown her in another way, buying dresses and bracelets and pearls.

Marite turned her face to the wall and wept bitterly, her sobs ripped from the depths of her body. She was dimly aware that Elizabeth was no longer sitting on the bed.

When she turned over again, she saw her grandmother sitting in a chair near the window, staring at the panorama of the mountains. There was a funny brightness in her black eyes, a little smile on her narrow lips.

"Grandmother." Elizabeth started at the sound of Marite's muffled voice; she stopped smiling. "Are you sad too?"

"Of course I am." Her grandmother got up gracefully from the chair, in a rustle of silken draperies, and came to the bed to sit down by Marite.

She took a fragile handkerchief from the little jacket of her dress and wiped Marite's face, then handed it to her. Marite blew her nose.

"Are you feeling better, sweetheart?"

"Yes. A little." Marite leaned back on the pillows as her grandmother offered her hand. She squeezed the smooth, soft hand, thinking: My grandmother is all my family now. She'll be the one, forever, to take care of me, tell me what to do.

Tell her what to do.

Marite wondered how that was going to be. But she couldn't think about that right now. Right now she wanted to know what had happened to her mother and father. "Tell me about the accident, Grandmother."

Elizabeth drew back from her and looked away. "They were in an accident in a car," Elizabeth said.

"But they don't have a car."

"It was someone else's." Elizabeth was flushed with vexation. "Why are you asking me all these questions, my dear?"

"I want to know." Marite sat up in the bed. "Why didn't you tell me when . . . when it happened?"

"I didn't have the heart. I just didn't have the courage. But when I saw you writing to your father, I had to, you see. I couldn't keep it from you any longer." Elizabeth was hugging her again, and Marite breathed the frail, lovely smell of jasmine and roses which Elizabeth said came from the meadows of Grasse.

Marite leaned against her, nestling in her embrace; Elizabeth felt silky and soft, and she was stroking Marite's hair, murmuring to her. Somehow things didn't look so black when she did that.

And yet something in her grandmother's touch, and the feel of her body, reminded Marite of her mother, Kate. And she had thoughts she had never had before—thoughts about how pretty her mother had been. How kind, even if she had seemed far away at times; how smart she had been, to paint all those pictures, like the one in Marite's room on MacDougal Street, of the peculiar and beautiful animals like nothing in any zoo; trees like no trees Marite had ever seen, against a rosy-purple sky prettier than any sunset over Long Island. It was strange to think about those things now, but they were vivid in her mind.

"What is my girl thinking about so deeply?"

"My mother." Marite stared out the window at the green slopes of the mountains. Elizabeth sighed.

"Now, darling," she said with sudden brightness, "I think we should take a nice long walk and get some air. Otherwise you will have an awful headache from crying. Why don't you wash your face now? After our walk we can have a lovely dinner."

Marite nodded slowly, got up, and went to wash her face and brush her hair.

Her solemn face stared back at her from the mirror. Everyone said she was "unusual-looking," with her black eyes and her golden brows and hair. Somehow her eyes never seemed to fit the rest of her face, with its short, tilted nose and small, round mouth. She supposed that was because she had Jewish eyes. That's what her brother used to say.

All at once she was struck by an almost crippling pain, thinking of her lost father. She threw down her brush and bent over, resting her forehead against the dresser top. She didn't cry, which made it hurt worse than ever.

Suddenly she wanted terribly to go back home, even to MacDougal Street, which had never seemed so wonderful or so nice as the house uptown. But it was too late for that. There was no "home" anymore, except the country house in France, and that seemed big and gloomy and empty now when she thought about it.

It was too late now. Maybe she should never have come with Elizabeth on the journey.

Marite opened her little jewel box, and fumbling in its depths, brought up the golden star on the fragile chain, the necklace her father had given to her mother and her mother had given her. She held it against her cheek for a second, then clasped the chain and slipped the star under her dress.

Elizabeth must not see it; she didn't like it when Marite wore the star.

"Where are you, darling?"

Her grandmother was calling her again. Marite couldn't

understand why that, too, reminded her of her mother. Marite had considered her mother indifferent, uncaring. But right now all she could think was that, unlike Elizabeth, her mother had not always been calling to her, looking at her. Her mother had let her feel . . . free.

"I'm coming," she said quickly, and closed the jewel box.

"Where are your pearls, darling? Are you getting tired of them? If you are, we can buy you lots of other necklaces." Elizabeth stared at her.

"Oh, no. I'm not tired of them at all." Marite went back to the dresser, got out the pearls, and put them on.

That evening at dinner it was hard to understand why Elizabeth seemed so gay, when Marite's parents had died such a short time before. She supposed it was because of what Elizabeth had told her—that she, Marite, was the dearest person in her life.

But she was very quiet as Elizabeth chattered on, telling her what they would be doing and seeing, where they would be this fall and through the winter. Marite would never have to go to school again; she would have a governess this fall, who would teach her the languages she needed, the arts and graces she must learn to be a proper young lady. The governess would go right with them this winter to the Riviera.

As Elizabeth went on, Marite's sadness began to lift a little.

"We're going to have a wonderful life, Marite."

Elizabeth smiled at her and patted her hand across the table with its vase of small white flowers, while in the background was the lilt of shining violins.

Chapter 18

On an early morning near the end of May 1927, David Barsimson found his mother standing at the door of the room with his sister's things in it. As much as he loved his mother, David felt his usual impatience. She had been doing this for more than two years.

They had given up looking for Marite in February 1925, after his Uncle Rafael had come to the house and they had had a long talk behind closed doors. His mother had cried all that day and into the night. David thought: At least she doesn't do that anymore. She hadn't even been painting many pictures; she had begun some, then said they were terrible, and stopped again. And he knew she had almost forgotten his birthday, a few weeks ago, and then remembered just in time.

"Mother." She jumped a little when David spoke, and turned around, smiling at him, but her eyes were sad. "You're going with us tonight, aren't you?" So many times lately she hadn't gone with him and his father when they went out. And she still wrote letters to his sister.

She looked blank for a minute; then her eyes cleared, and she answered, "To see the Lindbergh newsreel? Oh . . . yes. Yes, of course I am." This time she gave him a real smile, like her old one, and David felt good.

"Oh, that's great!" He hugged her, thinking how pretty she always was, how good she smelled, even when she was sad a lot and seemed to be thinking of other things.

When he ran down the stairs, his father called up from the kitchen, "David? No breakfast?"

David stopped and called down, "I had it real early, Dad. Gotta go. See you tonight." He ran out of the house, and just caught the bus.

The whole day seemed to drag; he was so excited about the newsreel he could hardly eat dinner. But finally he was sitting with his parents in the picture show, next to his father. His mother was sitting on the other side, holding his father's hand. That always seemed funny to David— his friends' parents never did that at the picture show.

But now he was finally going to see Lindbergh in Paris: there it was! Gosh, it was wonderful. David's eyes were glued to the moving picture. It looked kind of snowy— thousands and thousands of people, yelling, busting right through the lines of cops and soldiers, lifting David's hero right out of the cockpit of the plane.

And there seemed to be millions of people around the plane. Lindbergh sure looked tired. But he smiled anyway, and waved his hand. The soldiers were having a time trying to keep the people from just mashing Lindbergh; then an old dressed-up fellow was shaking his hand.

Now the picture switched to a wide street in Paris—the commentator called it a "boulevard"—with Lindbergh riding in an open car, and about a million more people standing on either side of the boulevard, waving. The camera got in close to people watching from hotels and other buildings, houses that looked like his Grandmother Wendell's house.

David heard his mother gasp. "Joseph. That was Marite!" She whispered so loud David could hear her clearly.

Then his father was whispering in her ear, putting his arm around her.

But David was so excited about the picture that he couldn't let it bother him right then. Only afterward when his mother hadn't said a word all the way home, and his father looked glum too, did it occur to David that his sister might actually have been one of the people in the picture, watching the Lindbergh parade.

Usually when they came home after a moving picture, they would all go downstairs to the kitchen and talk about it, and have a picnic. But tonight his father said, "You go ahead, David, and make yourself something. I want to talk to your mother for a while."

David's heart sank; he had looked forward to talking about the newsreel with his father and mother. But tonight she seemed to have her mind on other things again.

All of a sudden, something got into David. It was time his mother really paid attention to him. Marite was gone; she had been gone for nearly three years now, and she had never even written his mother a letter.

Instead of obeying his father, David followed his mother into the living room and began to shout at her, "Look at *me*, Mother! I'm still here, and she's *gone*! You still have me! Look at me, Mother . . . pay *attention*!"

His mother just stared at him, and his father strode into the room, grabbed his arm, and shook him. "David. That's enough."

His father said it loud. He sounded so angry David was scared: his father had never hit him, but he looked like he was going to now. David's mother was crying.

"Stop it, David." His father's strong grip loosened, and he said more quietly, "We know you're here. And you know we love you. Now go on downstairs. We'll be down there in a little while."

David kept his head down when he walked out, ashamed to let his father see his face all bunched up. He was about to cry, and he hadn't done that since he was ten years old. Fourteen-year-old fellows didn't cry, especially when they were as big as he was. His father said David would be the same height as him by next year, that he had shot up like a balloon, and that's why he was always hungry.

But David was damned determined that he was going to make his mother, and other people, sit up and take notice, the way all those people had noticed his hero, Lindy.

*   *   *

"What's all this?" Joseph walked into Marite's bedroom. Kate was taking down the fluffy curtains; the bedspread lay folded at the end of the bed, and there were full packing boxes all over the place. The high-school pennant was rolled up on top of one of the boxes. The closet was empty, the dressing table bare.

"What should have been done a year ago," Kate answered calmly. "Turning this into a guestroom. It's silly for David's friends to have to bunk with him, when we've got a whole house."

"Can I help?" Joseph went over to steady the low stepladder, stroking her neat ankles.

"Not that way," she teased him. "You can hold the ladder while I get down and up again, and hand me the new curtains. On the chair, over there."

"Nice. Very classy." He helped her up again with one hand, then handed her a curtain with the other. She hung a pair, then asked, "How's that?"

"I like it, Kate." The curtains were a heavy homespun material of oatmeal color printed with a bold geometric design in black.

"With touches of red and blue this summer . . . bright yellow and orange this winter. You think? And some of my circus paintings?"

"Perfect." He studied her, finding it hard to believe she was the same sad, stubborn woman he had talked to the other night. "What can I do?"

"Nothing. Just sit and talk to me, Joseph." She moved busily around the room, taking paintings down from the wall, smoothing a new bedspread on the brass bed. It was red, with a faint black stripe; Joseph marveled that in spite of the spread's brightness, it contrived to look cool. Kate was a wizard with colors.

"It's got blue in it." She grinned at him. She could also read his mind. He grinned back, as she took some pillows from a sack and scattered them in front of the bolster on the bed—the pillows were black with red and royal-blue stripes. She put one of the Wendell silver candlesticks on the chest of drawers and another on a small side table.

"Now," she said briskly, and picked up a painting propped with its face to the wall, a circus painting she had done when the children were small, and hung it above the chest of drawers. She hung her early painting of the courtyard washing in another bare space, then threw herself down on the red bed to look around. She squinted. "I think this will do."

"It'll better than do." He admired her against the background of vivid color. The royal-blue pillows made her eyes look even brighter than usual, and her face looked young and vital, framed in her brief drift of golden hair. "Kate, I feel like we've . . . got you back."

"You were right about this, Joseph. We've got to go on living, no matter what's happened. This is my symbolic letting go. No matter what I . . . feel"—her voice shook a little—"I've got to let go. I think I *imagined* Marite in that newsreel. And I'm going to stop sending her things."

They were silent, thinking of the greeting cards, the letters, and the gifts returned marked *inconnu*, "unknown."

"This house has been like a tomb because of me. I've got to get back to work."

Joseph was overjoyed; she looked renewed, vital. "Something about this room reminds me of the old place, Kate. When you first fixed it up, with the bright colors. And you look like the same Kate."

She smiled, adjusting a picture, and stepped back to judge its straightness. "I hope not. I'd make quite a sensation in the styles of 1910."

"You know what I mean."

"I do. And I thank you."

He thought: It's hard to believe she's thirty-seven. She looked very young in her funny dress with no waistline to it.

"You know," she remarked, "these are David's favorite colors. He might want this room for himself—we could put two beds in here. Then I'd have the perfect excuse to redo a whole new guestroom.''

"Good idea." Joseph looked around again with pleasure. "Speaking of David, isn't he a little late getting back from the park?''

"I don't think so," she said easily. "He said he and Jimmy Ryan might go to a picture. He'll probably call. By the way, we had quite a talk this morning. Things are a lot better, Joseph.''

"I'm so glad." He got up. "But I can't keep sitting here in idleness when you're working so hard. Where do you want the boxes and stuff?''

She told him. He hoisted two to take them to the attic, feeling a twinge when he looked at the pennant. Kate met his eyes, and he knew that both of them had assumed more cheerfulness than they felt. They would never quite get over this. But at least this way they were making a commitment to life, and not to perpetual grieving. The room was no longer a shrine.

He was halfway to the attic when he heard the doorbell, and wondered who it could be this close to dinnertime. David almost always came in through the side entrance, heading straight for the kitchen to have a wolf-size snack that would ruin anyone's appetite but his. Joseph smiled to himself as he stowed the boxes and started down the stairs again.

Faintly he heard Kate's voice and David's. And someone else's. "Mr. . . . Sweeney?" Kate sounded mystified.

Joseph went on down the rest of the stairs to the hall. An abashed David was standing there with Kate and a tall weathered-looking young fellow. He had ruffled sandy hair and the kind of eyes that would twinkle when he smiled, except that now he looked inordinately solemn. He wore a khaki shirt and trousers.

Kate introduced Joseph, but she still looked puzzled. "Please . . . come in, Mr. Sweeney. I'm afraid I don't understand exactly what this is all about.''

David shot a rather anxious glance at Joseph, who sensed trouble.

"Can I offer you a drink, Mr. Sweeney?" He flushed. It was an indiscreet question during Prohibition, when he didn't even know who the man was. "We didn't make it," he added, smiling.

"Oh, that's all right, sir." Sweeney laughed; his eyes *did* twinkle. "I'm not a federal man. I'm an aviator."

"An *aviator*?" Kate gasped, and glared at David. "From Garden City?"

"Yes, ma'am."

Joseph and Kate exchanged an exasperated glance. David had already been retrieved three times from the airfield in Garden City, where he had gone without their permission.

"That's why I'm here, ma'am." After Kate and Joseph had sat down, Sweeney sat down gingerly on the edge of a chair. He said reluctantly, "David, here . . . took one of our planes this afternoon."

"David!" Kate cried. " 'Took'?"

"Flew, Mother," David admitted.

"Oh, for God's sake," Joseph exclaimed.

"Look, I wanted to bring him home and have a talk with all of you," Sweeney said. "I told him sixteen's too young to fly, sir. We could all lose our licenses."

"Sixteen! He's fourteen," Joseph said angrily. "What kind of place do you run out there, to let a fourteen-year-old kid . . ." He stopped himself. "Well, a sixteen-year-old kid . . ."

"Lord!" Sweeney gasped. "David, you didn't tell me that." He turned to Joseph again. "We run an orderly field, sir," he said earnestly. "But one of the men slipped up today, and David took her up before we knew what had happened. Look, I'm sorry . . . both of you must know that. I assure you this won't happen again. Ever." Sweeney gave David a stern warning look. "I'm sure you'll cooperate, Mr. Barsimson."

After the man had gone, David's fearful down-at-the mouth expression melted Kate and Joseph.

"David, how did you know *how*?" Joseph couldn't help asking.

"There's nothing to it, Dad." David looked brighter. "And I really flew that little crate; I wish you could have seen me. Sweeney admitted I'm a damn good flyer."

"Well, Sweeney was right—that this won't happen again . . . for a long, long time."

His son brightened. "You mean until I'm old enough to get a license."

"Exactly."

"But, Dad, what do you think about what Sweeney said—that I'm a 'natural'?"

Joseph grinned at David. "Even if you were illegal as hell, I think I'm proud of you."

Marite wandered out of the half-empty hotel early one September morning, loitering aimlessly around the gardens. Nice was quiet this time of year. They usually came here in winter, but friends of Elizabeth's had persuaded her to come for the summer. It was still too hot in Paris to return.

Being sixteen in France was depressing. In France a well-brought-up girl was *jeune fille* until she was eighteen: a child prisoner. Marite did not feel well-brought-up today at all, and she thought how free she would be in America, by comparison. For the past several months she had been teased and tortured by peculiar emotions she knew were highly improper, emotions that had to do with boys.

Her grandmother seemed to watch her more closely than before. Marite was thankful she was still asleep. Bored with the prospect of another day like all the others and weary of the splendid monotony of the garden's cannas and palms, Marite decided to explore, even if her grandmother absolutely forbade her to go about alone.

She walked to the promenade quickly and found herself on the Quai du Midi, near some curious flat-roofed houses. The morning was hazy, not brilliant as morning usually was on the Riviera, and the sea looked gray. A great rock loomed before Marite. She climbed the big stairway that led up to the rock, discovering what seemed to be the ruins of a medieval castle, and she was thrilled.

But the ruins had been repaired and turned into a public garden; there were booths where tourist mementos were sold. The booths were shut, however, and the garden was deserted except for a few plainly dressed old people sitting on benches. Marite passed them, noticing that they looked at her with surprise; she supposed there weren't many fashionable young girls who came to this public garden alone.

She walked on to the other side of the ruins and sat down on the grass. The sun was coming out again.

"*Bonjour.*" Startled, Marite turned her head. A tall boy with dark hair, about her age, was standing a few feet away, smiling at her. He wore a carelessly buttoned white shirt and cotton trousers.

"*Bonjour.*"

She noticed that he had strange-colored eyes, almost amber.

"May I join you, *mademoiselle*?" he asked with great courtesy. He spoke with a city accent, not that of the natives of Nice.

She nodded, feeling that this had suddenly become quite an adventure. The only boys she had ever spoken to were the ones she met at carefully supervised entertainments.

The boy came toward her and sat down on the grass a little distance away from her. "I am André Schwarz-Brillon," he said, holding out his hand.

Timidly she shook it. "My name is Marite Wendell." He held her hand just a moment longer, then released it. "You have a very . . . unusual name."

"I keep both my parents' names. Schwarz was my mother's maiden name." He looked into her eyes, and she was charmed by the odd color of his. "My mother is Jewish."

Something made her say, "So was my father."

"And yet your name is Wendell. That is interesting." He sounded curious in a friendly, uncritical way.

"My grandmother adopted me when my parents died."

"I see." André Schwarz-Brillon drew up his long legs and clasped his knees with his hands. His arms, below his rolled-up shirtsleeves, were deeply tanned and muscular. Marite experienced an odd discomfort, looking at his arms. She had never seen anyone look so elegant in clothes like that, nor had she ever spoken so openly to a perfect stranger. In fact, she hadn't spoken to a stranger at all since they'd come to Europe.

"You're staying at one of the Cimiez hotels." He made it sound like a statement, not a question.

"Yes. How did you know that?"

He laughed. "A young foreign lady who looks like you, and speaks Parisian French, could hardly be staying anywhere else."

"Do you live in Paris?"

"No. Bordeaux." He smiled to see her expression. By now she had learned to recognize at once the French of the "boulevards," and that was the way he spoke. "My mother is a teacher," he explained, "and cured me of my accent. My father makes wine."

She did not know what to say then, and they sat in silence for a time, both of them looking ahead at the ruins of the castle. Finally he lay back in the grass with a contented sigh. "It is very peaceful here."

"Yes. But it is quiet enough at the hotel."

"Not among my family," he said wryly. "I have a brother and two sisters, and we're always fighting."

"That sounds wonderful." She couldn't hide the wistfulness in her comment; just now she longed so for the old days on MacDougal Street, the racket when she and David had quarreled, even for the loud enthusiasm of her Uncle Rafael, her grandmother Anzia's emotional outbursts. Her longing surprised her.

"You have no brothers or sisters?"

"I have a brother, in America."

"And he is not with you and your grandmother." André had a way of expressing curiosity with such gentleness that Marite had a desire to tell him everything. She couldn't understand how this could be so; yet it was. Perhaps it was because his dark hair, his sharp features, his strong leanness brought back memories of her father.

Marite began to talk to him; astonished, she realized that she had told him almost everything about herself. She stopped, chagrined: it was very rude and ill-bred to talk about oneself for so long.

Flushing, she said so, concluding, "I'm sorry."

"Nonsense." André sat up in the grass and, moving near her, took her hand. She knew that was very improper, too, and tried to disengage it. "Nonsense," he repeated. "You don't talk very much to people, do you?"

He knew so much, she thought, without being told. "No. Usually there's just my grandmother, and my governess. And the servants, and people I don't . . . know well." She felt tears gather in her eyes.

"People you don't care for, you mean?"

André pressed her hand, and she felt a different kind of warmth, a feeling she had never had before. A prickling hotness, a kind of ache. "I'm sorry. I'm sorry if I made you cry. Please don't."

His face was near hers and the amber color of his eyes seemed to blot out the very sky. His skin smelled like the pine trees in the sun, and as she lifted her chin, his mouth was almost touching her mouth.

He had put his hands on her shoulders, and they felt warm too, through the thinness of her blouse, as he lowered his head slowly, very slowly, and brushed his lips against hers. A mysterious heat seemed to shoot from her mouth right down to the middle of her body, like a shock of lightning, and then his mouth was on hers, over hers. She was being kissed for the first time in her life.

André drew back again, as quietly and slowly as he had kissed her; he was smiling and his eyes had a tender look that she remembered from long ago in her father's eyes.

"You have never been kissed before," he said softly, but it was not teasing, or a reproach. It was spoken with a kind of wonder, and he still held her upper arms in his strong hands with their long, narrow fingers.

"No," she admitted.

"It's nothing to be ashamed of. Now you have been. And now"— he kissed her again—"you have been kissed twice." The last kiss was different from the first—lighter, almost like the wing of a butterfly brushing her mouth.

"Would you like to take a walk around Nice?" he asked her, and the way he asked didn't sound abrupt or strange at all. It sounded simply as though he would like to give her pleasure. She liked that; in fact, she was glad, because she didn't have the slightest idea now what to say or do after he had kissed her. She only knew that she wanted to be with him awhile longer . . . a lot longer.

"Oh, yes. I *would*."

He sprang up and held out his hand to help her up. When she took it, she felt that incomprehensible warmth, that odd delight again. But then he didn't touch her anymore, preceding her down the stone stairs because they were steep, walking companionably by her side through the little streets.

This was a Nice she did not know; they were on a street with many restaurants, not the kind Marite was used to, but homely places. A menu, with prices, was fixed to each door. The blinds were open so passersby could see the brightness inside, the small tables with their clean white cloths.

André paused before one whose sign announced it as the Restaurant d'Espagne. "Let's try this one." he turned to Marite for approval. "It has Spanish food."

"Oh, yes! I've never tasted Spanish food."

"*Bien*. Then you will have another new experience." He smiled down at her, and her face felt warm around her ears; he was talking about the kiss. The kisses.

The little restaurant was full of working people in rough, plain clothes, speaking with the inflection of the Niçois;

Marite had heard that accent only from a distance before, when their car had stopped to wait for a passing wagon, or when the gardeners working in the hotel grounds had called out to each other.

André chose a table by the window. Near the table was a small canary, cheeping in its intricate cage; creeping vines were planted in other cages.

André looked at her. "You remind me of the little golden bird with your yellow hair, locked away from the world."

She marveled at that. No one she had ever met had talked like that. Except, perhaps, for her Great-Grandfather Dryver, whom she recalled dimly as a genial dark presence in the garden on Eleventh Street. A memory returned to her—her father laughing, teasing her mother, saying, "You sound like your grandfather. I've never heard anyone say the things he does."

Marite hadn't thought of her great-grandfather in years; she was astonished at the sudden rush of memories. She couldn't have been more than nine or ten when that happened. It was André who had caused all this.

"What are you thinking about, *petit oiseau*?" What was more astonishing was that his intimate tone seemed so natural to her, when she had known him only for a matter of hours.

"My great-grandfather."

"Your *great*-grandfather!" André's dark brows shot up. "He must have been an enormous age."

She nodded. "His name was Harry Dryver."

André looked awed. "But he is a famous painter. I know of him. Why, there are several paintings of his on exhibit in Paris. Of course you have seen them."

Marite hadn't, but she was ashamed to say so. Her grandmother and her governess had taken her only to the Academy and to the Louvre. She could hardly connect that genial, distant presence with paintings on exhibit in Paris. Someday she would go to see them.

The leisurely waiter appeared to take their order. Andre

told him to bring them something called *paella*; the waiter placed a carafe of white table wine and two thick glasses on the table. "This is only the *vin du pays*," André said, "but it's not bad." He grinned. "Though my father would say otherwise." He poured their wine.

Marite was not allowed to have wine with meals—her grandmother said it was not customary before a girl was eighteen—but she had had a glass sometimes on festive occasions and holidays. To be drinking it now, simply at luncheon, was another high adventure. She sipped it gingerly; it had a rather tart but stimulating taste. "It's good," she said, and drank some more.

The *paella* was good too, and Marite found that she was quite hungry. André seemed to enjoy her enjoyment, as she drank two more glasses of the pale wine, feeling her spirits soar.

"When will you return to Paris?" André asked her.

"Perhaps next week, or when the heat is over. And you?"

"We will return to Bordeaux in a few days." He looked doleful. "Next year I will come to Paris to go to the university, though. May I write to you?"

Her heart thudded. "Of course."

Eagerly he fumbled in his pocket. Then he put his hand to his forehead. "I am *fou*. I have no pen or paper. Do you?"

She shook her head, and he made a sign to the waiter.

Marite was feeling very light-headed. "André, I want to ask you something . . . What happened to our *noses*?"

"Our noses?" He was bewildered. "What do you mean?"

She leaned over and whispered, "When you . . . kissed me. Where did they go? Why didn't they bump into each other?"

André stared at her a moment; then he began to laugh.

"You're laughing at me." She was afraid she was going to cry.

"No, *no*." He took her hand. "It is just so . . . charming." His amber eyes had that tender expression again.

"The secret is—I simply turned my head to the side, you see."

The waiter was coming toward their table, when there was a commotion at the door. A policeman was talking to the proprietor, who was waving his hands excitedly, protesting with vigor: "This is insupportable. What is the meaning of this intrusion?"

The policeman made a placating gesture and said something in a low voice to the proprietor. Then, looking around the restaurant, he saw Marite and André and came toward them.

"You are Mademoiselle Wendell?"

Marite nodded.

"Please, then, will you come with me?"

"But why?" she demanded. André was on his feet, glaring.

"Your grandmother, Madame Wendell, is extremely perturbed. We have been scouring the city for you, in the fear that you had been abducted."

"Abducted!" André was furious. "Look here . . ."

"You have identification?" the policeman inquired curtly.

"Of course I don't!" André scoffed. "No one carries identification when he just goes out for a walk."

"What is your name?"

"André Schwarz-Brillon. I am staying with my family on the Promenade des Anglais."

"Ah! That is a very different matter, *monsieur*. I ask your pardon. All the same I fear the *mademoiselle* must let me take her back to the hotel."

"No!" Marite almost screamed the word at him. Everyone was staring at them now.

"Please, *mademoiselle*. I beg of you. You have only sixteen years, and you must understand that you are under the jurisdiction, therefore, of your grandmother. You must come with me."

Marite looked at André. He looked miserable, but he shrugged. "He is right. Neither of us has any power in this matter."

Marite got to her feet, resigned. "Then I will say good-bye, André." She held out her hand.

He took and held it, looking into her eyes. "No, Marite. Only *au revoir*."

She followed the policeman from the little restaurant and got into the back of his car. When it pulled away from the curb, she looked back. André was running after the car, waving his arms and shouting something.

He had never gotten her address in Paris.

But, she consoled herself, he might be able to get it from the hotel. It had all happened so quickly she had hardly had time to gauge her feelings. But they overwhelmed her now, and the strongest one was a burning indignation. Elizabeth was treating her like an intractable little girl, and she was almost a woman. It would have been so different in America.

With a light, respectful touch on her elbow, the policeman steered her into the lobby of the hotel, where Elizabeth was waiting with an exasperated face.

She rose and came toward them. "Marite, where have you been?"

"It is all right, *madame*." The policeman smiled at Elizabeth. "Your granddaughter was in a restaurant with a perfectly respectable young man, a certain André Schwarz-Brillon. His father is the noted wine producer of Bordeaux."

"*Schwarz*-Brillon, you say?" Elizabeth stiffened. The policeman assented and bowed to her, but her lips were tight and sour with disapproval. She thanked him coldly. He bowed again and went off.

"You picked up acquaintance with a total stranger?" Elizabeth took Marite by the arm.

"Yes!" Marite said defiantly. "And I had a wonderful time—a better time than I've ever had with you!"

Shocked, her grandmother recoiled. "You have *wine* on your breath. I think that you are . . . drunk," she whispered with horror. "You're coming upstairs with me, *now*."

"I don't want to go back to Paris," Marite cried out, beginning to sob. "I want to go back to America."

"Be quiet. You don't know what you're saying. We're not going back to Paris. We're going to the country, today. And we're going to stay there until October . . . or until you come to your senses."

October.

If André should write her in Paris, Marite thought in despair, he would not get an answer. She had a feeling she was never going to see him or hear from him again.

Chapter 19

When Kate looked back over the three turbulent years before David's seventeenth birthday in 1930, she often wondered how she had survived them. The answer was always Joseph. After two decades together, she could still look at him, and their marriage, as something of a miracle. He was the only constant in a country and a world of continuous, violent change, a whirl of anxiety-provoking events.

She wondered, too, how she had contrived to become the Kate Barsimson whose paintings now received increasing notice. During the economic disaster of 1929, which had depressed art sales alarmingly, Kate and other artists had formed an Artists' Union which demanded federal support for art. The union had not been wholly successful, especially for those artists like Kate who were mavericks in the new milieu of "social art," which she considered no more significant than crude propaganda posters. Like the independent Georgia O'Keeffe, Kate had continued to lean toward formalism without fully discarding realistic elements.

This year, artists' money problems were producing novel events in New York. Semiannual outdoor shows would establish an informal art market in Washington Square.

Her course had been a lonely one: other artists resented not only her rejection of "pure" social art but also the fact that she and Joseph had weathered the Depression with comparative ease because of the canny foresight of Wen-dell advisers. In 1928 her mother's lawyer had urged her to let him appoint Kate administratrix of certain portions of the estate; Elizabeth's absence was complicating matters unduly. He managed after some sharp maneuvers to have it done; Kate refused to enjoy the full proceeds of the estate, which were still held in trust for Elizabeth, but she consented to take the ten-percent administratrix fee to defray expenses. The great mausoleum on Madison Ave-nue had been sold. But even the modest ten percent was large, and with the remains of Dryver's estate, and the proceeds from pre-Depression sales of some of his valu-able paintings, Kate and Joseph found themselves secure while others faced hardship.

And yet Kate had had to enclose herself in a kind of protective shell, shutting the world out, to do her work. She went doggedly on with it, despite the graver matters that faced them all—the troubles in Joseph's union, the growing threat of Nazism throughout Europe and in Amer-ica, and always, her worry about David. There was so much to cope with that at times she almost forgot they had ever had a daughter.

Despite all Joseph's enthusiasm and support, Kate knew well that her work could hardly have the same meaning for him. In the four years since the union had taken over the wreckage of the cloakmaker strike, proceeding slowly and painfully to rebuild on the shambles, it was a wonder to Joseph that the union had achieved a kind of order. Com-munists had continued to hamper and obstruct the union, but they had been defeated. Last year the formation of a needle-trades organization had marked the end of Commu-nist disruption. But the ravages of that internal war were still being felt. Joseph was elected executive vice-president in 1928, and he brought back exceptional leadership to the union. But then the great crash of 1929 struck hard at the industry; Communist sabotage and scabbery went on. And enrollment was declining.

Worse than that, Joseph told her, the Jewish trade-union

movement in America was offering no more than a conventional response to the global Nazi threat. Both the
Zionists and labor were contenting themselves with impro-
vised, sporadic action.

Early this year, Kate was dismayed to learn, David had
involved himself in something almost as dangerous as
flying—forays into political meetings in the company of
rash young men Joseph called "wildcat Zionists." On
several occasions David had come home with cuts and
bruises, a split lip, and his clothes in tatters.

To top it off, their ostrichlike preoccupation of the last
few years was being dispelled by a gnawing terror—their
daughter was still in Europe, and they didn't even know
what country. Kate was haunted by the notion of Marite's
being in Germany; she recalled her mother's sentimental
attachment to that nation. Kate remembered her grandfather mentioning it before he died—his comment that it was
an attachment he had never shared.

That memory was like a dark cloud as Kate let herself
into the house that May afternoon, the day of David's
birthday. They were planning a party for him that night,
and she was laden with varicolored balloons, already blown
up and held by their numerous strings, and a bag full of
other decorations and favors. She had even bought some
toy airplanes, as a kind of apology for all the nagging she
had done during the past year when she suspected David
might be illegally flying.

She thought: I still miss Letha every time I step in this
house. The failing woman, who was nearly ninety, had
become too tired and old to work any longer. They had
insisted on her living with them for the last two years, as a
guest. Then last winter she had expressed a sudden, surprising wish to "go back south to see my people one more
time." It had broken Kate's heart to see her go; it was the
end of an era. Letha was still alive, but they knew she
wouldn't be much longer.

Kate squared her shoulders; she had to stop thinking all
these gloomy thoughts or David's birthday would be a

disaster. With the help of the maid, she started putting up the planes and the balloons.

A little later, when she was going to her room to change, she caught sight of a white rectangle on David's bed, through the open door. Puzzled, she went in and saw that it was a sheet of paper.

"Mother," the letter ran, "please forgive me. I've been given a chance I may never have again, to do barnstorm flying all over the country. I told them I'm nineteen, and they believed me."

They would, Kate decided bitterly. David was already as tall as Joseph and he looked far older than his age.

Trembling, she read on: "You and Dad can stop me, I know, if you want to, but I beg you not to. If I can't fly, I'd just as soon be dead. I know this is an awful time to run out on you, with my birthday and everything, but I had to go, because they wanted me to leave this afternoon. I'll let you hear from me, wherever we go. I hope you believe how much I love you, and Dad, and always will."

It was signed simply "David."

Kate was crying so hard that she could hardly make out his name. Her tears fell on the paper, and the ink started running. She set it aside, because she must show it to Joseph. It might be the last letter he ever wrote them.

She rocked back and forth in a paroxysm of grieving rage, thinking: Is there never any end? Is there never any peace? After all the trouble and exhaustion, the worry and work and pain, when they had just begun to rebuild their strength to cope with all that faced them, she might lose her other child.

She lay down on David's bed and cried it out.

Joseph found her there when the light was beginning to fail.

"What's happened?"

Kate sat up, wiping her swollen eyes. She held out the letter to him. He took it from her, scanning it rapidly where he stood. Kate saw his mouth relax with stupefaction, his skin turn muddy with shock.

"Oh, God." He sat down beside her on the bright-colored bedspread, staring at the letter. "Kate. Kate, the ink's all . . . run. Poor thing, poor darling."

Joseph let the letter fall and put his arm around her, pulling her tousled head down against his chest. They sat for a while in silence as he stroked her, rocking her a little to comfort her.

"Joseph, what are we going to do?"

"The first thing we're going to do is go downstairs and have a drink. I could use one, couldn't you?" His voice was tightly controlled, but she could hear the tiredness, the devastation in it.

"Yes." When she got up from the bed, she felt as if she had aged in the slender space of the last hour. Joseph retrieved the letter from the rug and they went dowstairs.

"Thank the Lord for your grandfather's cellar," he remarked, pouring a sherry for her and a whiskey for himself. "Sit down, Kate. You look done in."

She sipped her sherry, set the glass on a table, and sprawled on the gray couch by the window that had replaced the old "Baghdad corner" of Dryver's heyday, leaning back against the purple and orange cushions scattered there.

Joseph swallowed his whiskey at a gulp and joined her.

She closed her eyes and ran her fingers through her short, ruffled hair. "Joseph, what *are* we going to do?"

"Nothing."

"What?" Kate's eyes blinked open. "You can't mean it."

"I do mean it. You read the letter, darling. He meant it when he said he'd 'just as soon be dead' as quit flying." The smile he gave her was worse than no smile at all; it was more like a grimace.

"But good heavens, he's only a kid."

"He's been a man for four years already, according to Jewish tradition." Joseph spoke quietly but she knew that intonation, that conclusive voice she had heard him use before. "David's thought of almost nothing else since he

was ten or eleven years old, Kate. We can't deny him this
. . . as crazy, as dangerous as it may appear.''

" 'Appear'?'' she mocked him. ''Why, you said yourself those planes are like orange crates! How can you even
think of letting him do this?'' She jumped up from the
couch and paced the carpet, scowling at the ironic gaiety
of the bright balloons, the small toy planes. Angrily she
reached out and jerked one of the planes from its string,
throwing it to the floor. She stamped on the toy with a
childish vengeance, listening to the crack of the frail bal-
sam wood, and burst into tears again.

Joseph got up and grabbed her, holding her tightly
against him. When her sobs had abated he lifted her wet
face to his and kissed her. His glittering black eyes were
soft with compassion.

Finally he said, ''Do you remember how old I was when
I organized the jacket workers, Kate? I was twelve. And
for years before that I'd already been carrying bundles to
the factories, and pulling threads and sweeping up on
Essex Street. My father wanted to stop me, too, but I
never let him. I was fourteen when I won my first prize-
fight. David knows all that; what do you think he's going
to say if I try to find him and stop him? He's going to tell
me that I don't think he's the man I am.''

Listening, she relaxed a little. There was so much truth
in what Joseph said, although she was still aware his
arguments were specious. And she thought, with the first
flash of humor that day: This is his famous gift of gab . . .
the talent for persuasion that's won the union so much all
these years.

''I'm not convinced,'' she murmured, ''in spite of your
silver oratory, Joseph Barsimson. But I also know it's
pointless to argue with you now. Your mind's made up
and you don't want to be confused with banal facts.''

He leaned back and looked down at her; she couldn't
help the smile that twitched at the corner of her mouth.

''I knew you'd listen to reason.'' He grinned at her;
then he sobered. ''Look here, darling, I know it's a dan-

gerous game. But so were the young Zionists; so are football and diving from a diving board. And driving a car. All we can do is hope, since we don't pray.''

"I may take it up," she threatened. "All right, you've won your point." She gave him a mock slap on the cheek.

"I'm not as happy as I sound, you know. I knew he'd have to go away sometime . . . but I didn't think it would be this soon."

Kate sighed. "Neither did I." Then she said in a brisk, businesslike way, "I've got to start phoning, or we're going to have a houseful of guests tonight."

"And tonight," he said, caressing her face with his palms, "I don't want any guests. I want to start our next honeymoon . . . the first one we've had since 1924, remember?" Holding her face between his hands, he kissed her for a long, long moment.

"I remember." Whatever else they lost, they had each other.

For months after their meeting in Nice, André was seldom absent from Marite's thoughts. At first she waited each day for a letter from him, convinced he must have gotten their Paris address from the hotel on the Riviera. But no letter came, although Marite was careful to intercept the postman, fearful that her grandmother might confiscate any letter from André Schwarz-Brillon.

In desperation she addressed a letter to him in November, directed simply to him at "Bordeaux," not very hopeful that it would reach him. The letter was returned a few weeks later marked "Refused."

Marite was devastated. Crumpling the letter in her hand, she fled to her room. It was inconceivable that the gentle, concerned boy she had met in Nice could refuse her letter. Then it occurred to her, in a sudden flash of perception, that his parents might have confiscated her letter, as her own grandmother would likely conceal André's from Marite. There must have been talk in Nice, after the policeman brought Marite back to the hotel. And the Schwarz-Brillons would be no more eager than Elizabeth for Marite and André to know each other.

Marite became so despondent and thin that Elizabeth was alarmed about her health. It was time to seek a warmer climate again, she declared, and whisked Marite off to Italy.

By the next summer the image of André was fading; after her brief rebellion, Marite found herself becoming resigned to what her life had to be. But there was one important difference: she discovered that whenever she wanted her own way, the swiftest means of getting it was to tell Elizabeth that she wanted to go back to America. Inevitably Elizabeth came to heel.

When Marite complained that she was bored with her governess and that she had had enough of studies, Elizabeth dismissed the governess and conceded that Marite was quite "finished" enough to take her place in the fashionable world. Marite was fluent in French now, could converse reasonably well in German, and had even picked up a little Spanish and Italian in their travels.

Elizabeth had also relaxed the ban on *haute couture* clothes before the age of eighteen. By the time she was seventeen Marite had developed a passion for clothes; a midinette in one of the great dress houses told Marite, "*Mademoiselle* is better than *chic*, she has *élégance*." There was nothing quite so impressive, Marite decided, as the drawn-out sound, in French, of that prized compliment.

Over the next two years Marite began to discover in herself an odd duality: on the one hand, she looked as mature as a woman of twenty-five, with her highly developed breasts and curving body lines, her sophisticated apparel. On the other, her inexperience and fears turned her emotions inward; she had reverted to the fantasies and naive expectations of a thirteen-year-old.

This blend, apparently, created havoc in the hearts of the young men she met in those years—the stiff, correct young men of Elizabeth's world. But the young men made little impression on Marite. Her grandmother was overjoyed to observe her fastidiousness, her lack of response. What Elizabeth did not know was that no one since André had been able to arouse Marite's deepest longings. The man who could had not yet appeared to her.

Then in the spring of 1931, Marite sat in a box of the Berlin Comic Opera beside Elizabeth, surrounded by the sweetness of Lehár's music. The operetta was *The Land of Smiles*, which had a certain kinship to her favorite, *The Student Prince*, recalled from so long ago in New York.

Suddenly she remembered the disparaging comments her father had made about that romantic operetta. André had reminded her of her father—she hadn't thought of either of them in almost four years. But now the memory of André's clean male scent, his golden eyes, was so poignant that she was stricken with longing for a male presence in her life. Marite's breath quickened, and she fingered the lustrous pearls around her neck, the flawless pearls Elizabeth had given her for her twentieth birthday.

She thought of the men she had rejected: the French count, the British lord, even an Italian prince. Her grandmother had applauded the rejections. The young count was too much addicted to women, the lord had Communist sympathies, and the prince, like all his "race," Elizabeth concluded, was too mercenary and unstable. Here in Berlin, a city to which her grandmother was very attached, the men certainly looked wonderful.

Marite thought uneasily of their politics, but the tangle of European alliances and quarrels was a muddle to her, and a bore. Apparently Elizabeth did not have too clear a grasp of politics either. She called Hitler a "vulgar little man" and said he would get nowhere in government. The aristocratic Prussians would never allow the rabble to take over their country.

Anyway, at the moment, politics was the last thing on Marite's mind. The music was deeply affecting; she could feel it in the very center of her body.

Then she saw him, right there below her in the audience. The most beautiful young man on earth—and he was staring up at her. He wore his evening suit like a uniform. His hair was a lighter blond than Marite's, cut *en brosse* in the Prussian style; and his eyes were a stunning ice blue against his ruddy skin. Marite recalled something she'd read in a romantic novel of Elizabeth's: "the dark-eyed ever hunger for the fair."

The man was regal, lean as a whipcord, and he towered over his companions. He even had a scar, like a large crescent, extending from the middle of his left eye, down his cheek. It had to be a Heidelberg dueling scar. Marite's heart hammered so hard she was afraid it might be visible under the clinging white satin of her Lanvin dress, or in the very hollow of her ears, below her drawn-back hair. He was exactly like the "student prince."

At the intermission he disappeared, and Marite felt inordinately dismayed.

"The new operetta is charming," Elizabeth murmured. She raised her silver opera glass to her eyes and surveyed the theater.

Marite heard the slight rustle of parting draperies behind them and turned her head. The beautiful young man was standing there, framed in the wine-red velvet; his pale-blue eyes met her dark ones, and his hair was like winter sun.

"By your leave," he said. Elizabeth turned too, and smiled with recognition.

"Guten aben." He bowed, and there was a perceptible click of the heels. "Frau Wendell, I trust you may remember me. We were introduced at the home of Colonel von Lagen. Oberleutnant Rudi von Durning."

"Of course, Lieutenant. Your cousin is a dear friend of my own cousin, Madame Boerum. May I present my granddaughter, Fräulein Marite Wendell."

Rudi von Durning bowed again, with the same sharp click of his patent-leather heels, and Marite offered him her hand. He pressed his lips to her fingers, and even through her glove's white kid she was aware of the warmth of his mouth. There was a tiny, bubbling roar in her ears, like a miniature sea, and she felt a quick rush of blood to her face.

"*Fräulein,*" he murmured. The word had a peculiar softness but with it a lingering strength, conjuring up images she could barely comprehend—a tempo of the act of love which she had perceived in Wagner's music, that act she did not know.

He straightened to his imposing height and spoke courteously to Elizabeth. "Are you enjoying *The Land of Smiles*?"

"This country *is* my 'land of smiles,' Lieutenant von Durning." Elizabeth fairly simpered. It was obvious to Marite that her grandmother approved of him; she seldom put herself out to be pleasant to anyone.

"I had hardly expected to be entertained by wit, when so much beauty is reward enough." He complimented them both with a glance. It was a stilted little tribute, the kind of thing nobody said in 1931, Marite decided. But all the same it made him seem even more appealing, as if he lived in another century. And he was so clumsily masculine.

Marite was hard put to concentrate when von Durning asked for her impressions of Berlin. When the intermission was ending, he inquired if Elizabeth would let him take them to supper. She quickly consented.

In her state of high excitement, Marite had no appetite at all and talked little. But Rudi von Durning seemed to find that charming, like everything she did. When he took them back to their hotel, the famous Adlon on the Unter den Linden, he was obviously impressed with their choice. He asked to call on them the next afternoon, offering to drive them on a tour of the city.

Again Elizabeth agreed readily. Marite wondered why.

In their suite, she found out. Elizabeth gloated, "You've made a conquest. Rudi will be the next Baron von Durning. The family is a very old one; they have a *schloss*, a castle, near Königsberg, greater than the Hindenburgs'. Now you see what you missed that day . . . when you said you'd be 'bored' at the von Lagens'."

Marite had never seen her grandmother so excited before. But then, she had never been so excited about someone, either.

"You are very quiet, Marite. Don't you like him?"

"Of course I do . . . very much. But we only met
tonight. I can't know how he . . . really feels about me."
Marite could hardly believe that Rudi von Durning had felt
as deeply as she had. It seemed too good to be true.

"Nonsense! He was definitely smitten. Mark my word,
my darling, he will be your prince. I'm sure of it."

Rudi von Durning appeared at the appointed instant the
next afternoon, with a bouquet of flowers for each of
them. The roses he presented to Marite happened to be the
exact shade of her elegant suit, designed by the eccentric
young Chanel. "What a pleasing coincidence," he remarked, meeting her eyes under the shadow of her rakish
black hat.

He handed them into a magnificent sky-blue open car,
trimmed with black, extremely smart with its white-sided
tires. He fussed over Elizabeth's comfort in the rear seat
and opened the front door for Marite. She found his nearness even more disturbing than it had been last night. As
they drove off down the famous avenue lined with its
slender linden trees, she stole admiring glances at his
profile, on the pretext of observing the sights beyond him.
He was even handsomer by the light of day with his clear,
ruddy skin, marked only by the titillating flaw of the scar.
His eyes looked gray above his fine gray suit, and his
cropped hair was gold in the gentle sun.

The statues and buildings of Berlin had never looked so
lovely to her before; she had always preferred Paris and
London. But in Rudi's presence the cathedrals became
storied castles; the small side streets of workers' pointed
whitewashed houses, the old flower ladies in the Pots-
damerplatz were like the drawings from a storybook.

When she mentioned that to Rudi, he smiled. "You
have pleasant fancies. If Berlin strikes you like this, you
will be enchanted by our *schloss* in Prussia. Von Durnings

have lived there for nearly three hundred years. Perhaps you will stay there, later this summer. At this time of year my family is still in Berlin.''

They lunched at an outdoor beer garden. He asked Elizabeth, ''Would you honor me by visiting my family tomorrow? The house is near your hotel, on the Unter den Linden.''

Elizabeth beamed. ''We would be delighted, wouldn't we, Marite?''

''Of course.'' Yet Marite wasn't too sure she would be delighted. Rudi was one thing, but his family might be another.

They were invited for tea. Marite rejected one dress after the other, finally choosing a Lanvin afternoon dress with a creamy chiffon blouse and flared godets set into the brown crepe skirt. The blouse was almost the shade of her hair, and the long graceful jacket to the dress, matching the chocolate brown of the skirt, made her eyes look lustrous. As always she had a difficult time fitting the small brown skullcap over her luxuriant hair; the current hats cried out for a bob. However, she was glad she hadn't cut her hair; she had noticed Rudi's admiring glance at it.

Elizabeth was elegant in an ensemble of black crepe and bronze silk and a close-fitting black hat that almost hid her graying hair.

They learned that the von Durning town house was only four blocks away; nevertheless Rudi insisted on driving them there in his long pale-blue car. He complimented their clothes: ''This is like a visit to the Ruc de la Paix,'' but his glance lingered longest on Marite, taking her in from head to foot.

When they parked in front of a wide four-story mansion, she was oppressed by its gloomy liver-colored facade, even more so when they were admitted by a servant into a dim, overfurnished hall. The man, whose eyes and eyebrows were so light he seemed to be perpetually surprised, informed them stiffly that the *Baron* and *Baronin* were with the family in the salon.

He drew aside a massive, heavily carved set of double doors and they entered a huge room that was dimmer, if anything, than the hall. The windows were shrouded with dark-blue drapes, shutting out the sun, and pale lamps were already lit, although the dark had not yet come.

The manservant announced them as if it were a formal reception; Marite blinked a little. There were two men in the room, who rose to their feet as soon as the three entered, and three women.

Rudi bowed. "May I present my mother, the *Baronin*." This of course was the older woman, a hawkish-looking, slender, feminine version of Rudi. "My sister, Irmgarde" —the sister was a faded copy of her mother, with a rather pinched mouth. "My sister-in-law, Helge von Durning."

Helge was the greatest surprise of all; she had a bold red mouth and heavy-lidded hazel eyes the color of her short, shining bob. She was lounging in a high-backed chair and Marite noticed with shock that she wore very little under her blouse. But she smiled at the visitors with more warmth than the other women, regarding Marite with strong interest and something else Marite could not quite define; something that was almost pity. She was startlingly *chic*.

Her expression was so puzzling that Marite almost failed to acknowledge the last introductions to the baron and Rudi's brother, Friedrich.

She could see at once that Friedrich was a nonentity, which made the exotic Helge even more puzzling. They were oddly matched.

Marite made her observations swiftly as they took their places around the tea table while the baroness uttered some pleasantry about "English high tea." If she resembled a predatory bird, the baron was positively fearsome. He was seated now, but he still seemed immensely tall, a few inches taller than Rudi, who was well over six feet in height. The baron's mouth was a thin line which was sinister when he smiled. He regarded Marite with gray eyes so light she wondered if he could be going blind—

until the eyes, set close to his beakish nose, penetrated her like an X ray.

Seven years of European society had not left her easily intimidated, but this baron was a different matter. Marite was glad that her grandmother, the baroness, and Irmgarde carried most of the conversation; to talk much with the baron or Friedrich would be heavy going. Friedrich was amiable but silent; it occurred to Marite that the sleepy-eyed Helge must be generally bored to death in this company. At the moment, though, a veiled amusement touched her impudent face. And she cast an envious eye over Marite's slender Lanvin ensemble.

Marite was most sharply conscious of Rudi, standing behind her chair. His big hand rested with seeming negligence near her shoulder, but when she leaned back now and then, or changed her position slightly, she came into contact with that hand. She was astounded at the effect of his touch on her clothed skin: light as it was, it burned like fire.

She could not even see him, but his nearness was so powerful that in her mind's eye she clearly saw his blue stare fixed on the mass of gathered hair at the back of her neck. Marite was vibrant with his awareness of her, and for one incredible moment she yearned for him to stoop down, take off her small hat, and freeing her hair of its pins, run his hands through the long golden strands.

It was the strangest thought she had ever had. Her senses' long sleep, disturbed only once and so long ago by the innocent caress of André, was at an end. Almost fearful that the others could read her emotions, Marite deliberately leaned forward and picked up her cup of tea in its fragile saucer. Her face stung with heat and confusion.

When she lifted her eyes from the cup, she met those of the *Baronin* over the rim. The old woman's look was amiable, approving.

She murmured to Elizabeth, "I admire your views, Frau Wendell, and I heartily concur with them. Both the baron and I miss the days when Berlin was only a great, not a world city. It is regrettable that a world city includes so much that is unspeakable. The old traditions are dying. We are witnessing the spiritual death of Berlin, perhaps of Germany.''

"When men like this ruffian Hitler are becoming admired,'' Rudi commented. The timbre of his voice, so close behind her, thrilled Marite; she was hardly listening to the sense of the words. Now an odd chill succeeded the warmth of a moment ago.

"Exactly," said the baroness. "And to think what they plan to do with the East Prussian estates—''

"I think," the baron cut in hastily, eyeing his wife, "we should wait and see how that cat jumps, as the British say.'' The baroness flushed slightly, and Marite wondered why. There was some mystery here. Perhaps, though, it was only her lack of fluency in the language.

The baroness quickly changed the subject. "In any case, you understand us capitally, Frau Wendell. And I must say, it is good to meet a young girl like your granddaughter in such benighted times. Girls of such modesty and quietness are rare these days." She shot an annoyed look at Helge, whose eyes were glazed with boredom. Marite thought: The *Baronin* is discussing me as if I were ten years old; and surely Helge must have heard these sermons many times, to judge from her expression.

The unspoken addition to the baroness's statement— "especially an American''—trembled on the old woman's lips. Marite caught Helge's eye; the hint of a smile curved her bold red mouth.

But Marite ceased to follow the conversation at all. It was most convenient if her "quietness" impressed Rudi's parents, because she wasn't the least interested in the state of the world. All she could think of now was the resonant pull of Rudi's closeness, and hope that this evening they might contrive to be alone.

In a few moments Elizabeth rose, thanking the von Durnings for their hospitality, and there was a sedate flurry of good-byes. When Rudi delivered them at the hotel, he kissed Elizabeth's hand and cajoled her, "Would you trust this young lady to me for an evening at the theater?"

Elizabeth pretended to hesitate, but Marite knew that she would grant Rudi permission.

Later, dressed for the evening, Marite dismissed the maid and stared at herself in the looking glass. Her dark eyes blazed with anticipation; she knew she had never looked better, in her golden gown, with her golden, high-dressed hair.

She knew . . . she knew that Rudi would kiss her tonight.

And she hoped that his kiss would be only the beginning.

Four months later, the baron heard a familiar step in the hall and looked up from his book. His elder son strode through the open door of the library, grinning.

"Well, Rudolf? You look as if you have made progress."

"Better than that." Rudi went to the Buhl cabinet and poured himself a Scotch whiskey. "I have finally proposed marriage, and she has accepted."

" 'Finally'? Good God in heaven, my boy. You are a phenomenon." The baron's book, bound in tooled leather, fell from his knees to the Persian carpet. He retrieved it tenderly; it was a first edition. "The Americans are truly mad. But you've done splendidly, boy. I never dreamed you could move this quickly."

Rudi drained his whiskey. "She is mad about *me*. Will you join me?"

The baron shook his proud head, shaped exactly like his son's, and chuckled. "No, I thank you. Now, stop prancing around and tell me about it. When is the wedding to be?"

"I will tell you all about it at breakfast," Rudi said impatiently. "Some of the fellows are waiting for me at the White Mouse. Don't you think I deserve some relaxation? It's been a bore, squiring her and the old woman about."

"Ah!" The baron was wistful. "The White Mouse? Is that the cabaret where the young women dance naked?"

Rudi nodded.

"Remarkable. You have all the advantages these days. We could find nothing like that outside a brothel when I was a boy. Well, you must postpone your delights for a half-hour. If I have to wait until morning, I'll have apoplexy. Sit down and tell me."

Rudi sat down on the arm of a chair. "There's nothing much to tell yet. I have to see the old woman in the morning. No doubt she will make a great fuss over settlements and trousseaux, all the usual feminine nonsense."

"The settlement, my boy, is hardly nonsense," the baron retorted. "Maria von Lagen knows for a fact that Madame Wendell is indecently rich; Maria claims she got it from Kopf, the banker, when he was in his cups. The old woman transferred a staggering fortune from Kopf's bank to Swiss accounts. She is cannier than she looks, evidently. We have got to strike while the mark is high." He laughed. "Is the girl amenable to an early wedding?"

"More than amenable," Rudi boasted. "She quivers if I so much as kiss her hand. It is amazing, I tell you. She looks like a woman of the world, but I could swear she is absolutely pure. I can tell by the way she kissed me."

"A pure American, in these times," the baron marveled. "I have to give the old woman credit. The girl seems very credulous. We should keep her away from Helge as much as possible. That girl"—the Baron digressed, frowning—"is a disgrace. Friedrich should put his foot down."

"Friedrich." Rudi shrugged, dismissing his younger brother. "His father-in-law is too powerful. The old fool believes that his daughter can do no wrong. Anyway, it will be difficult to keep Marite away from Helge; there will be a dozen of these damned women's fetes before the marriage, you know. They'll be in each other's pockets."

"There is much to be said for elopement," the baron commented wryly.

"Shall I persuade her to do that? She'd do it for me, I am certain."

"No. No. On the contrary, it might be a bad notion. If the old Wendell is angered, she's capable of seeking an annulment. We will just have to chance Helge and her insolent mouth. The main thing is to get a proper marriage settlement before these thieves begin to partition the estates."

"It hasn't happened yet." Rudi's impatience was returning.

"It will. I see it coming, this very spring. Or at the latest, by next winter. The sooner we become solvent, the better."

"As to that, yes. But surely," Rudi protested, "Hindenburg will fight partitioning in East Prussia, with his own estate at Neudeck. I think it's all a tempest in a teapot. Our 'Cabinet of Barons' is safe enough with von Papen. He's smarter than that little jailbird will ever be."

"I wish I could dismiss Hitler that lightly," the baron responded gloomily. "But never mind that now. First things first, my son. Get yourself married to the Wendell girl. That shouldn't be too onerous a task. She's quite beautiful."

"Oh, she's beautiful enough."

"Well, then." The baron smiled at Rudi. "You're anxious to be off, I can see. But just one thing before you go—be careful with the old Wendell tomorrow. We can't afford to offend her. According to Maria von Lagen, she's kept her treasure safe from several improvident marriages, in three different countries. Apparently it took a von Durning to succeed," he added with pride. "The woman obviously approves of you, or she would have never agreed to such an unheard of arrangement . . . your taking the girl out unchaperoned all those nights."

Rudi mocked, "You forget that this is 1931."

"I am never allowed to forget it. Now, go, go. You've earned your relaxation. Kiss the dancers for me."

His son saluted him, smiling, and walked out.

Running lightly down the stoop, Rudi von Durning

hailed a cab farther along the Unter den Linden. "The White Mouse," he told the driver. All the cabmen knew where it was; no one ever had to say "Französischestrasse " a tongue-tripper when drunk.

He was already hot, picturing the dancers. They wore only necklaces, high-heeled shoes, and silk stockings rolled to just below their knees. His favorite number was the one Ilse and Erika did with the scarf and the umbrella. Erika was always so coy, holding the scarf over her body just below the navel, but the wild Ilse's little black triangle was completely exposed . . . and their breasts—their heavy, naked, rolling breasts.

Rudi could feel the blood pounding in his veins.

And after the show, late in the night, none of the girls had ever been averse to the more lucrative and private performances arranged in Schober's rooms. He had missed these parties in the last several months, missed them like hell.

But now that the matter of Marite Wendell was almost concluded, he could have fun again with an untroubled mind.

Chapter 20

*L*ate on a February afternoon in 1933 Marite von Durning stood at a narrow window of her boudoir at the *schloss*. The thickening snow threatened to isolate Königsberg from the world. It would not be pleasant to be snowed in.

Soon she would have to go down to the echoing dining hall for the ritual of family dinner below the tattered banners, the heads of slain deer and glaring boars. Marite was sorry the holidays were over. Sedate and gloomy as they were, the holidays summoned relatives who took some of the attention away from her. Now there would be only seven of them at the endless polished table. Marite would sit by Rudi in his place, as the eldest, near the baron. Rudi would be correct and handsome, looking at her with unseeing eyes. And her in-laws would study her appearance, ask her with that significant inflection how she was feeling, because she was still not pregnant after sixteen months of marriage. There had been little opportunity for that in recent months; Rudi was forever away on "business of the regiment." When they were together he was less than ardent.

Marite went to the tall cheval glass and looked at herself. Perhaps it was something lacking in her. The high-necked, long-sleeved dress was not very exciting. Helge in her forthright way had said it was "dull enough for Irmgarde." But the *schloss* was so cold Marite was daunted by the idea of low-cut evening clothes. The pale aquamarine velvet enhanced her hair but did little for her skin and eyes, which had lost some of their glow.

Irritably she struggled to remove the dress—she didn't welcome the idea of the stolid, indifferent maid at the moment—and looked for something else to wear. Finally she decided on a parchment-colored satin dress, clinging and cut on the bias to mold and expose the torso. Over it she could wear its companion jacket of golden-orange brocade. She had to change again from the skin out, down to stockings and shoes, but when she was done she already felt brighter and more appealing.

She added rouge and coated her lips lightly with a pale orange-toned salve, touching brown to her lashes. Marite did not have Helge's sure, subtle hand with makeup, so she was reluctant to do more. Rudi said he hated her to look "painted."

It seemed such a short time ago that he had considered everything about her "charming." She was amazed that she could have been so eager to marry him. She sat down by the window and recalled their first summer, incredulous that it had been only last year.

Marite had been so hypnotized by him, so besotted, that she had wept when Elizabeth flatly refused to allow a hasty wedding. "A four-mouth courtship," she declared, "is indecent enough. Now a sudden marriage will hardly give you time to collect a trousseau. There are forms to be observed. What will the von Durnings think? If you rush into this headlong, it will look as if you *must* marry, like some common servant in trouble."

Expecting Rudi to oppose Elizabeth, Marite was devastated when he did not. She endured long weeks in Paris, with fittings from morning till afternoon that made her almost drop with exhaustion; a round of fetes—tea dances, musicales, luncheons, receptions, and dinners—that left her hardly a moment alone with Rudi. The only consolation was that he seemed to be suffering as much as she. He often had dark circles under his eyes, and seemed irritable and gloomy. When she asked him what the matter was, he smiled and said, "I'll be glad when all this is over." That proved he desired her as much as she wanted him.

Finally, on the day of the wedding, all of it became worthwhile: Marite floated down the aisle of the cathedral in a fairylike drift of gauzy white on the arm of Colonel von Lagen, who, in the absence of a father, was giving her away, and when she saw Rudi and his uniformed attendants at the altar, he was once again the prince of her old imaginings.

The gigantic reception that followed, the bouquet of lilies tossed from the ballroom balcony at the Grand Hotel, the donning of travel clothes, and the entry into their compartment of the train for Paris—all of it passed in a golden blur, until they were alone, and close together. But the delight she had awaited never came, and still had not.

Her first experience of love had meant nothing but pain and awkwardness, a racking disillusion. Marite's untouched body had felt as heavy as a stone; she had known nothing of how to please him. And instead of the ecstatic closeness she had envisioned, their lovemaking became a perfunctory engagement, with a burning, gnawing emptiness for her, a matter-of-fact acceptance for Rudi.

At the end of their uneasy honeymoon, Rudi told her that he would be rejoining his regiment for maneuvers. Marite would go to the *schloss* at Königsberg. It was neither safe nor proper for her to live alone in Berlin. And he said he would be "running over to Königsberg now and then."

She ached with loneliness in the oppressive routine of the castle. Meals were served on a schedule of military exactitude, and there was little for her to do but read or take out one of the gentler horses. She spent the other long hours in strained conversation with Irmgarde and the *Baronin*, endured stiff visits of their acquaintances, or moped in her room. Life in the *schloss* made her days with Elizabeth seem carefree by comparison.

In all those months Rudi had been to the *schloss* only once, and even then seemed to devote more time to riding and drinking at the inn than he did to her. What was worse, he told her that the hunting season would soon begin, and he wanted to be on hand for that. The hunting season would go on through the end of November. Since Christmas was not long after, the family might remain at the castle until the new year.

Marite was afraid she might go mad, hungry for the bustle of Berlin, trapped in the desolate country with the family and a husband who was no longer the dashing, attentive lover she had married.

When her grandmother was invited to stay with them during that first holiday season, Marite was dismayed at how little Elizabeth's arrival brightened her mood. After the first novel flurry, their lives settled into the same gray routine. And when Marite hinted something of her disappointment to Elizabeth, she was uncomprehending. "Perhaps it is not very gay at the moment," she conceded. "But now you have *everything*. You will be the next *Baronin*. Besides, you are very fortunate to have an absentee husband," she added cynically. "It makes your burden all the lighter."

Marite was aware of her grandmother's notion of love—an onerous duty to be endured by all nice women.

"There are plenty of those . . . creatures to accommodate the kind of thing that men require," Elizabeth said smugly. Marite did not tell her it was that very notion that was making her miserable: Rudi, with his strong desires— she had seen the strength of them on their honeymoon— was not a man to live like a monk when he was away from her. She tried to picture the kind of women who would excite him. Undoubtedly whores, wearing all the "paint" that Rudi disliked seeing on her own face. "Besides," Elizabeth said brightly, "when you have a child, you'll be able to dictate everything. You'll see."

It was hardly marriage as Marite had imagined it; Elizabeth made it sound like a business arrangement. Perhaps her own was typical of all marriages; after the early kisses, the romantic ardor, below the lilies and the splendor this loneliness and weary cynicism were hidden in all men and women.

One feature of her grandmother's visit continued to puzzle her: in the early days the von Durnings had received Elizabeth with open arms. Now they were almost cool. And one night, passing the baron's library, where Elizabeth was conferring with him, Marite heard their voices raised in violent argument. Several times she heard the word "settlement." She knew it had to do with the marriage contract the attorneys had drawn up before the wedding, an affair that Marite had paid little attention to.

In the next few days, as she listened to the family's hints about staying in the country as a "'matter of economy," Marite reached a grim conclusion. The von Durnings had needed Elizabeth's money. Marite wondered why it hadn't occurred to her before. Now that she had the leisure to consider, it seemed strange for titled Germans to have accepted an American daughter-in-law so quickly, with such ease—especially one whose family origins were virtually unknown.

The idea of the deception, or Rudi's treachery, devastated her. But then, when he would come back to the *schloss* in the evenings, gay and debonair and flushed with the triumph of the hunt, she could almost forget. The old yearning, each time she saw him, would revive, even if he were not the strong, heroic figure she had fallen in love with at the beginning. It had not taken her a month to learn that Rudi was as weak as Friedrich, below his bluster, and totally under the baron's thumb. That insight edged her undiminished passion with new tenderness.

But that was last year, she thought, watching the swirl of snow. Her feelings were as different now as Berlin had been in November. The city had lost its quaintness and peace in the "final round" of the presidential elections; the baron and other titled men had supported Hindenburg. Yet when Adolf Hitler was made chancellor the month before, the von Durnings had accepted the inevitable with an ease that chilled Marite; this Hitler, she heard, had already built concentration camps for Jews.

She shuddered to imagine what the von Durnings would do if they found out her father had been a Jew. The irrepressible Helge, on the pretext of taking Marite to a museum, had taken her on a *sub rosa* visit to an exhibit of the pictures of George Grosz. Since Grosz was not only a Communist but also a Jew, Helge warned her to "say nothing of this at home." At the time, Marite had thought the pictures shocking, brutally ugly.

She understood them better now, sitting by the window in the prison of the castle. Grosz had delineated the absurdity that underlay the splendor of Germany's von Durnings. Such insights had come to Marite more and more since that afternoon in Berlin.

She recalled the immense trucks everywhere on the streets. Their sides were plastered with poster images of Adolf Hitler, and the legend "This is ADOLF HITLER the MAN . . . LEADER of the German PEOPLE." Passing one of the trucks with Helge, Marite had been almost deafened when a squat, black-uniformed Nazi trumpeter had blown a blast right in her ear. The Nazi flag, with its bold black swastika, was attached to the trumpet's shaft. Helge had laughed and told the trumpeter to "shut up." The man had stared at them suspiciously with hard gray eyes. Marite shuddered at the memory.

Suddenly her boudoir door opened. "How do you *stand* this tomb?" The question was in English.

It was Helge. She was scantily dressed as usual in a startling velvet creation the color of a tangerine, cut deeply to show the cleft of her breasts; the nipples were plain through the clinging silk velvet. In deference to the chill of the *schloss*, she was wearing the ensemble's jacket; the collar and the cuffs were edged in dark fur. But Helge wore the jacket carelessly, slung back to flaunt her splendid body. Above the vivid clothes her hair was like a polished chestnut; penciled black lines around her hazel eyes lightened and emphasized their rich color.

"You look wonderful," Marite said, smiling. Helge was callous and cynical, sometimes vulgar, but Marite could not help reacting to her vitality and impudence. She was like a pillar of fire in the cold, somber room.

"So do you." Helge eyed her approvingly. "I'm glad you've given up those pastel shrouds."

Marite laughed.

"Maybe you'll straighten Rudi out yet," Helge added.

"Straighten him out?"

"Keep him in line. Come, my dear, you know as well as I do that those 'maneuvers' are maneuvers around the Reichstag . . . and the whores." Helge still used English, her private language.

Marite flushed. "No, you don't have to tell me. I guessed, long ago."

"Well, you can do something about it. Get pregnant. As soon as I did, even the old buzzard came to heel." Marite grinned at Helge's description of the baron, but she was always taken aback at her sister-in-law's way of speaking. "Since I gave Friedrich a son," Helge asserted, "I do anything I damn please. Friedrich was beside himself, you know, to get ahead of his elder brother. Just grit your teeth, my dear, and give him a little baron."

"Grit my teeth?" Marite raised her brows. "You sound like my grandmother."

Helge laughed, exposing her little white teeth and pink tongue. "Well, I'm not going to give you any grandmotherly advice."

Struggling to find a polite expression, Marite asked, "You mean that . . . marriage is unpleasant for you?" It was the last thing she had expected from Helge.

"My sweet girl, marriage has nothing to do with pleasure, unless it's a man's. For my pleasure there are the Salome and the Eldorado."

Marite was stunned. She had heard about the Salome, a nightclub frequented by grotesque young men with plucked eyebrows and painted lips, women who dressed like men. The Eldorado was even more notorious: each table had a telephone so the patrons could get acquainted without the tedium of introductions.

Helge smiled at her shocked face, looking dainty and amoral as a cat. "I've always been that way."

"Why did you marry Friedrich? And have a child?" Helge's attitude toward her two-year-old son mystified Marite. She rarely mentioned him, and left him in the care of a nurse most of the time.

"For a blind, my dear. And to make my great father the general happy. It's all so convenient, with my father commanding Friedrich's regiment. Women are a commodity, Marite. We, too, have our heavy artillery." She read Marite's expression and said gently, "You are a dreamer. That's not your idea of love."

"No. I always wanted to live with a prince in a castle. Now I do and it's not what I expected."

"You poor darling." Helge smiled her bitter smile. "All your beauty and money have trapped you in the von Durning mousetrap. I never thought you'd stick it out this long. Wait!" The sudden exclamation made Marite jump. "Just wait a moment," Helge said. "I want to bring you something."

She got up and rushed out. In a few minutes she was back, with something black and filmy lying over her arm.

"What's that?"

Helge held the garment up. It was a perfectly transparent nightgown of black chiffon. "It's not just a nightgown. Look here." She poked an enameled nail through a slit in one breast of the gown, then the other; she repeated the gesture through an opening below the waist, and at the gown's sides. "It is conveniently made at salient points."

Marite flushed.

"Whenever I want Friedrich to toe the line, I put this on . . . or others like it, in perfectly outrageous colors." Helge giggled. "I think the black, though, is lovely with your hair. Wear this for Rudi; he'll forget his 'maneuvers' for a while. When he gets you pregnant, demand an apartment in Berlin." Helge offered the gown.

Slowly Marite took it and started toward the closet.

There was a staccato tap on the door.

"Irmgarde," Helge whispered. "She always raps like a little toy soldier."

Marite called out, "Come in," and opened the closet door.

Irmgarde poked her dun-colored head around the boudoir door and entered. Her small pale eyes darted resentfully from Helge to the gown Marite was hanging on a padded hanger. "I hope I do not intrude," she said in her high, careful German.

Marite thought: She heard us speaking in English, and that's always suspect to her. Helge was quite proficient in Marite's language; it had formed an additional bond between them.

Before Marite could answer, Helge retorted in German, "You always do."

"I'm sorry to disturb you, Marite," Irmgarde said with prim emphasis, "but you did say I might borrow your seed-pearl necklace."

How hideous the poor thing is, Marite thought. The features that were so impressive in her parents looked . . . melted on Irmgarde's sallow face. She had always lived in the shadow of her handsome brothers. Marite, out of pity, dealt with her gently; they had almost become friends. "Of course, Irmgarde. Please. Just help yourself. The case on the dresser."

While Irmgarde went gingerly through the jewel case, Helge chattered on in German about the weather, the guests expected for dinner. She got up and wandered to the cheval glass to examine her face and poke at her hair.

Irmgarde shut the case softly, holding the seed pearls in her knobby fingers. "Thank you, Marite."

"It's nothing." Irmgarde was staring at her strangely; her flat cheeks looked very pale. What on earth was the matter? Surely she couldn't have understood their conversation; the doors were too thick. And Irmgarde spoke no English at all. Marite was puzzled.

"Thank you," Irmgarde repeated, and hurried out with her head lowered, shutting the door.

"What's the matter with Irmgarde?" Marite still could not fathom the meaning of that quick pallor, that stare of dismay.

"Sheer envy, darling. That awful color of hers is not ill health; it's pure envy-green. Poor bitch, if she thought it would get her a husband, she'd stand naked in a window of Wertheim's department store."

"Helge," Marite reproached her, but she couldn't help laughing."

"Forget that poor thing. Now, my dear, a boyfriend of mine at the Salome taught me some perfectly outrageous tricks. Do you want to know how to positively enslave a man?"

Marite nodded, amused at Helge's tutorial air and distracted by curious thoughts of Irmgarde. What could have made her look like that, all of a sudden?

". . . just go right at it. It's absolutely overwhelming. But you must remember not to . . ."

Helge's voice faded; she sounded so far away she might have fallen into a well, because of the words abruptly shouting in the loud silence of Marite's mind.

The star. She had forgotten it was still there.

Irmgarde must have seen the Star of David.

". . . and of course a little rouge—the courtesans used to do that in France," Helge was saying.

Dear God, what would Irmgarde do now? Marite agonized. Go to the baron at once and tell him? I'll have to make up something. But what?

"Marite? Are you listening?"

She struggled to focus her attention on Helge. "Yes. Of course," she stammered. "But . . . tell me that last part again."

This time she listened closely to her sister-in-law's shocking directions. She knew now she would do whatever Helge suggested.

If ever there were a time to bind her husband to her, it was surely now. It might be her only hope.

"That is correct, sir." Rudi tried to keep the smile from his voice as he spoke into the telephone. "A matter of great family urgency . . . if I might extend my leave for only a few more days." He listened, his smile broadening. The major had snapped at the bait. "I am most grateful, sir," he said solemnly, and hung up.

He would just have a cup of coffee in the kitchen and then go right back upstairs. The cook greeted him respectfully but with astonishment; he never appeared belowstairs at this hour in a dressing gown.

Rudi sipped his coffee, reviewing the incredible, wonderful night. He had gone to their room with the intention of falling asleep. And then that apparition met his dazzled eyes: his wife. His pretty, dull little wife stood there at the door to meet him, bedizened and dressed—or undressed, he amended, with a twinge of lust—like a beautiful whore. The dim lights behind her frankly outlined her body through the thin black thing, and one of her round, magnificent breasts was bare. There was rouge on the nipple and on the aureola. His surprised hand found itself groping the breast, then caressing it with his mouth.

Titillated, he freed the other breast through its slit; she made a sinuous movement of her hips, and he realized that the gown had another slit. He glimpsed the golden luxuriance, and his body felt like burning steel. He kicked off his evening pumps and like lightning bared the lower half of his body. It was unbearably exciting, with his torso still clothed, the rest of him in nothing but his silk socks; it was like the first time he had had a girl, standing up, in that working-class alley.

He moved to her, but she laughed softly, like some nameless creature, and shook her head. The golden hair streaming down around her bare breasts fired him with new ardor, and he let out a pleading moan. But she still kept laughing, shaking her head, and moving so close to him that he was privy to all of her. Then she began to slide down slowly to the carpet, her hands sliding down from his waist to his knees to his ankles.

At once she had begun it, that incredible caressing. He had one swift, questioning thought: Where had she learned this . . . how? And then he had stopped thinking completely.

After that, during the long night, he had possessed her four more times, amazed at her own pleasure; she cried out continually, like a mewing cat.

This morning, watching her sleep, he wondered again where she had learned all that. The answer came to him— from that amateur prostitute, no doubt: Helge. That was all right, then. His brother Friedrich must have himself a time.

Rudi smiled to himself at the long kitchen table, ignoring the curious eyes of the cook and kitchen maids. He felt like a stallion. He would go upstairs again, right now. It was going to be a nice long holiday.

One month later Rudi heard his father calling out his name as he was on his way back to the bedroom. It was still early, and the corridor was cold with the chill of the winter morning. The baron stood at the door of his library; his face was like a stormy sky. "Come in here," he said curtly. "I must talk with you."

"Now?" Already burning with anticipation, Rudi was longing to get back upstairs. "I want to go back to sleep."

"Sleep?" The baron stared at him inquisitively. "You're never asleep at this hour. Come in, I say."

Sullenly Rudi followed his father into the cluttered room. "What is it?" he growled.

"You'd better take some brandy." Incredulous, Rudi noticed a half-empty snifter on the table by his father's thronelike chair.

"What is this?" he demanded. "Brandy before breakfast?"

The baron shook his narrow head and poured a brandy, offering it to his son. "You are going to need this."

Mystified, Rudi accepted the glass but did not drink from it.

Without inflection, the baron repeated to his son what he had just learned.

Rudi kept shaking his head. Finally he raised his glass with a trembling hand and drank from it. "There must be some explanation. Even if she has that . . . ornament . . . Marite cannot be a Jew. It is impossible. You have observed her features a thousand times—the fine nose, the small mouth, the shape of her jaw. The golden hair . . . ."

"And the fine dark eyes?" The baron sneered. "The soulful Jewish eyes that Frau Wendell tried to pass off as French?"

"No. It is impossible. She is too English-looking, too fine, to be . . . Perhaps," Rudi stammered with desperation, "perhaps it is a joke of Helge's! She is always making remarks, you know, about the Nazis, just to upset us."

"Helge is obnoxious, but she is not a fool. Why should she play such a perilous 'joke' on someone she obviously admires? No, Rudi, your wife has Jewish blood. Irmgarde found that disgusting . . . ornament, that star. She said it looked quite old. As a matter of fact, the kind of thing that might be worn by a small child. Your wife has had the thing for years; it must have been given to her as a child because she is a Jew, or at the very least has Jewish blood."

"I still don't believe it," Rudi protested. "I cannot."

"You must. I've made a few calls since Irmgarde told me about this," the baron said coldly. "Elizabeth became quite hysterical, but she finally had to admit that it was true. It seems the old woman took your wife away from a thoroughly disreputable background. . . . I can explain all the details to you later. The important thing now is that we will have to report this at once."

"*Report* . . ." Rudi whispered. "Turn in my *wife*, a woman who bears the name of von Durning? Have you considered the disgrace, the . . . kowtow to that *house painter*?''

"It's no good," the baron cut in. "It will have to be reported. Hitler is our *führer* now."

"You can't. I won't allow it." Rudi jumped up and threw the glass into the fire. He was shaking with anger. His father only blinked when the glass shattered, exploded. "She is my wife."

"You have never been so enamored of her," the baron said sourly. "And you *dare* to speak of 'allowing' me my actions?"

"It's different now." That was an answer to both the baron's comment and his question. Rudi's feelings were different now; the woman he had married for his family's convenience, on the baron's very order, had become precious to him in the space of just a few weeks. And at this moment he had no fear of his father; he could dare.

The ultimate weapon had not been aimed, he thought, and hope rose in him. "I have given her a child. Would you destroy the mother of the grandson who will succeed to the title?" Rudi got to his feet, fixing the baron with his stare.

"Succeed to the *title*?" The old man stood up, facing his son; a frantic pulse beat in his temple. "A child with the blood of a Jew? You must be mad!"

They faced each other with the stiff wrath of fighting dogs. Rudi knew he was within an inch of slapping his father across the face. "You will not betray my wife," he repeated coldly.

He turned on his heel and strode out of the room, quivering with anger, but even more with utter amazement at his own temerity, stunned by the abrupt knowledge of how much Marite now meant to him. After all the months of marriage he had crossed the threshold of their bedroom that one night a month ago and fallen in love with her at first glance.

It was a concept he had laughed at, always, in the company of other men; it was an idea fostered by silly women who got it from their silly books. But now it had happened to him, Rudi von Durning, the soldier who had always believed that one woman was much the same as another—that all cats were indeed gray in the dark.

He still did not believe, could not believe, that his well-bred wife could possibly be a Jew. Recalling with fury how his father had talked to him, Rudi thought: I will ask her and she will explain. The whole idiotic matter will be clear. I'll put my foot down and my father will acknowledge my proper position.

But as soon as he opened the door and saw her smiling at him from the great bed in the astonishing glow of her new beauty, the thought of explanations for the moment left his mind. A strange protective tenderness, an emotion he had never felt for a woman, warmed him like sunlight.

He went to her and took her in his arms, giving her a slow, affectionate kiss. "*Liebling*, have the maid pack your things. We are going to Berlin now. This morning."

Her dark eyes kindled. "Oh, Rudi, *together*?"

He could hardly credit his emotions when she asked him that. He felt now what he had only pretended to feel during their courtship days—everything about her was so utterly charming, even her English-accented German, which used to annoy him. "Of course together."

"I am so glad. But isn't the house closed?"

"We are not going to stay at the house. We are going to stay at a friend's apartment for the little time before I have to go away. Later we will have a house of our own."

She put her arms around his neck and he felt her softness against him, smelled the fragrance of her glorious hair.

And he said with a whole new sincerity what he had said only perfunctorily before. "*Ich liebe dich*, Marite." For the first time, with his whole heart, he loved her.

Marite parted the velvet curtains and watched Rudi walk away down the snowy street; his soft *Auf Wiedersehen* still echoed to her in the empty living room of the borrowed flat. This had surely been the happiest week of her whole life. It was agony to have to say good-bye.

When he was out of sight, she let the curtains fall together and turned away, sighing. She wished now that she had insisted on going with him to the train, but he had been so adamant about her staying here because of the freezing cold.

The flat had seemed cozy when he was with her. Now its modern starkness chilled her. The walls, the ceiling, and the fireplace were divided into geometric patterns; everything except the scarlet-covered windows was dark polished wood or white or gray.

Marite sat down in a gray velvet armchair close to the comfort of the fire, reviewing the miracle of her new delight. She had contrived, through Rudi's heightened senses, to arouse him to love, an emotion which she now knew had been alien to him. It was as if they had just met each other. These last weeks had been wonderful. Tenderly she recalled his shyness when he expressed his deeper feelings. Now she could dismiss all her early resentments, the painful clarity that had made her see why he had married her. There was no question now. He loved her.

The greatest miracle of all was Irmgarde's silence. Marite still puzzled over that. She must not have told the baron what she had seen; otherwise there would have been horrendous repercussions. The final proof was that Rudi had said nothing. Now Marite wondered if the naive Irmgarde, who led such a sheltered life, might not even have known what the star meant, incredible as that seemed.

She would not think about it now. Another happy idea had just occurred to her: lonely as it would be without Rudi, she would be possessed now of an unlooked-for treasure, a delicious freedom.

Marite hurried into the bedroom and telephoned Helge. Waiting for her to answer, Marite smiled. She had not let Helge know she was even in Berlin; a few days ago, she had wanted no interruption of the fresh honeymoon.

"Marite?" Helge's bright, impudent voice was full of

surprise. She demanded in English, "What's the matter? Are you calling from the *schloss*?"

"I am calling from Berlin." She told Helge something of what had happened. "Will you come to see me?" she asked excitedly. "Come at five and I will give you a drink. Then we can go out to dinner."

"That'll be splendid!" Helge sounded buoyant. "*You* are splendid, my dear."

Marite hung up, grinning with pleasure. She decided to tidy up the flat, wash her hair, and begin a letter to Rudi; there were hours to kill before Helge came.

By a quarter to five she was ready, dressed in the cocoa-brown skirt and overblouse of a warm Chanel suit and tall brown boots for the snow. Her blouse was ornamented with several long golden chains. When she had taken the chains from her jewel case, she had seen the little star. Some sense of perilous defiance had made her clasp the frail chain around her neck and slip the small star beneath the high round neck of the blouse.

As she mixed the cocktails, she wondered about that mysterious impulse. Why, tonight of all nights, had she done such a thing?

The doorbell interrupted her reverie. Helge was early. Marite hurried to the door with a wide smile.

Her smile froze on her lips when she opened the door.

Two tall, imposing men in jet-black uniforms, their peaked caps piped in dazzling white, towered above her. In a fleeting second she recognized the insignia on their lapels—the bright white eagles of the SS.

A coldness deeper than that of the wet, freezing wind struck her body.

"Frau von Durning?"

Marite nodded, unable to say a word. What did they want from her?

"May we come in?"

She nodded again, like a broken-necked doll, still voiceless with apprehension, and stood aside. It struck her as horrible that both the officers stamped the snow from their boots before they entered.

When she closed the door, one of them stood next to her, staring at her, while the other quickly walked around the flat. She could hear him opening drawers in the bedroom, pulling aside the shower curtains of the bath. "She is alone," he said to his companion when he returned, and for the first time she saw that both of them had their guns drawn.

"What do you want?"

"You will please come with us. There are certain questions we would like you to answer." They put the guns away.

Suddenly she was almost paralyzed with fear and her urge to urinate was agony. "I don't understand. By whose authority?" she managed to demand, steadying her voice. "My father-in-law is the Baron von Durning."

One of the officers gave her an unpleasant smile. "It is at the request of the baron that we are here."

She jerked backward as if he had hit her. The extreme shock had rendered her body even more vulnerable.

"Please," she said tightly, "may I . . . get my coat?"

"Be quick."

She rushed off toward the bedroom which adjoined the bath, and through it to the bathroom. When she was flushing the toilet, she thought of the star. With feverish haste she unhooked the chain and took off one of her boots; she pried up the inner sole with her nail and thrust the star and its chain under the sole. She had put on the boot and was zipping it up when one of the men began pounding on the door. "*Schnell!*" he shouted. "Quickly!"

She jerked the door open and rushed into the bedroom, snatching her jacket and fur coat from the closet. She was reaching for a hat whan the officer repeated loudly, "*Schnell,* I say."

"My . . . my *hut,*" she stammered.

"Never mind that. Come."

She saw that it was useless to argue; his face looked as

hard and immobile as stone. She threw on her jacket and put the coat over it, and followed the man from the bedroom. At the door, the officers flanked her, each holding one of her arms; they walked three abreast to a waiting car. One of them got in the back first, while the other still grasped her arm in a bruising grip. The one with her pushed her into the rear of the car and then got in himself, snapping at the driver, "Go on."

Marite sat so tensely between them that her muscles ached; she could not bear the thought of touching those hard-muscled thighs, or even the contact of her fur sleeve with the heavy wool of those black uniforms. It was hard to breathe; her chest hurt with the effort of taking that freezing air into her lungs, and her hair was wet with melted snow.

As the great car proceeded slowly down the Unter den Linden, she was almost blinded by the brightness of dozens of columns of light, surmounted by the Nazi eagle, lining the traffic island. They had been there all the time. In her bemusement, drugged by her newfound happiness with Rudi, she had not even seen them.

When the car was slowed by traffic beside Wertheim's department store, she saw four frozen-looking soldiers parading among the familiar columns blazoned with the brass name, N. Israel, which she had passed unheeding so many hundreds of times. The soldiers were bearing placards with enormous letters: "GERMANS! BEWARE!" And underlined in black below that warning, "DO NOT BUY FROM JEWS!"

I should have paid attention. The words were a silent mourning in her brain. *I should have paid attention, to all of it, long ago.*

The car picked up speed and turned a corner: Marite was thrown against the officer on her right. She held herself as stiffly as she could, but could not avoid the meeting of their bodies. She felt his stare on her profile and heard him laugh softly.

Now she was aware of another terror, one that had

escaped her before. What would they do to a young woman? She blinked back her tears, ashamed to let these arrogant bullies see her cry.

There must be someone . . . someone who could help her. Perhaps, when Helge found her gone . . . But what could Helge do, when the baron himself had betrayed her? Rudi was on the train, heading for a distant assignment. Elizabeth was en route to the Riviera.

In America there were lawyers . . . and justice. But now she was a German citizen by virtue of her marriage.

Abruptly all the images of her nights and days began to flash in her vision, like the sights seen by a drowning person; she was a child again, in the Village garden, and very clearly she could see the face of her gentle father.

Then Rudi's face flared in her mind.

At least it had not been he who betrayed her.

Chapter 21

The car slowed as it passed the Adlon Hotel—it seemed a century ago that Marite had stayed there with Elizabeth, received the ardent Rudi von Durning in the stately lobby—and made a swerving turn onto the Wilhelmstrasse.

"Where are you taking me?" Neither of the officers answered or so much as looked at her. The car proceeded on past the French embassy, turned again, and passed the French gymnasium. The world had suddenly gone mad: less than an hour ago, she had been a sheltered, loved woman of enviable status waiting for her friend, the general's duaghter, in a warm, luxurious flat. Now, in the freezing dark, she was nothing; worse than nothing, with less than the rights of a felon. The only reality left was the silky feel of the fur collar against her cold cheeks, the weight of gold on her breast, the oddly satisfying discomfort of the little star rubbing her stockinged foot through the sole of her finc Italian boot.

The Reichstag loomed before them with its immense ornate central dome, flanked by lesser domes on either side, the forest of the Platz der Republik just beyond. The plaza, before Hitler's election, had been called the Königsplatz, the plaza of kings. There were no more kings now, Marite reflected with despair, nor cabinets of barons; even the great Baron von Durning reported to Adolf Hitler.

When the car passed the Reichstag, too, and stopped outside the deserted park on Friedrich Ebert Strasse, she began to realize that they had not brought her here for questioning. Two enormous trucks were parked among the trees of the wooded oval; a small group of soldiers, in their long belted overcoats and steel helmets, aided by the Berlin police were shepherding a line of women into the trucks. Even in the half-dark Marite could see the pain and the terror on the women's faces.

Now she was almost gagging with fear: she could barely get her breath, and the hammering beat of her heart was like a giant mallet smashing at her body. She could feel the force of its thudding even in her arms and legs, smashing away at her very brain.

"Out." The man on her right had opened the door and was pulling her into the frozen night. She swayed on her feet, tried to force the cold air into her lungs. The officer was half-dragging her now toward the line of women, tearing her long fur coat away from her body.

"You won't need this now." He laughed. That laugh was the most hideous sound she had ever heard. She felt his hand fumble at the back of her neck; he was unfastening her golden chains. "Nor these." He put the chains in his pocket, holding the silky fur over his arm. He shouted, in her ear, "Let's go, Hans! We're through here. They're waiting for us at the Herrenklub."

Then he walked away. A soldier shoved Marite into the line of women, bellowing at them to hurry, to get into the truck. Marite, shuddering with cold, found to her horror that her legs no longer functioned; her knees buckled. "Come on, beauty. Get going." A squat young soldier with a snub, grinning face grabbed her around the waist and lifted her into the truck, whistling and laughing when her skirt rode high on her body, exposing her long, silk-covered legs all the way to her chemise of ecru satin. He squeezed her buttocks, shoving her headlong into the truck against the legs of another woman.

Marite cried out and struggled to her knees. A woman's hand stretched out to help her. She grabbed it; the hand was as cold as death, but it was like a lifeline thrown to someone drowning. It was the first gesture of compassion in this nightmare world where pity no longer existed.

"Get up." The woman's voice was harsh, without cruelty. "They already shot three women because they were sick."

Marite scrambled to her feet; her skin was wet with perspiration, and it was turning to ice on her neck and hands. Her knees stung, scraped raw from her entry into the truck. "Thank you," she gasped to the woman; they were standing breast-to-breast in the space jammed with other standing women. She almost recoiled from the woman's sour breath, but her black, cynical eyes were full of pity.

"It could be worse," the woman said. "They say Sachsenhausen's a resort compared to the other places. You're pretty. You'll do well there." The haggard woman gave Marite a grotesque smile, checkered with the dark hollows of missing teeth.

Marite's own teeth chattered with the cold; the nearness of the woman's heavy body was oddly comforting. It gave off heat.

There was another shout from outside; the rear leaf of the truck banged shut with a jarring impact and the engine rumbled to life. With a sudden swerve that threw the women against each other helter-skelter, the truck roared off into the night.

Its jolting threatened to throw Marite off her feet again; the heavy woman grabbed her arm. The interior of the truck was so crowded that Marite could neither move nor turn; her back was to the other women. All she could see was the weathered, painted face of the woman before her.

"I'm Tilli," she said. Another blast of her fetid breath, compounded of garlic and wine and tobacco, assaulted Marite's nostrils. "What's your name?"

"Marite von—"

"We won't have any last names anymore," Tilli cut in. "But I could tell right away you were a 'von.' " She grinned again.

"How . . . how can you smile?" Marite could barely speak from cold, the stiffness of fright. Besides, she was afraid the jolting of the truck would make her bite her tongue.

"To keep from crying."

For a time the rattling jolt of the truck was so severe it was foolish to try to speak at all. Then, during a lull, when the vehicle was moving more slowly, Marite asked Tilli, "What will they do to us?"

"What they do to me all the time." Tilli's word seemed squeezed from her with the renewed jouncing of the truck, which had picked up speed again. "We're lucky, girl. You're pretty. I'm good at what I do. They may even let us live for a while."

A cold fist closed about Marite's heart, a freezing ache possessed her entire body. Tilli was a whore.

Marite could not gauge how much time had passed before the great truck braked to a curt standstill, once more throwing the women against each other. Bruised and shaken, Marite grunted and moaned along with all the others. Someone cried out in pain, and Tilli let out a grieving oath, her huge breasts jammed against Marite's.

Two soldiers were opening the rear of the truck with an ear-splitting racket, shouting at them, "*Aus, aus!* Out! Make it quick!"

Marite's sweating feet were swollen inside her boots and her legs were so stiff from standing in one position that moving was agony. But she forced herself to move; the soldiers were irritable and impatient and she was afraid of what they would do if she showed weakness. Tilli had said they had shot sick women. She staggered to the lip of the truck, her feet feeling as huge and heavy as boulders and, crouching, jumped to the ground. The pain of impact was so great that she almost screamed, but she dug her nails into the palms of her gloved hands and righted herself.

A soldier jerked her by the arm with such force she thought the arm would be torn from its socket. "Move along! *Anstellen! Anstellen!*" For one horrified moment Marite could not understand the German word; her mind had just stopped working. Then she saw other women getting in a line; that's what it meant. "Stand in line." Her relief was so sudden and total that she began to urinate. Overwhelmed with shame, she felt the hot trickle of moisture down her legs and walked stiffly to the forming line.

"March!" An officer at the head of the line was leading them to one of the ugly wooden shacks that bordered a high wire fence.

Now she was past thinking; the important thing was to do exactly what she was told. Otherwise at any instant one of the soldiers might raise his gun and shoot her through the head. So she kept on doggedly marching, behind Tilli, into the shack. It was only slightly warmer than the air outside. She was aching all over, quivering with cold and shame, convinced that she stank from urine and sweat.

"Take off your clothes!" someone barked. Marite's heart seemed to stop breathing. Dear God, if they took her boots . . . and found the star . . . . Bile rose in her throat. She prayed that she would not vomit. Her mouth tasted horrible; she was starving, she realized all of a sudden, not having eaten since breakfast. "Take them off!"

A soldier was collecting the women's clothes, tossing them into a huge wooden box. He examined Marite's Chanel suit with interest and put it aside, apparently enjoying the sight of her in her brief chemise, perverse and bizarre with her outdoor boots.

"Take off everything!" the voice bellowed. Marite stood naked now, still in her boots. She turned her head painfully and glanced down the line. Fifty women stood there, naked, most of them with bare feet. "The boots too." The soldier who had taken their clothes was standing before her.

"No." The sudden command took the soldiers by surprise. A tall, imposing officer was standing in the doorway. Marite recognized, with some lucid, still-functioning portion of her mind, the insignia of a major on his uniform. "Leave them on," he commanded the soldier, with a terrible half-smile. "It is a most interesting effect."

Marite could feel his stare, like a palpable crawling, on her bare body.

"Issue a dress to this one," the major snapped. "Send her to the doctor first. Then to the Vergnügenhaus."

The soldier leapt to obey, taking a rough gray dress from another huge box. Marite put it on with frantic haste, glad to have anything to cover her nakedness, glimpsing a black number stamped on the breast of the sacklike garment. It felt as rough as sandpaper and swallowed her, the hem extending to her ankles, but it hid her. That was all she could think of; it was everything in the world at this moment.

Then the soldier led her out of the shack to another one; the front door opened directly into a kind of examining room. A thin, grim-faced woman in a nurse's uniform, her face deeply scored with lines and her graying hair cut like a man's, immediately came to Marite and pulled the dress roughly over her head. "Lie down there," she snapped, indicating a metal table with stirrups at the foot. "No. Wait." The woman looked contemptuously at the trail left by the urine down Marite's legs. "Go in there and wash yourself," she spat, pushing Marite through another door into a room with a sink and toilet. There was no washcloth. Marite washed herself with her hands in icy water and dried herself with a towel so thin it could not absorb the moisture.

The door opened with startling quickness and the nurse ordered her back to the examining table. The woman had still not looked at her directly.

Trembling, Marite got painfully onto the table and lay back, closing her eyes, with her legs pressed together.

"Now, now. Come on. I can't examine you that way, you know." The oily, almost gentle tone made her open her eyes. She looked up into the porcine face of a grizzled man; he had a monocle screwed into one of his little granite-colored eyes, and his skin was flushed.

"Come, come," he repeated, stroking her thighs. She winced back from the touch; he cursed and grasped her legs, pulling them apart. "Feet in the stirrups!" Fearfully she obeyed, enduring his fondling survey, determined not to cry out while he inserted his instruments and played with the flesh of her secret body. At last it was over.

"She is clean," he grunted. "Send her on." She got up, feeling a relief so immense that it lapped her senses like cooling water. Then she saw the soldier smirking in a corner: he had seen the whole thing, had witnessed her helpless humiliation. And no one cared. Furthermore, the "doctor" had ignored her scraped knees, which really hurt now.

A scorching anger followed the brief balm of relief. For the first time in her life she hungered to kill—to kill all these mocking, callous monsters who were less than human, to flee with the other hapless prisoners into the snowy night, even if they all perished from cold and starvation. She had been so paralyzed by fear before that there had been no room for anger; it possessed her now, totally, hot and sweet and vitalizing. That anger would keep her alive.

This time when the soldier barked at her to go with him she summoned up every ounce of her will to hide her reaction, to keep the expression on her face stiff and bland. No matter what they did to her, they would not defeat her. Above all, she was going to live as long as she could manage. At least she knew what to expect in the "Vergnügenhaus."

But when the soldier led her to a wooden structure a little apart from the others, and she saw its brighter lights, heard the gruff laughter of men and the *biergarten* music, her courage failed her. She was almost devastated by hunger and thirst—her mouth seemed to be stuffed with cotton, her head was one great pounding ache, and her arms and legs were shaking uncontrollably.

The soldier thrust her through the door and she stood there blinking in the light, blinded after the outer darkness. What met her eyes was like a scene from hell.

Five drunken, half-dressed men and almost a dozen naked women were in the big room. Two of the men sat negligently at a wooden table, drinking beer from enormous steins, their legs stretched out easily. Each of them fondled the woman on his lap. The other men were roughly caressing women on the floor. There was no place to turn her eyes from the sordid horror. There was such a racket of music and laughter, of groaning and shouting, that they had not even noticed her entry.

But in her savage hunger she was instantly aware of the food on the table—thickly sliced bread, great slices of rare meat—and she nearly fainted at the sight and smell of the food.

"What have we here?" One of the men at the table sighted her. Unceremoniously he dumped the naked woman from his lap and she fell to the floor. Her blank face showed no reaction; she stared at Marite with glazed, unseeing eyes, lying where she had fallen.

"We have a new guest at the party." The man rose and, staggering, bounced against the wall. He laughed at his own drunken gait. He was wearing the jacket of his uniform unbuttoned, revealing an undershirt beneath. There was no clothing on his lower body. He lurched toward Marite.

She shrank back, but she could not help staring at the food on the table, at the steins of beer. She had always hated beer and never drank it, but now it looked like nectar. She could feel saliva gather at the corners of her mouth, and raised her hands to the edges of her lips to hide her humiliation. It was insane; the man could rape her where she stood, but at that instant all she could see, or think of, was the food.

The man grabbed her by the arm and dragged her toward the table. "Are you hungry?" he mumbled, grinning. "Then beg for it, like the others. Sit up and beg like the Jewish bitch you are."

He forced her to her knees and bellowed at two of the women who were lying back against the wall, "Show her! Show her how the Jew dogs are fed!"

In frozen horror, Marite watched the women. Their eyes were as blank and dead as those of the woman who had fallen on the floor without reaction. Both of them were dark and young, with full but slender bodies. Matter-of-factly they crawled toward the table and sank back on their haunches. Then they sat up a little, holding up their grimy hands like a dog's paws. Shouting with laughter, the man tore a piece of beef apart and tossed a fragment of it to each of the women. One of the women caught it in her mouth and chewed hungrily; the other failed to catch the meat and it fell on the floor. She snatched it up eagerly and ate it.

Marite's legs could no longer support her: she collapsed into a sitting position on the floor.

"You see now, bitch? You see?" Grinning horribly, the man threw her a chunk of bread. It struck her on the face. She made no move to catch it and let it fall to the floor. Bile rushed upward in her throat. Hungry as she was, she knew she would never be able to swallow.

"It's that or starve. It's up to you." The drunken soldier turned away from Marite and threw himself down on the floor beside another prisoner and began to fondle her body.

Marite lowered her head in despair, crouched where she was, waiting for the inevitable moment when one of the men would take her dress from her; the others were observing her. And there was no place to run, no place to hide.

"Come." She felt a rough grasp under her armpits, urging her upward. Now it would begin.

She looked up with apprehension: the major was looking down at her with glittering eyes. Her back was to the door and she had not seen him enter. For the first time she was able to see his face clearly. His narrow lips were set in one thin line; his predatory nose, his granite eyes, reminded her of the baron. Another cold wave of fear washed over her.

"Come," the major repeated. Numbly she stood and felt his hard arm encircle her body, his steely fingers squeeze her breast. "Kopf, you are a pig," he called out in his deep, gruff voice. The half-dressed man on the floor, who had made the women beg, laughed at the major. "Listen, all of you. and remember. This one is mine."

There was no more laughter. Kopf and the others were silent.

The major pulled at Marite's waist, and she followed him, stumbling, into a smaller room in which there was only a cot and one dim light, an ugly, naked bulb suspended from the ceiling. He closed the door. "Sit down," he said curtly. She sank down on the cot; there were black flashes in front of her eyes. The sudden quiet, her deep exhaustion, and her painful hunger aroused such a shuddering along her body that it felt like a seizure. "Wait here."

He went out, snapping the door to. She heard a key turn in the lock. In only a moment, the key turned again and he was back. He was holding a plate of bread and meat in his hand. "You are no good to me if you starve," he said coldly. "Eat this. Slowly, or you will vomit."

She took the plate with trembling hands and tore off a piece of the bread, stuffing it in her mouth, gulping it down. She almost gagged; there was a sharp pain in her throat and chest.

"Slowly, I said." Marite nodded, trying to obey, but she wanted to gobble it, her hunger was so fierce and all-encompassing. She didn't care anymore that she was a prisoner, that her captor was standing before her, watching her tear at her food like a savage animal. All she knew was that she was eating at last. Food was the only thing on earth that mattered.

When she was finished, the trembling subsided a little. He held out a stein of beer; she took the stein and drank from it.

"That's better." He smiled. It was a vulpine smile, but now that her deep, terrible craving had been eased, it no longer looked fearsome. "Now. Let's get rid of this."

As he pulled the sacklike garment over her head, making her naked once more, and began to undress before her, she thought: I played the whore to win Rudi's love. Now I must do so again to keep my life. When he entered her with brutal quickness, she made sinuous motions to hurry him to the conclusion. But he repeated the performance again and again throughout the night. By then she was already learning the art of separating herself from this other woman's body that was being used while another part of her observed the woman with compassion and endured. Finally, in sore exhaustion, she fell into a death-like sleep.

Marite awoke to a morning of almost sinister silence: the room had no window, but she knew the night was over because the overhead bulb had been turned out and brightness penetrated the cracks of the shoddily built walls. The major was gone. She was very cold, and huddled for a moment under the thin blanket of the cot. There was little sound outside the room, only the occasional murmur of a woman's voice, a passing footstep less heavy than a man's.

She got out from under the blanket, and snatching her prison dress from the floor, put it on. This time she noticed the numbers on the pocket—17072. A shiver ran over her. She was a number now, no longer a name.

And she was terribly hungry again, and dirty-feeling. There was a sink in the corner, boasting a ginger-colored bar of harsh soap, a stringy towel, but no toilet. Marite was amazed to discover warm water in one of the taps; the prisoners' washroom in the doctor's office had offered only icy cold. The soap stung, but she was grateful for the feeling of cleanness after she'd sketchily washed herself. But she needed to go to the bathroom desperately.

She went to the door. It was locked from the outside. She hit the door with the palm of her hand, and waited. No one came; there was not a sound from outside. She thought, in rising panic: I displeased him. He has locked me in here to die. She began to sob convulsively; her convulsions set off a rumbling pain in her lower body. She tensed her muscles, leaning against the door in utter misery. To her dismay, she was unable to control her defecation.

She observed the results with a numb horror, starting to cry, utterly paralyzed, not knowing what to do. Then, in a little while, after her sobs had abated, she lurched to the sink and washed herself again and tried to clean up her feces with the sodden towel. She hid the laden towel under the cot and lay down again with a sense of total despair.

The sound of the key in the lock a few minutes later sounded sweeter to her than any music she had ever heard. She was going to be let out; she was going to see someone. Perhaps she would not be left to die. It must be the major. Suddenly, insanely, she was sick with shame about the awful smell.

An enormous woman, dressed in a khaki shirt and skirt, with short flaxen hair, poked her head around the door. She came in then, studying Marite with tiny gimlet eyes the color of slate. Her size was intimidating; she must have weighed at least two hundred pounds. "So," she said in a harsh alto like a young boy's. "So this is the treasure the major is hiding." She smiled and her small eyes almost disappeared in the folds of her fat cheeks. Then her smile died and she wrinkled her nose. "Phew! Where is it?" she demanded abruptly.

Marite felt the heat of shame flood her whole skin's surface. "Under the bed."

"Bring it to the latrine," the woman snapped. "Come." Marite followed her, glad to be out of the fetid room, into a cold and evil-smelling place with tiny sinks about the height of her knees lined up against the wall. The woman waited while Marite rid herself of the disgusting burden in one of the stalls. " Pick up that towel. You will have to wash it in the laundry." Almost gagging again, Marite obeyed and went to one of the tiny sinks to wash her hands.

The hideous woman started laughing. "Idiot! Those are urinals. The sinks are over there." Men and women used this place, then, Marite realized coldly. "Never mind that now. Bring that filthy thing to the laundry. I will show you your duties. If you work well, you may get some breakfast."

In the laundry room, Marite saw a number of women bending over steaming tubs. Some of them were naked. She saw one of the naked women lift a sodden lump of gray from the water, and knew she was washing her prison dress.

"You'll stay here until the washing is done," the huge woman said. "After that the big whore there"—she indicated Tilli, and Marite was so glad to see a familiar face she almost cried out, but Tilli did not look at her—"she'll show you how to iron. Then there are the floors to scrub. If you show that you can be trusted, you may get to work in the kitchen. It's too soon for you to handle forks and knives."

At once Marite understood; she had a quick, urgent desire to stick a knife in this fat monster. But she did not answer—silence seemed to irritate them less than a reply—and lowered her eyes to hide their vengeful expression.

"Go on then, Jew bitch." The woman gave her a playful swat on her buttocks, but her strength was such that the blow stung. Nauseated, Marite felt the woman's big hand linger. Then she was pushed toward one of the tubs. She dropped the fetid towel into the steaming water and plunged in her hands, studying the others out of the corner of her eye to imitate them. The water was so hot it burned, but the heat of the laundry was almost luxurious after the cold of her room, the latrine, and the gloomy halls. When she was through with her tub, Tilli approached her with a neutral face, without recognition. Marite was bewildered until she glimpsed the fat woman standing at the door surveying them all with her gimlet eyes. Following suit, Marite acted as if she did not know Tilli.

But there was a split second in the ironing area when the big woman's attention was distracted long enough for Tilli to whisper, "Don't let them know we're friends. They'll separate us." Marite was too cautious even to nod; she indicated she understood by a swift glance, and Tilli showed a wary relief.

They were scrubbing the floor of the common room when another chance came. Marite was awkwardly squatting down; the contact of her scraped knees with the splintery floor had been too painful to endure for long. Tilli whispered, "Elephant Foot's got her eye on you. If you're nice to her, it'll go better for you . . . you understand?"

Marite nodded once. Considering the gross body, the slitlike eyes of the matron, she felt a new queasiness.

"Take my advice. Play up to her. The major won't care . . . women don't count." Tilli gave her a furtive, cynical smile.

Later, in the kitchen, she was astonished at the ease with which she could smile at the gross matron. The woman's eyes glinted; she allowed Marite to have two bowls of the gruellike mess that was to be their twice-daily ration. When she was told grandly that she would have "free time" that afternoon, Marite knew what to expect. When the key turned in the lock to her cell-like room, it was the hideous matron.

As one grueling day and hollow night succeeded another, time took on a whole new face. There was no time anymore; Marite never saw a clock or calendar. The hours were measured by the key turning in her door in the mornings, by their labor and their sketchy meals, and the major's visit at night. Marite learned to dismiss her longing for a breath of outdoor air; the women of the Vergnügenhaus were not allowed outdoors.

No one, except Tilli and Marite, called each other by name, or even knew the others' names. One day the matron told Marite her name was Elke. As much as Marite loathed the sight of her, knowing the woman's name somehow gave her a semblance of humanity. She learned, too, that using Elke's name brought her unusual benefits—a little wall mirror and a comb. The women bathed in long, open showers without partitions or privacy; Marite became accustomed to Elke's fondling her whenever she bathed, relieved that none of the other women seemed to notice. There was a tacit arrangement among them to give each other a form of privacy by never acknowledging anything.

Tilli was Marite's sole source of information; the soldiers apparently talked a great deal when they were drunk, and Marite learned from Tilli something of what was going on outside the camp. The men, Tilli informed her, hated the major as much as the women resented Marite. "He's a 'von,' too. His name is von Bulow." Once again, knowing her captor's name made him seem less like a machine.

Tilli advised her, "There's an off chance you could get out of here if you played your cards right. One time when an officer was transferred to Berlin, he took one of the prisoners with him." Marite's oppressed spirits rose slightly. It had happened once; it could happen again.

One anxiety, however, plagued her: it seemed a long time since she had menstruated and didn't even know what month it was. She took all her courage in her hands and crept into the room Elke called her "office." A newspaper was there, and the date on it was March 15. Marite smelled it; it had that unmistakable new smell that a fresh newspaper always had. Resisting the desire to steal it—to have something, anything, to read—Marite went hurriedly out again. Uppermost in her mind was the damning date; her menses should have appeared at the end of February. She must be pregnant.

Pregnant women were sent to Auschwitz for the "experiments." The only consolation was that if she died, she would die carrying Rudi's child. It could be his; it *must* be.

Passively, Marite accepted Elke's attentions during her "free time," thinking how little it all mattered when she was bound to die within a few months. But later, helping prepare the dinner for the visiting soldiers, she found a bottle of vanilla in a cupboard and slipped it under the loose armhole of her dress. Holding the bottle tightly under her arm, she smuggled it into the shower, where she bathed and washed her hair. As the major's favorite, she was allowed to bathe more frequently than the others.

She dressed, concealing the bottle again, and went to her room. There, naked, she rubbed the vanilla into her hair and on her naked skin. It smelled so fresh and sweet she was incredulous. That night she met von Bulow at the door, naked above her boots—she had been allowed to keep them, for they pleased something dark and perverse in him. Smiling his thin smile, he murmured with pleasure and took her in his arms, breathing the fresh vanilla scent of her body. Fired with hope, Marite recognized that she had stirred a depth in him she had not reached before; she took great pains to pretend affection and employed all the devices that Tilli and Helge had taught her.

The next night he did not come. Tilli heard he had gone to Berlin. But on the following night he entered with a flat wrapped package, presenting it to Marite. It was a box of chocolates. She was incredulous; it seemed a lifetime since she had tasted such a luxurious, such a fantastic treat, and she wept over the gesture. He observed her with a new look in his granite-colored eyes that was almost pity.

"What is your name?" he demanded abruptly.

"Marite," she answered, wiping her face. "Marite von Durning."

"Von *Durning*?" he repeated. "You cannot be the *daughter* of the Baron von Durning."

"I am his daughter-in-law."

"Gross Gott!" He stared at her a moment, then went out, slamming and relocking the door.

She did not know what it meant until the following evening. When he came into her room his eyes reflected the same odd expression that they had the night before, that strangely reluctant pity, a look resembling tenderness.

Without a greeting, he sat down on the bed. "My name is Reinhold von Bulow," he said quietly. "I went to the academy with your brother-in-law, Friedrich von Durning."

She studied him, hardly knowing how to answer.

"I was born in Prussia," he went on. "I was reared to be a soldier, not to torture women."

"That is why you always look so unhappy," she said slowly.

"Yes. And because I have formed . . . an attachment to you." His face fell; the admission apparently shamed him.

"And I to you," she lied, smiling into his eyes, "even though you are my captor." He leaned toward her with a groaning sound and kissed her savagely. With cold skill, she helped him remove his clothes and started to caress his eager body.

During his next brief absence in Berlin, a wild, unlikely plan formed in her mind. He had told her he had an "attachment" to her. She decided to tell him that she was pregnant with his child. There was no way she could prove the child was his, except to lie. There was no way he could prove it was not.

This time he brought her a pretty, warm dressing gown from Berlin and a pair of slippers. She thanked him profusely and was more accommodating to him than usual. Gasping in the aftermath of pleasure, he held her as he had not held her before.

"I have something very . . . bad to tell you," she murmured.

"Bad?"

"I am pregnant. They will be sending me to Auschwitz." The bald statement made him wince.

"They will not send you to Auschwitz," he responded. "You've been to the doctor, then?"

"I dared not. How could I? No. I just know. From other . . . evidence."

He straightened and sat up in the bed. "Is it . . . von Durning's child?"

"It couldn't be," she lied. "He rejoined his regiment last November. You are the only man who has touched me since."

"What is his regiment?" von Bulow asked blandly, and she wondered if he had seen through her lie. If he checked it . . . . She gave him a false number. "I see."

He held her close to him again and embraced her. "They will not send you to Auschwitz."

There must, she exulted, be some kind of God. He appeared to believe her.

Her mad hopes rose and fell again a hundred times during the nights that ensued. Time, and von Bulow's whims, were still incalculable. But she continued to try to please him in every way she could.

Then at last, a month or so later, he entered her room one night with a pleased face, carrying a soldier's uniform. "I have been posted to Berlin. I am going to smuggle you out of here. We must use great care. I am not a favorite of the high command, you see," he explained with a dry smile. "Otherwise I would not have been sent to this post. But now a friend has helped me, a friend who fought for the Kaiser with my late father. Put this on."

Trembling, she donned the uniform, evidently cut to the measure of a small soldier, because it was a passable fit. She stuffed her hair under the peaked cap. He pulled the bill down over her brow.

"A car is waiting. We must exit in a hurry. Try to walk like a man."

That was all the preparation he gave her. They rushed down the corridor and through the front door of the shack. He pushed her into the rear seat of a waiting limousine with small Nazi flags attached to rods on its windshield.

She sat back in the shadows, keeping her head down while they drove past the stiff, respectful guards at the gate. Marite hardly dared breathe.

But they passed through the guard and the gate. Within moments the powerful car was speeding toward Berlin and freedom.

Chapter 22

"Will you stop that listening, Esther?"

Herman Grieb stood at the door of their kitchen, observing his wife with affectionate exasperation. Her ear was pressed to the wall; her soft dark eyes mirrored her anxiety. In the six-story apartment building in a cul-de-sac off Berlin's Krausenstrasse all the kitchens faced each other. The sociable, gossipy Esther had learned that seven years ago, when they had first moved in and life for Jews had been pleasant. In November 1933, life was not only unpleasant but also perilous. The artist George Grosz, whose family had been threatened, had emigrated to America the previous year. The musician Fritz Busch left Germany "after a series of indignities at Dresden." The Griebs, who were not prominent in any way, had fared better through their lack of prominence. Herman kept an obscure shop, Esther was a hospital nurse. But by September, the boycott of Jewish stores had told heavily on Herman's profits. He would no longer be allowed to make a living. They were going to Switzerland the day after tomorrow, to start all over again with the help of Esther's family.

Herman reflected that they didn't need any more trouble now, not this close to their departure. He said gently, for the hundredth time, "This is no time to be helping a Nazi." He came into the kitchen and sat down on one of the old wooden chairs that would be left along with the rest of the furniture; they could take only their clothes and a few precious small things. With the bitter rage in his heart Herman had no pity to spare for a Nazi's wife, pregnant or not.

"I don't think she *is* a Nazi, Herman. How could they be loyal and move into a place like this . . . and never have any company? You yourself said they had to be hiding something." That was Esther's constant refrain. The whole affair did look odd—a high-ranking Nazi moving into a fourth-floor walk-up with a pregnant wife, when they could have afforded better; an apartment house where last year Communist flags had outnumbered the Nazi banners displayed outside windows before the elections. The man had a furtive air, unlike the other cockadoodle Nazis who walked the streets like kings. And then they had stopped seeing him at all. Esther said she had heard the woman crying at night; they assumed he had left the woman . . . or was dead.

Esther told Herman the Weber woman had to be at least seven months pregnant when her husband had stopped coming home. Count on Esther to be right, Herman thought with a rush of tender pity; she ought to know, as an obstetrics nurse, and as someone passionately interested in other women's pregnancies, since they couldn't have any children of their own. It wasn't so bad for him, but his wife still hungered for a baby. The way things were these days, though, he was almost glad they didn't have a child to worry about.

Esther had taken food to Frau Weber many times; she couldn't stand to see the woman struggle up and down the stairs. Obviously there was no one else to bring her anything. "I don't care if she does have a Nazi husband," Esther asserted. "She's a human being." But now he said, "Esther . . . please."

"Don't 'please' me, Herman," Esther retorted. "The woman could be in labor. I'm an obstetrics nurse. God will punish me if I don't try to do something." She was on the verge of tears.

"The Nazis will be quicker than God," Herman countered, "If we get arrested for breaking and entering."

"Well, I'm going over there."

He knew that tone; when she sounded like that, Esther was immovable as a boulder. He sighed. "I can't let you go alone."

Herman followed his wife, still uneasy and reluctant, waiting behind her as she tapped at the Webers' door. Finally they heard a slow, awkward movement; the door opened. Young Frau Weber stood there, and Esther exclaimed. The poor thing was on her last legs; even Herman could see that. Her eyes were huge with terror and her face was white as paper.

Esther gently went into the apartment and took over; she put a few brief questions to the pregnant woman, nodded, and made her lie down on the bed. "She's in labor," Esther said calmly.

"Oh, my God," Herman whispered.

"Don't pray, Herman. Help me." The young woman was moaning horribly and the sound chilled Herman's blood. But he followed his wife's directions, marveling at her commanding efficiency. This was an Esther he had never witnessed, in all the years they had lived together. Swallowing his nausea, Herman did what he was told. At last the Weber woman emitted an awful sound between a grunt and a scream, and Esther was elevating a ratlike creature by its feet, slapping it on its buttocks. It gave forth a wail.

Herman swayed on his shaky legs and sat down on a chair. Esther ordered him to take the baby and wash it, so she could see about the mother. He obeyed, terrified that he might injure the fragile little thing. It was a girl. After he had washed it delicately, it began to look like a person. He wrapped it gently in a towel, and cradling it, went back into the bedroom. The mother lay with staring eyes and Esther was crying.

Esther bent over to shut the woman's eyes. "She's dead."

Wordless, Herman sat down again in the chair, holding the baby. When he could get his breath, he whispered, "Did she . . . say anything?"

"Only a few words . . . they sounded like an English name—Windom or something like that. And she said 'the star' . . . 'give him star.' " Esther drew the sheet over the woman's face.

"What could it mean?"

"We've got to find out. We'll go through her things. She must have some relatives . . . somewhere. They'll have to know about her. They'll want the baby."

The woman had had few possessions; there was nothing in the small closet but a few clothes. But in the bureau Herman found a letter from Frau Weber to a Frau Elizabeth Wendell in Zurich. It had been forwarded from a hotel to a clinic, then stamped "Deceased" and apparently returned to Frau Weber. Herman opened the letter. It began, "Dear Grandmother," and pleaded for help. Skimming over the letter, Herman saw a reference to New York.

"Esther! Look here!"

But his wife was staring at something on her palm; Herman caught the glint of a frail golden chain hanging from Esther's palm. "Herman. This is a Mogen *David*. She was a *Jew*," Esther marveled. He went to her and she held out her hand. He looked at the tiny star with a minuscule diamond in its center.

"Good God," he breathed. "*That* was their secret. But here, read this. It was 'Wendell,' not 'Windom.' That's a funny name for a Jew," he muttered.

Esther was still holding the baby; he held out the letter for her to read. "There were no other letters, no papers?"

Herman shook his head. "Listen, Esther, we've got to make some decisions, and make them right now. We can't just . . . leave her here," he whispered, turning his eyes from the thin mound covered by the sheet. "But as soon as we report it, the hospital will have to let the police know."

Esther nodded. "Of course. They always do that in the

case of sudden death. And if the police find out we're involved . . ." She didn't have to finish the sentence. They both knew how the Berlin police would treat a Jewish couple entangled in even a slightly questionable situation. They might just call Esther's intervention negligent homicide. Then Herman and Esther would never get away.

"We've got to leave tonight," Herman said abruptly. "Right away. At least we'll get out of the building; Steinman knows places to stay. As soon as we're out of here, I'll make an anonymous call to the hospital."

"All right. I'm ready." He loved her for her calm, her courage. "But, Herman—the baby?" She was staring at him with her soft, hungry eyes.

He started to say: We'll have to leave it at a hospital. But his heart sank. He knew he couldn't say that to her. Maybe this was God's way of giving her the baby she had always wanted. It was risky, it was insane. It could cost them their lives. "We will take her with us."

The happiness shining from Esther's eyes was his reward.

Chapter 23

"We're nearly home!" The Washington train crawled into the dark tunnel that signaled Pennsylvania Station. Kate started to collect her things.

"Well, we *could* have done this in about an hour, you know," Joseph said. It was a perpetual but friendly debate between them—train versus plane. Besides Newark, New York had its own airfield now. Three years ago Floyd Bennett Field had been opened in Brooklyn.

"An hour," Kate retorted, "and another one in traffic from Newark or Barren Island."

"You never give up, do you? I love the way women exaggerate everything. And I love that hat. It makes you look about eighteen." Joseph's dark, brilliant glance admired her small royal-blue beret that hugged the soft waves of her brief hair. "Your eyes look as blue as neon."

She squeezed his hand. "Now I know why the union has two hundred thousand members. After all this time, you can still talk anybody into anything." She saw him beam with pleasure, marveling at the new appeal that middle age had given him. At forty-eight he was far handsomer than he had been at twenty-three; time, work, and their worries had scored lines on his forehead, from the edges of his nostrils to the corners of his lips. But there were smile lines there too—on his cheeks and at the ends of his eyes. The gray in his hair only made the contrasting blackness more striking, and he had an even more noticeable look of authority since he had been elected president of the union last summer.

But his eyes, she thought, his wonderful eyes, as black as anthracite, had not changed a bit since 1909. They smiled down at her as she murmured, "It's like the old days, Joseph . . . union business on Thanksgiving."

He raised her hand to his cheek, understanding all that her statement implied. They had both reminisced over that first Thanksgiving dinner during the stay in Washington, where he had testified on the controversial Reed Amendment. There had been a honeymoon feeling about their private time together and Kate had been sharply aware of the way women covertly admired her tall husband.

"Yes, it was," he responded softly. "It was, and it wasn't."

Kate glanced up at him apprehensively.

"Oh, with *us* it was a thousand times better, darling," he hastened to say. "But I mean the hearings, the whole atmosphere of the union these days. I was never meant to be such a politician, Kate."

"You were *brilliant*," she protested.

"Thanks. What I mean is, sometimes I miss the old ways so damned much, being right on the line, in the heart of things. And even now, after twenty-five years, with all our advances, we've still got shoestring sweatshops, for God's sake. And we—"

The train lurched to a grinding stop, jerking them forward in their seats. "End of lecture." He grinned. "We're here . . . finally."

He hoisted their bags from overhead and they moved forward in the car. "I still say you're worse than your son," she teased him, holding on to his arm. David was stubbornly airborne, and Kate had accepted it long ago. She decided if he had survived barnstorming, he would survive his present job. Last August he had become a copilot for the Lindbergh Line, an overnight service between New York and Los Angeles. At least they saw a lot of him now; it was an immense improvement over post-cards from Nebraska and Mississippi and Idaho.

When they stepped out into the station, a black man called to them eagerly, "Redcap, sir? Redcap, ma'am?"

"Sure," Joseph said, surrendering their bags. Kate smiled: the bags were no weight for Joseph at all, but he always said he liked to "give people employment," and he tipped outrageously now that they could afford it. In this year of 1934, while the rest of America was recovering from the fears of '33, their own finances were even better. Rafael Simson's bequest and proceeds from the sales of some of her grandfather's paintings had brought them phenomenal benefits.

"Uh-oh," she heard Joseph say. "I thought they'd let us alone at least until tomorrow." A trio of people who were apparently reporters converged on them.

"Mr. Barsimson! Could we have a word from you on the Washington hearings?" A raffish and eager young man approached Joseph. Another young man snapped their picture; a young woman with them was eyeing Kate.

"Just a very few words," Joseph said firmly. "We're tired and we'd like to get home. Walk along with us, and ask away."

Kate dropped behind, as Joseph responded to the reporters, "The hearings made one thing clear—'housedress' manfac-turers are not manufacturing only housedresses. They're working under the cotton code, but they're making higher-priced dresses out of wool and rayon—"

"Mrs. Barsimson?" the smart-looking young woman was at Kate's side, giving her an ingratiating smile. "I'm Donna Rubin, of *Women's Wear Daily*. Do you mind if I describe your outfit in my fashion follow-up to the Reed story?"

"No, not at all." Kate had become accustomed to such requests. She was a rich source of copy, she knew, as Harry Dryver's granddaughter and Kate Barsimson the painter. But she always managed to insist that she was primarily Mrs. Joseph Barsimson.

"Your suit looks like a Schiaparelli," Miss Rubin remarked, "and yet it doesn't, somehow."

"That's because I designed it," Kate told her. "I may have been influenced by Schiaparelli . . . not enough" —she twinkled—"to be sued. Don't quote that," she said hastily. Miss Rubin shook her head, smiling. "I learned to sew a long time ago," Kate continued, "before the Depression. But I found the patterns didn't exactly suit me, so I started designing for my own pleasure, making up my own patterns."

"That's very exciting. Do you think you'll ever do it professionally?"

"I doubt it. But look here, this makes me out as a kind of . . . scab," Kate confided. "I should be wearing ready-made."

Miss Rubin laughed. "I'll fix it up," she promised. "We love you and your husband at *Women's Wear*, Mrs. Barsimson. You couldn't get a bad press from us at the point of a needle."

Kate chuckled. "I'm glad. I'd hate to get a bad name on Seventh Avenue."

"Just between us, I have to confess that my question was personal, not for the article. That's just a *gorgeous* suit." Miss Rubin gave Kate's ensemble, with its slender black skirt and its graceful black-and-white tweed jacket, another lingering glance. "You're a fashion editor's dream . . . you always look just right. When you're at a workers' rally you're always understated, and then at those big dos you look sensational." Miss Rubin sensed Kate's controlled impatience. "But I'm holding you up," she apologized. "Just let me ask you what you thought of the fashion scene in Washington?"

Kate summoned up all her tact. "I never saw so many pretty, well-dressed women in one city. On the other hand, my husband's union *does* want to make New York the country's fashion capital. So I was glad to learn that most Washington women still shop in New York." That should do it, she thought with satisfaction, bidding the admiring reporter good-bye and hurrying off to meet Joseph.

When their taxi was hurtling down Seventh Avenue at last, Kate felt herself begin to unwind. "Oooh," she said, "we're on the way." She leaned back and closed her eyes.

"Tired?"

"Very." At forty-four her boundless energy sometimes seemed a bit less boundless, and Washington hadn't been all vacation and honeymoon. Lately, the European situation arose in everyone's talk; the obscenity of Hitler's growing power, like a dark cancer already threatening to engulf the body of the world, underlay their daily concerns.

Kate had been strangely relieved when Joseph was so absorbed in his union work that he had hardly had time to follow the European news. Now they would return to it; a depressing headline leapt from the folded newspaper on Joseph's knee. In these last years they had developed a reaction that almost approached denial, trying not to drown in their fear for Marite and Elizabeth. Kate knew that Joseph brooded about it perpetually without telling her. He didn't have to. She could see it in his eyes, hear it in his calmest words.

She wondered if he were thinking about that now. His glance dropped to the paper.

The cab lurched onto Greenwich Avenue, heading east, and was caught by a traffic light at the corner of Greenwich and Tenth Street. To her right was a small pink stucco apartment building that reminded Kate of Left Bank houses in Paris. She fervently hoped that was where Elizabeth and Marite were by now. Even if Paris had had its violence and uprisings in recent years, they would be better off in France than in most countries. Maybe they were in England.

Kate realized that the cab had overshot their destination. Joseph hadn't noticed either; he *was* preoccupied.

"That was *Eleventh* Street," she said to the driver.

He swore under his breath, swerved into an illegal turn and shot across Tenth Street, turning again onto Sixth Avenue. When they were on Eleventh, and Kate saw the familiar red house beyond the Sephardic cemetery, she had an almost fey sensation of happiness. They were home. And David would be coming to visit tomorrow.

She rushed up the stoop ahead of Joseph, and without bothering to ring, unlocked the front door. The cats, Tarf and Kwan, came into the hall.

"Hello, *hello*." Kate leaned down to pet them. She heard the maid, Loreen, coming up the stairs from the kitchen. "Welcome home." Her smile was wide in her dark face. "There's a gentleman waiting to see you. A Mr. Burgess. He's been here for quite a while. He says it's important."

"Mr. *Burgess*?" Kate and Joseph looked at each other. They hadn't seen the Wendell lawyer for several years; they received occasional letters from him or spoke to him on the phone about estate matters. A personal visit like this was an oddity.

"Where is he, Loreen, in the living room?"

"Yes." Kate pulled off her beret, tossed it on the side table, and made a careless pass at her hair. She was in no mood for company right now and knew Joseph wasn't either. But he put the best face on it he could.

Burgess was standing in the living room. Joseph held out his hand, greeted the lawyer cordially. But Burgess did not smile; Kate thought he looked much older.

He took her hand. "I'm sorry to break in like this, but I have something to tell you that I could not write you about, or tell you on the phone."

Her heart misgave her; she'd been feeling almost too happy when they got home. "Please . . . what is it?" she asked with rising panic. It couldn't be David: Burgess would have nothing to do with an accident of his.

"Sit down, Kate." She did not move. "Marite and Elizabeth are dead. They both died months ago; I only learned of it this morning."

She couldn't take it in. Joseph shook his head. She had never seen him look so bewildered. All Kate could think of right then was how he felt; she was too shocked to have any feeling of her own, too numb.

"Dead?" Her voice cracked on the word.

Burgess nodded, and she saw that he was crying. "Please," he said, "you must sit down."

She allowed Joseph to coax her down into a chair. He pressed her shoulders with his hands; she could feel them trembling. "What happened?" His voice was level and controlled, but she knew it was near to breaking. She raised one of her hands and clasped the hand on her shoulder. She still could not quite believe what Burgess had told them.

The old lawyer sank down on the couch. "Elizabeth died in August of an inoperable brain tumor, in a clinic in Switzerland."

A brain tumor: it explained so much—her mother's rages and caprices, the kidnapping of their daughter. Their daughter.

"But *Marite*?" The desperate question tore from Kate like a cry.

Burgess wiped at his eyes, cleared his throat. "Marite was sent to the concentration camp in Sachsenhausen. She . . ."

Concentration camp. The grim words echoed: Kate felt her body take their impact, like an explosion. They were all she could hear now, blotting out the rest of what Burgess was saying. Kate felt Joseph's hands squeeze her shoulders in a paralyzing grip, then relax, grow limp.

". . . did not die there," Burgess was saying. "She escaped, but only to die later in Berlin." He cleared his throat painfully again. "I have . . . I have brought all the evidence."

Kate felt a scream rise, heard it tear free, as if someone else were screaming. She leapt up from the chair. "What does it matter?" she screamed. Joseph grabbed her and slapped her face.

Brought to her senses, Kate collapsed against him. Joseph held her, stroking her head. Then he walked her toward the stairs, burdened with her sagging body, helped her to their bedroom.

She lay down and closed her eyes; her head whirled like a drunken person's. Then she felt the weight of Joseph's body sink onto the bed next to hers.

Faintly, from below, the murmuring sound of Burgess's voice, and Loreen's, reached them through the open door.

They lay there wordless.

Kate felt Joseph take her hand in his. His fingers trembled, but she clutched them; they were the only lifeline remaining where the universe was a sea of despair.

Late that night, finding Joseph absent, Kate went downstairs and saw a light in the living room. He was sitting on the couch with a thick folder opened across his knees. He looked at her with hollow, reddened eyes.

Silent, she sat down next to him and they read together. There was a letter from Burgess advising them of the deaths, a letter from Elizabeth to Kate and Joseph, asking their forgiveness for what she had done. The letter said pathetically, "At least she will have a good life as the Baroness von Durning."

"She didn't know, then," Kate whispered. "She didn't know what happened."

At least there was that. And it was apparent from the uneven tenor of the letter that Elizabeth had had only flashes of rationality.

Finally Marite's name penetrated: the Baroness von Durning. Elizabeth had achieved one of her foolish dreams for Marite, Kate thought bitterly.

She leaned back and closed her eyes, aware that Joseph was still reading.

"Kate!" She opened her eyes again. "Kate . . . look at this."

He was pointing to the report from Elizabeth's Paris attorney. "Read it, darling. Read it all." Joseph handed the folder to her.

She took it in numb hands, trying to concentrate.

The Paris attorney, a Jew, had enlisted the aid of the Jewish underground in locating Marite in Sachsenhausen, where she had been admitted as a "Jewess." The irony of that was unbearable. Marite had not even been a Jew. Another prisoner who later escaped informed the underground that Marite had escaped too, although she did not know how.

At last, through an anti-Nazi friend in Berlin, the French attorney, tracing Marite as Elizabeth's heir, had been informed that the body of a young woman answering Marite's description had been brought by the police to the Berlin morgue. The police had found no identifying papers in the dead woman's flat except some rent receipts made out to a Major Weber, and an unmailed letter from "Frau Weber" to one Elizabeth Wendell, at a clinic in Switzerland. The dead woman had apparently died in childbirth.

When Kate looked up, Joseph was staring at her with wild hope in his eyes. He even had the trace of a smile on his lips. "Kate . . . do you see what this means?"

Her heart thudded. She looked back at the report: "Of the baby, no trace was found. It is my belief that the infant was taken by neighbors of 'Frau Weber.' On the very day after her death, four Jewish families moved out of the apartment building where the dead woman lived, and all four families disappeared. Generally immigrants flee to Switzerland. But after all these months, the family, or person, who took the baby could be anywhere in the world."

"Joseph!" Kate looked up again, infected by the hope she had seen in Joseph's eyes. " 'Frau Weber' had to be Marite. Otherwise why would she have written to Elizabeth? And she left a *child,* Joseph. She left a child, and it must be alive somewhere. It must!"

Joseph put his arm around her, saying gently, "We can't be sure, darling. But there is a chance."

"How can we find the child?"

Joseph was leafing through the rest of the report. "Look here, Kate," he answered with rising excitement. "The

French lawyer has provided several sources, and so has Burgess.''

''We must find the baby, Joseph. Think what it will *mean.*''

They looked at each other. They didn't have to say it, because they both knew the answer with all their hearts.

A part of Marite would be alive for them again, their last and only hope of atonement for the intolerable loss of their daughter, who lay in some anonymous and unreachable grave.

PART III

Rachel

Chapter 24

Group Captain David Barsimson, RAF, emerged from the Warner Cinema on the last Sunday evening of 1940 into the foggy dusk of London's West End. He felt a bit low; the Bette Davis picture, instead of diverting him, had made him homesick for the States. And his leg hurt. He found himself limping along on a rather aimless course. In another half-hour it would be dark, everything blacked out for the night.

People were not encouraged to wander about then, but David's uniform seemed to give him *carte blanche*. The wardens were good fellows; they would give him a wink and a thumbs-up when they saw him. He wished to hell he could get back to Kent and the squadron right now: the little soreness in his leg wouldn't keep him from taking up his sweet Hurricane. But that medico at St. Bartholomew's was a damned stubborn chap; this leg didn't need another week.

David limped from the fog into the grateful, golden warmth of a small pub he knew well to have a "pint." Someone was playing a tinny piano. The twang of the old-fashioned tune mingled agreeably with loud chatter, the smell of smoke and ale and whiskey. He felt better at once. It had been too quiet outside—a quiet that was beginning to get on his nerves.

David joined the crush at the bar and called out his order to the genial fat barmaid. "Right away, luv."

"AWOL, old boy?" David felt a hand on his shoulder, and swiveled around. It was Hamilton, a Spitfire pilot he had met a few months before at a party. His arm was in a sling.

"Good tó see you, Geoff! What'll you have?" David clapped him on his good shoulder.

"*Have* it, old fellow." Hamilton held up his pint. "When you've got yours, join me over there." He nodded toward a small empty table. "I'm on my own."

"Thanks, I will. I'm on my own too, worse luck." David waited for his pint of ale as Hamilton returned to the table. It occurred to him now, how odd it was that the British expressions came so easily from his American tongue. After three years in England, he frequently forgot he *was* American. Until he would see an American film or hear FDR on the wireless . . . or read a letter from his mother and father. Then he would get that nostalgic twinge again, faint as the twinge in his leg tonight but still very much present.

Hoisting his pint, David paid the barmaid and started to make his way toward Hamilton's table. He was glad there was a table—standing up tonight for a couple of hours wouldn't exactly be fun. He moved aside politely for a pretty WAAF to pass. He felt quite another kind of twinge, and it was clear she admired him. But he caught a rather desperate wildness in her blue gaze that put him off. David always went for dark-eyed women. Anyway he was not quite in shape for that tonight. So he just smiled and went on to the table.

When he sat down, Hamilton asked, "Why are you at liberty, Barsimson?"

David took a swallow of his ale. "Caught something in my knee last week over France. Can't go back till Saturday. Those bastards really knocked up my beauty, too. The plane won't be back in commission for another week or so." He had an uxurious passion for his Hurricane fighter.

"Bad luck. But you fellows did a bang-up job, if you'll

forgive the pun"—Hamilton's white grin slashed his ruddy face under his neat blond mustache—"and your luck was better than mine. Who needs a leg? These quacks tell me I need two arms for the Spit."

"Too right. I didn't see you around Bartholomew. Where've they got you?"

"University. How are you otherwise? What's the news from the 'colonies'?" Hamilton demanded.

David chuckled over his term for the States. He had had a couple of long conversations with Hamilton about their respective families, had shown Hamilton pictures of his mother and father and told him a lot about them, bragging a little about his mother's mural that had graced one of the buildings at the New York World's Fair last year. "Very good, fortunately. And your parents?"

"Top hole, I'm glad to say."

They were silent for a moment, looking around the pub.

"What have you got on tonight, Barsimson? I'm going to the Windmill for that nude revue. Want to join me? Unless you have something more interesting, of course."

"Some hope."

"*Well*, then."

"Think I'll give it a miss," David said. "I'm always afraid one of those girls is going to lose a limb during a raid; the last time I was there the poor girls looked so bloody frightened it took all the zing out of it."

"Well, old boy, I never got a very good look at their *faces*," Hamilton quipped. David's laugh was a little hollow. Hamilton was good company, but tonight, somehow, David was feeling very Jewish and gloomy. He wondered why. Maybe it had something to do with that uneasy feeling he had had when he first stepped into the pub, that sense of an impending thunderstorm that one has under certain barometric pressure; that, and the desperate wildness of the WAAF's pretty eyes. And his own damned fastidiousness about women.

"I say, is there anything the matter?"

David realized he must have been looking distant, rather

sour. "No, no, not at all. Just a . . . pre-raid feeling, I think."

"Oh, Lord, old man, not tonight, please! We've had enough of those lately. After all those hours upstairs, it would be the final irony to catch it on the ground, like a poor ruddy civilian." Hamilton looked so downcast David was sorry he had mentioned it.

"Look here, I *am* sorry. Forget it. I'm not psychic." David tried to sound light. "I should 'wash my mow-uth.' " He gave a creditable imitation of a Mississippi accent that he'd heard in Biloxi during his barnstorming years. It worked. Hamilton guffawed.

Looking brighter, he said, "Well, I'm longing for the fleshpots, Barsimson. Sure you won't go along?"

"Quite, I'm afraid. I'm really not feeling great this evening, with this idiotic pain. Not supposed to be out at all, really, but I couldn't take confinement any longer. But at the moment, it seems they might have had a point," David said. He had an abrupt desire just to sit there alone for a time, and think about things.

"I say, that's too bad. I'll be off, then." Hamilton rose. "It was jolly nice to see you, Barsimson. Here's hoping the next time we meet it'll be in Kent. Keep your pecker up, old boy."

"Do the same." David saluted Hamilton with his pint, and watched him thread his way through the smoky gathering toward the door.

Leaning back and looking around him, David thought how much he admired the British people, with their courage and their self-effacing ways. He admired the way they kept going about their business with Jerry two-pounders popping around their ears. David had attended concerts at Albert Hall, where a signal light had been connected to the right of the stage. When it turned red, that meant a raid was on. Most of the concert audience would stay on while the light was red, enrapt in the music. David had stayed too, figuring that if he were going to get it, he might as well die to the sound of glorious music.

A waiter walked by his lonely table, eyeing his almost-empty pint. "Do it again, sir?"

"Please." The man brought him another pint, and David sipped a little of it, half-closing his eyes. The scene before him seemed to fade into a one-dimensional picture, like a living poster; he was the still but three-dimensional observer, not a participant. He had had that feeling more and more during the last year. As much as he loved flying, finding the air as natural as the earth, there was something horribly impersonal about war from aloft.

At least a fighter plane was better than flying a bomber, he decided. Better to creep up on a Heinkel or a Junkers and blast away at men than to drop a load of death on a city of women and children and houses and animals.

Animals. All of a sudden he had a painful, heart-wrenching image of his parents' garden on Eleventh Street in Greenwich Village . . . the garden where he had lounged with his long-legged father, his incredibly beautiful mother, watching the cats romp among the flowers or leap after a butterfly. The cats. His own black-and-whites, with their star-names, most of their sleek bodies shining black; Shing with her seductive eyes, the white spot under her nose, like a trace of vanilla ice cream, and Dar's white line between his wide green eyes. And the younger ones, the relentlessly mischievous Tarf, and the lovely ginger Kwan sitting on his haunches like a little beaver when David's mother spoke to him.

David let his memory drift to those rough years after they had gotten the news about Marite. Both he and his father had been afraid that David's mother was never going to pull out of her spin into that paralyzing depression. She had, though, bless her. By last year, his father had written him that she was in command again. So much so that the big mural, of which his father sent a picture, was not his mother's only contribution to the Fair. Several paintings of hers—and of course Harry Dryver's—had been exhibited in the contemporary-arts building, and her dress designs appeared in the fashion section.

His father was still the same ball of fire, too, David mused. Into everything—running around everywhere to advise in strikes, coping with all the wartime headache. It looked as if the garment union was leaning now toward rejoining the AFL.

The last pictures David's father had sent him revealed that those years had taken their toll on him, but Joseph and Kate Barsimson were still the best-looking damned set of parents David had seen. He recalled a remark of Hamilton's: "Good Lord, old boy, that's your *mother?* She's smashing. My mother, bless her, looks as old as the dowager queen."

Kate Barsimson was a wonderful woman. The way she had kept on looking for Marite's baby, all this time, never getting discouraged, never giving up, even when his father was ready to throw in the towel. Maybe so wonderful, David decided, that he would never be able to find a woman of his own who came up to her standard. There had been so many near-misses—the brown-eyed, golden-haired girl in Mississippi whose skin and voice had been like honey. She couldn't cope with David's being half Jewish. And the one in California, with her gorgeous, sleek body, who swam like a seal, and wanted him to give up flying to go into her father's business. Actually, though, he just hadn't loved either woman.

So he had gone on until he felt married to planes. There was nothing he couldn't fly. His mother had taken it pretty well when David announced he was going to join the RAF; America was too reluctant to get into the show. David smiled to himself, recalling how flabbergasted his RAF instructor had been with the quality of his first test. Now he had so many hours of combat he had stopped keeping track; he left that up to the record boys.

His leg felt stiff. He had been sitting too long in one position; better give it some exercise. David was so accustomed to the blackouts now that he could find his way about like a cat. He had a sudden urge to walk to London Bridge and look at the Tower.

The leg felt better in motion, but it was a long hike, so he opted for the Underground. That prickly feeling he had had earlier returned: many Londoners seemed to be seeking deeper shelter in the Underground instead of in their basements. And by now Londoners had developed a sixth sense about raids; they had endured more than four hundred since September.

David emerged from the Cannon Street Station, near the Southwark Bridge, a few minutes later. It was not quite six o'clock.

He heard approaching aircraft. His trained ear registered engines that were out-of-sync. The Jerries kept their planes' engines that way to confuse British tracking equipment. David knew the planes were Heinkels. The sirens sounded.

The Germans' He-111's were almost on top of him, with less warning than he had ever known before. A cluster of two-pound fire bombs flared in the dark, striking the steeple of a church beyond; a half-block away, there was a glittering shower of molten white, splintering, flying out in all directions through the blackness.

A sudden renewing hatred, a savage frustration, drove away David's fear. The men of the Eighty-fifth, his squadron, would be taking off right now from Gravesend, going after the Luftwaffe. And he was stuck here with a lot of helpless civilians. Well, he wasn't going to cower in a shelter.

Beams of antiaircraft light were trying to pick up the invaders, but a thick cloud cover gobbled up the light. David watched orange bubbles of antiaircraft fire shoot through the clouds.

London's gallant LFB—the London Fire Brigade—was already trying to put out the fires, but everywhere new blazes sprang to sinister life. Fire bombs punched their way through surrounding roofs, smoldering at first, but then becoming the spark for major fires.

David saw that he was near an air-raid warden's post; the building's wardens and fire watchers were collecting all the sandbags they could find and carrying them up to the roof. He joined a line of men passing sandbags from hand to hand. With that job done he was about to join a bucket brigade when he saw the woman—the young, slender woman in a nurse's uniform, huddled in a dark scarlet-touched cape.

A ray of passing antiaircraft light struck her face: even in her terror it was beautiful. Her huge dark eyes blazed against the whiteness of her skin. She looked lost, disoriented.

"Take cover!" David shouted, running toward her.

She shook her head and started off up the street. David dashed after her, still shouting, hardly knowing whether he could be heard in the hellish din. She might have taken a knock on the head, she looked so dazed.

He caught up to her and grabbed her arm. "There's a shelter right here!" He indicated the Cannon Street Underground entrance.

"You don't understand!" she shrieked. David saw that she wasn't dazed at all, only frightened and impatient, her impatience apparently stronger than her fear. "I've *got* to get to work! The University Hospital!"

The look in her eyes was so determined he decided it was futile to argue, even while the sky was falling around their ears.

"Let's go, then!" he bellowed. "I'm going with you!"

The woman had sense enough not to argue; another incendiary bomb exploded only yards away. He pulled her behind a fire truck for an instant, then along toward the west; her small overnight bag banged against him. She made no resistance, apparently relieved that she had someone to guide her. He had a feeling she had been detoured from her usual route and had gotten lost.

He took the bag from her hand. In a lull, he said, "We'll have to go the long way round—the Guildhall's burning and St. Paul's has gotten some bad ones . . . Holborn viaduct, maybe."

They ran toward the viaduct. He was astonished that his leg was holding up at all, but he had forgotten all about it until now. It caught a little. He gritted his teeth and slowed to a fast walk, aware of her frightened dark gaze upon him.

The sky above St. Paul's Cathedral bloomed like a monstrous orange flower behind billows of swirling smoke. They made their dogged, steady way across the viaduct to the Gray's Inn Road. "Not too long now," he said, to encourage her. He noticed that she was walking with a different gait, as if every step hurt her. "You're all-in! Here, wait. There's a public shelter. You can rest a minute in there."

Reluctantly but with a certain resignation she preceded him into the shelter. It was almost deserted. The pavement shelters were highly unpopular—they were drafty, damp, and all the noise of bursting bombs and incessant blasts of antiaircraft made the walls rattle. He led her farther back into the shelter and started to unbutton his overcoat. It would do for them to sit on.

"Wait," she said, and smiled. She took her bag from him, opened it, and pulled out a heavy, voluminous bathrobe. "Use this, Captain. I can wash this at the hospital . . . there may not be any cleaners left tomorrow."

Her ability to smile in all this dazzled him, and the smile showed her straight white teeth, lighting up her sorrowful dark eyes. She was even more beautiful than he had thought; the grim humor, the practical sense of her statement almost did him in. It took every ounce of his control not to kiss her, then and there.

"You're very kind," he said, and spread out her robe. She sank down on the garment with a loud sigh of relief.

"My feet are almost gone," she confessed. "They put us off the train at New Cross Station, and all the wretched buses were locals. There wasn't a hope of a bus to Central London, they told me. I walked all the way along the Old Kent Road. Then, when you found me, it was so dark and so chaotic that I suddenly got lost."

"Good God! the Old Kent Road. And New Cross is *miles* away!"

"I counted every one," she retorted with the same dark humor as before. He couldn't quite place her accent.

"You're not English," he said, lowering himself rather stiffly to sit beside her.

"No. And you're American, Captain. What's more, you've hurt your leg. How long have you been out of the hospital?" she demanded. She offered cigarettes; he lit them.

"A day." She shook her head. He was able to see her hair clearly now; under her nurse's cap it gleamed bright auburn-brown. She wore it center-parted in loose waves to just above her shoulders. With some of its color regained, her skin was not white, but rather rosy, and utterly flawless. By his lighter's flare, her red lips shone.

He snapped the lighter shut; the heat was burning his hand.

"You'd better let them have a look at it at University," she murmured.

"I have a feeling they'll have more important things to do," he said diffidently.

"It may be bad," she admitted. David was still trying to place her faint accent. His glance dropped to the gloveless hand she was smoking with; he saw no gleam of a ring. She was not only lovely and supremely feminine—her stretched-out legs curved into rounded hips, and her upper body was softly curved too—but also matter-of-fact and intelligent. She had not fluttered, protested, or said something coy in reply to his disclaimer.

"I must go soon," she murmured. "My shift has already started."

He rose at once, but with enormous unwillingness, holding out his hand to help her up. She sprang up with lithe, vital grace, and the hand in his was strong and warm, yet very soft. David could not let it go.

Gently she withdrew her hand from his grasp and said, "Please don't think you have to come with me any farther. It's not far, and you have been most kind."

He smiled down at her. "I'll see you to your door."

She stared up into his eyes, and her eyes looked deep and dark enough to spin down into, like a sweet oblivion. Without replying, she gathered up the robe, shook it and repacked it, and they went back to the street.

"It's over," he said, "at least for tonight." The antiaircraft guns sounded more distant; the bastards' bombers were flying away. But the fires weren't, he thought darkly. All over the place they were still burning, and they looked like they would burn until day.

"Thank God," she exclaimed. "I don't think the hospital got much, do you?"

He studied it. "No. It's a minor miracle. I hope St. Bart's fared as well."

"That's where you were."

"Yes." They were at the hospital entrance. David's heart sank at the thought of seeing her go.

"Thank you, Captain. Thank you very much." She held out her hand to shake his. This time when he took it, it was worse than ever. He wanted never to release it. "Good night," she said with a significant inflection. "Good luck."

"Wait, you can't go yet!"

"I must," she responded, pulling her hand away.

"But I don't even know your *name*. Mine's Barsimson, David Barsimson." She seemed to react to that.

"I'm Leah Berg."

"May I see you again?" he asked in a rush. "When is your shift over?"

"Usually at three A.M. But I may have a double one tonight."

"But may I see you?" he insisted. "May I come back at three and try, Miss Berg?"

She hesitated a split second, then smiled her wonderful, warm, generous smile. "Yes, Captain Barsimson. Come back at three and try." Then she left and he stood there gazing at her as she walked away. He saw her snatch off her cape as if to prepare for action. He was charmed by her retreating back view: the snug uniform clung to the shapely back above her slender middle, hinted at the blooming curve of hips, revealed her long, well-formed legs. She was willowy without boniness.

David was convinced, beyond any doubt. He had just met the first woman he could love.

It was nearly two in the morning before University was back on an even keel. Sister Leah Berg had little time to think of anyone but the injured. She was relieved to hear that the loss of life had been incredibly low—only one hundred and sixty-three people, in all the great city, had died. There were more than five hundred injured, but most of the injuries were cuts and minor injuries to eyes. All but twenty-five of University's patients were released; St. Bart's had taken up the slack, too, treating half of the two hundred and fifty wounded firemen.

The matron eyed Leah. She had been told of the nurse's trek along the Old Kent Road from New Cross. "You look like you're about to drop, Berg. Why don't you lie down for an hour? I'll check on your regulars." Two of Leah's colleagues had been injured, so her station was shorthanded. She was touched by the matron's concern; under usual conditions Matron was a perfect tartar, hiding her preference for Leah, one of the few nurses who came up to her exacting standard.

"Thank you, Matron. But I think a half-hour will do it."

She lay down on a cot in the nurses' lounge, thinking that it was heaven to have her shoes off for a while. The dedication that her superior admired was real enough, yet it was also compensation for Leah's lonely life and starved emotions. Leah and her widowed father, who had been first violinist with the Berlin Philharmonic, had fled Germany seven years ago in the month that Hitler took power. But Max Reiss, the young cellist Leah had planned to marry, had not.

When Max's letters stopped coming in 1934, she had received word through the Jewish underground that he had been taken to the camp at Dachau. The next year Leah's father died, and she had no family left aside from some cousins in America. Leah stayed on in the big flat she had shared with her father, and studied to qualify as a nurse. She yearned to dedicate herself to life. She had focused all her unsatisfied longings on the care of the patients; work had been a perfect anodyne.

She had kept herself remote from the other young nurses, and from men. There would never be anyone else, she decided, after Max, even if her strong feelings at times had demanded release to the point of torture. But she knew she could never sleep with anyone she didn't love. So she had kept her feelings at bay by working even harder, working so hard sometimes that she fell asleep as soon as her head touched the pillow. Her willingness to take shifts for other nurses, and her wry, unfailing humor made her well-liked among her colleagues.

And yet she was always a little alien from them; her losses, her past, had made her older than most twenty-three-year-old women were in England. Anyway, no man she had met had ever really moved her. Until tonight.

Leah considered the man she had just met—David Barsimson. Something about him reminded her of Max—a gentle seriousness, a clean sincerity. Americans were so much more open than Englishmen, and also somehow more masculine. Of course, he was also Jewish. David Barsimson was the handsomest man she had ever seen, with his deep black hair and his proud, sharp features like a Spanish grandee's. His bright blue eyes, in contrast, were positively startling. And of course he had that dashing air common to RAF pilots, a charm that Leah was wary of.

But she hadn't felt so wary with him . . .

Good heavens. She glanced at her watch through half-closed, sleepy eyes. He might be downstairs right now, asking for her; he had said he would be back at three. It was too bad; there was nothing for it now but to accept her situation. Leah hoped he wouldn't be put off . . . strange how much she hoped that . . . she floated off into the bliss of sleep.

It seemed only minutes before she felt Matron's firm, carbolic-smelling hand on her shoulder. It was already four.

Her nap had refreshed her, but by the time she had done her half-tour that ended at seven in the morning, her eyes felt gritty and she moved with a sensation of floating. Now she would have to find out if her flat was still there, after the raid. It was a daunting prospect to face alone. But surely the handsome captain had given up on her by now.

She was incredulous when she saw him waiting for her outside the hospital.

"Good morning." He grinned at her and gave her a mocking salute. He was better-looking, if anything, by the gray morning light, but his eyes were reddened from lack of sleep.

"You look so *tired*," she blurted.

"So do you, but the difference is, you look beautiful." He said that with such gravity that she knew he meant it. "I thought you might need an escort home . . . and I assume you're going home, after that extra tour."

"You came *back*. I *am* sorry."

"Of course I came back. And there's no need to be sorry. Now"— he became brisk—"have you had breakfast?"

She nodded.

"Fine, then I'll see you home . . . wherever that is." She reacted strongly to his grin. It transformed his austere face, making him look rather clownish in a way that tugged at her heart. "Is it in London?" He was unbelievable; he was ready to take her anywhere.

"Yes. Chelsea. I was visiting a friend in Brighton yesterday."

"Then we're practically neighbors. My hotel's within spitting distance of Chelsea."

She laughed at the funny foreign expression. "You must

have been the despair of St. Bart's. You haven't slept at all, and you should be resting, Captain."

"First things first. You must be worried about your flat. Cheer up. I took a bit of a tour this morning, and the Chelsea end seems to be in better shape than this one. Come on, now. I'll see if I can summon up a taxi." He took her elbow, and she went along with him almost as a matter of course, as if they had known each other all their lives. She had never felt such a thing before.

He even found a taxi. As it proceeded laboriously toward Chelsea, Leah observed the grim results of the raid. This one had been the worst so far—there was row after row of blackened shells of buildings, free-standing walls and mounds of rubble. As always, the morning after a raid made a chaos of traffic. The firemen were still battling fires.

At last the taxi drew up in front of her apartment building. "Thank God," she breathed. "It's still there. It's all right." Aside from a few broken windows and charred streaks on the walls and roof, the building was intact.

"I'm glad." David Barsimson took her hand. "Driver, will you wait a moment, please?"

"Absolutely, Colonel. Take yer time."

"I'll leave you now to get some rest. May I call you later?"

"Absolutely *not*, Colonel," she retorted in imitation of the driver. "You can't go off without a cup of tea, at least. Not after what you've done for me."

He looked overjoyed. In his excitement he outrageously overpaid the fare. "Well, *thank* yer, Colonel, indeed!" The pleased cabman turned around and grinned at them. "And lots o' luck to you and the lady."

When Leah let them into the flat, she saw that he looked dead on his feet. Before she even took off her cape, she went to a closet and took out a blanket.

"What's this?" he asked sleepily.

"You're going to lie down. Now. I noticed you were limping, Captain." She gestured at the sofa.

"Now?" he protested. He was swaying with fatigue.

"Now."

He obeyed her. She took his overcoat and hung it in the closet with his cap. When she came back to the couch, he had taken off his shoes and jacket and was stretched out, fast asleep. She felt an overwhelming tenderness when she covered him with the blanket.

David felt a light touch on his forehead and smelled distant flowers. A woman's hand, a woman's faint, subtle scent. His eyelids fluttered open.

Leah Berg stood beside the couch, smiled down at him. There was a dim, warm light behind her like the light of a fire; her glowing hair was also like a fire, her dark eyes less sorrowful. She was wearing something dark brown that made her rich coloring even more vivid.

"Good Lord! What time is it?" He felt hot with chagrin. He must cut a pretty sorry figure, dazed and rumpled, passing out like an invalid before this beautiful woman. "I say, I *am* sorry." He sat up and began to put on his shoes.

"Don't be foolish." Her slight German accent, with its dragging consonants and full-bodied vowels, made the words sound soft and cozy. "Would you like some coffee? I know most Yanks detest tea."

"Coffee? Real coffee? That would be splendid." He stood up. "As soon as I get myself in order."

"The bathroom's there. Then come into the kitchen."

After he had washed up, combed his hair, and straightened out his shirt and tie, he followed the appetizing aroma of coffee into a bright, neat kitchen, where the blackout curtains were already drawn tight.

"I can't believe it's evening." he blinked, sitting down at the table. She turned off the overhead light, leaving the glimmer of a candle, and poured the coffee. It tasted magnificent. "How did you manage this?" There had been a long coffee shortage, among many others, in war-time London.

"A treasure from a grateful patient. Her husband's in the coffee business." When Leah grinned at him, David felt warm all over.

"I still can't believe how late it is." He shook his head, glancing at the drawn curtain. "I feel like a perfect fool, going out like that."

"I'm a nurse . . . remember? You just got out of the hospital and you went all night, I assume, without sleep. I was . . . feeling your head for fever," she added hastily. Her blush delighted him, telling him in an instant what an innocent she was.

"That's too bad," he said deliberately, keeping his gaze on her lovely face.

Slowly her cheeks became a deeper red. At last her long brown lashes rose, unveiling her big, expressive eyes. Her generous lips parted a little, and her eyes met his. She seemed unable to look away and yet so shy, so unpracticed in flirtation that his whole body heated with tenderness.

He got up from his chair and stepped around the table to stand behind her, putting both of his hands lightly on her shoulders. He could feel the narrow shoulders tremble, the silkiness of her hair brush his fingers. That silky tickle galvanized him into desire. But he hesitated even to move his hands; he sensed her inexperience, and the idea of frightening her, offending her, was hideous.

And then, with utter wonder, he watched her tilt her head until her cheek rested against his hand. In all his life no woman had ever made an act of surrender so poignant.

His shaky hands, with this new license, caressed her shoulders, stroked her hair, drew her head back gently against his throbbing body. She said his name, softly and rose to stand beside him. He turned her around and captured her in his arms, holding her so tightly that their bodies joined like brazed metal; he could feel a longing hot and wild as his, and when she raised her face, he learned at long last the form and taste of her generous, sweet mouth.

Gasping from the kiss, he held her closer, moving his half-open lips over the glowing filaments of her hair, running his hands down her vibrant sides. All her flesh seemed to answer his.

Shakily he loosened his hold, and leaning over, snuffed out the candle flame between his thumb and index finger. She whispered, "Come," and he walked close beside her from the kitchen, through the firelit sitting room, into a room beyond.

There was only a faint light burning, but it cast an aureole around her auburn head; he could just make out the sweet curved outline of her dark-clad body. With a shy smile that touched him all over again, she put out that light too. Now he could only feel her presence, smell the faint flowers of her subtle scent in the resonant dark.

By touch he found the fastening at the neck of her dress and pulled the zipper down. As her dress fell away, he savored her bare shoulders and arms with his fingers, felt the swell of her breasts under satin. Dimly he watched her complete her undressing, almost too excited to breathe; began to rid himself of his clothes, flinging them down and away.

When they met flesh-to-flesh he thought again of the white heat of the brazing of metal and knew that this encounter could not leave him the way he had been before. With an enormous effort he braked his runaway need: her innocence was patent in her light, tentative touches. In all the world she had become the thing most precious. He could not hurt or hurry her. He must go slow, go slow.

With the gentlest of touches he began to fondle her body, tracing with delight the shape of her generous breasts, her narrow waist, the pillowed bones above her sweetly shaped upper legs. She made a sound of wondering pleasure, quivering under his caress.

His stroking hands met the downiness of her secret body, and its smooth, trembling flesh, and she cried out with an urgent intonation. Sliding onto the floor, he knelt before her, and began to bring her desires to an even greater life: she was moaning now with an incredulous joy, trembling and swaying while he held her tightly, savagely. David was possessed by feelings he had never known with another woman—a wild lust in giving her pleasure, so strong and deep that he could feel her pleasure in his own drumming skin. Her outcry, her slackening flesh struck like a cymbal against his nerves, like a little release of his own even while his body drove him onward with its own demand.

He pressed his face against her body, kissed her hip bone gently, and heard her gasp his name. Still holding her to him, he slowly rose, caressing the inward curve of her waist, her breast, her shoulder, and her tumbled hair, urged her to lie on the nearby bed and cradled her to him. His flesh stung and shouted with his need, but now he owned an infinite, tender patience, although her hands' caresses were sending him to frenzy.

The part of his brain that still functioned, that was a little rational, sang out: This is what it's like to love. This is the glory—the pleasure of the beloved.

And then she was guiding him, urging him, and he knew at last that it was time: his driving body found a silken corridor, a hidden and enchanted place. His mind stopped, there was only gigantic sensation; far away he heard a slight cry from her throat, felt her wince. A narrowness eased: he was drowning now in a honeyed sea, in a flashing explosion while her hands pressed his back. Triumphant, he felt her shudder, heard her wondering, incredulous exclamation.

After his bursting heart had slowed, he moved from her and lay beside her with his arms about her body. Her smooth haunch felt like a silky pillow; he stroked it and she made a little growling murmur that reminded him of a loud-purring cat.

"I love you, Leah." The words astounded him. "I have never said that to a woman."

But he did. He knew it now. It had happened with the lightning suddenness of the raid.

"And I love you." She spoke against his chest, her warm breath tickling the dark, moist hairs, the warmth thrilling his nerves almost as sharply as her declaration scraped at his very heart. He had been the first man to love her. And he decided he was going to be the last. "You have set my whole heart free," she whispered. Then, after a pause, "Oh, David, I hope we have this one night without a raid."

"We will, my darling. Listen."

Wind rattled at the windows, soon bringing with it the welcome patter of rain.

The Luftwaffe would be grounded tonight.

Chapter 25

"Your eyes look so big and bright they're a hazard," David said. "Don't go near the blackout curtains." They were sitting at the kitchen table again, smoking cigarettes and drinking coffee.

Leah put her hand over his. She still felt dazed after what had happened—ecstatically dazed, almost tipsy. "In just a few hours, I have become another person. This is a whole new life, David." She was surprised at how happy he looked when she said that small thing, even more surprised at the ease of their content. "You look handsome in my father's old bathrobe." It was the only garment she had been able to give him; she had kept the robe out of sheer sentiment when she had given his other things away.

"Until I stand up." David grinned. Her father had been almost a foot shorter than David; the robe struck him at the knees, like a Japanese kimono. "But it feels very good." He ran his long fingers over the heavy wool. "Oh, Leah, I feel very greedy."

"Surely not so soon." She raised her brows and he laughed.

"No, no! I mean to know you, to know everything about you. Tell me."

She got up briskly. "I'll tell you while I cook. I'm starving. Aren't you?"

"*Cook*! On New Year's Eve!"

She had to laugh at his inflection. "Yes, you know, prepare food. Women do it . . . your mother did it, and—"

"*My* mother?" His mockery sounded affectionate. "As a cook, my mother was always an excellent painter . . . designer . . . and general fashion plate. Darling, I don't want you to cook for me; I thought we might go out and explore, see if some restaurant might be open."

"Some hope. I'd *love* to cook for you. It's easy, and we won't have to get dressed." He made a pleased sound. As she took meat from the fridge and put two potatoes on to boil—wishing steak and herbs weren't so unobtainable—he asked, "Can I do anything?"

"Stick to your last, Captain. Men make too much noise in a kitchen, and they always put everything back in the wrong place. Enjoy your coffee." She felt his gaze on her as she searched for something to flavor the food. "Your mother sounds very interesting."

"She's that, all right. A rich Gentile who fell in love with a poor Jew on a union picket line and gave up everything to marry him. We were poor for a lot of years, but now, with one thing and another—all kinds of complicated deaths and bequests—they're not poor at all."

Leah smiled and produced the last of the wine, reflecting how fine it was to watch his sharp, austere face, his strong features relax, then light up with boyish excitement. Every time she put something else on the table she had to touch him. Their elation was like a string of phosphorescent bubbles; it was impossible to settle down to eat until they had both had several glasses of the red and vivid wine.

Finally, they ate ravenously, in companionable silence. She observed the amount of food he put away with a maternal tenderness; he was so lean, so ascetic-looking. It was another agreeable paradox. They stared at each other, big-eyed, over the candle flame. When she was setting a fresh pot of coffee on the table, he said softly, "Tell me what you were like when you were a little girl. What a darling little girl you must have been."

She touched his hair lightly and sat down. "A terribly solemn little brat whose house was full of music." Sketchily she outlined her life, told him about her father. And Max. "I was engaged to someone, but we never . . . we didn't make love to each other." David nodded, squeezing her hand. "He was sent to Dachau."

"Oh, God." He held her hand harder. Then he said, "My sister was in Sachsenhausen."

"Your *sister*! An American?"

He told her Marite's story, ending with his parents' seven-year attempt to find her child. "I think what happened to my sister was the final push for me . . . to England and the RAF. Since my own country," he added bitterly, "has been so slow."

"I see. It must have been awful for your parents."

"It was." He brightened. "But they're very strong people. Just a minute. I've got their pictures in my billfold. Let me get it." He came back from the bedroom with his wallet, held it out to her. "This is an old, old picture of my sister, Marite." She studied the face of the beautiful blond girl with black eyes. David flipped over one of the glassine folders, saying, "As you see, she looked exactly like my mother, except for their eyes." He handed the wallet to her.

"Your mother's beautiful," she exclaimed. "She has *your* eyes. So this is your father. Good heavens, he looks like your older brother, David. They both look so young."

"I think they always will be," he said, smiling. "They married young; my mother was only twenty and my dad twenty-four. He's the head of a labor union. He was only an organizer when they met."

David chuckled. "My mother's family was Tory and rich, but she's a corker. She married my father anyway."

"I like that." Leah passed the wallet back to him.

"You know," he confided, "in a way they met the way we did. In their case it was only a riot," he added dryly. "There weren't any bombs falling on Washington Square. People had more time in those days."

"Yes. They did." Her velvety eyes met his, brightened by the candle flame, and he could see bitter knowledge in them, the fear that his next flight might be his last.

And he had a feeling that when he compared his parents' meeting to theirs, he hadn't done so lightly.

"Happy New Year, Leah."

He hoped they'd have a New Year's Day.

"Thank *you*, Captain." Out of the corner of her eye, Leah Barsimson saw her husband practically slam the door of their suite on the grateful attendant.

She smiled and closed the closet door, where she had pretended to be intent on hanging up her coat.

Then she and David were in each other's arms; he was kissing her again. Leah could hardly credit what had happened: it was two weeks, to the night, since they had met in the raid. And they were married. She nestled against him, glorying in the strength of his arms and body.

He loosened his hold and stepped back to look down into her face. His bright blue eyes were earnest, profoundly solemn. He kissed her again and it was like an unalterable vow.

"I can't believe this," she whispered. "I can't believe this happened so quickly, David. My wild, impulsive Yank."

He grinned and whirled her around, keeping one arm around her waist. "Look, Mrs. Barsimson, we've got the bubbly waiting." He led her to a small round table set with elaborate hors d'oeuvres and a green bottle nested in an ice bucket. "Madam." He seated her with a flourish and opened the wine. "Will you?"

"I will." The reply was so much like the wedding vow that they smiled at each other, looking into each other's eyes.

When they lifted the thin-stemmed glasses and drank, she murmured, "I don't know how you did all this in the middle of a war. I hardly knew champagne could be had anymore."

"We Yanks are truly wonderful," he teased her, reaching for her hand. He lifted it to examine the topaz-and-diamond band on her wedding finger.

"Or my ring," she added, "or this lovely dress, without a single coupon."

"I played on the heartstrings of a motherly assistant at Harrods, pleading with her to ornament the bride of this dashing American." He laughed softly. "You look heavenly in that dress."

It was a model gown of thin, fine wool just the color of the topaz birthstones in her wedding ring; simple and exquisite, wonderful with her dark eyes and hair.

"And I can't believe you consented," he said, looking serious again. "I think I knew I wanted to marry you the first night we were together. But if you'd said no, I would have just kept asking."

She looked into his remarkable eyes and said, "I don't think I could have said no, David. I've waited all my life for you." It was true; even what she had felt for Max seemed a childish infatuation in the face of what she felt for David.

She smiled. "It's as if . . . as if flowers, and not bombs, fell out of the sky that night."

His eyes shone so at that, she knew there was moisture in them. His strong mouth twisted with his powerful feeling. He lifted her hand and kissed it.

"I'm drunk, I'm drunk already," he said, grinning, as he poured two more glasses.

He was in the midst of pouring his own when the telephone startled them both. He set down the bottle with a puzzled frown. "Who on earth could be phoning us?" he demanded.

He got up and strode to the telephone, saying grimly, "If this is a joke of Hamilton's, I'll kill him."

"Surely not." It didn't seem the sort of thing Geoff Hamilton would do; she had met him only that morning, when he had stood as a witness for them, but she had liked and respected him at once. Besides, he had already gone back to Kent.

"I knew it was you," she heard David say. "Bugger off, old fellow."

Then she saw his exasperated face change, grow serious. He was listening intently. "What? Yes, for God's sake, open it and read it to me." He looked so apprehensive that Leah got up and went to stand beside him. David put his arm around her but his eyes were absent and glazed, listening. She felt his shock. He fairly shouted, *"What?* Good God! Why, that's . . . unbelievable," he stammered. "That's perfectly splendid!" He was grinning from ear to ear.

Leah was weak with sudden relief.

"Thanks, old boy! Thank you!" David hung up with a clatter, lifted Leah in his arms, laughing wildly.

"What *is* it?" she demanded.

He set her on the carpet again, hugging her. "They've found my sister's child!"

"Oh, David!"

He let go of her, pacing excitedly as he babbled on. "That was a cable from my mother. Of course Hamilton thought it might be an emergency, otherwise . . ." David grabbed her upper arms, squeezed them. *"Think* of it! She was in England all this time . . . and my mother traced her from America." He shook his head, wondering.

"Darling, that *is* splendid. I'm so glad. But for heaven's sake, calm down. Sit down. Tell me the whole thing." They sat on the sofa and he slipped his arm around her waist.

"Well, you remember I told you my parents kept searching all these years?" Leah nodded. "She's in a children's shelter in Suffolk. Apparently the people who adopted her were killed in a raid. I don't remember all the details . . ." He spoke in a hectic rush. "Some agency must have notified my mother. She's cabled the shelter, saying they should expect me. We can go tomorrow to get Rachel. Oh, that's her name. I didn't tell you."

"Let's go now, David. Right away. It won't be dark for hours. Maybe they'll put us up at the shelter tonight!"

David looked at her. She knew what he was thinking. This was their wedding night. And they had so little time. Only four more days. "Do you mean it?"

"Of course I mean it, David."

"Oh, Leah . . ." He gave her a tender, lingering kiss, and her whole body melted. "I love you, I love you so much."

"I love you, David." She stroked his face. "I never knew what it was to love before."

He put his hands up to cover hers. "I just thought of something. We might be cutting it close, in case there's another raid. It could be safer to go tomorrow; I could go alone."

"We *met* in a raid, remember," she reminded him softly. "Besides, I'm not going to be away from you again." *Until I have to*, she added in bitter silence. "Never."

He pulled her close and kissed her again. "You get better every minute."

They were both too excited to sit down when the woman went to get Rachel.

David paced before the hearth; to relieve his tension, he glanced around the spacious room, which must have been a drawing room before this "stately home of England" had gone to war.

When the big double doors slid back, both he and Leah stood perfectly still, just staring.

A small, delicate girl with golden hair was clutching the nurse's hand. Gently the woman let go of the child's hand and took her by the shoulders. "This is your Uncle David, Rachel, and your Aunt Leah."

David couldn't say a word; he could only smile. For an instant he was five years old again, and he was looking at his sister.

But this little girl wasn't the one he had quarreled with

and resented and teased all those long years ago. This was Rachel. Her dark eyes, which were Marite's, stared back at him in disbelief, as if afraid to hope, afraid to believe. And her whole terrible history was in them.

Then he saw, against the neckline of her shabby little dress, a frail golden chain that held a tiny Mogen David. Marite had kept it all those years, and passed it on to her daughter. David's eyes blurred.

He went to the solemn little girl and knelt down to take her in his arms.

"It's a hell of a good campaign, Jules." Joseph addressed the general manager of the Dress Joint Board. "What we've got to come up with is a holeproof plan to back the step-up idea. Maury? Can we start with yours?"

Before the board member could speak, the door opened abruptly. Kate stood there, gesturing to Joseph.

He was flabbergasted. She hadn't been to the union office in years; she always said a president's wife shouldn't be too visible at the office.

The other men goggled, with expressions varying from bewilderment to disapproval to friendliness. Mostly friendliness; Kate was very popular with them and their wives.

Joseph panicked.

David was dead.

But that couldn't be it: she looked too happy.

"Go ahead, Maury. Excuse me a minute." Joseph went to the door, took Kate's elbow, and urged her out, shutting the door.

"My god, darling, what's happened? We were right in the middle of—"

"David's married!" Kate took a cable from her coat pocket, thrusting it at him. "And Rachel and his wife are coming here!"

Joseph read it. "Our son was never dull. His messages are like firecrackers." He let out his breath. "And his wife and Rachel will be here *next week*."

He looked back at Kate: she hadn't looked so renewed,

so glowing, for a long, long time. He grinned. "That doesn't give you much time, does it?"

"It gives me another challenge."

Joseph laughed. She was already prepared for Rachel; as soon as she had learned where Rachel was, Kate had had Marite's childhood furniture moved into the guestroom and had transformed it into a child's paradise of bright yellow, balloons, and circus decorations.

He recognized the same fanatic light in her eyes now, could almost hear the small wheels turn with numerous lists and plans, with new designing.

"So you see why I couldn't just *phone* you," she said, patting his face. "Now, I've got to get busy. Apologize to the board."

"They'll understand."

When he got home that night, she was already busy with David's room. "I'm going to redo it for Leah," she told him. "So she can feel closer to him, living in his own room."

"That's a great idea." Joseph hugged her, infected by her élan.

A few days later a long airmail letter from David arrived. "Rachel's resemblance to Marite is uncanny," he wrote. "And she wears the little star that must be the same one you gave Marite."

Kate and Joseph looked at each other. The Christmas star of 1909.

There were pictures. The one of Rachel was a little fuzzy, but they could still see the astonishing likeness. She might have been the twin of the child Marite.

Then they looked at the picture of David's young wife. "She's lovely," Kate said. "And she must have enormous courage. Listen to this." She read David's glowing description of Leah, their meeting during the raid, when she risked her life to get to the hospital.

David went on to say he had "pulled some wires," managing to get space for Rachel and Leah on a plane to Newfoundland, a safer route. The implication chilled Kate and Joseph; David wasn't flying "safer routes" over Germany and France. As if by tacit agreement, they did not comment on that sentence. From Newfoundland, the letter said, Leah would cable them the arrival time of their commercial flight to New York.

"Thank God they're all in the country now," Kate murmured. Joseph agreed, thinking that it was a pathetic form of denial on her part to imagine him "safe in the country" for the present. They both knew too well where David flew from Gravesend.

The remaining days were frantically busy. Kate, as Joseph put it, had bought enough clothes for the new arrivals to stock a store; she proudly showed him the renovated rooms. As always, Joseph was dazzled by the speed with which she accomplished so much beauty.

The room that had been David's was transformed; somehow Kate had contrived to make it look feminine while retaining much of its former character. A dressing table had been added, and the autumnal colors of the rugs and hangings enhanced David's old and treasured artifacts— his books, his old model planes and childhood photographs in tawny wooden frames. Kate had placed russet candles in brass holders on the mantel, and hung over it a new painting she had recently done for David: an exciting abstract collage of World's Fair scenes, with the hangarlike Aviation Building, designed to embody "flight in space," prominent. The painting showed the subtly shifting colors of the floodlights that had been used at the Fair, from the reds of Constitution Mall to the golds of the Avenue of Patriots, the Avenue of Pioneers' deep ultramarine.

Kate had let her rich imagination run wild in the room for Rachel: it looked like a miniature circus of yellow and scarlet and green and blue, and there were matching balloons strung around the moldings under the ceiling. An impressive array of clown dolls and other dolls of every sort, bookshelves filled with other toys, completed the picture.

"She'll love it, Kate."

"I think so. After the austerity of England, I want to surround her with color and warmth and everything good."

Before they knew it, the day of the homecoming was upon them.

Joseph's heart tripped like a hammer as he stood beside Kate waiting for Rachel and Leah to appear. He saw Leah first, a beautiful young woman whose bright auburn hair flamed over her wool coat. Then the child who had to be Rachel.

Both of them looked tired and dazed and uncertain. But when David's wife caught sight of them, she raised her hand in greeting and smiled a wide, brilliant smile. Clutching Rachel's hand, she rushed toward the barrier.

The little girl, with her golden hair and solemn black eyes, was the image of Marite. Kate gave a low cry.

Rachel caught sight of Joseph, and breaking away from Leah, come running toward him, shouting, "David! David!"

"Beloved," Leah wrote to David, seated at the pretty desk in the autumnal room. "By now the sun must be rising in Kent, but here in your parents' house, in New York, it is three in the morning. Done in by the grief of our good-bye, and the flights and the strangeness and excitement I fell asleep soon after dinner, then woke just a little while ago, with a longing for you so sharp it was like a physical ache.

"It is better now, writing to you, a ritual I am going to repeat nightly, without fail, until the time when we are at last together. Your wonderful and sensitive mother has put me in your 'guest' room, and here among all your old treasures, you seem less far away. A very touching picture greets my eyes when I look up—Shing is sleeping on my father's old bathrobe. I think she smelled your scent on it, since you wore it so often in London. When I was unpacking I put the robe on the chest at the foot of the bed; your cats smelled it and immediately reacted. Dar has now gone off on business of his own, but Shing, with the fidelity of our sex, is immovable, as if she is sleeping on your lap. I wonder if I will ever have the heart to move the robe at all.

"Oh, David, I miss you. I miss you so much that I feel as if a part of my body has been amputated. We had so little time, and we had just begun to be happy. And yet the reason you gave me for sending me away—the last one on your list, the first on mine—was the only one that could really reach me. When you said that bit about needing every ounce of your concentration to come through missions safely, that if your worry about me distracted you, it could cost your life and those of your men, I had to accept it. And you were clever enough to know that, weren't you? When you are home again I shall watch out for such tricks."

She wrote this with a lightness she was far from feeling, but she knew how much he loved teasing, and the beginning of her letter had been so somber. She went on.

"There is so much to tell you, I hardly know where to begin. Perhaps for now with our arrival." She described Rachel's mistaking his father, at first, for him. "Then, when she saw your father's face up close, she said, 'You're not David!' Your father smiled and lifted her up to his shoulder, telling her who he was. I was as agog as Rachel, seeing New York for the first time. All great cities are *not* the same! The air is so sharp here, so thin and bright, that it took my breath. And where Berlin was golden-brown, Paris silver, and London gray, New York looked blue, with a bright, bright blue sky, a lavender-blue shadow on the buildings.

"But the first thing I thought when I saw your parents was how really beautiful they are. They are both in perfect health and look so amazingly young. Your father's likeness to you caught at my heart. Something very poignant happened when the taxi brought us to the house. Rachel said, 'When will I have to go to the country?' Your parents were utterly bewildered. I explained that in London most children are sent away from the city because of the raids. I thought both your parents were going to cry.

Your father, who was holding Rachel on his lap, hugged her and said, 'Never. Not without all of us. You see, you're in America now, and we don't have air raids.' Rachel seemed reassured, but when we got out, she still looked up at the sky with an anxious expression. I think that one incident, more than anything, moved us all.

"And, David, the *house!* the beauty, the comfort, after London, seem almost unreal. We actually had steak for dinner, and butter. So *much* butter. Also, I found it remarkable that a woman of your mother's elegance should also have the gift of *hamishness* . . . we dined in a relaxed way in that wonderful area adjacent to the kitchen, and everyone took it for granted that the cats begged for morsels and occasionally even jumped up on the table. It is wonderful. I admit I was a little afraid of the idea of your mother until I met her. but she is everything you described, and more."

Leah briefly described her room and Rachel's. "When I was unpacking and putting my things away, opening closets and drawers, I was overwhelmed by what I found— incredible quantities of sweaters and blouses and underwear, *nylon* stockings, and several pairs of fine leather gloves as smooth as London's nonexistent butter. To crown it all, there were suits and dresses and slacks in the closet; shoes, boots, night things. And a lovely coat lined in *mink*. Your mother said very casually that the things are only for my approval, that if anything is not right she'll have it returned. I saw your fine hand in this; everything seems to fit. I've never known such a generous woman in all my life. Rachel's drawers and closets are equally full.

"The cats, of course, are just splendid. Rachel was most charmed with them, as I am. Shing, however, remains my favorite, because of her loyalty to your scent. I must admit I brought the robe for the same reason, wanting to wear it as long as it keeps your special essence."

She was abruptly stabbed with a painful lust, and wrote on rapidly, reminiscing over their private times together, ending with "I long for you with a savage desperation. I send you my deep, unchanging love. You will never know the desolate hollow that your absence leaves in my very soul, how fervently I pray for your safe return. You are all my life.''

As Leah signed the letter, a piercing shriek ripped through the silence.

Rachel. She flung on a robe and ran barefoot into the hall. Joseph and Kate were rushing into Rachel's bedroom.

The child sat upright in the gaily covered bed, her pallor, her staring eyes in dreadful contrast to the bright balloons, the vivid colors, the circus jollity. Kate went to Rachel and put her arms around the small, quivering body, kissing her hair, murmuring. Rachel began to cry.

Leah sat down on the bed, and Rachel struggled in Kate's grasp, reaching out to Leah. Leah took Rachel on her lap and rocked her. "Would you like to stay with me tonight?" she asked her quietly?

Rachel nodded. Leah gave her parents-in-law an apologetic glance. "She's used to me," she whispered over Rachel's head. She was saddened by the look in Kate Barsimson's eyes. "It will change," Leah whispered again, smiling, "when she realizes she's really safe."

Rachel nestled in her arms, not reacting much to goodnight kisses from Kate and Joseph. When they had gone out, Leah said, "Let's put on these pretty slippers, all right?" She slipped the small fuzzy bedroom slippers, with their toes like the faces of yellow kittens, on Rachel's cold feet, and picked up her yellow robe from a chair. Taking the child's hand, she led her to her own room.

The little girl stared curiously at David's model planes, but her eyes were getting heavy. "Go to bed, now," Leah said. Rachel got in the big bed and snuggled under the covers.

After she had turned out the lights, Leah got into bed and hugged Rachel to her body. The small warm form was comforting to her, too, in her loneliness. "Leah?"

"Yes?"

"David's not dead, is he?" The seven-year-old's voice

was anxious, yet it had a tone of precocious resignation that wrung Leah's heart. Rachel equated "going away," already, with dying.

"Of course not! Of course he's not, Rachel. He's going to call us on the phone, in just a few days. You will hear his voice."

The child relaxed a little, and soon Leah heard her even breathing. but she herself lay awake for a long time, staring into the dark. By now he could be dead, she admitted in agony. But he couldn't be. He couldn't be. If he were, there was nothing left for her, nothing at all.

At ten the next morning Kate paused in the upstairs hall, thinking she heard faint stirrings from Leah's room. She tapped softly. Leah opened the door. Glancing beyond her daughter-in-law, Kate saw Rachel, still asleep.

"If you're ready for breakfast," Kate whispered, "come down to the kitchen. Don't dress, if you don't want to. There's just us."

"I'll come right now."

Leah followed Kate quietly down the stairs, admiring her slender form in its high-necked turquoise robe, the exquisite sculpture of her silver-blond hair. The appetizing smell of strong coffee drifted up from the kitchen, and bright sunlight flooded the ground floor of the house.

When they reached the kitchen, Kate said, "I'm so glad to find you awake. I wouldn't have disturbed you for the world. I know the time change . . . and everything else . . . must have exhausted you. Sit, my dear, I'll have Loreen make you some breakfast. I've already had mine."

The gentle-faced black woman brought them coffee. "Good morning." Leah smiled at her.

"I've got some hot tea, too," Loreen said, smiling. "I understand English ladies like that."

"Coffee will be fine. I'm not really English. I was only living there." Loreen nodded and poured their coffee. Leah thought what a lovely voice she had, soft and brown like chocolate. She'd had very little experience of black people. The coffee tasted wonderful; Leah poured real cream into it from a jug.

"You can have all kinds of breakfast," Kate said gaily. "Loreen cooks the best waffles and pancakes in the world. And if you're not kosher, there's bacon, sausage, or ham."

Leah shook her head in disbelief. "It sounds like a fantasy. I can't remember the last time I had bacon. And I'm not kosher at all."

Kate grinned at her with bright eyes. She loves to make people happy, Leah thought with a rush of warmth. Leah could sense also that Loreen was taking it all in; she had a compassionate expression. America was a country of incredible riches. "Some scrambled eggs and sausage would be fine. And toast, if it's not too much trouble."

Loreen and Kate began to laugh. "You should know what a small breakfast that *is*," Kate said.

"That's the truth!" Loreen chuckled. "Lord, Mr. Joseph puts enough away in the morning to feed an army. I told him he eats so much it makes him poor to carry it."

Leah liked the free-and-easy ways between Kate and the servant. It was as if they were friends instead of employer and employee. Maybe that's the way everyone was in America . . . or more likely, that was the way Kate was.

"I know, more and more, what David meant when he said there was no one else like you. I don't think I properly thanked you for all the lovely things you've given me, Kate. They're so *perfect* "

"Are you sure, now?" Kate's bright blue gaze was probing. "For heaven's sake, don't be polite, if anything doesn't suit you. I must confess I went wild. I've never done that before . . . I mean, buying for another person. It's so damned presumptuous."

"Presumptuous!" Leah stared at her. "Really, I don't know how you did it—colors, styles, everything. I don't know how you *knew* so well."

Kate looked inordinately pleased. "Cross-examining my son over the telephone. He picked up his ideas from me and his father. You see, Joseph's father was a tailor, and

Joseph was a tailor's apprentice for a while. On top of that, he's had more than forty years in the clothing trade. David, unfortunately, has two words for women's clothes— 'nice' and 'funny.' When he told me that you always look 'nice,' and never 'funny,' it was easy enough to translate.''

Leah laughed.

''You're feeling a little better today, aren't you?'' Kate asked, suddenly serious and concerned.

''Oh, yes, Kate. Yes. So much better. I wrote a long, long letter to David in the middle of the night, and it helped so much.'' She attacked her breakfast with enormous appetite, while Kate sipped coffee, seeming to discreetly enjoy watching Leah eat. Like a real Jewish mother, Leah decided with affection.

''Which reminds me. There's a post office on Tenth Street, right around the corner. And I've got a wad of airmail stamps in the living-room desk. David's a horrible correspondent. Now that you're here, though, we're hoping there'll be more letters,'' Kate teased her.

After she'd eaten and was having another cup of coffee, Leah took cigarettes from the pocket of her robe and offered one to Kate. Kate lit their cigarettes and said, ''When you get your breath, my dear, sometime maybe we can have a talk about Rachel. What we're going to do with her—school, and all that.''

''Of course.''

''Not today, though.'' Kate twinkled at her. ''For a while I need a holiday. There are so many wonderful things to see and do, Leah. And we natives don't even see and do them until someone comes from out of town. I don't think I've been to the Statue of Liberty or ridden the Staten Island ferry for twenty years!''

''I just can't wait to do it *all*.''

The cats wandered in, as if from nowhere, looking sleepy. Leah caressed each one in turn. Shing jumped on her lap.

''Ah. She knows the closest one to David,'' Kate murmured. She looked at Leah.

A sudden poignant longing for him struck Leah; she could see his pitch-black hair, his bright eyes that were the exact eyes of the woman across the table. Kate seemed to know what she was feeling; she reached across the table and took Leah's hand, stroking it.

"You must have wondered why I hadn't even mentioned him much this morning," Kate said softly. "Maybe you've guessed that's one of my ways of . . . handling it. Otherwise I think I might go mad. David's one of the reasons I go rushing around, working a lot, doing things, buying things. My way of warding off the . . . 'demons.' "

"I understand." She did. She planned to ward off her own demons by keeping frantically busy herself. "Why don't I go up and check on Rachel?" she suggested. "Or let's both go," she added. "Maybe you and Rachel can do the next breakfast tour in this splendid hotel"—Leah grinned at Kate—"while I get dressed and mail my letter."

They got up and Kate put her arm around Leah's waist. "I like the way you think," she said lightly, but Leah could hear her gratitude. It would be a good chance for Kate to get acquainted with her grandchild. When Rachel got to know Kate, Leah decided, she would have to love her.

After she returned from the post office, Leah noticed that Rachel seemed a bit easier already, and they had a delightful day together. Kate had a way of hurrying without rush, a mysterious gift that Leah decided she would like to emulate. Kate suggested that they spend the first day exploring Greenwich Village, not wanting to subject Rachel yet to the roar of the subway trains, the crowds of rushing people "uptown."

The weather was milder than the day before; warmly dressed, they strolled about the twisting streets in the brilliant sun and looked into charming byways and visited many small shops. At almost every shop Kate bought some little thing for Rachel, and they lunched at a restaurant just like an English inn, on a quiet corner amid old trees; then strolled to a huge motion-picture theater, the

Sheridan, to see *Fantasia*, a new Walt Disney movie. When they were coming out of the theater, Kate asked Rachel how her tummy was—she'd had a candy bar as well as a whole box of popcorn.

"Fine," Rachel said. "I'm hungry." Kate's glance met Leah's; the child had probably never had quite enough to eat in England.

To mask her deep concern, Kate said, "You're as bad as Jonah and the whale. We'll get you something else right away. Do you know what a hamburger is?" Rachel shook her head. "Well, you're going to find out. Right this minute."

Rachel burrowed down under the cover with the clowns on it, hugging the big black-and-white panda bear, feeling very sleepy. She was beginning to believe that there was nothing to be afraid of anymore. Leah had not been telling her a story; David had talked to her on the telephone the other night just before she went to sleep.

And she was getting used to her fourth *mutter*, the lady with blue eyes and yellow hair like her own, who scared her at first. The lady was Nan now, and Joseph was Zayde. They laughed when Rachel called him that at first, and made a joke about Rachel being a "real Jew," but that was what her first *mutter* had told her the word for "grandfather" was. When they laughed, though, it wasn't mean. They all looked and sounded happy. Zayde always picked Rachel up high in the air when he came home at night; she liked that, because no one had ever done it except David. Rachel's first *fater* had been kind, but fat and sad. Nobody seemed sad in America, except sometimes when they talked about David; Rachel would be awfully glad when he came back.

Right now, though, she was having a very good time. Leah, her third *mutter*, and Nan and Zayde still hadn't gone away. No bombs had dropped out of the sky, the way they did in England before she lived in Suffolk. Even there, she remembered, the children never had the wonderful things Rachel had in America—the warm hats and coats, the toys, the oranges and candy and popcorn.

Or *katzen*. Rachel opened her sleepy eyes and petted the little black-and-white cat lying beside her. She liked all the *katzen* a lot, but Tarf seemed to be her special friend, and he was warm, too. Sometimes he slept curled up to her legs.

Rachel loved most of all to be warm. It was nice to come into the house out of the cold outside. Even outside she was never cold, with all her new clothes. There was always something to look forward to. In Switzerland and England, there had only been her birthday and Hanukkah. Here there were days like that all the time. Nan said there would be another celebration pretty soon, something they called Valentine's Day. People gave each other heart-shaped boxes of candy and other presents. Rachel hoped she would get a lot of candy; she just couldn't get enough of it. She thought maybe one reason she liked Loreen so much was that her skin reminded Rachel of chocolate. Once Rachel asked Loreen if she tasted sweet, too. Everybody looked worried for a minute, but Loreen just laughed and hugged Rachel.

Rachel went over in her mind all the other good things that were supposed to happen later on—the holiday called Easter, which her Zayde said was really "Pesach-Easter," when they had toy rabbits and chickens and baskets of eggs made out of candy. Nan also said when it got really hot they might all go to a house by the ocean where they could swim.

It seemed as though every day something nice and different happened. And she hadn't had a bad dream for a while—that dream with the noise and the screaming and the bombs coming from the sky.

Rachel was getting so sleepy now she could hardly think about things anymore. Her eyes closed, feeling heavy, shutting out the dim little light which Nan always left on at night for her.

* * *

Leah sealed her nightly letter to David and leaned on her elbows to look at his photograph. She had longed to hint to him of her new high hopes, but didn't dare. It could be a false alarm, the interruption caused by deep emotional upheaval and change.

But she had always been like a clock, almost to the hour. If nothing happened by Valentine's Day, she was going to be tested.

Don't let it happen, God, she whispered. She had never wanted anything so much as David's baby . . . except for him to be here, at this minute.

Leah read through all his letters again, lingering over the passages she couldn't share with Kate and Joseph.

There had been another raid the night after she and Rachel had left. "Field Marshal Sperrle's boys," as David called them, scored a direct hit on the Bank Underground Station, creating an enormous crater in front of the Royal Exchange—a crater so deep and wide that the Royal Engineers would have to build a bridge across it.

"Don't worry, my love, I didn't see it this time," he had written. The rest of the sentence was blacked out by the censor; she inferred that he had said "not from the ground." She rubbed her sweaty palms on her robe: every newsreel she saw, every newspaper account of RAF dog-fights over London or sorties over France, brought fresh terror. There was no way to find out what really happened, with the tight censorship of both the news and his letters.

All she could be sure of was that he had been alive on the last date he wrote to her; London was so besieged now that it was almost impossible for him to get clearance for a personal transatlantic phone call.

Leah got up and paced the carpet, back and forth and back and forth again, trying to tire herself into sleep.

He must make it through, she repeated over and over in wretched silence, listening to the winter wind buffet the house.

Leah had memorized a phrase from one of the thin sheets scribbled in his bold, black hand: "Your letters are a quiet light for me in the loud dark. They sustain me, Leah, like the very oxygen in my blood.''

She concentrated hard, in the hope that he would hear her answering, as he rose in the light of the English morning: So do you, my love, so do you. and soon another part of us may be alive.

Chapter 26

Almost every day was like a birthday to Rachel. Nan and Leah and Loreen were always nice to her, never sad like her first *mutter* or impatient like the ladies in Suffolk. But the part of the day Rachel liked the best was when Zayde came home and picked her up in the air the way David had done.

Rachel was still waiting for him to go away, because men always did. First her *fater,* and then David had. It had happened to the other children, too. Another girl in Suffolk had a father in the RAF and she said his plane had fallen down and he had died. Rachel lived in terror that David's plane would fall down too, and she would never see him again.

There were so many things they didn't tell her; sometimes Zayde would stop reading David's letters when Rachel came into the room, and Nan acted very funny at the picture show. Between the cartoon and the movie, she always took Rachel out to walk around the lobby, sometimes saying she wanted to see if the snow had stopped, other times that it was time for popcorn or she was tired of sitting. Rachel could always hear a kind of marching music from inside the picture show then, and a man's voice talking loud.

Sometimes when Rachel would say something, all the grown-ups would look at each other strangely. That had happened when they showed her the circus bedroom and she had asked Nan where the beds were for the other children; it happened again when she pulled her curtains together at night so the Germans couldn't see her light.

Most of the time, though, it was like a birthday or Hanukkah, or what some of the English children called Christmas. Valentine's Day was just wonderful. Rachel put on her red dress before Zayde came home, and when he did, there were a lot of presents. Loreen gave Rachel a little box shaped like a heart with different-colored heart candies in it, Leah gave her a bigger satin box of choco- lates, and Nan and Zayde gave her a bracelet with a gold heart on it. Nan said it was a charm bracelet and on every special occasion she would get another charm to wear on it until she had a lot of charms.

Leah's eyes were very big and shiny. She got three presents from David, two letters and a ring that had wings above a heart. Rachel's feelings were hurt that David hadn't sent her a valentine; a valentine meant you loved someone. She knew David still loved her, though, because at the end of his letters that Zayde read to them, David always said to give his love to Rachel. Of course, he always said to give it to other people, too . . . and to the cats, so maybe that didn't mean anything.

The week after Valentine's Day all of them seemed to act different. Leah's eyes were bigger and shinier than ever, and one afternoon she whispered something to Nan and Nan laughed and cried happily and hugged Leah. Right after that Nan went uptown and came back with a lot of packages. All of them, except one for Rachel, were Leah's. That night Nan whispered to Zayde and he looked very happy too. Rachel wished they would tell her what it was all about.

But she had plenty to do now that the weather was getting warmer and Nan and Leah took her to a lot of new places. They went uptown to see two very old ladies named Aunt Bertha and Nanzia, who was Zayde's mother. The old ladies hugged her and kissed her a lot and gave her good things to eat. The food Rachel liked the best was a candy that tasted like roses. While they were there some other children came; they all had black hair and let Rachel play with their toys. She waited for them to start crying, the way the children did in Suffolk, but they never did.

At Easter, Nan gave Rachel an egg for her bracelet and a new spring outfit and Nan and Leah took her to the Easter Parade on Fifth Avenue. It was a funny kind of parade; there were no flags or bands, just a lot of people in pretty clothes. When they came home, Nan told Rachel there were secrets hidden in the grass in the garden, and she found toy rabbits and candy and real eggs in all different colors. Rachel decided she loved Easter better than any of the other days.

Rachel couldn't understand why nothing bad had happened yet, but she was glad. The bad dreams were going away and she didn't wake up at night anymore. But she couldn't understand why Leah was getting so fat. She asked Nan about it, and Nan said it was because she was going to have a baby in October, a little before her own birthday. (Nan had asked her, when she first came, when her birthday was—she couldn't understand that, because parents always knew, but of course Rachel had told her November 13.)

"If I'm going to get a cousin, why is Leah fat?"

Nan gave her a funny smile and said that's the way women get before they have babies. Then she asked Rachel, "What's the matter?"

"Are you all going to love the baby more than me?"

Nan gave her another strange look and hugged her and said, "No, no. Never." Still Rachel didn't think she was going to like the baby much; there had been one in Suffolk and it didn't do anything but cry.

Summer was even better than Easter. They all went to a house by the ocean on Long Island. Nan and Zayde came back to the city after a while but Leah and Rachel stayed. There was a dog and miles of sand and Rachel loved to play in the ocean; it wasn't like the ocean in England at all, that had no sand, only rocks.

Before she knew it, it was time to start school, which was just around the corner from home. It was still warm, and Rachel had a lot of pretty new cotton dresses to wear. She didn't like the other children much, but she was used to a lot of strange children, after the home in Suffolk and the other school in England. The teachers were nice and the questions they asked were easy to answer. Her first *mutter* had taught Rachel to read when she was only four, so she read very fast. When the other children read slower, she got sleepy. They didn't like her because she could read so fast, but Rachel didn't care much; after school she could go home, where people did like her.

One girl really didn't like her, and tried to stick her face with a pen. Rachel slapped the girl—her name was Dorian, a silly name—and then later dipped one of Dorian's curls in her inkwell. It was easy, since Dorian sat right in front of Rachel, and it made Dorian cry a lot when she saw her red curl all blue at the end. The teacher took them both in the cloakroom and told them they mustn't fight, but Rachel felt fine because Dorian never bothered her again.

The girls were jealous of her because of her dresses and her bracelet. Nan had given her a little apple for the bracelet to celebrate the first day of school; on her birthday she was going to get a cake for it, on Halloween a pumpkin, on Thanksgiving a little turkey, and at Hanukkah-Christmas a tree. She had a lot to look forward to.

One day in October she came home from school and Nan and Leah were gone. Loreen said they were at the hospital. Rachel said she wanted to go too, but Loreen told her that children had to be twelve to visit. Zayde didn't come home when he usually did, and Rachel was very lonely. Finally Nan and Zayde came home, almost at the time Rachel was supposed to go to sleep, and told her she had a new cousin named Jacob.

About a week later Leah and the baby came home. Leah was still very sweet to Rachel, but Rachel decided she hated the baby. Everybody paid more attention to him than to her, even the cats. Leah let the baby feel the cats' heads, and the baby made a silly sound and the cats purred.

Rachel had another fight with Dorian at school, and also hit a boy and made his nose bleed. Nan came to school with her one day and went off to talk to the teacher. After that people paid more attention to Rachel. She decided they would look at her more if she was bad; it was something to remember.

Her birthday was nice, too, with the gold "cake" for her bracelet. She hated the fuss they made over the baby, and began to wonder if being bad had helped. It was very confusing, even when Leah and Nan tried to explain things to her. And after the fight at school, Zayde talked to Rachel in a different kind of voice. Nice, but different. Rachel heard him and Nan talking about her one night—they left her door open so she would feel less lonesome—and she couldn't hear it all, but she caught words like "spoil" . . . "hard on her later, Kate" . . . and "too much." Rachel heard Nan answer, sounding kind of mad, "What is too much . . . after what happened to Marite?"

It was like a mystery story. Rachel made up her mind to ask Nan about the person named Marite. Maybe she would do it right now. But it was so cozy in the bed, and Tarf was asleep on her legs, and she hated to make him move. Rachel decided to ask Nan in the morning.

While they were having breakfast, Rachel suddenly said, "Nan, who is Ma-reet?"

Her grandmother was putting her fork right up to her mouth and the fork just stopped; her grandmother held the fork in a funny way, looking at Rachel. Her eyes got sad. She put down her fork and touched Rachel's arm.

"I heard you talking last night," Rachel said.

Nan nodded, still sounding sad, and said slowly, "Marite was your mother, Rachel. Your real mother."

"Where is she?"

"She . . . died, Rachel. When you were just a baby, in Germany. And the Griebs took care of you after that, because they were kind people."

Rachel nodded. She knew about people dying; a lot of people died all the time in England. But she wished she could have seen her mother. "What did she look like?"

"Exactly like you, Rachel. I'll tell you what—when you come home from school today, I'll show you all her pictures. Would you like that?"

"Yes."

When she got up from the breakfast table, Nan hugged her. "Rachel . . . are you okay? I hope you won't let this make you too sad, darling."

"It doesn't, Nan. Just about everybody's mother and father, in the shelter, was dead. We were all orphans. I just wanted to know."

Her grandmother gave Rachel a funny look and hugged her harder.

That afternoon Rachel studied the pictures. It was all true. Her real mother had looked just like Rachel when she was a little girl. Rachel noticed that Nan and Zayde kept looking at her that night, and the next few days, a lot more than usual.

But what Rachel had told Nan was the truth: she didn't feel that bad. It was so long ago, and there was so much else to think about. Rachel was getting along better at school. She didn't fight now. If she didn't like one of the children, she had learned to just look right through her, like she was glass, so Rachel got left alone. The teachers began to like her better because she was "smart" and could answer questions.

She was really looking forward to Christmas-Hanukkah, and sometimes she even liked Jacob a little, because he *was* cute. He had a little mop of reddish hair and eyes they said would be as blue as David's.

Then one Monday morning, a few weeks before Christmas, Zayde had the radio on before Rachel left for school. A man with a deep, solemn voice announced that the Japanese had bombed a place called Pearl Harbor. He said it was a day that would live in infancy.

"Infancy" meant "children." Rachel heard Zayde say, "My god, we're at war."

Rachel stood at the kitchen door staring at the others. They had lied to her. They had told her America was not going to be in a war, that there would never be bombs falling from the sky over New York.

Now there was. And soon Zayde would go away, like David had, and Nan would cry over him the way Leah sometimes did over David. And Rachel would have to go to the country with Jacob and sleep in a bed in a long row; the bombs would kill people and burn up the house and the cats and all of Rachel's beautiful dresses.

She dropped her book satchel on the floor, she was so scared.

"Rachel. Rachel," Zayde said in a soft voice. "Come here, darling."

But she couldn't move. And when she tried to cry, or say something, nothing came out of her eyes, nothing come out of her throat except a kind of a horrible croaking, like a big bird in a cartoon.

The doctor came into the hall and shut Rachel's door with a quiet click. All three of them were there, too anxious to wait downstairs.

"There's nothing organically wrong with her throat, " he said. "From what you've told me, my guess is that it's purely hysterical. If this symptom doesn't disappear, I can recommend some very good people for her to see. I've given her a very mild sedative, by the way, to make her sleep. Try not to worry too much." His sharp, rather sad gaze touched their faces, one by one. "Children are very resilient. I've heard of English children having these hysterical symptoms and getting better almost overnight."

"What do you think we should do? I mean tonight, right now?" Kate asked him anxiously.

"Just be as calm and natural as possible. See that she goes out as much as possible, so she can see for herself that things are still okay in America . . . and New York."

"With any luck at all they'll stay that way." Joseph sounded grim.

The young doctor's smile was no lighter. "Let's hope so. I have a feeling I'll soon be treating sailors, but my associate will be around to help you."

Kate wished him luck and offered him a drink. Declining, he hurried away, saying he had another call.

When they went downstairs, Leah murmured, "I still can't believe it. It all happened so fast."

"I can't either." Kate sounded so disturbed that Joseph asked her, "Do you want me to stick around for a little while?"

"No, darling." Kate kissed him. "I can imagine what's already waiting for you. Go on, please." The unions and the factories would already be mobilizing, too, she was sure. There would be military uniforms in production instead of civilian clothes, and with the changeover the union would have to face a whole new set of problems.

Joseph, who had been helpless in the face of Rachel's condition, looked relieved, in charge again. He hurried out.

"Oh, my God." Kate felt her strength drain away. "Let's talk, Leah."

"I'll get the baby."

Kate waited until Leah came back, holding Jacob. After a brief look at Rachel, she led the way down to the kitchen. Loreen was subdued and solemn when she brought them coffee, although she managed a smile for Jacob, ruffling his tiny thatch of reddish hair. He gurgled at her and held up his small hands.

"Oh, let me take him a minute, Miss Leah. It's a mighty sad day, and this little boy has feel-better built right into him." Loreen grinned at them.

"He sure does." Leah handed the baby to Loreen. He settled happily against her wide breasts.

"Good Lord," Kate said, "he's barely two months old, and already I can see David in him, Leah. That outgoing sweetness, that confidence with the world." She lit a cigarette. She had been smoking more and more, ever since the summer when the RAF had been flying raid after raid over Germany. She couldn't even imagine what Leah must have been feeling.

"But I'm so glad he has your hair. I hope it stays that way." Kate smiled at Leah and leaned over to pat her face. The dark eyes which had been twinkling at the baby were somber. "You're quite something. I don't think I could have been as strong as you, through all this."

"From what David told me, you've done all right for a number of years, Kate." Leah took the baby back from Loreen so she could start breakfast.

Kate shook her head, observing the easiness of Leah with the baby, thinking back to the time when David and Marite had been infants, and of her own lack of expertise. "I admire you so much," she said softly. "I had Joseph with me both times, when David and Marite came, and yet I never managed half so well as you."

"You didn't have a Kate, for one thing."

"Oh, Leah. What a dear thing to say." Kate was so touched by that, her voice shook when she went on. "I can't help feeling that Rachel's illness started with *me*."

"With *you*? Kate, that doesn't make sense."

"It does, Leah. If I had been a better mother, my daughter would never have run off in the first place . . . if I'd found her, her daughter wouldn't have been born under those horrible conditions."

"Kate." Leah took her hand and squeezed it. "David always said that even if you'd found Marite, there was no guarantee that she would have *wanted* to come back; that she'd been under her grandmother's . . . spell since she was a little girl."

"That's what it was, all right. A spell," Kate said. Loreen had put their breakfasts before them, but the food had no appeal for Kate. "I wonder how much of Marite's . . . strangeness has survived in Rachel. Compounded by all the poor little girl has gone through. What *are* we going to do, Leah?"

"Exactly what Segal told us, Kate. If she's not all right by tomorrow, we'll take her to see that other doctor."

When Rachel woke up that afternoon, she was still silent, and was reluctant to come out of her room. Kate decided not to press it, and allowed her to have dinner there. She noticed Rachel was reading avidly when she went in to say good night, and the child reacted indifferently to their caresses.

The morning after that she submitted to the idea of getting dressed for the visit to the doctor. But when they got to the front door, she dug in her heels, obviously afraid to go outdoors, and only relaxed a little when they were inside a taxi.

After she had been examined and had her history taken, the doctor recommended a special school that offered something new called speech therapy, born of the European war. It had helped combat veterans, Kate and Leah were told.

Thereafter Kate took Rachel to the school every day and was there waiting when it was time for her to go home. She was still silent. Kate learned of another specialist and took her to him, with no more success than before.

As Christmas approached, the whole household adjusted to the small, silent, ghostlike Rachel. All of them tried in every imaginable way to coax some life from her, waiting moment to moment for her to laugh or speak. Even her Christmas presents, which were more elaborate than any others had been, evoked only a small response. It was a subdued festival; the only bright spot was the baby, who gurgled with delight when he was shown the brightly decorated tree.

One morning in January, Kate rushed to answer the doorbell. A messenger handed her a yellow envelope. Her heart leapt to her throat and fluttered and she thought she might faint. Leah stood anxiously behind her with the baby in her arms. Dear God, Kate thought, is it David? Her hands were shaking so she could hardly sign for the telegram. She saw that it was addressed to Leah.

"It's for you," she quavered.

"Open it for me, Kate. Please."

Kate tore it open and shrieked joyfully to Leah, "He's coming home, Leah! He's coming home!"

Leah started to cry. "Oh, Kate!" She took the yellow paper from Kate's hands and read it over and over, as if she were unable to believe her eyes.

"Oh, Loreen!" Kate called out, running toward the kitchen stairs. "David's coming home!"

"Oh, Lord, thank the Lord." Loreen was halfway up the stairs, clasping her hands together before her breast, smiling widely.

When Kate turned back to the living room, she saw Rachel standing on the stairs, staring down at them. She went to the child and encircled the small body in her arms. "Rachel, David's coming home. He'll be back next week!"

Rachel stared at her, unbelieving. Then she smiled, and repeated in her normal voice, "David's really coming home."

Chapter 27

The week before David arrived was full of festive anticipation. Rachel could talk again, and each night when
Joseph came home for dinner it felt like a party.

Now as they waited together at the pier for David's
ship, their excitement was almost unbearable. Rachel finally saw David waving at them. He looked just the way
he had looked when he came to take Rachel away from
Suffolk—tall and handsome in his uniform, except now
there was a black patch over one of his blue eyes, like a
dashing pirate.

Rachel broke away from Nan and ran toward him,
grabbing at his legs. But he didn't even see her, at first; he
was holding Leah in his arms, kissing her and kissing her.
Rachel yelled out his name, still clinging to his legs, and
finally he looked at her. He was laughing and crying at the
same time. Instead of scooping up Rachel in his arms and
whirling her around, he just bent down and kissed her,
keeping his other arm around Leah. Then Nan and Zayde
were hugging him and kissing him too, and everybody was
talking all at once.

They got in the big car, which Nan said they had rented
so they could all get in together with David's baggage.
David laughed and said he only had the one big suitcase;
he had given a lot of stuff away, left a lot of things behind,
because he wanted to ''travel light.'' He let Rachel sit in
his lap on the way home, and then there was more

excitement—David was hugging and kissing Loreen and petting the cats, and holding Jacob. He walked all around with Jacob in the bend of his arm, and the other arm around Leah, kissing them both over and over. Rachel wanted him to kiss her again.

After a while Zayde opened a bottle of champagne and the cork banged, and he said everybody had to celebrate, that even Rachel, this once, could have some champagne. He gave her a glass with just a tiny bit at the bottom; when they all drank it, she did too. It tasted awful, like medicine, and tickled her nose. She sneezed and everybody laughed and David *did* kiss her again.

Loreen brought plates of tiny sandwiches and all kinds of other good things and asked David if she could cook him up something, and he said no. Rachel noticed that he was looking kind of nervous, and he kept looking at Leah.

Zayde smiled at him and said, "It's time for you two to go." Leah got all red, and nodded her head. She said she was going to run up and get her bag, which was all packed. David's bag was still sitting in the hall, by the front door.

Rachel was terribly frightened. "Where are you going?" she almost yelled at David. He put his arms around her, stooping down, and kissed her again.

"Just about two blocks away," he said in a soft way. "We're going on our interrupted honeymoon, you see. And we'll be back real soon, tomorrow or the next day."

"Oh, please come back tomorrow!" Rachel couldn't help it; she was crying. "I don't understand why you have to go away again, David."

David took out his handkerchief and wiped her face. He kissed one of her eyes, then the other. "You will, when you're a grown-up lady." He stood up again, towering high above her, and she grabbed his legs.

Leah was back, and Zayde was saying, "Now, Rachel, honey. They'll be back soon. Really." Nan was kind of frowning. She had never done that before and it scared Rachel.

"Will you forgive us?" Leah asked, but she was smiling and she didn't sound like she was sorry at all. She and David were looking at each other, and didn't even seem to see Rachel anymore.

"We will if you get out of here right now, and don't let us hear *anything* from you till you're ready," Nan said. "The Fifth Avenue Hotel's not going to hold your reservation forever."

David and Leah kissed them all over again, and then they rushed out the front door. David had not looked back, not even once. Rachel's heart felt sore.

Nan and Zayde were sweeter to her than ever that night, but Rachel felt so awful when she went to bed that she wondered if she might be sick again. She was awfully tired, from the long, thrilling day, but she couldn't fall asleep. Nan and Zayde were still in the living room. She could hear them talking.

She got out of bed and crept barefoot into the hall and to the top of the stairs to listen.

"Oh, sweetheart, I'm so happy for them," Nan was saying. "I can't even imagine what it would be like to be away from you all that time, knowing you were in such danger."

Everything was quiet for a while; then Zayde said something. "We've been damned lucky in that way, haven't we, darling?"

There was some more quiet, then Nan said, "If that apartment on Charles Street works out, they can start to move right in. Heaven knows we've got enough Wendell treasures in storage to furnish three apartments, so we can tide them over."

Rachel shivered. What was Charles Street? They were going to go away again. She didn't listen to anything else; she couldn't stand to. She crept back into her room and got back in bed.

David and Leah would just have to take her, too. She remembered how people had been when she had had the bad dreams, and then when she got sick, and couldn't talk. They did everything she wanted then. Maybe she could pretend she couldn't talk. Then they would feel sorry for her, the way they had before.

That was what she would do. Because she was determined she would never, never be away from David again.

Rachel smiled, snuggled down into the covers, and fell asleep right away.

"You two have enough to cope with," Kate persisted. She lowered her voice a half-note: Rachel was with Loreen, down in the kitchen, but all the same she felt the need for caution. "The baby . . . the new apartment . . . and everything you have to adjust to, David. You both need time alone."

They'd been going over and over this. Joseph made an impatient gesture. "Darling, Leah's already told you they have lots of room; you've seen the place yourself. It's not that far away. And we can baby-sit anytime."

"Believe me, Mother, every 'adjustment' I have to make is ecstasy compared to what I was doing." David grinned; his eye patch gave him a rakish look. "The old blinker will be okay in a few months. I'm only a crock as a pilot, sweetheart, not as a civilian. They're already fighting over me at Curtiss and at Wright."

That was true enough. With fifteen years' experience of planes and flying, with a degree in aeronautical engineering awarded him before the European War, David had his choice of jobs. He was opting for Curtiss, so he could commute from New York rather than, as he put it, trap his wife and child in the "boondocks."

"There's nothing to cope with, Mother," he repeated.

"Really, Kate, it'll be no problem to have Rachel with us for a while," Leah added. "It'll be good for her and for the baby to have each other. Besides, you were sweet enough to offer to handle the therapy end of it."

"Why, of course. There's no question. I can pick her up and take her every day and bring her back."

"Well, then. What's the problem?" Joseph asked her.

The problem was, Kate admitted to herself, that she was

just a plain hypocrite. She was more worried about herself than about David and Leah, even if their convenience did enter into it. She still felt Rachel was her responsibility, somehow; still her atonement for Marite. But she had to face the fact that David and Leah might be better for the child. "All right," she said. "I was just being silly."

"Great! Why don't I go downstairs right now and tell her?" David suggested.

When he came back upstairs, his face was transfigured with happiness. "Tell them what you told me, Rachel."

" 'Tell' us?" Joseph demanded, astonished.

Rachel was smiling at them. "I want to go with Leah and David," she said awkwardly, as if she were testing the sound of her voice.

It had happened again, Kate thought. Like magic. The other time Rachel, after weeks of silence, had cried out David's name. Now that she knew she was going with them, her voice had come back to her.

Like magic.

A little too much like magic. The sudden thought shamed her. How could she be suspicious of an eight-year-old child, her own grandchild, who had suffered so much insecurity and deprivation?

But when she caught Leah's eye, there was a strange, reluctant look of half-doubt in those dark eyes, too.

Rachel loved the new house on Charles Street, which Zayde said was really two apartments put together so they could all have plenty of room. Down in the basement was a kitchen that looked out on a little garden, much smaller than the one on Eleventh Street, but still very nice. Dar and Shing had come with them, since they were "David's cats," Nan said. Shing paid more attention to David now than anyone else, but Rachel didn't really care. David was in the same house, right down the hall from her room, and she had breakfast with him every morning and dinner with him every night. That made life seem almost perfect.

Her new room was pink and very pretty. Nan had fixed

it for her, and she still brought Rachel things every time she came to see them, about once a week. On Sundays they always went to Eleventh Street for dinner, and everybody had a good time. But the best part was going back home, and having David come in her room to kiss her good night the way he did every night.

And she loved the mornings now, when it was time to go to school. Leah had to stay with Jacob, so most of the time, especially when it was cold, David was the one to walk her to school before he took his train to work. Rachel was disappointed when the weather got warmer that year, and Leah would walk with her instead, wheeling Jacob in his little cart.

Rachel knew now that she was in love with David, and that when she grew up they would get married. She didn't know quite how Leah fit into the picture, but Rachel decided Leah would just go on taking care of Jacob and everything would be fine. Rachel had an idea that eight-year-old girls were not supposed to be in love—that's what Leah and Nan and her teachers all said—but she was in love, all the same. She would read in books about the things people felt when they were in love, and the feelings sounded just like hers, even if the girls she read about were much older. In fact, Rachel had read a lot more books than other children, because she had started so early. She remembered hearing her first *mutter* tell another lady that Rachel was already reading books at four that other children didn't read until they were nine years old.

All during that first swiftly passing year on Charles Street, Rachel's feelings continued to be a closely guarded secret; she couldn't speak of them to anyone. David and Leah paid a lot of attention to her, and acted interested in her, worried about her. They asked her whom she wanted to invite to her ninth-birthday party, from school. She told them she would rather have a party with just them and Nan and Zayde, too embarrassed to admit that she had so few friends the party would be very small.

After that David looked more worried than ever, and

one night she heard him talking about her real mother, Marite. But Rachel forgot about it. There was so much to think about that was her own secret that most of what went on around her didn't seem very real. Only David was real. He was the only thing in the world that made life better; she hated school now. It was still so easy and boring and she heard the other children whispering about her, calling her "teacher's pet."

Even the war didn't really seem to be happening. Everybody talked about it, and there was rationing and "cutting down and cutting out," as Leah said. But it was still nothing like England. There were no bombs, and Rachel and other children still rode their bicycles and walked along the streets without being afraid. Rachel was already so used to blackouts that she didn't pay any attention to them anymore. And the "air-raid alarms" weren't really alarms, David told her. They were just for practice. He said America wasn't going to be bombed and she believed him. The soldiers and the sailors she saw had come back home from a lot of distant places; the war was like a story. There wasn't that much difference in the food they had, either.

One night Nan and Leah had a big argument with David and Zayde about sending Rachel to a "special school," a school for "extra-bright" children. Nan said things about "holding Rachel back," and Leah agreed with her, but David and Zayde used words like "democratic" and "adjustment." They never really won the argument, any of them, because David and Nan continued to discuss it from time to time. Meanwhile Rachel stayed in the same school, which didn't make any difference, because she thought a special school would be as bad as the one she was in, anyhow.

The only thing that mattered was that she was living in the same house with David. He was like her *fater*, but much handsomer and younger, and he wasn't going away like her first *fater* had. She liked Nan and Zayde a lot better now, since she didn't see them every day. Going to

their house was a real treat, like having a birthday every
week. Nan still gave her something every Sunday, and
Zayde teased Nan about it, but he sounded like he really
didn't mind.

The only big thing that happened to Rachel before the
end of the war in 1945 was the sickness she got when she
was eleven, which turned out not to be real sickness after
all. One morning when she was working on one of her
poems that she had been writing for a year, she felt a sharp
pain in her lower body, a terrible breaking inside her.
Then the sharp pain went away and she just felt a dull,
steady ache in the bottom of her stomach. When she went
to the bathroom she saw that she was bleeding, from
inside. Rachel knew then that she was very ill, and was
probably going to die. She couldn't face telling David and
Leah; it would make them so sad. The thing to do was to
keep it from them as long as she could. She carefully
washed out her panties and took them to her room to let
them dry in the closet so Leah wouldn't find them.

She put on fresh panties and went downstairs to breakfast. She was going to be very good until she died, so they
would have nice memories of her. But the thought was so
sad—dying when she was only eleven years old—that she
could hardly keep the tears from her eyes.

David and Leah kept looking at her all through breakfast. She was so glad it was Saturday and she wouldn't have
to go to school. If she was going to die, she hoped it
would be tomorrow, after they had gone to see Zayde and
Nan. Then she would never have to go back to that awful
school again.

David said he was going to the hardware store to pick
up some things so he could fix a leak in the kitchen. When
he got up Rachel ran over to him and grabbed him around
the legs the way she had when he had come home from the
war. If she died this morning, she would never see him
again. "Good-bye, David. Good-bye!"

He laughed. "I'm only going to Eighth Avenue," he

teased her. "I'll be right back." He patted her shoulder and went out.

Rachel burst into tears.

"Rachel, what's the *matter*?" Leah came to her and put her hands on Rachel's shoulders. "*Tell* me. You were upset when you came down to breakfast."

Sobbing, Rachel told her. She had never seen Leah look so surprised; her eyes were as big as saucers. "Rachel." Leah took her hand and led her over to the chairs by the window. Jacob was playing in the garden and Leah always watched him when he did. "Honey," Leah said softly, and kissed Rachel. Then very quietly she explained to Rachel what had happened to her; a natural thing that happened to girls, but usually when they were thirteen or even fourteen. "My goodness, I would have told you already, Rachel, but I didn't think it would happen to you for two years yet."

Leah talked to Rachel for a long time, explaining everything to her. Some of it Rachel still didn't quite understand. Then they went out and got Jacob and Leah put him in his room and shut the door for a minute while she took Rachel to her own room and gave her a Kotex. She told her that as soon as David got back she would go to the drugstore and get some special ones for Rachel that would be her size. Leah still looked sort of shocked and worried but she smiled and asked Rachel if she felt better, not so scared now. Rachel nodded.

"I'm glad I'm not going to die." When she said that, Leah looked like she was trying not to cry. But Rachel felt much better: not only was she not going to die, but she was becoming a woman faster than other girls usually did. It was something to be proud of.

Leah was glad Loreen had the day off; helping Kate with the dishes was a perfect excuse for some privacy, while Rachel played Monopoly with Joseph and David upstairs in the living room. Leah hadn't had a moment to call Kate since yesterday morning. When she had told

David about Rachel the night before, he had been astonished, as she was initially, and saddened, saying over and over, "The poor little kid."

They were starting the dishes when Leah said to Kate, "My dear, I have something perfectly phenomenal to tell you." Succinctly she told Kate, waiting for the reaction she herself had had.

"I've never heard of anything so extraordinary." Wide-eyed, Kate sat down again at the table, staring blindly at the dishes. "God heavens, I was nearly fifteen."

"And I was halfway between thirteen and fourteen," Leah offered.

"It explains so *much*, Leah . . . that odd maturity, that reticence. Over and above her traumatic experiences," Kate murmured.

"I know. But I feel so *guilty*—not preparing her for it. But good heavens, who would have expected it? I didn't think I'd have to talk to her about it, even, until next year."

"Of course you didn't. How could you know? You have no reason to feel guilty, darling. But, good Lord, I didn't think we'd have to face sex education this early on."

"Who did?" She watched Kate smile at her raised brows, her strong Jewish inflection. "Besides that, of course, something else worries me. She seems detached enough already from her peers, because of her brightness and her poems and her early reading. What will *this* do to her sense of herself, Kate? She's more alien to the others now than she was before. Technically she's able to bear a child, and the others are still children."

Kate nodded, looking somber. "I'm afraid it means we're going to have a whole new set of problems."

Chapter 28

Only three more months, Rachel exulted one evening in February 1947 as she was dressing to go to a Broadway musical. In June she would graduate from that silly grammar school and start high school, though she was only thirteen. At least in November she would be the same age as other people, even if she was years older in other ways. And there would be older boys, juniors and seniors; she just knew she would be the first freshman they would ask for a date, because she looked sixteen right now.

Rachel leaned toward the dresser mirror framed in moviestar pictures, carefully outlining her mouth with a dark-red lipstick she wore away from home. Tonight she was going to wear it *at* home; let them all scream and yell. She was going to look glamorous for David if hell froze over. Rachel put mascara on her lashes, pleased with how long they looked. Then she took the rotten barrette out of her hair and brushed one side of her hair so it would hang over her eye like Veronica Lake's.

She couldn't believe how good she looked, how old. She got up and went to the full-length mirror on the closet door, turning this way and that to admire her figure in the new dress. Leah didn't even know she'd bought it. Rachel had asked Nan for some money to buy records, and of course Nan had given her too much, as usual. So Rachel had gone over to Klein's and bought a really snazzy dress—black crepe with a black net top, covered with sequins and lined in flesh color so it looked like your breasts through it.

The trouble was the bras she wore were white and had straps, so she wasn't wearing one. With the black ankle-strap shoes the outfit was super-glamorous. She knew David would think she was gorgeous. For the whole last year he had been acting different, she decided. He didn't seem like her father so much anymore. It was almost as if he was embarrassed to be around her. That had hurt her feelings at first, but then after she'd read some novels about older married men falling in love with younger girls, she began to think about it a lot. Maybe David finally was falling in love with *her*. The idea was almost too good to be true. But maybe . . .

Leah was tired a lot lately, taking care of Jacob and the new baby, Saul. The books said when wives were "too tired" for their husbands, it meant big trouble.

Rachel made a kissing motion at her own image; a big, luscious red mouth kissed her back from the mirror. She really did look like Veronica Lake, except a little taller— her dark, slanty eyes, her "luscious" lips, and her smooth blond hair. She practiced a low, husky voice—what they called "sultry" in the magazines.

She put everything in a little black purse and remembered to put Evening in Paris on all the bare places. Leah had bought her some Bond Street cologne but she hated it; it smelled as fresh and unseductive as shaving lotion.

David was still dressing, she guessed, when she went down to the living room. Leah was there, with the baby-sitter, and she was wearing one of those awful plain dresses that Nan had designed for her. It fit all right but there was just no glamour to it. Leah didn't even have any earrings on, only a topaz brooch that matched her topaz wedding ring. It was her birthstone. Rachel had recently discovered astrology; when she found out that Scorpio women were "seductresses," it pleased her very much, but she couldn't believe that Leah was one too.

Rachel was wearing her good-as-diamonds earrings from

Klein's that she had bought the same day as the dress and the ankle-strap shoes.

When Leah saw her, she turned absolutely pale. "Rachel!" The baby-sitter, a bookworm in her class that Rachel just couldn't stand, was gaping at her. "Hello, Amy." Rachel used her Veronica Lake voice and smiled.

"Rachel, I want to talk to you." Leah sounded very stern. "Excuse us, Amy." She grabbed Rachel by the arm and practically pulled her upstairs. David was coming out of their bedroom and the three almost collided. "My God!"

David just stood there staring at Rachel.

"Do you like it, David?"

He was staring at her body, especially her breasts. "No," he said bluntly. "That looks terrible."

Rachel felt as if he had hit her in the chest. She gasped, and ran into her room, slamming the door in Leah's face. She heard Leah calling out. "We won't be long." The door opened abruptly.

Rachel was lying facedown on her bed, crying. Big black streaks of mascara had already stained the flowered bedspread. Rachel wished she were dead. David had told her she looked "terrible."

"Rachel." Leah's voice sounded softer now, and Rachel felt her weight on the bed, Leah's hand on her hair. "I'm sorry David hurt your feelings. But you don't look as attractive that way as you do in your own clothes. Come on, now. Put on your pretty turquoise dress. It makes your eyes and hair look *lovely*. You really can't go to the play like that."

"Why not? Because you're jealous?" Rachel sat up and met Leah's shocked eyes.

Leah didn't say anything for a minute; then her eyes got sad. "No, Rachel. I'm not jealous. But I've got to speak plainly. You're dressed up like a prostitute; it's not pretty at all. Now, please get changed, or we'll be late for the play." Leah's voice softened a little, and she added, "I'll help you. I'll show you just how pretty you *can* look.

We'll leave your hair that way, but maybe use some light lipstick and *brown* mascara. Hurry. You know how mad David gets when we're late."

That did it. Rachel didn't want to displease him any more than she already had. She rushed into the bathroom and washed all the stuff off her face, snatched off the dress, noticing that Leah averted her eyes at the sight of Rachel's big, bare breasts. Rachel got into her underwear and pulled on the blue-green dress. It annoyed her to admit that Leah was right; this dress *did* look nice on her. Rachel put on her plain black patent pumps and then smoothed on her regular lipstick.

"Wonderful." Leah smiled at her and found her little flat box of brown mascara, moistened the cake in the bathroom, and then carefully applied some to Rachel's lashes. "See there?" Leah smiled at her in the mirror. "You look *beautiful*."

Rachel put on the copper-and-turquoise necklace that went with the dress and sprayed on her Bond Street.

When they got downstairs, David was pacing impatiently, but he smiled at Rachel and said, "You look more like yourself now . . . very pretty. And you smell good, too." He leaned over and kissed her lightly on the cheek. "Okay, girls, are you ready? If we don't get out of here, they'll be into the second act."

All the way to the theater Rachel puzzled over his reaction. David just liked plain women, that's all there was to it. Leah and Nan were very plain and wore very little makeup, and he always complimented them. She guessed the dress had been a big mistake. And still, there was the funniest look in his eyes when he had stared at her breasts under the black sequins. Was it because he found her "seductive" and didn't want to? That was the way it happened in so many of the books.

That idea, mixed with the music of *Carousel* and its romantic story, but most of all the nearness of David, excited her more than ever before. David always sat between her and Leah at movies, concerts, and plays, so he could be "surrounded by his girls," as he put it. But tonight was totally different. He held Leah's hand but didn't hold Rachel's. A few years ago this would have hurt her feelings; now it gave her the strangest sense of triumph.

There were some pretty racy things in the musical, and it thrilled Rachel more than any play she had attended. That night, in bed, she started thinking of what Julie and Billy Bigelow had been about to do, even before they were married. It excited her and she started to do that thing she had been doing for more than a year now, the satisfying practice a girl had showed her at school in the rest room. The girl said it would make her feel great. And it did, every time. If she thought of forbidden things at the same time, it was even better. Tonight she pretended David was doing it to her, and they were naked together in a place where there was no Leah, no Jacob or Saul. She gasped with pleasure.

She could hear Leah and David talking in their room. And a few minutes later she heard their door open and David's footsteps in the hall. He was going downstairs.

Rachel got up, put on her robe, and opened her door without making any noise. Leah's and David's door was closed. Leaving her door a little ajar, Rachel crept down the stairs in her bare feet. There was a light on from the floor below. He must be in the kitchen.

Rachel padded down the kitchen stairs. David was standing by the refrigerator, drinking a glass of milk and eating a doughnut.

When he saw her he looked a little uneasy, but he smiled and asked, "Are you hungry? What would you like?"

She didn't answer. She just walked up to him and put her arms around his body. He was holding the doughnut in one hand and his glass of milk in the other; she had trapped him for the moment. She pressed herself against his body and said in her Veronica Lake voice, "I want *you*, David."

He reddened. Then he leaned over to the side and put

his milk and doughnut on the table. She was still holding on to him. He put his hands behind him and took her wrists, loosening her hold on him.

"Rachel." He sounded very gentle, almost sad. "You don't know what you're saying, honey. I think you're just imitating the play." He smiled at her crookedly. "Sit down a minute. Let's talk about this."

Numbly Rachel obeyed, feeling like she wanted to die. He hadn't kissed her back, hadn't held her. Hadn't wanted her at all. And right this minute he was looking at her the way he had that day he came back from the war, when he had told her she would understand why he and Leah were going away when she was grown-up.

Still standing, David asked her, "Are you sure you don't want something to drink?"

She shook her head, mute, still staring at him in bewilderment.

He sat down across from her and said, "Honey, I think maybe that play gave you a lot of funny ideas. You're getting to be a big girl now. You were feeling romantic, from the music and all that. And I just happened to be the nearest fellow in the house." He grinned at her.

"That's not true," she said bitterly. "I'm in love with you, David. I've always been in love with you, ever since you came back from the war."

"Rachel, you still don't really know what being '*in*' love is." He still hadn't touched her, but his eyes, his voice, were gentle and affectionate. She felt a whole new wave of hot feelings. "Of course you love me," he went on, "and I'm very glad. I love you, too, as if you were my own daughter. Leah loves you, and Nan and Zayde and the boys. But that's not being *in* love, you see. That's when you love someone the way Leah loves me, and I love her; the way Nan and Zayde love each other. It's when you marry the one you love, and never love anyone else."

"That's not true," she retorted. "In a lot of the books I've read, people fall out of love with one person and in love with another. They get divorces and marry the new people because they're better, more exciting than the old ones.''

David looked sad when she said that. ''Those books are full of baloney. When people fall in love for sure, they don't fall out of it, Rachel. And people generally get divorced and marry new people because they think the 'new people' are going to solve all their problems and make them better than they are. When an old guy marries a young girl, she's not going to make him twenty again. Honey, you've gotten hold of some pretty lousy books. Do you understand what I'm saying?''

He looked earnest and worried. Rachel hated to worry him but she had to make *him* understand.

''No. Why did you look at me like that, in my black dress, if I didn't look better than Leah?''

''I looked at you that way because you looked *awful*, Rachel. You looked like a girl no nice guy would ever ask to marry him. If that sounds old-fashioned to you, it's because I am.'' David smiled a little; then he got very solemn. ''I'm your uncle, Rachel. That's a lot like being your father. An uncle can't love you the same way that your husband will someday. Do you see?''

She did and she didn't. But to please him, she nodded yes, nodded just to see him smile his beautiful smile.

''That's good.'' He still seemed a little worried. ''The thing to remember is that all this was just a mistake, a big misunderstanding on your part. And also remember that we all love you very, very much and want you to be happy, to have a good life, Rachel.'' He studied her and, after a moment, suggested, ''Why don't you go back to bed now?''

''Will you come and kiss me good night?''

''I'll kiss you good night right now. I'm going to stay down here for a little while and read.'' He got up and came to her side of the table, kissed her lightly on the forehead, and ruffled her hair. ''Now, run along.''

That wasn't the kind of kiss she wanted. Her heart was

heavy as she obeyed him and padded back up the stairs and into her room. She was so warmed now by his touch that she was more wakeful than before; she knew she'd have to do that thing again to still her excitement, to feel lazy enough to sleep. This time there was a whole new wickedness in it, which she really liked, because he had told her her feelings about him were "wrong." Her pleasure and her relief were overwhelming.

David was wrong: people did fall out of love with each other. And the men who had been married, with children, always told somebody how wonderful it was to be "free," to have fun with some young girl. Rachel decided she was going to be just like that girl in *Nana* that all the men ran after. That girl got naked and rode a fat old man like he was a horse. She beat him on the back, and he loved it. David wasn't old and fat, but she would like to do that to him. She was sure he would love it, too.

The best way to show David how much fun she could be was to get every boy she could to run after her. When David saw that, next time maybe he wouldn't tell her it was "wrong."

Leah set down the vegetable peeler and went to the kitchen window to look out into the garden, where the boys were playing under the watchful eye of their young maid, Pam. The girl was invaluable, good-natured and gentle, and her duties had evolved more into those of a nursemaid than a maid, which was fine all around. Leah didn't need that much help with the house, apart from the cleaning woman's visits.

The open window admitted mild April air; Leah found New York lovely in the spring. David called it "the *day* we have spring in New York."

Jacob looked more like David every day, she thought, watching her six-year-old son teach his younger brother how to put the Erector set together. The dexterity of the four-year-old Saul, who looked like Leah but had David's temperament, amazed and gratified them all.

Saul, with his dark eyes and black hair, had the agreeable placidity of May-born children, like David. And David swore that he was going to be either an artist or an engineer. His favorite toys were finger paints and any kind of vehicle or metal gadget.

Jacob, on the other hand, who was David's clone except for his hair, already showed promise of height and leanness, and he had a passionate curiosity about everything. Zayde had already taught him a lot of old union songs and told him he was born to be a troublemaker.

He wasn't making trouble at the moment, thank heaven. Leah heard him instructing Saul, "You have to do it that way because I'm the union *pres*-e-ment."

Leah laughed out loud; Pam looked up from her textbook and smiled at Leah. Pam was putting herself through college with the strong encouragement of Leah and David, and also their extra help at times.

"I'm going to finish this salad," Leah called out, "then pick up around the house. Are you okay?"

"I'm fine. It's great to have this time to study."

Leah went back to her task, thinking how much she liked the neat, serious girl with her *café au lait* skin and her black, curly hair cut into a neat little cap on her head. She was so cheerful and helpful.

So is this house, Leah added mentally with one final glance at the attractive kitchen before she went upstairs. This house . . . my children, my husband, my life. And Kate and Joseph and America. Guiltily Leah realized she hadn't listed Rachel.

Rachel was the only cloud on their horizon in these perfect, peaceful days. Everything else was idyllic. The horrors of the war were almost a memory; the country was prosperous again. With the increasing enthusiasm for air travel, the changeover at David's company had gone smoothly. The airlines needed more and more planes; people were buying small private craft, companies were even using them for commuting. The aviation industry was booming, the number of airline passengers now about twenty million. With the boom David's value to the company rose; he was amazingly inventive, knowledgeable, and at the same time rooted in experienced practicality. He could always, as he put it, tell when it was time to stop, to "keep the guys from shooting off into the stratosphere." Yet he was now in the midst of testing something quite revolutionary called the "jet."

He was so perfect as a husband that Leah could hardly believe it—more of a husband than a father, really, although he was never anything but affectionate with the children. Leah knew he patterned his idea of a perfect marriage on his parents', and he often said his own parents' benign neglect had made him into a man early on. Leah had to agree with that; no one was more manly and self-reliant than her husband, except possibly his father. If her sons turned out half so well, she would be thankful.

Leah had to admit she envied Kate a little sometimes for the cachet her work gave her, and occasionally missed the satisfaction being a nurse had brought her. For the time being, however, it was enough to pour all her emotions and energy into her house, her husband, and her sons. When she had said this to David, it made him very happy. "I hope you never get the idea that I think of you as a 'boring housewife,' lady. I adore Kate, but I never wanted to marry her twin. And I'd be miserable if you didn't enjoy what you're doing. Anyway, look here—you can always go back to nursing, after the boys are in school. Why not?"

She had retorted that she would be rusty. David ridiculed her. "You have a natural talent for it. You could always brush up, take some courses to catch up with what's new. I can see you now, as an older lady . . . one of those gimlet-eyed head nurses, as scary as any matron was at St. Bart's."

That had encouraged Leah no end; when she mentioned the conversation to Kate, she had agreed completely. So that, too, was a pleasant challenge to look forward to.

Leah finished picking up in the living room and gazed at it fondly before going up to the next floor. She had learned so much about decorating from Kate that David once said she was "every bit as good." Kate had responded generously, "A thousand times better. With my low boredom threshold, I do a room and forget it. Leah pays attention to everything, every day, in loving detail."

It was true. Their house had a perfection that even Kate's didn't, and yet people always felt comfortable there. The children played happily among all the old Wendell and Dryver treasures that blended so nicely with their new pieces.

In their bedroom Leah felt a fresh wave of love for David. His military neatness made her life so much easier.

The boys' room, of course, was another matter, although Jacob was very good about putting his toys away and helping Saul. A real organizer, that Jacob. Leah grinned as she put the boys' clothes away and collected the dirty ones for the laundry.

She went into Rachel's room with that vague sense of oppression which she tried so hard to ignore. She smelled her horrible Evening in Paris perfume all over the place again, and sighed. Rachel had been doing so well, ever since that night they went to *Carousel*. Leah was deeply disturbed when David had come up that night and told her what had happened. They had both taken extra pains with Rachel for the next few months, asking for help from Kate and Joseph too.

Rachel had calmed down so much that their relief was enormous. She was acting almost like any other normal teenage girl, except for a deeper reticence that still bothered them. Leah, with Kate's approval, decided to allow Rachel to wear her light lipstick and a small amount of brown mascara to school, even if most "nice girls" weren't using such things. They felt they had to make some concession to her extraordinary glandular difference from the others.

They were also allowing her to have certain "dates" in the Village—besides the regular school dances, Rachel was now permitted to go to the movies with a boy her age, and have something to eat afterward, as long as she was home by a reasonable hour. Most of the boys who asked her to go out were the sons of people they knew. One of them was Barry Weiss. His father, Dan Weiss the labor lawyer, worked for the union, and David had known Dan since they were in high school. Leah had thought Barry was something special to Rachel, but she hadn't seen much of him lately.

Barry was already a dedicated Zionist who constantly talked about Israel. David said dryly that it was all to the good—it would give Rachel something to think about. She seemed impressed by Barry's ideas and had begun to talk about Israel herself. She was annoyed, though, when Barry's studies kept him from seeing her. Maybe that was why she had recently been favoring other boys.

She had a Saturday date this afternoon with a cute boy named Johnny Riley, a member of the football team. They were going to a movie at the Sheridan and have an early dinner afterward. Rachel had looked so pretty when they went out, Leah reflected. Her short plaid skirt and long Sloppy Joe sweater flattered her narrow-hipped form; the sweater looked as chic as a tunic on Rachel. But oh, those horrible saddle shoes, deliberately smeared with dirt to make them look "right." An insane fad. But no crazier, she supposed, than the craze over Sinatra. He did have a lovely voice, but when all the little girls screamed over him, it was so pathetic.

Still smiling, feeling better, Leah hesitated over Rachel's desk. She didn't ever want to be accused of "snooping," so she usually didn't even look at Rachel's rather disorderly papers. Her poems were very private to her, and she rarely shared them with the rest of the family. However, Pam wouldn't be able to vacuum with all the papers on the floor. Slightly annoyed, Leah bent over and picked up several pieces of paper. A phrase caught her eye and she couldn't stop herself from reading what was written there.

The names of Village restaurants and after each name a dish the restaurant specialized in . . . the names of movies Rachel had mentioned seeing over the last two months with her dates. And the running time of each movie. Why had she written these things down? Was it a kind of diary? But why the running times of the films?

It seemed senseless.

Unless Rachel wanted to . . . cover herself somehow. Unless she was really somewhere else. Leah recalled another odd thing that hadn't struck her until now. Twice when Rachel had come home after dinner with Johnny, she had snacked about a half-hour later—snacked substantially. At the time Leah had put it down to the endless appetite of the young. But now she wondered. Maybe Rachel hadn't even gone to dinner. Or to a movie.

Leah was struck with a shameful suspicion: Rachel must have been somewhere she had no business being. It was horrible to think that of a fourteen-year-old child. Except that Rachel hadn't been a child for the last two years.

Leah resolved to talk with her as soon as she came home. And to David, too. Something was going on and they had to get to the bottom of it. Right now.

Leah's head began to ache. She felt heavy and sore. The whole thing was her own damned fault. She had been so complacent in her own happiness, wrapped up in David and the children . . . so preoccupied with Rachel's exterior self that she hadn't tried to get inside her, where it counted. If they had really been talking for the last few years, nothing could have gone this far without her knowing about it. That sweet and needy little girl would not have grown into this stranger.

"You don't have to walk me all the way," Rachel said to Johnny Riley when they got to the corner of West Fourth and Charles. She wanted to get away from him as much as he seemed to want to get away from her. Rachel had felt this way almost as soon as it was over, in that room on Hudson Street. She wished she could stop going there, but she couldn't seem to help herself. Especially after what had happened between them in the balcony at the movie—she hadn't been able to wait to get to Hudson Street.

It was always like that, afterward, with Johnny. Rachel hated the getting-dressed part, and walking home, because he hardly ever looked at her and they had very little to talk about. Besides, they were always starving because the room took all his money, so they couldn't go to dinner.

"Really you don't," she said.

"Geez, what will your aunt and uncle say?" Johnny seemed eager to take advantage of her offer.

"I'll make up something."

"Well, I don't know . . ." He shuffled his feet.

"It's okay. I'll see you, Johnny." Rachel started to walk away.

"Yeah," he said guiltily. "See you, Rachel."

She walked on down Charles Street without looking back, going over what she would tell David and Leah, in case they noticed that Johnny hadn't brought her home. David was always so strict about that. Rachel guessed she could tell them they had had a fight, and she had just walked away. That would be okay, because it wasn't even dark yet.

She was opening the grilled gate outside their small front yard when she heard a boy call her name.

It was Barry. He was walking up Charles Street from the west, and his face looked grim.

Rachel's hand gripped the gate. She had told Barry she was going to study that afternoon.

Rachel couldn't think of a single word to say.

"I want to talk to you, Rachel."

"I've got to go in, Barry," she said weakly. "They'll be mad if I'm late. You know that." Rachel glanced at the front windows, grateful that her aunt and uncle weren't looking out. Maybe they were already having dinner.

"This will only take a minute," he insisted. His dark gray eyes looked like slate, hard with hurt and anger. All of a sudden she knew he had seen her and Johnny coming out of the rooming house on Hudson. He stepped closer to her and took her arm. "Come on, Rachel. We've got to talk. Right now."

Her heart sank; there was a cold, empty feeling in her stomach-pit that had nothing to do with hunger. If Barry had seen them it was all over. And she couldn't bear for it to be over. She loved him so much; just seeing him now made her want to kiss him, to put her hands on his hair and hug him close to her. She wished fervently that she hadn't done it with Johnny today . . . or any day. But she got so lonely, and Barry was always studying; he was never there when she needed him.

There was no point in postponing this, though. He would just keep standing there until she talked to him. One thing Rachel was sure of: she wasn't going to admit to anything until she found out just how much he really knew.

"All right." Barry stepped away again, toward the west, and she walked beside him. He didn't try to touch her or even hold her hand. That was a sign he was really mad.

They sat down on the stoop of an empty house. They had sat on that stoop before, on the way home from different places, and Barry had said such wonderful things to her there.

He looked straight ahead for a minute, still not touching her. Finally he said in a funny voice, as if his throat were sore, "I saw you coming out of the place on Hudson Street with Johnny Riley."

"So what? You know I date other boys. We went to see somebody."

Barry's mouth twitched. He still wasn't looking at her. "Don't lie to me, Rachel. I know what that place is. Because I went there one time with a girl, before I knew you."

Her stomach felt even colder. But she said, "I'm not lying."

"Yes, you are. And I know it now. The guys have been saying things around school. I didn't believe 'em before. I nearly got in a fight about it yesterday. But now I do believe 'em.'' Finally he turned and looked at her. She had never seen his face look so sad. "You said you loved me, Rachel. How could you . . . do that with someone else when you say you love me?"

"Because you won't make love to me!" she cried out, abandoning all ideas of caution now. "Because all you can think about is school, and studying, and Israel. You say you love *me*, but where are you when I'm lonesome and miserable and need you so much? Besides, who are you to ask me that when you went there yourself with another girl?"

"I told you that was before I knew you. Anyway, it's different for a guy."

"Different!" Now she was really angry. "*Why* is it different? Girls aren't supposed to have feelings? What do you think we *are*? Why is it different?"

"I don't know," he said miserably. "I didn't make the world, Rachel. That's just the way it is, and we can't change it. But that's not the point. The point is, you say you love me and then you go off with other boys and . . . I can't understand it. I can't *stand* it, either."

She wanted to touch him and kiss him and say she was sorry. But her shame had made her too angry. She was on the defensive. "So what am I supposed to do, sit around and wait forever . . . until we get married? About a hundred years from now, when I'll be too old for . . . anything?"

Barry put his face in his hands. "I don't know, Rachel. I just don't know." He dropped his hands, looking defeated and wretched. "But I trusted you and you've been lying to me all the time, and my 'girl' is somebody people laugh at."

That last remark was too much. Rachel jumped up from the stoop and snapped, "Well, that's no problem, Barry. I don't have to *be* your girl. Then you won't have to worry about your precious reputation anymore. As far as I'm concerned, you can go straight to hell.''

Rachel flounced away and hurried toward the house. Barry was still sitting there, on their special stoop.

She hadn't walked a half-block before her anger turned into a searing pain. It felt as though her heart were cracking right inside her body.

Chapter 29

*I*t was Sunday afternoon. Kate had been painting since she woke up. Now, glancing at the clock, she saw that it was nearly four. Joseph must have been up for hours, must have made his own breakfast. Kate shook her head, amazed at her ability to lose track of the time while she was painting.

She massaged her stiff neck, moved her shoulders to ease her back, and stood up to view the canvas. Damn, it was good, she decided—a city scene, but a city of deeper mystery, richer shadows, greater beauty than the city she lived in. It almost had the quality of the fantasy jungle scene she had done so many years ago. She cleaned her brushes, put her materials away, and snapped out the light.

Stopping in their bedroom to wash up and brush her hair, she was touched to notice that Joseph had made the bed, to help her, since it was Loreen's day off. Kate smiled to herself; the way a man tidied up a bed still left it rough and askew. After she had scrubbed the blue paint from her hands and face, she smoothed out the bed and ran down the rest of the stairs.

"Joseph? Where are you?"

"In my office, honey."

She shook her head and went in. His desk was a litter of papers. "I thought this was your day of rest."

He smiled up at her over his glasses. "You know very

well I'm not entitled. I'm only the president; if I don't work overtime, the members will have to. Without pay.''

Kate kissed his head. "I'm sorry about breakfast. You cooked it yourself.''

"So what am I? A cripple?''

"No, but it's the only day I ever get to cook you a breakfast, damm it.''

"How did the painting go?'' He took off his glasses and leaned against her.

"*Well*.''

"That's great. I'll take a look at it in a little while. May I?''

He always asked that, and she always answered the same way. "Of course.''

He swiveled around in his chair and put his arms around her body. She loved the sweet weight of his head against her. He raised his head and their eyes met. She thought: A lifetime cannot weaken that spell, the spell of those deep, dark eyes. She took his face in her hands and kissed his lips, then hurried away to take care of things, already feeling a little resentful that she had to see to dinner right this minute. She wanted the whole day and evening, and the night, to be theirs.

But as the hour for the visit neared she found she was slipping into her other persona, buoyed on Joseph's anticipation.

"What a nice surprise!'' she said when she saw Rachel with David, Leah, and the children. Rachel hadn't observed the Sunday ritual for a whole month now. "There must be some brokenhearted boys in the Village tonight,'' she teased Rachel while Joseph scooped Jake high in one arm and Saul in the other.

"Good grief! You guys have gained a ton in a week. You're breaking the old man's back.'' Joseph grunted dramatically. The boys were delighted. Jake grinned and made a muscle, and Saul giggled. "How are the ladies? You both look so pretty.''

They did, Kate thought. "Like spring,'' she said. "Those

gorgeous *colors*." Rachel was wearing a leaf-green skirt with a matching sweater and, Kate noticed with pleasure, her star on a more substantial chain. Leah's smart wool dress was the color of a new crocus.

"I knew you'd notice that." Leah smiled at her affectionately, but her dark eyes didn't quite. They telegraphed some sort of message to Kate. She knew Leah was dying to get her alone to talk to her.

Dinner was a pleasant interval, although Rachel didn't eat very much and seemed more silent than usual. Kate thought David and Leah were trying to hide their tension, talking and laughing a little too much. Kate wondered if Joseph had noticed, but he appeared to be engrossed in the boys.

Kate tried to draw Rachel out but had no luck at all. After dinner they went upstairs and wandered casually into the living room. Joseph and David were talking about the fight against the Taft-Hartley law and Kate and Leah were discussing clothes; once again Kate tried to include Rachel but she was sullenly uncooperative. It was obvious now that Rachel was the problem.

After Joseph had made them all drinks and provided Rachel with a soft drink, the boys clamored to see their daddy's planes in his room upstairs. He had asked Kate to keep them until the boys were older. It seemed the perfect chance to talk to Leah. "Come on," Kate said to the boys. "Let's go upstairs. I've got a surprise for you there." She had bought some new toy planes for the little boys, to divert them from David's treasured and fragile models, which Jake would be allowed to have when he was seven. "Leah?" Leah nodded eagerly. "Rachel, you want to come too?"

"No. Thanks," Rachel amended. "Zayde and David and I'll probably play Monopoly."

In David's old room the women settled the boys down to their planes, then sat in the chairs by the window.

"Something's worrying you," Kate said, lighting Leah's cigarette and taking one for herself. Jake and Saul were making zooming and crashing noises and she was sure they couldn't hear her. "Is it Rachel?"

Leah's eyelids dropped over her eyes for a moment; then she slowly raised them. Kate saw worry and pain and shame in their soft brown depths. "Yes."

"What happened?"

Haltingly, flushing, Leah told her about how she had found the movie running times and the restaurant listings in Rachel's room, indicating that Rachel had been spending her "dates" somewhere else. And how somewhere else turned out to be an empty room on Hudson Street, rented by the high school's band promoter to his friends— and their girlfriends—for recreational purposes.

Kate could literally feel the blood drain from her face; her head spun. At first she was speechless. Then she cleared her throat, asking huskily, "You're . . . sure? What did Rachel *say* when you confronted her with the evidence? Did she actually . . . *admit* to that deception?"

"Worse than that. She *gloated*."

Kate was appalled, confronted with the extent of Rachel's secret life—the savage sexual appetite of a girl so young.

Leah observed her with those clinical, compassionate eyes. "Are you all right?"

"Oh, yes. Of course." Kate wasn't: she felt queasy. A migrainelike pain shot through her head. It wasn't fair to expect Leah to cope with all this; Kate was going to have to do it herself. Leah had her own family to raise, and after all, Rachel was only her niece. But my God, Kate thought, I didn't think I'd have to cope with Rachel's sex life *this* early in the game. She had just finished getting Rachel's childhood problems under control.

"Yes," she repeated wearily. "In Tahiti a girl like Rachel would be married. But since we're not in Tahiti," Kate added in a dry voice, "we'll have to cope with this in another way. First of all, I think she should come live with us, Leah."

Her daughter-in-law started to speak, but Kate forestalled her with a gesture. "You owe your attention to David and your children, Leah. You've done enough. You've had no time at all for the last seven years. It's time for me to face the fact that I must share the responsibility for what's happened to Rachel."

"But, Kate, are you sure?" The relief in Leah's eyes was pathetic.

"Very sure. I'll talk to Joseph tonight, and then we'll arrange it. Whatever has to be done will be done. I'll tell Rachel, too, if you think that's a good plan."

"Maybe it would be, Kate. She and I haven't been close for a long time. I don't know who *is* close to her, except that nice boy, Barry Weiss. And I'm afraid he hasn't called her, either last night or today. He was in the habit of calling her every day before."

"I see. Poor child." Barry, Kate decided, must have gotten wind of Rachel's activities.

"Yes. She's so old and so young."

When they went downstairs again, that phrase echoed in Kate's mind. She went to the game table, where Rachel was sitting with a blank, shuttered face, waiting for her roll of the dice.

She hasn't been given many lucky numbers, Kate reflected. She squeezed Rachel's shoulder. The girl looked up at her with wary eyes, then answered Kate's smile with a tight little smile of her own. She must have known what Kate and Leah were talking about. She probably expected a lecture. But when Kate stroked her hair with a gentle hand, Rachel relaxed ever so slightly.

For a second Kate could see the little girl at the airport whose eyes already said there was nothing certain but uncertainty, who was always waiting for the fire to fall from the sky.

Rachel was not deceived by her grandmother's "asking" her if she would like to live on Eleventh Street: she knew there was no choice in the matter. David didn't want her any longer, so that was the way it was going to be.

Rachel couldn't run away without money; she had heard of the things that happened to girls who did. She had seen them on the streets uptown when she was passing on the bus from a school visit to the museum. The men who sold the girls, she had heard, beat them and took their money. Anything was better than that.

Anyway, her grandmother was so old she would probably be easy to fool. Rachel remembered how her grandmother had fluttered over her when she was little, and bought her things. It might not be too bad, especially since David hated her now.

And Barry. She winced, remembering their final horrible fight. Now that he knew all about Hudson Street, Rachel was sure everyone else at school would know by now, too. It had been three days and he hadn't even called.

Going to school Monday was the hardest thing that Rachel ever had to do. She felt that everyone was staring at her, that she was naked and cold in the path of all those eyes. As a matter of fact, the girls were already whispering about her; she knew they were. Johnny, and the others, must have confirmed Barry's reports by now. She was almost sick with humiliation. The only way to show them was not to show she cared, to be as smart as she could in class and make them look like a pack of fools. *That* wasn't hard; school had always been easy for her—so easy that she still got sleepy waiting for the other students to come up with some dumb answer.

She had seen Barry only once, in the hall by the lockers. He hadn't even looked at her. And just last week he had said he loved her. It had only been the usual lie. David had said he loved her, that he would never go away, but as soon as she had tried to kiss him that night, he had gone away in his mind.

Johnny and the other boys claimed they loved her, only so she would do what she had done with them in that room. Now they were just saying, "Hi, Rachel," and getting red and laughing and walking away.

And this was only April. She would have to face almost two more months of this before summer.

Her grandmother and grandfather—she didn't think of them anymore as "Nan" and "Zayde"—were very nice to her when she moved in. But they were nervous, too—so nervous she felt sorry for them. They really didn't know what to do with her. Her grandmother was looking really old; there were lines in her face and she seemed almost afraid when she looked at Rachel. Rachel's grandfather didn't look as much like David anymore, either. He was just tired a lot and unhappy.

Her grandmother offered to take Rachel to one of the department stores on Tuesday evening to pick out some new curtains and things for her room, but Rachel said she had to study. No one seemed to understand that she was not a little kid anymore, that curtains and skirts and sweaters didn't make it easier at school. It just made it worse that she had such pretty clothes; the girls at school who had been jealous of her before were absolutely vicious now.

Today two of them had quit the school play because Rachel was in it. Rachel had gone into the girls' rest room and cried. Quietly, so no one would hear and laugh at her again. She knew she could not face one more day at that school. But there was nowhere else to go.

Rachel began to sob and put the covers over her mouth. The house was so quiet she was afraid they could hear.

They had.

The door opened and her grandmother looked in. Rachel's heart sank.

"Rachel?" Her grandmother spoke very softly, but she looked really terrible, as if she hadn't slept for a long time. She didn't say anything else, but came in and sat down on the bed, putting her hand on Rachel's face.

No one had touched Rachel like that since Barry had. It wasn't as good, of course, but it made her feel a little less awful. Her grandmother smelled nice; it was like smelling very sweet flowers from a long way away.

"I'm sorry you feel so bad, darling. Is it . . . because you're not living with David and Leah, Rachel?"

Rachel shook her head.

"Is it Barry . . . and school?"

Rachel was surprised that her grandmother had guessed. She turned and looked at her. Her grandmother had very smart eyes; Rachel wondered why she hadn't noticed that before. But she had to be smart; she had always been so happy before, and she knew how to dress and paint pictures and make Rachel's grandfather love her.

"Yes."

"You feel betrayed by Barry."

Rachel nodded.

"And they haven't been nice at school."

She nodded again.

"Can you tell me about it?"

Rachel turned her head away. "I'm too ashamed."

Her grandmother was stroking Rachel's head. "You don't have to be ashamed of anything with me."

"But you've always been good."

Her grandmother smiled for the first time, really smiled. "Not always. Your Zayde and I made love before we married."

"You and Zayde?" Rachel was stunned.

"Yes. We weren't so different then. What was different was that I was a lot older than you . . . nearly twenty . . . and I knew we were going to be married. Sex is a very important thing, and everybody wants it. It's just natural. The only problem is, the world is cruel, Rachel. And if you throw sex away on undeserving people, there are those who will be judgmental, and mean, and make you feel miserable."

"It's not fair! The boys can—"

"No, it's not fair. And yes, the boys 'can,' " her grandmother agreed, with a funny little smile. "In my lifetime it probably won't ever be different, Rachel. I hope it will in yours. It probably will be. In the meantime there are other ways to relieve your feelings. Have you thought about that?"

Rachel hadn't.

"There are other kinds of love, for instance. The love we feel for you and David and Leah and the boys . . . the cats." Her grandmother grinned, then got serious. "And there's work."

"Like your painting."

"*Yes*. Did you know that sometimes when I paint it's almost like making love?" Her grandmother didn't look so old now; she was almost the Nan Rachel had first met when she was a kid. "It's true, Rachel. A person can have the most wonderful feelings about something that has nothing to do with anyone else, that's all her own."

"Not like . . . Israel. That's Barry's." Rachel hurt when she said his name.

"That's not true, Rachel. Israel isn't 'Barry's' . . . or any one person's. But your personal vision of it is *yours*, no one else's. Have you been to the Jewish Museum uptown?"

"No. Barry was supposed to take me, but he didn't." Rachel was bitter about that, especially.

"*I'll* take you. And maybe you'll do something for me."

Rachel just looked at her. What could *she* do for anybody? But she said Okay.

"Good. You can tell me about Israel. I haven't kept up, and I know there's a lot I've missed." Her grandmother looked very serious; she meant it.

"Sure."

"That'll be wonderful. And we'd better go to the museum soon. It's closed in the summers, and it's only five weeks until June."

"It seems like a long time." It was an eternity to get through, Rachel thought.

Her grandmother's eyes looked smart again. "How would you like it if you didn't have to go back to school at *all*, except to take the exams?"

"But how could I do that?" Rachel was mystified.

"I can have you coached right here at home. I've

already looked into it. Then next fall you can go to a new school.''

"Oh, that would be . . . wonderful.'' Rachel felt like crying again, but this time because she was so relieved. Not having to face them, not to be whispered about, laughed at. "A school where no one *knows* me,'' she blurted.

"A school where they will get to know you . . . know the new Rachel. A lovely, intelligent girl who knows about Israel and David Ben-Gurion!'' Her grandmother was kind of laughing, but her eyes looked shiny.

"At least you know his name.'' Rachel found herself smiling. Now her grandmother was holding her, and it felt good, in a whole new way.

"Now you'd better get some sleep,'' she said, and let go. "Starting next week, you're going to be working pretty hard.''

"Next week? Oh . . . oh. Thank you, Nan.''

Her grandmother got up, looking down at Rachel. She was crying. Maybe because Rachel had called her by the old name she had used when she was just a kid.

The next Monday Rachel woke up feeling lighter than she had felt for a whole year. Nobody would laugh at her that day, nobody would whisper behind their hands or make her cry. She could hardly believe it.

As it turned out, she had three coaches, and they all came that day—Miss Johnson, the English and language coach, who was very ugly but had a beautiful smile and nice eyes; Mrs. Harper, a fat, pretty woman who would coach her in history and civics; and Mr. Whyte, a really old, solemn man who would be handling science. Rachel would have the same schedule as school, nine in the morning until three in the afternoon, with an hour off for lunch.

Nan had been right: Rachel was going to be working very hard. But she didn't mind, because all her subjects were easy except science, and she wasn't going to need much of that when she went to college. She was already thinking of becoming either a writer or an artist. Miss Johnson was very impressed that Rachel had already done this year's required reading and some of next year's. Rachel heard her tell Nan that Rachel's reading ability was "phenomenal."

The five weeks seemed to fly by. Nan would paint in her studio in the mornings while Rachel was being coached, or go over to Leah's to baby-sit. In the afternoons they would go places together, to a museum or shopping. Then Rachel would do her homework in the evenings. She became so absorbed with preparing herself for the exams that she hardly realized or cared how constricted her life had become. Her new schedule kept her safe, sheltered from the cruel world of her contemporaries. At times Rachel felt like a small child again, grateful for the security her grandparents offered.

In the middle of May the Zionists proclaimed the new state of Israel, which was recognized by President Truman. Tel Aviv was bombed and Egypt ordered invasion. The New York Zionists were mobilizing, collecting funds to send arms to Israel. "I want to help," Rachel told her grandparents. But she was fearful of joining a Village Zionist group because she would confront Barry. Her grandmother seemed to understand that without being told and encouraged her to join a Young Zionist group on the Upper West Side. Rachel did, and in the afternoons after her coaching and most of the weekends she worked with the group.

She could hardly remember now how she had felt about "fooling" Nan; that had been the ambition of another Rachel. The fact that they trusted her to be where she said she was going to be made her feel proud and gave her a sense of renewal. Several of the boys in the group asked her for dates, but she refused them. They seemed so young and naive, they didn't attract her; she already knew so much that they had obviously not yet experienced. Besides, there was something almost frightening now about going out with boys. Rachel couldn't forget what had happened before. She was liked, she was respected by these people who didn't know about her, and she wasn't going to spoil it.

It wasn't easy; it was one of the hardest things she'd ever done. Her body still made its urgent demands, but she returned to her private appeasement, clinging to what Nan had said about the substitution of work for "love." Rachel knew she had never loved anyone but Barry and never would. What she had felt for the others was a physical thing. She was going to prove herself to Barry someday, she resolved. Someday they would meet again, a long time from now, and he would see that she had changed, that she was a whole new person.

The strangest thing was how her feelings for other people were changing: she was coming to love her grandmother more and more, liking Leah and the children better, feeling that David was her uncle again. And everyone in the family, in turn, treated her with great respect.

The frightening part was going in to take the exams. Now she was more "different" than ever, having had private coaching all this time, not having been in school at all. She took special pains with her appearance that first scary day, wearing no makeup at all except a little light-pink lipstick, getting into a covered-up cotton dress that was really too warm.

But it was better than she had expected; nobody was allowed to talk, of course, or even look at each other much during the exams, so she felt enclosed in a safe privacy. And best of all, when the tests were over and the results were mailed to her, Rachel discovered that she had made all A's and only one B in science, which she had expected. When she told her coaches, they were all delighted. Even the sour Mr. Whyte said she hadn't done "badly," and Miss Johnson told her there would be no problem now at all in being admitted to the difficult new girls' school, with its high standards, in the fall. Rachel knew that a good school record would be essential if she decided to go to

Israel; everyone in the Young Zionists talked of almost nothing else. A person had to have something to offer.

That summer was the happiest one she had ever had. She and Nan spent a good part of it on Long Island, and it was heaven to laze in the sun, after all her hard work; do more reading; dream her dreams of the future and of Israel.

She and Nan met with the director of Miss Prewitt's School late in the summer to find out what the school was like, what the girls wore, and so Rachel could take a placement test. Rachel scored so high that even the poker-faced director, Mrs. Hope, was deeply impressed.

By September they were all ready and Rachel's uniforms had been tailored. In the warmer autumn the uniform was a white or pastel shirt and a lightweight skirt of the student's choice; when it got colder they would wear the school blazer over the shirt, or a sweater. "We don't want the girls to be distracted from their studies by a study of each other's clothes," Mrs. Hope said dryly. Of course, on dates and at the dances they would be allowed to wear whatever they chose, but Rachel was eager to look like the others, to be accepted, so she listened carefully to what Nan suggested about dress clothes.

At first, even with her good record, she was terrified of the classes. The teachers required so much, after the relatively low standards of the public school. But by October Rachel knew she was going to meet the standards, even exceed them, because she overheard one of the teachers say to another, "Rachel has one of the finest minds I've ever encountered." Rachel glowed at that, and when she told her grandparents, she thought they looked happier than they had in a long time.

The habit of celibacy had grown easier, too; she was pouring all of her energies and emotions into study and into the Young Zionist work, which was still pursued one night a week and on the weekends.

However, she was not like the other girls, even if she looked like them now—wearing the same quality of clothes, the allowable amount of pale lipstick—she was both older and younger than the other students. When some of them giggled over the boys from St. Mark's and Goddard who would be coming to the dances, Rachel kept quiet. With her history it was hardly a thrill to think of being kissed. On the other hand, she knew they thought she was too innocent and too studious.

She went to the first school dance, before Thanksgiving, with an indifference that surprised the others. All that mattered was that her dress was right, that she could dance well and not be too noticeable. The idea of "romance" with any of the boys left her cold. Perversely, her indifference made Rachel enormously popular with the boys, and she could hardly dance two steps without being cut in on. But she was so cool, so discouraging, that she didn't arouse the other girls' jealousy; after a few tries the boys went off in pursuit of their former prey.

All Rachel wanted now was acceptance and respect. And she was getting it, at last.

No one had heard about her yet. No one knew. All they knew was that her grandfather was the big labor leader, her grandmother the painter and designer, and that her parents were dead. The Village seemed a world away. None of the girls at school had dated boys from the Village, evidently, and that was just the way Rachel liked it. Her secret was still safe.

She had made only two close friends by her junior year—Rhoda Carlton, whose mother was Jewish, whose father was a Gentile, and Carol Landau, who wanted to live on a kibbutz after graduation. The three came to be known as "the grinds." Plain Rhoda, who rarely dated, was more intent on becoming a writer than anything else in life, and Carol, a passionate Zionist, hoped to teach small children on a kibbutz.

Though she spent a good deal of time with them, Rachel decided she could never tell either of the girls about her past. She and Carol went to Zionist meetings together and the three of them occasionally went to a movie on Saturdays, to a museum or shopping. They rarely visited each other's homes; Rhoda's father was a Wall Street financier to whom Joseph Barsimson was anathema and Carol's parents disapproved of Rachel's "mixed" background. Both the girls envied Rachel's closeness to her family.

Neither of them could understand Rachel's indifference to boys. There was a group of fairly nice boys who sometimes left school early to hang out around the corner near Miss Prewitt's to ask Rachel to go out with them. Rachel nearly always said no. Once in a while she accepted a date, though, so the others wouldn't think there was something wrong with her. But she had a particular phobia about movies; she still couldn't forget the wild, nighmarish scenes at the Sheridan.

Once Rhoda asked Rachel what her mother had been like and Rachel answered, "She looked just like me." It occurred to her for the first time since she had come to America that she hardly thought about her real mother, and never asked Nan about her anymore. She supposed that Marite had never seemed real to her; the others were her true family. And life had been too full to linger on the ghosts of the past.

That night, however, Rachel found her curiosity aroused. What *had* she been like, the mother who died so long ago? Had she had the same wild feeling that Rachel had . . . suffered the same confusion . . . left her weaknesses to Rachel?

After she had done her homework that evening, Rachel went into the living room and said abruptly to Zayde and to Nan, "Will you tell me about my mother?"

And they told her. It took a long time, because the story went all the way back to the day Rachel's mother was born in 1911, the same day as the terrible fire. Nan said Zayde had saved people's lives in the fire and couldn't even be at the hospital at the time Marite was born.

They told Rachel how her mother had loved pretty clothes and pretty things, how close she had been to her own grandmother, Elizabeth Wendell; that Elizabeth had actually stolen Marite when she was fourteen and taken her to Europe.

"Did you try to get her back?" Rachel asked.

Her grandparents looked at each other. Zayde said, "For a very long time. She didn't answer our letters or anything. We went to France, to Paris, to try to see her, but her grandmother had taken her away again. Finally we felt there was nothing else we could do . . . and we thought your mother wanted to be with her grandmother more than she wanted to live with us."

"And then, much later," Nan said in a shaky voice, "we found out that your mother had married a German; that she'd been sent to a concentration camp because someone must have found out her father was Jewish. She still had the little star that the Griebs found in Berlin and gave to you." Nan got up and came to sit beside her, putting her arm around Rachel's shoulders.

"A concentration camp," Rachel said. "Oh, that's *horrible*." She felt like crying, but she still couldn't, and that was an awful feeling. Her grandmother seemed to understand. She didn't say anything else for awhile; she just held Rachel against her.

"We assume," Zayde said at last, "that she must have escaped from the camp somehow, to end up in Berlin, living next door to the Griebs. That's where you were born. Mrs. Grieb was a nurse—like Leah." He smiled at her. "Which was lucky, under the circumstances."

"But who was my father?" Rachel demanded. "Does anyone know?"

"He was a German named von Durning. Heir to a baron's title. We can't even conjecture what he looked like, because you look so much like your mother," her grandfather said. He peered at Rachel.

"What I want to know," Rachel said, "more than anything, is what kind of person my mother was. I mean, did she . . . act the way I did," she flushed, "when she was in high school? Did she have the same kind of feelings I've had?"

Her grandparents looked at each other again. After a moment, her grandmother answered, "No, Rachel, she didn't act much like you. I believe she felt her grandmother's ideas were the right ones, and her grandmother was very strict about things. But we don't really know what she was like later on. Because we weren't with her." Nan looked at Rachel sadly.

"I can't understand why anyone would want to leave you." Rachel put her arms around her grandmother's neck and kissed her. "Thank you for telling me the truth . . . straight out. That makes me feel good, like I'm a person, and not a kid."

Her grandmother held her close.

"You *are* a person, Rachel. Definitely a person."

Her grandfather was smiling at her, and she could see the love in his eyes. Somehow, her mother's history didn't matter quite so much as it had a few minutes before.

When Rachel stepped into the garden on a balmy evening in June 1950, her clothes and hair were a pale blur in contrast to her lightly tanned skin. By the late dusk of daylight savings time, Kate observed her trim body in its shirt and Bermuda shorts, the wheat-colored fall of her hair, newly cut to brush the delicate neck just below her earlobes. The ideal Fifties Girl, Kate decided with a smile.

"Hello, Miracle," Joseph said. His long body reclined in one of the garden chairs; one of the old cats lay on his chest, another on his stomach.

"Don't get up," Rachel said in a close imitation of Blanche Dubois. "I'm just passin' through." She went to kiss Joseph and then Kate, and settled on the grass between them. "Thank you so much, both of you. That was a wonderful dinner."

Kate reached out a lazy hand to touch Rachel's hair. "I'm glad you enjoyed it. We've had a lot of good celebrations there, when it had another name." She caught Joseph's eye in the dimness and saw his own eyes sparkle.

"We certainly have." They had gone to the same restaurant where Harry Dryver had taken them for their wedding breakfast. "Do you know how proud you've made us?" He smiled at Rachel.

"I think so." Her face was solemn, very touching. Kate recalled the odds against her—against *them*—when Rachel had moved back to Eleventh Street. They way she had almost held her breath for three whole years, the sleep she had lost, waiting for the ax of regression to fall; the constant attention, the anxiety and exhaustion. The times Kate had confessed to Joseph that she wasn't a psychiatrist, that maybe she was handling it all wrong.

Kate glanced at Joseph, the source of her strength and hope, remembering how he had backed her up and reassured her when she worried about Rachel's becoming too studious, too obsessed and isolated.

But she had come through, that brave, determined child; come through with flying colors at the top of her class. Any college would be glad to get her now. On the other hand, she might decide on art school. Kate would never forget how Rachel had come to her one afternoon in the studio and asked her so eagerly if Kate thought she could learn to paint.

That, Kate reflected, was the greatest miracle of all: her granddaughter might take up where Dryver, and then Kate Barsimson, left off. Most of all it might distract her from Israel.

But that was too much to hope for. Rachel had been talking for a long time about an artist named Ari Reisel, who had been a kibbutznik since he was nineteen and who had lived on the Kabri kibbutz for the last two years while he took part in exhibitions in Israel, Europe, and America.

Kate couldn't help her probing remark. "I guess it's way too soon to know what you're going to do."

"Oh, Lord, yes," Joseph protested. "You've got a vacation coming. Maybe we could go someplace different this summer."

Rachel was silent for an instant; then she said, "I'm glad you brought it up, Nan. It makes it easier for me to ask you."

"Ask us what?" Kate's heart failed her. She thought she already knew.

"If I can spend a year in Israel before I start college." She sounded almost fearful.

There was another uneasy beat of silence; then Joseph said mildly, "It's not exactly the safest place in the world, Rachel. And it's a tough life, in the desert."

"What is safe anymore?" Rachel asked softly. The U.S. was sending more troops to fight in Korea; the shadow of another war was on them all.

"This country still is, fortunately." Joseph sounded very calm, primed for debate. But Kate had a feeling it would be useless. Ever since they had told Rachel about Marite, her dedication to the Jewish cause had been more fervent than before.

"I want to go, badly. So badly." The child was so much in earnest that it touched Kate's heart. She knew what Joseph didn't—that Israel had become a kind of Grail for Rachel, a vision that had to do with her feeling for that boy, Barry, a feeling that apparently hadn't changed. If they didn't allow her to go, she would be miserable.

"We can't be too happy about sending you to a war zone, Rachel." Joseph's voice was still calm, still reasonable, but Kate could hear his underlying anxiety.

"We *picketed* in a war zone, Joseph." It was nearly dark now but Kate could feel their surprise. "You lived in one when you were twelve, and David started risking his neck when he was fourteen. So Rachel's behind schedule."

Her voice was so level they probably thought she was joking; Joseph's impatient movement sent the disgruntled cats leaping to the grass. Kate recognized the graceful outline of Kwan as he padded toward Rachel and rubbed against her leg. The girl rubbed his head and waited, leaning toward Kate while Joseph said, "Very funny."

"Who's laughing? This whole cockeyed family has swum against the tide for the last forty years. It's a miracle that you're alive or that I'm sane. My daughter-in-law strolled through air raids, and now our grandchildren are going the same way you and David went. Why should Rachel be excluded? Don't women have any rights?''

Rachel turned and looked up at Kate, smiling uncertainly in the path of light from the kitchen. Joseph was very still. Clearly they were puzzled by Kate's mockery, but aware that everything she had said was true. Jake had already begun visiting the union headquarters, declaring he was going to be another union man, and Saul hung around David's workplace every chance he got.

Encouraged, Rachel prodded Joseph. "The war was over in 1949, Zayde."

"And the Arabs never agreed to an armistice with a country they don't recognize," Joseph countered. "There are always 'little' wars."

"Joseph, do you remember what you told me when David went off barnstorming? Have you discouraged Jake from a new future of broken heads and *tsuris*, or told Saul he couldn't fly someday?"

"That's different. They're not girls."

"But I was, when I took the plunge with you . . . and told you not to accept Rafael's offer."

Joseph sighed. "You're still a twister. I can't win with you. I'd still hate like hell to have you across the table in negotiations." He couldn't hide his exasperated fondness.

"I think Rachel deserves her chance, after working so hard all this time. Don't you, Joseph?"

"All right, all right. But you're awfully young."

"Please . . . *please*, Zayde."

"I can't fight you *and* Kate."

"Oh, Zayde!" Rachel propelled herself up from the ground and went to kiss Joseph. Then she embraced Kate. "Thank you. Thank you. I've got to call Carol right now."

She rushed into the kitchen, and before she disappeared, Kate got a glimpse of her lithe young form and swinging golden hair.

"Kate, I thought you'd oppose this."

"So did I, Joseph. But I've had a lot of practice bowing to the inevitable . . . and ignoring advice about marrying a 'dangerous Jew.' We'll just have to start hoping again."

Chapter 30

Eight-year-old Jake Barsimson spooned the last of his tricolored ice cream, admiring his grandparents up on the platform they called the day-is. His grandfather was sitting right in the center of the long table, Jake's grandmother right next to him. It sure was exciting to have a grandfather who was a celebrity. He was wearing a black tuxedo and looked as sharp as that old guy in the movies with the French name—Monjoo or something. Jake's grandmother was awfully pretty, too, even if she was an old lady.

Behind his grandparents there was a great big banner stretching all the way across the top of the stage, glittering and gold, with a big "Fifty" in the middle, and on either side, "1900" and "1950."

Jake tried to imagine what fifty years were. It was more than six times his whole life. And his grandfather said it had been fifty-seven years since he was eight like Jake.

His mother smiled at him. "Having a good time?"

"Great. They look wonderful, don't they, up there?"

"They certainly do." His mother's eyes looked very big and shiny tonight.

"You do too, Mom."

"Well, *thank* you." She leaned over and roughed up his hair. She'd stopped kissing him so much when he had told her he was too old, but he still liked it when she did that to his hair. It felt nice. "How about you, Saul? Did you get enough to eat?"

"Do you think I could have some more ice cream?"
Jake's younger brother was such a *kid*. He didn't even
realize what a big thing this was. All he ever really cared
about was football and airplanes and eating. He was okay,
though, and he was really strong. When they wrestled,
Saul could already throw him. But Jake was going to do
something about that; his grandfather was already teaching
him how to "duke" with his hands.

"I don't see why not," their dad said. He must have
been listening. He held up his hand and a waiter came
right away. Jake liked that; it was exciting to feel so
important. People were looking at him and Saul and his
dad and mother. An old lady had stopped by their table
during dinner; his dad had stood up, and Jake and Saul did
too, the way they had been taught. The old lady said she
was an old friend of their grandmother's; her name
was Rose Nathan. She kept looking at Jake and his dad,
and said it wouldn't be long before Jake looked exactly the
way his grandfather did in 1909.

Boy, that was sure a long time ago. He wondered what
it would be like to be so old. Jake hoped he would be
famous by that time, and maybe married to somebody
famous, too, like his grandmother.

Their table was right by the stage. Jake looked up there
again. His grandmother was smiling and her hair was
pretty, kind of foamy and silver like that angel hair they
had on their Christmas-Hanukkah tree. She saw Jake and
waved to him. It was terrific.

Someday, Jake thought, I'm going to be sitting on a
day-is, too, when I'm rur...ing the union.

Kate thought: It's incredible how much that child looks
like Joseph. She gave him another little wave, fondly
studying his black, tousled hair, his rapt and serious face,
his bright blue eyes big as dollars with excitement.

She turned back to the board member on her left,
apologizing.

"Don't be sorry," the man said genially. "That's one

of your grandsons. The future president.'' He chuckled. ''I know him well.''

''You should,'' Kate retorted, ''the way he haunts the office. I hope he's not a nuisance.''

''Never. He's a delight. He *works*, does all kinds of things for the people around the office. I've never seen a kid that young who knows so much about the labor movement.'' Kate's dinner partner beamed at her. ''He's a chip off the old block.''

Gratified, Kate laughed softly and turned to her right, glancing at Joseph. *Though much is taken, much abides*, she quoted to herself. He was a hundred times more appealing now than he had been that afternoon in 1909; his black, white-threaded hair sprang back from his forehead with a young, vigorous growth. The lines and sharper planes of his fine face made him positively majestic; the brilliant black eyes, she decided, had never changed at all, even if he complained about the absurdity of having to wear glasses to work.

Sensing her attention, he turned and looked at Kate.

Sixty years old, Joseph thought, and she's still the loveliest woman in this whole big ballroom. With the young flesh melted away from her face, the magnificent structure of her delicate bones was even more apparent above that blooming mouth. Her mouth was the true indicator of what she had always been; it had never thinned from habitual stinginess of mind and heart, or drawn down at the corners from lack of humor or of hope. What a young mouth it still was.

Slender and elegant and upright, with her downy cloud of short, silvery hair, and her simple outfit—he liked that suit-thing she had on, with its blue jacket almost like a man's tux, and the long, graceful skirt instead of trousers, the shirt ruffled up around her neck, twin sparkles of diamond studs in her ears—she made most of the other women look . . . noisy. Kate never jangled or poked out or insisted to the eye.

He had never loved her so much.

Joseph smiled to himself. And he was going to tell them all tonight, when he made his speech. Kate had let him practice on her, but he had left out the part about her. That was going to be a surprise.

He was glad his dinner partner was talking to someone else right now; it gave him a minute just to sit, to be quietly happy. To look at Kate, and smile.

To look down the dais at the men and women there. He had worked with some of them the whole fifty years.

And then to turn toward the sea of tables out there in the ballroom, and look at the faces of the members. They were a world away from girls like Clara Lemlich and Rosa and Gertrude and Elvira. And was he glad.

To look at his son and grandsons, his lovely daughter-in-law. Leah looked lovely too, he decided, with her red hair, in her brown dress with the coppery trim around the neck and cuffs. Probably something devised by Kate.

That name still rang in his heart like a sudden little bell. He glanced at his wife again. Her profile, with its wide, expectant eyes and slightly parted lips, still reminded him of the young princess in the picket line.

Kate knew almost every word of Joseph's speech by now; she was free to enjoy the respectful, breathless silence, the attentive and inspired expression on the people's faces.

". . . from one little three-story building, with rickety stairs, to twenty-six buildings throughout the country, east and west, north and south. From sixteen hours a day and three dollars a week to some of the lowest work-hours in organized labor, for earnings in the front rank of American industry.

"From stifling rooms without sanitary facilities to welfare and medical plans, retirement pensions, vacations with pay, and activities in education.

"Yes, times have changed since the bad old days, since 'Home, Sweat Home.' " Joseph's mellow, resonant voice began to ease.

"I was not quite fifteen when I went to work for the union. I made one bagel a week."

Laughter bubbled in Kate and she could hear a wave of laughter rising from the audience.

"I was the hottest organizer in the children's jacket union. Marty, over there, was a hotshot poster-maker. Today he's our 'creative director.' " Joseph shook his head over the fancy title, and there was more laughter. He pointed out other board members who had worked with him at the beginning.

"And then there's this lady." Joseph bowed his head in Kate's direction. She recovered from her startle and managed a smile. "Forty-one years ago I found her on the Triangle picket line. And being a pretty good talker, I talked her into marrying me. The surprising thing is that all these years she's stuck to me . . . and helped me stick to the union. She made posters, *too*."

There was a good-natured, chuckling murmur from the audience and a spatter of applause. Kate marveled. That was very sly of him. He's never lost the gift of surprise.

". . . my son and daughter-in-law and grandsons," Joseph was saying, "and my granddaughter in Israel.

"This is a whole new world. There's a new generation of workers here tonight, thank God, who've never known what it was like to carry forty-pound bundles at the age of six or seven. Times are good and they'll get better.

"But make no mistake. We can never afford to grow complacent. There will always be another union-busting law, another power front in a sophisticated guise rising up to destroy us. It's no longer a matter of fire escapes; it's a war of laws and propaganda. The union is equipped to fight it.

"Many of us here are Jews. And we remember a holocaust that came thirty years before the monstrous holocaust in Europe. The holocaust of the Triangle Shirtwaist Company. You will say, perhaps, that it is foolish, grotesque to compare that fire with the destruction of millions of people. But I do not speak of numbers. I speak of the disregard of the lives of oppressed peoples, in whatever number, whatever circumstance, it may be shown. And I say, with the survivors of that infinitely larger holocaust . . . we must stay strong and vigilant . . . it must happen never again . . . *never again!*''

His voice rang with the final mighty words, and the listeners rose to their feet; there was a titanic wave of wild applause, the cheering cries of men and women.

Kate could barely see her husband for the tears flooding her eyes: she wiped them away with an impatient hand and gazed at him, standing there in the bright, golden path of light, his dark eyes glistening with his own emotion, with his relentless triumph.

From the moment the plane banked above Tel Aviv, the "hill of the springtime," and Rachel saw the spreading seafront dotted with small white sails, the buff-and-silver city along the shore, she fell under an enchantment that was to last for almost a year.

Her first months were spent in that white-hot city; part of her bargain with her grandparents had been to stay in a form of youth hostel in the city, with Carol Landau, who was in Israel for the summer. Only a month would intervene between Carol's departure and Rachel's admission to the Kubbutz Sharon.

Almost impervious to heat, and never forgetting the cold of Zurich, the wet chill of England, even in summer, Rachel took to the climate, Carol said, like a lizard. In some ways it was school all over again for Rachel, with Carol urging her to join more in the city's active social life, the long, lazy afternoons of swimming or drinking the insidious *arac* under an umbrella.

But if Rachel had not forgotten the cold of other climates, she had also not forgotten that gnawing need to prove herself. She was an American in Israel, not even a full Jew at that; hearing random references to "spoiled Americans" had given her a horror of living up to that title. Once again, she wanted to belong, to fade into the scenery, to feel secure.

Furthermore, within a week she was enrolled in the studio of Ari Reisel and began to immerse herself in work. Mr. Reisel was traveling that summer and the studio was run by his able assistant, Emanuel Boker. Boker was impressed by Rachel's seriousness and industry, and one landmark day informed her she had talent. Rachel glowed with his praise, working harder than ever. At least six hours of every day were devoted to her work and study.

At odd times she would feel a faint twinge of attraction for one of Carol's "sabras" or some tanned and strapping fellow on the street or in a café. Once in a while she even went out on a double date with Carol, yet the old reluctance, the old wariness remained. She clung to the vision of her reconciliation with Barry. She had heard rumors that he was already in Israel.

It would be the ultimate irony for him to see her with another man, assume that she was still the same as she had been years ago, when his image was never out of her heart. Carol teased her now and then about seeming to "carry a torch," saying it was already too hot in Tel Aviv for that. Rachel always made some evasive reply or other. Close as she was to Carol, she still hadn't told her about Barry. Carol didn't even know his name.

The one suggestion Rachel always agreed to was sightseeing: they traveled all along the coast that summer, from Gaza to Haifa, until Rachel felt that her very blood had been dyed with the colors of Israel, its solemn joys and its sad laughter. Unless the tours were short ones, Rachel opted for the weekends only; nothing could induce her to miss a session with Boker.

She found a new generation was forming in Israel. A combination of the idealists of the past and the realists of the present. Some of the old Jewish anguishes remained, but most of them seemed to be disappearing, and the street festivals were more orgiastic than religious. But the shadow had not completely lifted; less than a decade before, millions of Jews were being slaughtered. Many a deeply tanned arm bore, still, the trace of a blue number.

And everywhere, in spite of the fact that the war was over, were khaki-clad men of the Haganah. At first the Arabs seemed sinister, frightening to Rachel. But the peaceable Arabs in Jaffa, who sold exotic foods from little carts or hawked the wares spread on counters before their shops, had nothing at all to do with war. In a way they were no different from the Jews with pushcarts and stores on Orchard Street.

One of the places along the coastal route that Rachel found charming was the little seaside resort of Nahariya, built by German refugees who were saved from the death camps. The resort was ponderous and neat and slow, and embodied what one of the sabras called the "yekké spirit."

"What's a yekké?" Rachel asked.

"A German Jew. Very pompous, buttoned-up."

So I'm a yekké, Rachel thought, in more ways than one. She did not share the confidence of this with the unbuttoned sabra, whose casual shirt was open to his navel. Rachel looked away from his broad, hairy, mahogany-colored chest and studied the scarlet sails of the little boats in the water between Nahariya and Rosh Hanikra, their next stop.

Later she painted from memory a scene of that part of the coast, and the sea of blue-gray-green splashed with blood-red sails.

The summer passed as fast and smoothly as a lovely dream, and before she could credit it, her birthday came after the most joyous of the holidays, the Feast of Sukkos, the Ingathering. She had harvested her own treasures in the past brief months, which would remain with her forever. She came to the Sharon kibbutz with solemn anticipation.

Her first sight of the low concrete buildings, the sweeping fields below the mountains, the tractor sheds and primitive arrangements, was one of the greatest thrills of her life. Here was the ideal community, where all the residents were sisters and brothers, and the children were free and merry.

Rachel's rosy vision darkened a little when she saw the dormitory where she would sleep, the tiny corner allotted for her belongings. All of the women she met seemed so tough and self-reliant, so full of the juices of life, that they made her feel frail by comparison. She was thankful that she had already spent some months in Israel. At least she had not been obliged to join them with a pale, decadent-looking skin.

And that night, eating at the communal table, welcomed by the others, her dedication and enthusiasm were renewed. After dinner, dancing hand-in-hand in the *hora*, she began to feel that she might come to belong.

The next morning she was awakened at six o'clock; immediately after breakfast she joined the other women in the cotton fields, for picking. By noon she found her hands were sore and blistered; she ached over her entire body, neck and back and limbs and haunches. With enormous relief she went back to her painting in the afternoon; she was allowed a half-day of "artistic" work under the rules of the kibbutz. But it was rough going, painting with her sore hands, and she almost wept with frustration.

A voluptuous, strong-looking girl named Roberta, in the next bed to Rachel at the dormitory, observed the new kibbutznik with pitying eyes. "Reisel and Boker are coming at the end of the week," Roberta said. "Why don't you talk to them? If you're an artist, it's idiotic to foul up your hands."

Though it was a sensible suggestion, Rachel stubbornly maintained that she wanted to stick it out. By the end of the painful week she was gratified to find that her hands were better; she had learned the proper technique of picking, and already her tensile young muscles were adapting.

When her art instructor from the summer, Emanuel Boker, arrived at the kibbutz that weekend, he observed Rachel's hands. "I admire your dedication. But you're going to get calluses like an elephant's hooves. If you want to work, I strongly suggest you work in the house, and help out in the nursery.''

With a guilty relief, Rachel assented. She told Boker the story her grandmother had told her—how her grandfather said it was foolish for Kate Barsimson to walk a picket line when the union needed artists, that it was like a skilled tailor carrying a bundle.

Boker laughed. ''My father was a tailor. That's exactly right.''

''I don't want to be . . . apart from the others, though.''

''Your grandmother must have also told you that an artist is always 'apart,' Rachel. I'm a kibbutznik just like everyone else. I was born on one, like Ari. But I do the work I'm meant to do, and so will you. That is, if you're serious about being an artist.''

''I think you know I am,'' she said quietly.

''Yes, I do know. So please, no more of this happy peasant routine. This is 1951. There's plenty of work to do that won't cripple your hands. Helping me teach the kids art, for instance.''

She was a little shocked by his remarks, but her heart was high when he made the last suggestion. And from then on she alternately worked in the kitchen, the nursery, and taught the smaller children twice a week in the mornings.

Rachel knew her talent set her a little apart from the other women, even here, where the emphasis was on equality and sisterhood. But she was too busy, too content to care. She was well liked and respected; even the more nervous wives, who had looked a little askance at her beauty, relaxed with her now. Rachel had made it abundantly clear that she had no more than a friendly, distant interest in their husbands or, indeed, in any of the men on the kibbutz. The single ones had given up on her by the time she had been in residence for two months.

And she made an extra effort to be helpful and cooperative, to wear the uniform the others wore. It seemed an age since she had even considered anything other than Bermuda shorts with a sleeveless shirt, or a plain blouse and cotton skirt sometimes in the evenings. Early on she realized that the primitive bathing arrangements made even her ear-length haircut a nuisance. She asked one of the other women to crop her hair very short, into the boyish cut that many of them wore for cleanliness and convenience. It was good, she found, to be able to wash your hair and then just go about your business as it swiftly dried in the hot desert air.

Even with her less rigorous tasks, Rachel saw that she had grown deeply tanned, lithe, and healthy-looking by her fifth month in the kibbutz. And she looked upon the fields and mountains now with a surpassing love; this was her country; Israel was in her blood and bone.

The nation was crude and young, but the earth it occupied breathed with memories of ancient splendor, bore the imprint of heroic feet. At Sharon she felt that she had finally become an integral part of something infinitely greater. The kibbutznikim were her family, even more than those of her own blood. And after all, the people of Sharon *did* have the same blood, the blood of Jews.

Best of all, no individual here seemed to have a past. There was only the present, and the future. It didn't matter what anyone had been, only what one was now. In fact, individualism had no place at all at Sharon. Money was shunned, if not unheard of, and almost everything was shared. Rachel learned to look on her painting as her contribution to the kibbutz, her present to its walls. She was honored when Boker chose to hang some of her paintings in the dining hall and dormitories.

She was friendly and at ease with almost everyone, and became quite close to Roberta because of their sheer proximity. Roberta, who came from Brooklyn, had none of Rachel's poetic ideas about Israel. Her passion was politics. Israel was not a blue-and-gold vision to Roberta; it was the Jews' rightful land which must be won and held at any cost.

Rachel agreed in principle, of course. It was the "any cost" that bothered her. She had seen a captured Egyptian tank on display in Tel Aviv, guarded by a young soldier who looked no older than Rachel. The soldier, surrounded by hero-worshipping little boys, wore a black patch over one eye.

She had seen other young men: with a leg amputated at the knee, a hand at the wrist. It made the war of 1948–49 seem less holy.

And then there were the refugees. When they had toured the coast last summer, the northernmost stop had been Rosh Hanikra, on the Lebanon frontier. There they had had to turn back; in the far distance she had glimpsed a refugee camp. There were camps like that in Jordan, Syria, and along the Gaza Strip controlled by the Egyptians, harboring some of the million Arab refugees. To Rachel the refugees looked wretched, pathetic. A lot of them looked like civilians, not soldiers.

But she tried to repress her disloyal feelings: they were the enemy, and Israel was her country now. Furthermore, the Arab governments openly declared that they would not stop until Israel was destroyed. And there were plenty of Jewish refugees, too, driven out of Iraq and Yemen, Egypt and Morocco.

Rachel knew that Roberta was right; she *was* politically naive. There were still clashes between Arabs and Israelis on the borders, and the Gaza Strip began to serve as a base for Egypt's Fedayeen—self-sacrifice—commandos. The Fedayeen were mainly recruited from the Palestine Arabs, eager to escape the life of refugee camps. A successful commando raid was rewarded by money as well as military honors. Rachel was sickened to learn that Fedayeen success was allegedly rated by the capture of "trophies" such as a finger or an ear. These raids were increasing in intensity and scope, and there were times when Rachel felt deep apprehension: Sharon was not all that far from the Strip.

She looked back on her heedless, almost frantic attitude as a teenager, when she was helping raise money for Israel's arms, and thought what an innocent she had been.

Death and suffering and displacement were the same, no matter which side they were on. And yet she was horrified by her own treachery: the Jews were the people who deserved the greater compassion. The Jews were the oldest refugees in history. Her grandfather's people had been driven from Spain, her great-grandmother's from Russia. Her own mother had been in a concentration camp in her own adopted country. It seemed the killing had to go on.

Rachel was ashamed to tell Roberta her thoughts; Roberta had driven a jeep for the army in the war of 1948–49, and the man she was going to marry had been killed at Beersheba.

The lusty, matter-of-fact Roberta had no interest in or the slightest comprehension of art. Rachel knew that her own remote and celibate ways were also strange to the other girl. At first Roberta had looked a bit askance at Rachel, expecting her to fail the tests of endurance. But in a very short time she began to see that Rachel was tougher than she looked, and warmed to the new kibbutznik.

They had grown very friendly. Roberta took an amusingly maternal attitude toward Rachel, acting like a very advanced Jewish mother in her attempt to persuade Rachel to "find someone" and "enjoy the good life."

Dodging as best she could these discussions of sex, Rachel was not offended. She had become very fond of the big, voluptuous girl. With her fierce loyalties and her greenish, sleepy eyes, her love of food, petting, and the sun, Roberta reminded Rachel of a large, bumptious cat.

Then one afternoon as they were doing the kibbutz washing, and Roberta brought up the subject again, Rachel found herself confiding in her companion. All of her early history of wildness with boys came pouring out.

"All that must . . . disgust you," she faltered.

"*Disgust* me?" The affectionate Roberta wrung out a garment and threw it down on the table. She turned to Rachel and put her arms around Rachel's back; she could feel Roberta's big, wet hands through her thin cotton blouse. "It makes you *human*, Rachel." Roberta laughed.

"I was beginning to wonder if you were." She let go of Rachel and dipped into the soapy water again, rubbing the collar of a child's shirt. "Before, you seemed so cold, so remote."

"Well, now you know." Rachel took a little girl's red cotton skirt from the tub and checked it for cleanliness.

"There's someone special, isn't there?"

"Yes. Oh, yes. We lost touch, a long time ago. I think he's here in Israel, but I have no idea where. It's crazy, but I still feel the same about him." Rachel said softly. Roberta didn't say anything else, but Rachel could feel her staring.

One evening, a few weeks later, as Rachel and Roberta were walking back to their dorm to change into clean clothes for dinner, Rachel saw a group of soldiers getting out of a "sandwich car." The Haganah had no armored vehicles, so they substituted commercial trucks, with steel plates fixed to the chassis, the plates joined by poured concrete. Rachel had learned the term from Roberta.

"That looks like the Palmach," Roberta said.

The Palmach, "striking companies," usually patrolled the kibbutzim, but this was not just a patrol. They looked like they were setting up a defensive line.

"And . . . that must mean they're expecting a raid," Roberta added grimly.

Rachel felt cold with terror. She stiffened, stopping in her tracks to stare at the soldiers.

"Don't be afraid." Roberta took her arm. "It may not happen. They have to be prepared. And we still have to eat dinner." Raids, then, did not upset the routine.

It was incredible how casual she was, Rachel thought. But then, she had seen the real thing; Rachel hadn't.

Roberta tugged at her arm and she started to walk away. She glanced back once more at the line of soldiers. One of them, tall and wiry, had his back to her. He looked oddly familiar.

He looked like Barry.

Rachel's heart thumped and began to flutter rapidly, high in her throat. She could hardly breathe.

Barry.

It couldn't be, and yet that lean, wiry body, that stance was so familiar. It couldn't, yet it had to be.

Instead of her customary blouse and skirt, Rachel decided to put on a pretty cotton dress, one she hadn't worn since she had been in Tel Aviv. Watching her slip the wires of some Yemenite earrings into the lobes of her pierced ears, Roberta said, teasing her, "What's this? Are you coming out of the cocoon at last . . . is this for the soldiers?"

"For one of them." Rachel's voice was hollowed out with excitement. It sounded hoarse and strange in her own ears. "I think he's here, Roberta. I think I saw him out there with the Palmach."

"Oh, Rachel." Roberta looked at her with sparkling eyes. "You look beautiful." She surveyed Rachel's brief cap of pale blond hair, bleached almost silver by the sun to blend with the long, intricate silver earrings; glanced at the leaf-green, simple cotton dress that made Rachel's bare tanned arms and shoulders glow. "Let's go to dinner." Roberta grinned at Rachel, practically pulling her out of the dorm, across the hard-packed sand to the dining hall. The evening was rose and scarlet from the setting sun.

As she followed Roberta into the hall, the smell of food was abhorrent; her stomach pitched with the turmoil of her emotions. She blinked in the reddish light, suddenly sensitive to the loud buzz of voices, the laughter, the scrape of wooden chairs. It was such nervous laughter.

She saw him.

He was sitting with other members of his platoon at a tableful of soldiers and kibbutznikim, and he hadn't seen her. Rachel took her usual place at a table of single men and women, blessing the happenstance of her chair's facing his table.

Rachel could barely hear the remarks of the woman on her left, who was asking her something about the nursery.

She noticed that the sly Roberta had left an empty chair on her right. When Roberta's male companion murmured a question to her, Rachel heard her say, "None of your business, buddy," and chuckle.

Rachel tried not to stare too obviously, tried nobly to follow her companion's conversation. She could hardly believe it was Barry. He looked ten years older than when she had seen him last, a thousand times more appealing. The thin-necked boy-scholar look was gone. He was tanned almost walnut from the desert sun; his arms and shoulders had the heft of maturity. And he was only a year older than she was.

His face was even more transformed than his body: there was a determined set to his narrow mouth. He looked tough and able and undaunted—every inch the soldier.

Suddenly he looked up and saw her.

Their gazes locked; his lips parted in utter stupefaction. Then a slow, wondering, tentative smile blazed white against his swarthy face. Her heart was hammering so painfully she had to take a quick, shallow breath to force oxygen into her lungs, to still the trembling of her astonished body.

She saw him say something to the soldier next to him and get up quickly, with a loud scrape of his chair. He strode toward her table. Watching him walk toward her, Rachel felt the frail young passion of her yesterday stir from its long drowse, slowly, slowly, then very swiftly find its consciousness. What she felt now made the old feeling seem thin and ghostly by comparison. She had been a girl then. Now she was a woman. And he was very much a man.

"Rachel." Even his voice was different, older and deeper. "I can't believe it." Barry put out his hand and she took it: the strong, callused feel of it scraped poignantly along her aroused, awakened nerves. "Is . . . someone sitting here?" He indicated the empty chair. "May I?"

"Of course." She swallowed, trying to steady her shaky

voice. "It's . . . good to see you, Barry," God, how inadequate that was.

"I hardly knew you," he said in a low voice. "You seem so . . . grown-up, so different."

She realized joyfully that he was feeling as inarticulate as she. "So do you. How long have you been here?"

"I caught the end of the war in forty-nine." He grinned. "The truth of it is, I just ran away. There was hell to pay at home, but I finally persuaded my parents not to try to drag me back."

For a long moment they couldn't find anything else to say; they just stared at each other. Finally he murmured, "Rachel, you're so . . . different. You're even more . . . beautiful this way."

She looked down and away from him, wanting to say how altogether different she was.

She heard Roberta say, "Here we go." There was the rattle of a spoon against a coffee cup. Jakov Kaufman, the kibbutz head, was standing at his table to say what they already knew.

He told them that the women and children must take cover by dark, that there would be no "entertainment tonight after dinner." The announcement was merely a matter of form; the whole kibbutz knew what was expected. Kaufman seemed to be directing his remarks to the new kibbutznikim who had never experienced a raid.

And Barry, Rachel thought, would be out there in the dusk, in the thick of it, standing by the wall with his rifle trained at the desert.

"You'd better get back to your dorm," he said. "Let me walk you. I have a minute or two before I have to . . . get back."

She rose at once and they walked out of the dining room, pacing slowly along the few sandy yards to her dorm.

"Rachel, there's so much I want to say. But there's no time."

"I know." She looked up soberly into his dark, pleading eyes. "Everything is different now, Barry. *Everything*."

She felt that she must tell the whole four years in that one word. Miraculously he seemed to read her fervent wish, to understand how much the simple declaration meant to both of them.

"I want you to know something," he said earnestly. "I want you to know, Rachel. I've always loved you. I've never stopped."

Abruptly he grabbed her in his arms and kissed her; she clung to him, oblivious of everyone around them. Just as suddenly he let her go, turned, and walked away.

Her whole self resonated with his remembered words; it had been like the clap of a huge brass cymbal close to her vulnerable, dazzled ears, and now she rang with it, and trembled.

She stood there in the setting sun for a while longer, watching him walk to the barricade. And then she turned and went into the dorm, threw herself on her bed, and closed her eyes.

Roberta came in softly, without speaking; Rachel heard the squeaky springs of her bunklike bed, consoled by her friend's presence and her understanding silence.

It might not happen. It might not happen, Rachel repeated to herself in desperation. But she could feel the gathering silence on the settlement, the tension of heavy air before a thunderstorm.

All at once, without warning, she heard an ominous rumble. She opened her eyes. Those were not trucks.

"That's light armor. At least two small tanks." Roberta's exclamation chilled her blood.

"Tanks. Tanks are impregnable."

"Not quite. A few Molotov cocktails will turn them into stoves . . . and nobody stays in an oven. When they come out, they won't be impregnable at all. For God's sake, stay away from that window, Rachel."

Rachel stopped in her tracks, standing with her back

against the wall. There were explosions now, far louder than the crack of rifles. They must be using bazookas.

She heard the shouts of men, the horrible grinding sound of the tanks, the shattering of glass, the constant firing.

Rachel shuddered with fear; her teeth chattered uncontrollably, threatening to pierce her tongue. She had an urgent, shameful need to urinate; she tensed her muscles.

"It'll be all right, it'll be all right." Roberta soothed her as if she were a wild, frightened animal. "Sit down. Sit down on the floor. Draw up your knees and hold your legs. It helps. I don't know why, but it helps."

Hypnotized, Rachel obeyed. It did help, a little, but her whole body was one vast shudder, and she was drenched in cold sweat; her flesh felt sticky as glue.

Barry was out there, in the line of fire.

She heard men scream, and the sound was horrible beyond any horror she had known—except for London, when she was a little child, and the fire had rained from the sky.

She put her hands over her ears, trying to shut out the screams and bellows, the endless firing, firing.

Then suddenly there was no grinding of tanks; the shots grew random, fading into protracted silence.

And shouts and cheers tore the dark fabric of suspenseful quiet.

Someone shouted, "It's over! It's over!"

"We got the bastards, every one!"

There was wild laughter, and a group of men were singing. The girls at the other end of the dorm, who had been huddled silently together, clapped their hands and then joined them for the *hora*. Laughing hysterically, Roberta pulled Rachel up from the floor. "Rachel! Let's go!"

Stumbling, Rachel let herself be dragged along.

Doors were being flung open; the kibbutznikim were clapping their hands.

It had all happened so fast; Rachel swayed and blinked,

snatched out of her stuporous terror so suddenly that she was dazed.

The scene was one of utter confusion; in the midst of the triumph and hysteria, the medical crew was attending to three of the soldiers. Others of the platoon were standing on the captured tanks.

Rachel's mind cried: Barry. Where was he?

He was nowhere among the sweating, victorious soldiers.

The lights were going on again.

She broke away from the others and began to run along the barricade.

Ahead of her a small knot of men stood solemn and silent above the supine body of a soldier.

One of them knelt over him, feeling his neck and chest and wrist with slow, careful hands. He shook his head and turned the body over.

Rachel froze.

It was Barry Weiss.

Chapter 31

Kate paused at the corner of Tenth Street and Fifth Avenue, waiting for the traffic light to change. She felt unaccountably exhausted from the two-block walk. It certainly couldn't be the weather; the temperature was a perfect seventy and the humidity almost nothing. A lovely September day.

I guess I have to face the fact that I'm getting old, she thought, and feeling out of it. The outdoor art exhibit of 1959 was a far cry from the exhibits of thirty years ago—the paintings and sculpture she had looked over seemed commercial, passionless. A young boy, his transistor radio blaring rock-and-roll, brushed past Kate, jogging her arm without apology. That was something else that had changed, she decided with gloom; she watched him stroll out into traffic and hold out his leg like a dancer, laughing, daring a taxi to hit him. The young people these days seemed so *crazy*. Not daring anymore. Their daring was expressed in petty, childish ways. She *was* getting old, and grumpy.

The light turned green and Kate crossed Tenth Street slowly, still puzzled by her unusual reactions. But she readied her face for a smile: Rachel's spot was just ahead, about a half-block down Fifth. A prestigious location. All the artists in this area had achieved a certain status. Kate wished Rachel could believe it was her merit and not her name that had won it for her. They had been touched when

Rachel asked them to adopt her legally when she came back from Israel, so their surname could be officially hers.

Rachel was deep in conversation with a potential buyer, standing with her back to Kate and the other passersby. Kate sat down in one of the canvas chairs by the apartment building and enjoyed the sight of her granddaughter and her granddaughter's work. From the rear Rachel looked almost boyishly slim in her narrow blue jeans; her delicate tanned arms, bared by a sleeveless yellow shirt, were slightly extended away from her body as she gestured with long-fingered hands. Kate inferred that Rachel was talking about Israel to the interested woman; she was making sweeping motions with her hands at one of the Israel canvases, a semiabstract version of a terrace café overlooking the sea at Jaffa. The modern pleasure-seekers drinking under bright canvas umbrellas on top of an ancient biscuit-colored fortress contrasted sharply with the ruined stone and changeless sea. The sea itself was that indescribable blend of blue and gray and green that Kate always thought of as "Israeli blue"—the shade of Herodian artifacts, of unearthed vases from Byzantium. Jaffa, the city of Japhet, the son of Noah.

Kate was glad that Rachel still hadn't seen her; it was pleasant to sit there for a moment in the gentle sun, unobserved, to survey the versatile riches of her granddaughter's display. Besides the "Israel period," there were paintings born of other phases. The "blue ghosts," for instance—painted during that long, terrifying period of deep depression, soon after Rachel had come home, devastated by the death of Barry. She had lost her golden vision, lost it for three whole years, and said she could not paint any pictures of Israel, not ever again. The grotesquely comic "gross period" was also represented, expressing that time of cynicism when Rachel was emerging from melancholia; the "gross" paintings were of heavy-breasted, defeated women, always solitary, staring out of city windows. And yet each of these psychological souvenirs had great artistic merit. From the blue ghosts a delicate sorrow wafted; for Kate they expressed the poignancy of loss. She could see Marite in them; they made her hear the wind, and harpsichords in empty houses. The fat, gross women, all orange and purple and crimson, were creatures of bitter anger, as if that were the only heat that warmed them anymore, staring out at the world with tired eyes. Rachel had made the viewer feel the heaviness of their bodies.

Two years ago the Israel paintings had come out like the sun: Dr. Mendel, who had treated Rachel after her return, bought one of the paintings, telling Kate that it was the barometer of a healed mind. The psychiatrist had seen new sensuousness, new vitality in the picture, and so had Kate.

She sighed. It was about time. Rachel was twenty-five years old, and they were wondering if she would ever marry. She was certainly a drastic creature; someone had told Kate that the extremes Rachel had experienced as a child accounted for her passionate nature. Kate had dismissed the idea as nonsense at first, until she examined Rachel's history again—supreme sensuality or sainthood. There didn't seem to be any middle ground. No one could label Rachel's art as passionless; it fairly pulsed with sublimated emotion.

The interested woman had taken out a checkbook and was tearing out the check, she handed it to Rachel, then walked away, beaming, with the painting under her arm.

Rachel took a propped painting from the sidewalk and hung it in the empty space. Turning, she saw Kate.

"Nan!" She came toward Kate, smiling. Her lightly tanned face was lovely, framed by her smooth cap of silver-blond hair. Rachel's black eyes were stunning in contrast to her pale hair and slight, tilted nose, the full lips like a child's, they were so narrow from corner to corner. Under the open collar of the shirt Kate caught a glimpse of the golden chain from which the small star hung. For one startled moment Kate saw the little girl at the airport.

"Nan? Are you all right?" Rachel was bending over her, peering with loving anxiety into her face.

"Of course I am," Kate said calmly. "How could I not

be? It's a glorious day and my granddaughter just sold the Jaffa painting." She put all the gaiety she could into her voice, but she didn't feel all right at all. What had just happened was like some kind of scramble in her brains; she hadn't merely remembered the past. She had been *in* it. "Why?" She went on the offensive, to distract Rachel. "Do I look *that* haggard?"

"You never look haggard, and you know it, you fake." Rachel sat down in the other chair and took her hand. "That's a great dress, by the way. I've never seen anything like it."

Kate glanced down at her dark-blue denim dress. "It's a new 'Kate' experiment. My answer to blue jeans for the geriatric set. I hate the wretched things"—she glanced at Rachel's—"if you'll forgive me. But I notice they wear like iron. I'm going to do this in other colors, too. New Yorkers are going to look like a bunch of farmers in a few years if denim continues to catch on."

"You may be right. I don't like the damned things either," Rachel admitted, "but jeans are great to work in. And they last forever."

Kate was feeling no better, but she made an effort to keep talking. "Joseph said he'd let me do the honors today, since he was here yesterday. He'll be so happy to hear about your sale."

"Actually, it's my *second*."

"Oh, wonderful! And the day's not over." Kate squeezed Rachel's hand.

"It's about time I made some sales. I've felt like such a leech, Nan . . . being the oldest college graduate in the world." Rachel hadn't entered college until she had been back for almost a year, in the summer of 1952; she had dropped out for a long time because of her emotional difficulties and confused goals, then finally got her degree last year, at the "advanced" age of twenty-four.

"Not quite. You're not exactly senile."

"Three years more senile than most people," Rachel countered.

"But you were in Israel for more than a year."

"My calendar's always been different from other people's," Rachel conceded.

Kate smiled. "You've been working up to being young, instead of the other way around. I like the results." She squeezed her granddaughter's narrow shoulder. But she thought: I wish she weren't so solitary, so remote. In that she's like Marite. But at least Rachel has her work to absorb her, not her mother's empty, pathetic fantasies. And she doesn't have a snobbish bone in her body.

An interesting-looking quintet was assembled in front of Rachel's exhibit—three young men, a beautiful black woman holding the hand of a small girl with skin the color of pale mocha. The young woman's classic, thoroughly Anglo-Saxon features were striking in her dark face. Kate felt a desire to paint her. The young men looked very strong; there was a dashing, foreign cast to them.

"Attractive group," Kate murmured.

"Yes. She looks like a Yemenite. I think the men, two of them, anyway, are sabras." Kate was familiar with the nickname for Israelis. Rachel had told her it originated from the name of a desert cactus, which, she said, was "very tough and prickly on the outside, soft and sweet within." Kate had remembered it because the first time she had heard about it, it reminded her of Joseph.

"They certainly look it," she said. One of the men, shorter and more gentle-looking than the other two, had his arm around the lovely dark woman. Presumably he was her husband—or lover, Kate amended, the way things went these days. The second man, who had a strong family resemblance to the short man, was not so deeply tanned. But the third young man, to whom Rachel's glance clung, was apparently not related to the others.

He was astonishingly handsome, Kate thought, with his great height and heavy muscularity. He was tanned as dark as copper, making his reddish-brown hair burn; he had a strongly aquiline nose and a short, neat beard. He reminded Kate of a young conqueror; he had an air of calculated fearlessness. Like Joseph, she decided. Even if he really didn't look like Joseph at all.

And Kate was assailed by another wave of images from the past. Her head ached, and she was suddenly dizzy. For a moment she was looking at Joseph Barsimson on the picket line; not merely recalling it, but actually there. She shook her head, and tried to dispel the vision. There must really be something wrong with me, she decided.

With an enormous effort she focused again on the present, and said lightly to Rachel, "I think I'll run along. It looks like you might have clients."

"Oh, no!" Rachel protested. "You've been out here; you know how it is. People linger and then they go on, mostly. If you go, you'll have gone for nothing. You just got here. If they're really interested, they'll come to me."

Kate knew that very well, but she was feeling so strange she didn't want to get sick right here and ruin Rachel's day. Already the lighter-skinned, American-looking man was starting to wander up Fifth, the couple and child about to follow. But the "handsome warrior," as Kate thought of him, called out, "Shelly . . . Jay. Wait a minute." And he turned and looked at Kate and Rachel.

His eyes were amazing—a rich amber-hazel against the coppery darkness of his skin. Wise, fearless eyes for a man who seemed so young; sad and penetrating. When his look collided with Rachel's, Kate could sense the immediate impact. And she thought: This is what happened the first time Joseph and I looked at each other. She knew this was not an old woman's romantic imagination; it was real. She could feel the shock of discovery emanating from Rachel's smooth hand, still enclosed in her fingers. Kate let the young hand go.

The burnished man walked toward them. "Which one of you ladies is the artist?" His English was faintly accented, that of an expatriate.

"Both of us," Rachel answered at once. "But I'm the one who perpetrated this lot."

The big young man did not smile much but his eyes

glittered. "That's not exactly what I'd call it." Aside from one quick, courteous nod to Kate, he had not taken his eyes off Rachel. Kate glanced aside at her; she seemed quite self-possessed, but Kate, who knew her so well, sensed her tension. "I see two I'd like very much. Could you help me make up my mind?"

"Of course." Rachel was all business. She excused herself to Kate and followed the man to the Israel display. Kate thought: He's very clever. I'll bet he's never had an indecisive moment. And the prices of the paintings were clearly marked. It was an obvious and civilized way to prolong their encounter.

Over the babble of traffic and the conversation of passersby, their talk was inaudible, but Kate saw Rachel wax enthusiastic again, smiling widely when the young man pointed to one painting, then to another.

Smiling to herself, Kate got up and walked away, heading for Eleventh Street. She had a strong feeling that this was not the last she would see of the young giant with the reddish beard and hazel eyes, young and old at the same time. Just like Rachel. And Joseph.

Eager to get home she quickened her pace.

The house was very quiet. Kate found Joseph, as she expected, in the garden. Her rubber-soled shoes were soundless on the kitchen tiles; he hadn't heard her. She stood at the open window looking out at him.

He was sprawled on one of the long chairs, with a discarded book and a portable radio softly playing Vivaldi's *Four Seasons* beside him on the grass. The ancient black-and-white cat Tarf was asleep on Joseph's stomach; the other, ginger-colored Kwan, lay stretched out next to the radio. Both Kwan and Joseph were observing the two new kittens boxing with the thick ivy on Harry Dryver's urn.

Just the way Joseph watched the young men who would take over when he was no longer president of the union . . . soon, maybe. The comparison brought tears to Kate's eyes: sometimes she imagined she saw the same bewilderment in Joseph that she sensed in the cats, whose joints were getting too stiff to leap with the kittens. She went out into the garden.

"Hello! I'm glad to see you." Joseph's wonderful clownish smile transfigured his stately face. "But you'll forgive me if I can't get up." Tarf opened one smug green eye for Kate, as if to comment that it was only right he shouldn't be disturbed.

"I wouldn't dream of it." Kate kissed Joseph and ran her hand over his thick white hair; its vitality and spring belied the apparent languor of his body.

"There's a metaphor here," Joseph said as Kate sat down. "We're watching the new terrorists take over."

The black adopted kittens tore away at the ivy in a frenzy of demonic pleasure.

"They're destroying my vines." Kate was exasperated but she couldn't help laughing at their shining, devilish little eyes. She got up and pulled them gently away from the vines, bringing them back to her chair, where she tried to coax them into her lap. Freed by her left hand, one kitten curled up and stayed; her right hand tingled, and its grip could not be maintained. Her hand wasn't working.

Luckily Joseph hadn't noticed. "That one's a real wigglyworm." The escapee rolled over and over in the grass, fixed by Kwan's disapproving gaze.

Kate and Joseph fell into the familiar silence that had always been companionable. He closed his eyes, listening to the music. But Kate's quiet was born of fear: that was the second time this week that had happened to her hand. And she couldn't dismiss the odd experiences of a little while before, when her memories became more vivid than the living present, as if the clock of her consciousness were broken, and time, as Hamlet had put it, was "out of joint."

Fifty years of time had shot by her like one of those jet planes that barely seemed to move across the sky and yet flew at an incredible rate of speed.

How much time was left to her . . . to them? She glanced

across at Joseph, smiling with closed eyes, enjoying the sound of Vivaldi and, she knew, her silent presence.

She wanted to tell him about her hand, and the frightening memory experience, but she couldn't bear to break the peace. She was not going to tell him at all. Not until she knew for sure that something was wrong. It could simply be nerves. Not that she had much to be nervous about. Joseph had found a certain *modus vivendi* in the new unionism, helped along by the prospect of Jake's future—their seventeen-year-old grandson was already working as a union organizer in the summers and on odd days and nights while he finished high school. The rest of the family was fine. And now Rachel had met that boy; Kate had very positive feelings about him. "Nerves" was a weak explanation.

She and Joseph would celebrate their golden wedding anniversary in the spring. But spring seemed a lifetime away. Kate thought: Our real marriage was Thanksgiving 1909, and it took place in Marie's Café, with that congress of glances, that final commitment of the heart before we ever even touched each other. That was the day to celebrate. And, she decided with a sensation of sudden, paralyzing coldness, she had a better chance of being here for that.

"Joseph?" She steadied her voice to sound casual, easy. "Why can't we have our fiftieth on Thanksgiving, instead of waiting until spring?"

He opened his eyes and examined her face. She smiled to try to hide her fear, but she could feel the smile tremble a little. "It's a unique idea," he said gently. "But why, darling? Are you planning to leave me for a younger man?" His teasing question did not disguise a note of concern. "What's behind all this, Kate?"

"Just a whim." She decided to drop the matter. She had never been able to fool him for very long. "Would you still like to see that Jacques Tati movie? It'll be gone by next weekend."

"Yes, I would. But how about Rachel? Won't she be

coming for dinner?'' Joseph was trying to puzzle out her feelings. She wished she had never brought up the other thing.

"I have an idea she may be very busy tonight."

"Oh? That sounds interesting." Joseph scooped up the kittens and clicked his tongue to the old cats to follow them into the house. While they fed the cats and locked up, Kate told Joseph about the sabra.

At about the time Kate stepped into the garden, the big man with the amber eyes said to Rachel, "You know it all so well. How long were you in Israel?"

His nearness was so disturbing that Rachel barely comprehended the question for a second; she was listening to the resonance of his voice. "A . . . a little more than a year. I was in the Sharon kibbutz."

"I'd never figure you for a kibbutznik." He stared down at her; his eyes looked as tawny as quartz, and as clear and brilliant, with a certain smoky shadow. "The women I ran into had faces like saddles. But of course that was in the—"

"Ben," the taller man called out. "Are you staying? We want to get Tovah to the zoo before it closes."

"Go ahead. I'm going to hang around for a little while."

"Please," Rachel said perfunctorily, "don't let me keep you. I can put those paintings aside for a few days."

"I hate zoos," he said solemnly. "It makes me sick to see the animals prowling, shut up like that. Besides"—his look bored into hers—"I'm very happy to be 'kept' here. I mean, if you don't mind."

"No. No, of course not." Rachel tried to keep cool, but it was very difficult. Her heart thumped in her throat, and she could feel an almost painful magnetism between his bare, tanned, muscular arm and her own slender one. She hadn't ever felt like this about a man, not even Barry. Not even David, during that agonizing phase of her childlike confusion. It was frightening. She had been repressed, wary for so very, very long. And now she felt herself weakening, opening up to this stranger.

To create a diversion, she said quickly, "You were saying, 'that was in' . . . the what?"

"Oh. The Haganah."

"So you fought for Israel." That explained it, then— that look of extreme toughness, that wise expression in his eyes.

"A couple of times." His dismissive tone told her a lot; she had heard that intonation in the voices of men who had been in Korea. The worse it had been, the more reticent they were. "But look here, are you sure it's all right? I don't want to intrude on you. Or some other guy," he added.

He was prodding. It delighted her. "There's no 'other guy,' except my cousins, who helped me set up." Rachel smiled and saw his look drop to her mouth.

When he looked up again, his eyes were bright. "That's great, even if it's hard to believe."

She felt her face heat. "Let's sit down, shall we?" Leading the way to the canvas chairs, she saw that her grandmother was gone. "Oh, dear."

"What's the matter?" His concern was instant.

"Nothing, really." Rachel sat down. As he sat down beside her, she noticed for the first time the big, slick, pink scar on his left knee, below the khaki of his Bermuda shorts. The scar was blatant, measured against the tough coppery skin of his powerful leg.

He caught her glance. "I got that in Sharm-el-Sheikh. I hope it doesn't . . . turn you off," he added with boyish openness.

She knew she was flushing now. "No. *No*. How could it?" Realizing what she had said, her embarrassment grew. "I mean, it's a badge of honor, isn't it? You were with Dayan, then." Even during the depths of her depression years she had still read everything she could about Israel. Even when she couldn't paint it, it had never left her mind.

"Oh, yes." He looked away from her for an instant, a faraway expression in his eyes. "It was incredible. The Egyptians had all the numbers, all the equipment. But they didn't have a Moshe Dayan." Ben's glance returned to her, and he said, "You're pretty knowledgeable about it."

"I've . . . kept up."

"You love Israel, don't you?" He moved his big arm abruptly, and the warm, tough skin brushed hers. She felt the contact in the very depths of her body.

"Yes. I always will."

"When did you leave, Rachel?" His abrupt use of her first name startled her into wider warmth. It was suddenly an acceptance of intimacy between them, almost a commitment to it. "*Why* did you leave?"

"Because of death . . . even between the 'real' wars. Because of the 'little wars.' " Her quotes were bitter.

He leaned toward her. "You lost someone, then. I thought so."

"Why do you say that?"

"You're not wearing a ring. When I first laid eyes on you, I knew a woman like you had to have *been* married, somewhere along the line."

His comment almost disappointed her. This sounded like the usual prelude to seduction. She moved away from him.

But he sensed her withdrawal. He was very perceptive, she thought, a quality she valued. Maybe she had made a snap judgment. She was sure of that when he spoke.

"You still didn't answer my question. Something's been bothering you."

He sounded as if it mattered to him. "I was a little worried about my grandmother. She didn't seem well today. And then she just disappeared."

"The beautiful old lady who was sitting here with you. Would you like me to look around? Which direction would she have taken?" Ben started to get up.

"Oh, no. I don't think that's necessary. Kate Barsimson

doesn't like being looked for," Rachel said with wry affection.

Ben settled down again. "Kate Barsimson? The painter. Good Lord. I've seen her work all over. As a matter of fact, I could swear I saw some of yours in Israel, in Tel Aviv. Did I?"

She nodded. "I studied under Ari Reisel's assistant, and we had a few students' exhibits." Rachel was relaxing, beginning to feel open and confiding. "It runs in the family. My great-great-grandfather was Harry Dryver."

Ben looked impressed. "Some family. I saw a Dryver in Paris." For the first time he really smiled, and it lightened the craggy fierceness of his face. "I feel as if I know all of you." She could feel a quality of gentleness in him; some of her tension loosened. She leaned back in the chair, and they didn't talk for a while. A transistor carried by a passing girl emitted a glowing wave of Mozart.

"Nice," Ben remarked. "I'm getting a bellyful of rock-and-roll."

"I've *had* one." She grinned. Fewer people were lingering in front of her paintings. The sky was turning gray. "Uh-oh."

Ben followed her upward glance. "Think you'd better pack up?"

She nodded.

"I'll help you."

"Oh, please . . . it's okay. My cousins will be showing up pretty soon."

"Maybe not soon enough." He was already on his feet. He must have been an officer in the Haganah; he seemed to take it for granted that his suggestions were orders. But she submitted thankfully, admiring the delicate speed with which he dismantled her little show, the care he used in handling the paintings and wrapping them. He hoisted a half-dozen at once, holding the rope with one huge hand; then he picked up the others. She was thrilled by the strength of his arms. "Where to?" he asked her matter-of-factly.

"My car's right down there." She pointed, and he walked off with his burden, as casually as if he were carrying so many sheets of paper. When she unlocked her compact car he stored the paintings carefully in the rear. "Where to now?"

"I usually store them at my grandparents' house . . . on Eleventh Street. I live over on Bank, and it's easier."

"I'll give you a hand. May I?"

She stifled her perfunctory refusal. It would be O.K. Her arrangements with her cousins were always casual. "I'd like that." His eyes gleamed at her; he looked inordinately pleased.

Rachel was uncomfortably aware of his big body's closeness while she drove slowly down Ninth Street and turned onto Sixth Avenue, turning again to crawl along Twelfth, back to Fifth again before she could get back onto Eleventh. To cover her unease, she said lightly, "Anybody who drives in New York *has* to be crazy."

"It helps." She wondered how long he had been back in the States; there was an underlying intonation of New York. She started to ask him, but there wasn't time. She was pleased to find a parking place right next to the house.

Ben laughed when she offered to carry some of the paintings. "My *gun* was heavier than this." She glanced at him, noticing that he seemed chagrined, perhaps for bringing up such a brutal subject. To help him out, she said quickly, "I don't think anybody's home. But that's all right. I have a key."

She let them into the basement entrance and led him through the kitchen to a little adjacent storeroom that had been cleared for her paintings. Ben set them down with the same tender care he had taken from the first. "Leave them wrapped?"

"Yes. Fine."

"Well, he*llo*!" The cats were trickling in, in their liquid fashion. Ben squatted down to pet them. "Hey, these are *old* fellas, aren't they?" His touch was feathery on the animals' bodies, utterly tender. Rachel's heart turned over. The cats were rubbing against Ben's hand, then his leg. There was a sudden patter of minuscule claws against the tiles, like the percussion of tiny beads on the softness of the floor; the kittens made a dashing entrance.

"Well, look at this." Ben grinned with pleasure, and lifted the kittens to his hard, bent legs. They wriggled at the confinement and he let them go, still smiling.

"You like cats," she said softly, studying the pleasant picture.

"I *love* them. I could never have them in Israel . . . not where I was. That's the first thing I'm going to get when I'm living somewhere again."

She wondered about that cryptic statement, but she was silent, filled with new warm feelings for him. She stooped down and petted the old cats, making a playful grab for the kittens. They eluded her, skittering off across the gleaming linoleum tiles, losing their balance and rolling over, righting themselves again.

Rachel stood up. "Please let me give you a drink, or some coffee. You deserve some payment for all that work." Then she thought: That was a leading comment.

But he didn't take her up on it at all, as some men might have. She was beginning to believe that he was not "some man," that he was different from any man she had known, outside her family, even men she had met in Israel.

"No, thanks. Not right now." Her heart sank. He must have a date with someone later. She had probably been reading too much into his attention. Maybe he was just a kind, friendly person who didn't mind helping people.

But in the very next moment he proved her wrong. "I was thinking of having an early dinner," he said tentatively. "Would you . . . join me?"

Her heart thudded again. "I'd love to."

His look of pleasure dissolved her doubts. He seemed to think it was an enormous favor. "That's wonderful." Those amazing amber eyes were boring into hers again. "Do you know a place you like, where we can go in this gear?"

"Lots of places."

When they came up to the street again, he said, "Just a

minute. Do you mind?'' She followed him to the little burying ground. "Every time I pass Eleventh Street, I stop by here," he confided. Once again his openness, so at variance with his heavy dignity, the sad wisdom of his eyes, moved her. They stood together staring at the ancient stones behind the low wall.

Ben was peering at one of the stones. "Is that 'Barsimson'?'' he asked her, sounding excited. "I never saw that before."

"Yes. One of my grandfather's ancestors is here." Their shoulders touched; she had a strong desire to move even closer to him.

"My people are Sephardim too." He started. "I haven't even told you my name. It's Sforza. Ben Sforza."

"How do you do, Mr. Sforza." She put out her hand to shake his, glad of the excuse.

He held her hand tightly in his. "Rachel, I'm Ben."

She looked up at him, hearing the rain-bringing wind begin to stir the trees above them. Astonished, she realized she wanted him to kiss her, right this minute. She wondered if he knew that, and drew back a trifle, slipping her hand slowly from his grasp. "Shall we go? If you've been thinking of dinner, you must be starved by now."

She couldn't let him know how much she felt. Not yet. But she had a feeling he had read her eyes, because he murmured, "I'm not that hungry. But lead on."

She headed toward Sixth Avenue and he followed close beside her, with their arms brushing again. Rachel had a feeling he wanted to hold her hand as much as she wanted him to, but was inhibited by control as she was by shyness. "Do you like Italian food?"

"I love it. I can't get enough of American food." They both laughed. In New York, Chinese and Italian, she supposed, were American food. "Chinese is too Jewish. And I've had enough corn and *falafel* to last me a lifetime."

As they walked down Sixth Avenue, he asked, "Where is it, exactly?"

"On MacDougal. Maybe you know it. Allegro's."

"It's still there!" She saw him smile, glancing at the brightly lit confusion of Eighth Street. "God, Eighth looks like Coney Island now. Let's walk on down Sixth, okay?"

"Gladly." Rachel didn't like Eighth Street on the weekends, either. The crowds of young tourists from New Jersey and the other New York neighborhoods hung out there in wild-eyed bunches, many of them smoking pot, carrying their perpetual blaring transistors. It was darker, quieter, more peaceful farther down. A delicate drizzle began to fall.

"Oh, this is nice." Ben lifted his head. "This is New York for me. The little rain, the lights shining."

He told her he had been away ten years. That meant he had fought in both wars. "You were born in New York," Rachel guessed.

"East New York. Brooklyn," he added, seeing her blank look. "A very tough neighborhood. Jay and Shelly— those guys with me this afternoon—and I used to fend off the Irish and Italian kids together. A strange neighborhood for big-deal Sephardim. We were the 'poor branch.' "

"So was my grandfather." Rachel felt a strong kinship with Ben. "Who was that beautiful girl with you . . . Shelly's wife? She looks like a Yemenite."

Ben chuckled. "That's what they always thought in Israel. They lived on a kibbutz for a while, but they hated it. She was Ruby Johnson, from Chicago. Her brother's Lightning Johnson, the boxer. But what about *you*? We haven't talked about you at all. What made you give up the kibbutz, Rachel?"

"It's a long, long story. Mainly, I guess, because it just wasn't for me. I think I'm a city person." They were on MacDougal now and he slowed his steps, staring down at her intently.

"What do you think of Arizona?" he asked abruptly.

"Arizona? I've never been there. Talk about *relevance*," she teased him. But he wasn't smiling. "Why do you ask?"

He gave her another mysterious look. "That's a long

story, too. Let's have dinner.'' They went into the merry, casual restaurant; he put his big hand lightly on the small of her back, and she reacted at once to the faint, respectful touch of his strong, warm fingers. While they were being seated she noticed that the other diners were staring at them, some of the women with frank admiration. Ben was so big and ruddy and imposing, he made the other men seem small and pale, insignificant.

He was staring only at her, across the table. He made quick business of ordering, seeming eager to get it out of the way, because he said, ''Now. What *about* you, Rachel? We've had enough of me. Were you born here, too?''

''No. In Germany. In 1933.'' Embarrassed to be in the spotlight, she put both her hands around her water glass, playing with it. He reached over and gently uncurled her fingers, took one of her hands in his. She felt a hot aching, sudden and narrow, shoot up her arm from her wrist.

''That was a hell of a time for a Jew to be born in Germany,'' he said softly.

''Except that I'm not really a Jew.'' And she told him all of it—the kidnapping of her mother, her mother's marriage to that unknown German, the internment in Sachsenhausen, and her grandparents' subsequent failure to find out more.

''Berlin and Zürich, London and New York. No wonder you're a city person.'' Ben's eyes were tender.

Their food and wine arrived. Rachel took a swallow of Chianti, eyeing the food with indifference. She had no desire to go on with the rest of her biography with this good-looking stranger. And yet that stranger's touch had set off such wild, outrageous feelings. ''Do you plan to go back to soldiering?''

His eyes darkened. The lightness of her voice had distanced them again. ''No way. I'm an engineer by trade, and now I'm going to build things instead of blowing them up for a change. I've had enough death for a lifetime.''

The remark made them both laugh, and she felt herself relaxing, floating back to a kind of closeness to him.

Her appetite returned and they ate with enjoyment, the talk easier, more impersonal. She was impressed by his wide-ranging knowledge, surprised that such a tough and massive man had a passion for chamber music. And she enjoyed telling him about the changes in New York.

"Some of them I can do without," she said. "Rhinelander Gardens, for instance." She had always loved the New Orleans-style Rhinelander mansion on Eleventh Street, across the avenue from her grandparents', with its wrought-iron balconies. It had been converted into apartments, and on summer evenings a creative cacophony emerged from the windows—sopranos and typewriters, clarinets, actors projecting lines in rehearsal.

"They're tearing it *down*?" Ben was dismayed. "I always liked that place, from the time I was a kid. The first time I ever read a play by Tennessee Williams, I figured it had to be set right there."

"I'm such a sentimentalist," she confided, "that I wanted to get some kind of . . . souvenir. But all the rubble looked so *heavy*."

"Come on." He got to his feet. "Let's go get something right now." He left some bills on the table.

"You're crazy!" She laughed. "But nice crazy."

They found an old man wandering the rubble-scattered yard before the gutted mansion. "Did you live here?" he asked Rachel dolefully.

"No, but I've always loved it."

"I was the super here since 1935," the old man told them. He sounded very sad. "Here, take something. They're just going to throw it all away. Just throw it all away." He lifted a heavy baluster from among the rubble, a lovingly carved, fine piece of nineteenth-century work. He handed it to Ben.

Ben thanked him solemnly. They said good night to the sad old man and walked away. "Where should this be delivered?" Ben asked Rachel.

"Bank Street. Oh, thank you. This is marvelous." She was immensely moved by the whole thing—Ben's love for the old building, his desire to do this sentimental thing for her. And his enormous gentleness and strength—as they strolled west, she noticed, as before, that he held the heavy baluster in one hand without effort.

She felt very nervous, unlocking her door. What would happen now? She wondered if he would think the "delivery" was a ploy to get him into her apartment.

"Just put it anywhere," she said with tense, false brightness when they were inside. He set the object down, looked around her living room, and murmured, "Your place is lovely."

He straightened up and stood there, staring down at her. The very air between them sang. Then he said, surprising her, "It's far too early to end this evening. Maybe you feel like going to a movie."

"Yes. Yes, I'd like that." She knew he had been about to kiss her, and she was puzzled.

And strangely relieved. There was a depth in this attraction that could deepen with postponement. Besides, she was afraid. It had been so long; she feared her own awkwardness.

She could almost see his knowledge of her in his tender scrutiny; that quick, mysterious understanding that dazzled her, making her sense that this would be no light encounter.

Chapter 32

"Rachel, Rachel. This has been the longest two weeks of my life." Ben's arms tightened around her. She pressed her face against him, her skin singing with the resonance of his growling baritone. She stroked his bare, hair-roughened chest and he made a humming pleasure-sound.

"And to think you hadn't even kissed me, until tonight." She sensed his quick reaction to the tickle of her moving lips on his flesh; his big, hard hand traced the slender, naked curve of her.

"I didn't dare. I knew I wouldn't want to stop with kissing you."

"I knew I wouldn't either." She raised her hand, outlining the shape of his firm, handsome mouth with her fingers. He kissed the fingers and they lay for a time in happy stillness. Bank Street was very quiet, so quiet Rachel could hear their own breathing. Then a small breeze began to stir the old trees' branches outside her window; the bright silver of the full autumn moon dusted the leaves with its silver.

"We had this appointment from the beginning," he whispered.

She smiled at the variation of the line from Tennessee Williams. "I know. I knew it from the first."

"And I was so afraid of scaring you away." He made a move as if about to rise, and she started to move backward to release him. "No." His hard arm tightened around her. "Don't go away. I'm not going to let you go now." His tone was serious. She moved toward him again and lay against him, enjoying the play of his muscles as he reached over beside the bed for cigarettes. With one hand he shook a cigarette out for her, put it between his lips, and lit it before taking his. He set an ashtray on his flat, muscle-knotted stomach and leaned back to expel gray smoke, still holding her.

"How good this tastes." She smiled, exhaling. "I feel like all my senses just came to me."

It was true. Her whole body—bone and blood and nerve and muscle—seemed to have a tingling aliveness that she hadn't felt since she was a child.

He had been tender with her beyond all words, brought her to a pleasure-place that had been unimaginable. What had happened with Ben made those frenzies of long ago no more than the lurid nightmares of an instant. Their pleasure had been so close, so deep, her skin felt burnished with it now.

And suddenly she recognized, with a kind of terror, that she would not be able to live without him anymore.

"My little Spanish pilgrim." He kissed her on her head. She took the ashtray from him and put out her cigarette; he tamped out his. Replacing the tray, he turned her in his arms so that their bodies faced, pressing her to him, caressing her face and head and neck, her back and haunches.

"Rachel, Rachel. You've got to know I want you to come with me to Arizona.

"Oh, Ben. Oh, Ben." She kissed his neck; there was a quick, strong pounding beat below his ear.

"Will you Rachel? Will you?" His hands were hard and urgent on her back; she felt his tension.

She began to cry with utter happiness.

"Don't cry, don't cry." He kissed the top of her head. "If you're crying, you can't answer me. And I want an answer. Will you let me take you away from all this to the desert of Arizona?'' He was trying to tease her out of crying, she knew, but the question was very earnest.

"Yes. Yes, I will.''

She could feel how overjoyed he was by the way he held her.

At last, at last, she exulted, I belong to someone.

The morning when Kate's hand started to tingle, and her sure brush stroke went completely out of control and wiggled across the canvas, she knew it was time.

Time to check out of her fool's paradise and find out what was wrong. Whatever she was told, she would have to face it.

Nevertheless, she was quite worried when she entered the reception room of Dr. Lester Margolies, the specialist her own doctor had sent her to see.

She was relieved to find that there was no one else in the room. She gave her name to the receptionist and sat down in a chair by the window to look out at Washington Square. The memory of the happy hours she had spent there with Joseph, so long ago, was like a fist against her heart.

Restlessly she got up and went to the table bearing magazines. Their bright colors were meaningless; the topics they offered were cruel in their irony. How to live to be ninety, new resort fashions for the winter. She might not live to see seventy, or see another December.

But that was useless morbidity. She still didn't *know*.

A pleasant middle-aged nurse poked her head around the alcove arch. "Mrs. Barsimson?''

Kate nodded tensely.

"Dr. Margolies will be right with you.''

Kate thanked her and continued to pace. Her agitated gaze wandered over the walls and stopped.

One of her own city scenes, perfectly lit, was hung on the opposite wall.

"Mrs. Barsimson?''

A man's voice this time, rumbling and calm, Russian-accented. She turned her head and saw the white-haired old man with thick features and sleepy-lidded eyes. It was hard to credit that he was one of the best neurologists in the East, until she noticed the compassionate sharpness of his scrutiny.

He smiled, uncovering a jumble of tobacco-darkened teeth. "I see you are admiring my gallery." His ponderous consonants retarded the words. "It is a pleasure to meet the artist herself, at last."

Kate gave him a courteous smile, but it seemed to her that Margolies' greeting was very calculated, like a lollipop offered to a frightened child; his keen look already diagnosed her.

"Please, come in, come in," he murmured easily, and she followed him reluctantly into an imposing office.

He stood by his desk and invited her gently to sit down. "Make yourself comfortable. Do smoke if you wish, and so shall I." He smiled at her companionably, noting the eagerness with which she took out her case and lighter before he could offer her the leather box on his desk.

Margolies sat down with a sigh and lit his own cigarette. He blew out a cloud of smoke with apparent gratification, and said, "Well, now. It astonishes me, you know, that I never met you before, admiring your work as I do."

She murmured uneasily, wondering if he were postponing some horrible disclosure.

"I have other work of yours at the hospital, and in my home."

In spite of herself, Kate felt a slight relaxation. Perhaps he was wise, after all, to begin this way. "How nice," she said. "Which ones?"

He described them. "Doctors are human too," he confided suddenly, showing his stained smile. "And I must admit that you are a very special patient." She noticed that he glanced at her hands.

"Thank you." She was afraid she was going to cry at any moment. This was infinitely more reassuring than she had expected; at least he was a close friend of Dr. Segal's and he had a particular interest. Absurd as it might be, it made her feel less desolate, less lonely. And she knew that Margolies knew that.

"You have come without your husband," he said abruptly.

"He doesn't know." Margolies studied her sharply. "Or rather, he might suspect, but I haven't told him."

"You are a very brave woman. Now," Margolies added in a brisk tone, putting out his cigarette and taking up a folder in his long-fingered hands. "Dr. Segal has given me an excellent preliminary report . . . together with a relevant personal history." Those old, keen eyes looked up at her again.

Margolies was hardly much older than she, but his tone was so fatherly and encouraging that before she was aware of it she was pouring out almost her entire history. It was an astonishing relief to talk about it; she rarely talked about herself at all, and she could feel her trembling abate.

He nodded now and then, studying her as he leaned back in his chair with his long hands folded over his chest, asking her to go on when she hesitated.

"So," he said gently after she finished, "during these last years, in particular, you have subjected yourself to an almost intolerable burden of guilt and atonement, after the loss of your daughter." There was nothing reproachful in his comment. "You have worn your guilt for years, like a blue number on your arm." He shook his silver head. "I understand, I understand so well, Mrs. Barsimson. One of my relatives died in Sachsenhausen, others in camps in Russia and Poland." He had a faraway look for an instant; then he returned to the present with a start.

"Now, today I think we should give you an EEG." He said reassuringly when she looked startled, "It is nothing to fear." He explained the process to her. "If you will just step into that examining room. The nurse will take care of your things for you."

To her surprise, Margolies conducted the examination himself; she had understood that it was usually a routine matter conducted by a technician. She tried to read his expression but it was perfectly blank.

"If you'll kindly wait for me in my office . . . after you've put yourself back together." He smiled paternally at her stocking feet and her head, from which the nurse was removing the apparatus. He stood with his back to her, then, intently examining the paper that rolled from the machine.

Kate sat in the chair by his desk; her heart thudded sickeningly in her ears and her palms were moist with fear.

She turned and saw him enter. She was hoping to see him look reassuring. He did not. Her heart gave a frightened thump and the weakness of dread crawled over her legs and arms.

Margolies sat down at his desk and looked at her over his glasses. "I believe we've found the culprit."

"What is it?" she asked shakily.

"The tests and other factors indicate the presence of a tiny lesion on the left side of your brain, Mrs. Barsimson. Or rather that is my conclusion, you see, based on my long experience with these difficulties." His voice was gentle and calm; he seemed to be choosing his words with care to try to lessen her terror, which, she felt, must be naked in her eyes.

"However, we cannot be sure without exploratory surgery."

She was too appalled to answer. But finally she managed to ask, and her voice came out in a squeak, "What . . . *caused* this? I've never had any injuries or . . ."

"Extreme mental stress can cause this difficulty."

Kate covered her eyes with her hand. "I realize there's . . . a risk in surgery, especially at my age." She marveled that her voice was so steady now, and she saw a melancholy admiration in his eyes. "What will happen if I . . . don't have it?"

"Within the next two to five years your present symptoms will worsen. You will lose the use of your hands entirely and there will be great lapses in your memory."

He spoke with such reluctance that she could feel his deep compassion.

"No brain, no life at all." Her voice sounded high and pained and angry to herself; she was fighting not to break down.

"I'm sorry. I'm truly sorry, Mrs. Barsimson. In all the years of my practice it has never become easier to tell a patient something like this. Naturally, you may want to see another doctor . . . or as many as you wish. I encourage you to do that. But my own feeling is that surgery is the answer. There is every chance that after surgery, you will be as good as new." He smiled at her for the first time since he had come into the office, and she felt the stirring of hope.

"It would be an utter waste of time to see another doctor," she said with an ease that astonished her. "Dr. Segal told me you're the best."

He retorted, sounding immensely human, "I'd like to be better. We still have a long way to go in these matters. I told you—it is highly unprofessional of me, but you are a very special patient, Mrs. Barsimson." He sounded almost abashed. "You are a magnificient woman." He cleared his throat.

"And you're a magnificent doctor." He bowed his head once and they studied each other. "Will you . . . perform the surgery yourself?"

"Of course, if you wish me to. I will be honored. I have performed this procedure many, many times, and in almost every case with perfect success."

"It's the 'almost' that bothers me."

Her grim humor made him smile. "There is never any perfect guarantee. It would be wrong of me to give you one. But I strongly urge you to have it done, my dear lady. It is your best hope, in my opinion."

She hesitated. Then she sighed and asked, "How soon?"

"As soon as possible. Naturally, you will want to discuss this with your husband."

Poor Joseph. She dreaded telling him, more than she

dreaded the operation itself. "Yes. Yes, of course." Then she added with dark flippancy, "I'd like to be in shape for my granddaughter's wedding."

She caught a glint of respect and exasperation, too, in the heavy-lidded eyes. "God. A *wedding.*" She almost laughed in the midst of her anxiety and wretchedness; he was obviously picturing a huge, orchestrated affair. "What are you *saying*?"

"I'm not talking about the Temple Emanuel, with eight bridesmaids and flying doves." Kate had not ceased to be amazed at her ability to keep talking like this, but somehow it relieved her enormously. "I'm talking about a small, quiet affair at the Brotherhood Synagogue, with an even smaller reception afterward. Everything's almost done, anyway."

He smiled. "The Brotherhood Synagogue. Ah, yes. The one on Thirteenth Street, where the synagogue shares the premises with a Presbyterian Church. Most interesting, very unique."

Kate knew quite well he was chatting with her as a purely therapeutic device, and she liked him for it.

He asked her with anxious abruptness, "Are you feeling a bit better now? I know this had to be an awful shock."

"Yes. I am."

"If you'd like to have a cup of coffee . . . sit awhile in one of the rooms before you go . . ." he began delicately.

"No. No, thank you," she added. She rose a bit unsteadily but straightened her shoulders, and saw him notice that as well. She found his sharp perception very reassuring.

He got up too, and walked with her to the door. "May I expect, then, to hear from you soon, so I may make the arrangements?" His voice was gentler than ever.

She nodded. "Very soon."

Kate felt her shoulders slump when she left the building. She caught sight of herself, reflected in a polished window, and straightened her back again. At first she had been glad she could drop the gallant pose which had held her together, thinking it must be like taking off a girdle—which, thank God, she had never had to wear.

But now she would have to assume it again, for Joseph. Keep it up until after the operation was over.

She walked east past Washington Square, seeking the sparser pedestrian traffic on Fifth Avenue, fighting the tears that gushed to her eyes, blurring her vision.

This might be the last time she would have with Joseph: one of the last times she would walk up Fifth Avenue, look up its blue-gray vista telescoping to the north, narrowing into the castles of Manhattan. The city that for her was the enchanted city, whose scenes she had painted for so many years, whose streets she had walked with Joseph.

Extreme stress, Margolies had said.

"You have worn your guilt for years, like a blue number on your arm." That tragic poetry struck her deeply now. It was true. So had Joseph, but he was much stronger.

Thank God he was stronger. There could still be years of life left for him. And her years, now, were just so much roulette.

It isn't fair. It isn't fair, her mind shouted.

But it was just. Eminently just: her life for Marite's.

Grim, perfect justice that the years of guilt, and then the years of battling for the life of Rachel, should rub this fatal sore upon her brain.

She was paid in full.

Joseph leaned forward when the cab slowed up at Eleventh Street and Fifth Avenue. "Go on a couple of blocks, would you? Down there by the arch."

His sudden urge was too strong to be withstood. He had to take another look at the old Asch Building, where the Triangle had been. His head still jangled with the meeting, the talk of expansion, promotion, and public relations. Sometimes the union business reminded him of Madison Avenue. Or Wall Street.

He had looked down at the trousers of his Brooks Brothers suit, his polished English shoes, and seen the baggy pants and worn shoes he had worn in 1909. Nostalgia ached in him.

When the taxi released him, Joseph got out and walked eastward, remembering how unconscious he had been of movement those long years ago. Now he could feel his tired bones and muscles fairly creaking, like rusty gears.

The old building loomed ahead. Gray now, not white. But smoothed, renewed several times. Hard to believe the fire had ever taken place, even if he had dreamed about it until long after World War I.

What a world, where world wars had numbers, like wings of buildings. With the bombs they had now, they might as well not bother with World War III.

Joseph moved his shoulders as if to physically shake off the awesome darkness of that notion.

"Oh. Sorry." A tall boy in jeans and a herringbone jacket, with his arm around a girl's waist, had cannoned into him.

Pleased to receive an apology, Joseph smiled. "Okay, son." The boy and girl strode on with matching steps. Her long, untidy hair streamed down her shapely little back; her blue jeans, under a brief jacket, curved snugly around her hips and blatantly outlined her buttocks.

God, Joseph thought, where have the women gone? He remembered their enticing, mysterious curves in the long fitted jackets, the ankle-length skirts of the old days. They still curved, but without enticement or mystery.

He had a sudden vision of Kate that first day on the line, on this very street where he now stood. The sap had sprung in him then! Now he was just standing here, staring and dreaming like a lobotomized old relic. A few minutes ago he had been ready to take a sentimental stroll through the square and on to MacDougal Street past the old flat. One of those beatniks probably lived there now. The plan had no appeal. As Ben said, MacDougal *and* Eighth were getting more and more like Forty-second Street. Or Coney Island.

It was heartening to recall Ben. Joseph smiled. Now,

that was a *mensch*. He was going to make Rachel very happy. She absolutely glowed now, and they weren't even married yet. With Rachel so happy, he had thought that Kate would be too. But the last few days she had had an almost haunted look. She was sweeter, gentler than ever. But it occurred to him she hadn't laughed for days and days, and she was always so full of infectious, good-natured laughter.

Joseph had put it down to preoccupation with the wedding. Kate had always thrown herself so single-mindedly into every new project. And he had been preoccupied himself, with the union, and with Jake. That boy was a natural. He had put the *cojones*, as the Spanish kids said nowadays, back into the union.

Joseph asked himself abruptly: What the hell am I doing here, moaning about how everything has changed, when everything that means anything is waiting for me right now on Eleventh Street? A sentimental stroll was empty, idiotic without Kate. She was so much a part of him that he felt like an amputee when she wasn't beside him.

He wheeled around and walked back toward Fifth, heading uptown.

Good God. Maybe something was wrong with her. Something physical. Joseph's heart gave a knock and palpitated. If anything happened to her . . . Life was unimaginable without her. As long as she opened the door for him, and he could see her smiling at him, the world would still revolve. Otherwise . . . No, he couldn't even imagine it. He couldn't bear to.

The city and the streets, the people and the buildings, even the union movement had all changed, were now alien to him. Only Kate was the repository of his lifelong hopes and dreams. She still shared them with him. There was absolutely no one else who could. Not even his son, his grandsons and granddaughter, as dear as they were. They were just too new; they didn't know.

Only Kate could know, because she shared his dreams. She *was* his dream. And he had kept her waiting for him while he stood like a fool on an alien corner, trying to understand an alien time.

Impulsively he turned onto Eighth Street and went into one of the finer jewelry stores. He couldn't really *tell* her all she meant to him. But he could pay for some fine, imaginative craftsman to deliver his message. He saw a beautiful diamond ring, glittering and intricate, shaped somewhere between a snowflake and a star.

Both were appropriate. The first gift he had given her had been the star of his people, the star on the flag of Israel. And they had declared their love for each other, that night in the glittering snow that fell on Eleventh Street, on the little burial ground where an ancient Barsimson lay. She was so sensitive, so quick, she would perceive and be touched by the symbolism.

Joseph bought the ring, paying with a credit card, and slipped the little velvet box into his pocket. At the corner he bought a dozen yellow roses—even if her hair were not that color now, he always thought of her that way—and hurried up Fifth to Eleventh Street.

His heart was high when she opened the door to him, smiling.

"Oh, Joseph, I'm so glad you're home." She hugged him before she even noticed the roses, and he felt an overpowering wave of emotion. She had always told him, during their poor years, that he was her gift.

He held her with one arm and kissed her.

When he let her go she saw the roses. "How *beautiful.*" She held them in the crook of her arm while she brought him his drink. He tossed off his hat and sat down on the couch to enjoy the cold, tart flavor of his drink, and the sight of her arranging the roses in a blue-green Rockwood vase, one of the old Wendell treasures. The vase was the color of her dress. She and the room and the flowers were so beautiful. Like a defiant declaration. "No matter what the world does," she had often said, "we must always keep our private dream."

"Sit by me," he urged her softly. Smiling, she brought

her wine with her and sat down close beside him on the couch. He reached into his pocket and brought out the small velvet box, handing it to her in silence.

Opening the lid, she gave a little gasp. "Oh, Joseph. Joseph." She whispered, then, "It's like a snowflower. A *star*flower." She looked up at him with wide, young-looking eyes and his heart turned over. He had known so well that she would know why he had bought this particular ring.

She slipped the ring from the box and, glancing at its tiny circle, put it on the little finger of her right hand, a finger it seemed made for. She observed its delicate glitter again and then looked back at him. "We think the same thoughts, Joseph." She took his face in her hands and kissed him. "I can't tell you how this *touches* me."

He put his arm around her. Slowly he began to tell her about his little walk to the Triangle, and all his recent thoughts. As he spoke, she stroked his chest. "I was so worried, all of a sudden. About you, Kate. You've been so . . . different lately. I had the feeling you've been keeping something from me. Have you?"

She was silent, tensing in his embrace.

"*Have* you?" He pressed her shoulder with rough anxiety.

"Yes." Joseph felt her body resign, softly, and lean against him, as she said, "And now I know I must tell you."

Joseph kept one arm around her, covering his face with the other hand. Right then he remembered vividly the first time he had been knocked unconscious in the ring. It was nearly sixty years ago, but he could feel it physically—as if his head were being knocked right off his shoulders, with a stunning, tooth-jarring impact. He was even slumping a little forward.

Her hand caressed his back and he came to his senses. Hot chagrin showered his body. She was the one who faced that terror. If ever he had beén a rock to her, he must be one now.

He straightened and gathered her close to him.

"I hated, I *hated* to tell you," Kate murmured against him. The muffled words flayed.

"I wish you had told me from the very start. To think that you went through all that alone . . ."

"Oh, Joseph, I wanted to do that, at least, for you. To spare you all the extra days and nights of worry."

" 'That'?" he demanded. "*That*?" He made a dismal attempt at a smile. "What do you think you've been doing for me, a half-hundred years? You've given me all the . . . all the beauty and happiness I've ever known. Oh, Kate. Kate." He hugged her closer and said desperately, "I wish I could *express* it. Even when I told you you make my heart 'dance like the rams,' those were another man's words."

She was silent, but her hands spoke softly to him, loving, accepting.

"That's why I bought the ring, you see. I thought it would be like giving you a . . . little poem that I couldn't write, or say."

She moved out of his arms and grasped him gently by the chin, pulling his face to hers to kiss him. When she opened her eyes, they were wet and shining.

"I knew that, as soon as I saw it. It was our star, all over again; it was that Christmas, and the snow. A flowering of the snow and the star, a flower that will last forever."

"I loved you from the minute I saw you, Kate. But now love seems an inadequate word for the way I feel. You'll come through, Kate. You'll *have* to. You always have. If you . . . didn't"—his voice shook, and he steadied it with effort—"I wouldn't either. I told you what I was thinking, when I was coming home to you—as long as you're here to open the door, and smile at me, the world will keep on turning."

She was looking down with a small, wistful smile. He had a sudden ache to see her eyes.

As gently as he knew how, he lifted her chin.

Those blue, unchanging eyes, that still looked like the summer sky to him, were hopeful, shining.

He felt so thankful, so relieved it hurt. He had found the words, the way to keep that light in those beloved eyes. He had given her a whole new goal, a solemn challenge—to survive for him. Joseph knew her, through and through. She wanted to come through, more than anything, for him. And the poignancy of that brought quick, stinging tears into his eyes.

He had given her the same courage she had always brought to him—the hope that had been the thrust of both their lives. That very hope would increase her chances a thousandfold.

Unquenchable, it had sparkled to him from the Star of David he had given her years ago; from the "starflower" she now wore on her slender hand. And from her constant, loving eyes.

About the Author

The Constant Star is the author's debut novel as Patricia Strother. She has published eighteen others under various pseudonyms, ranging from astrological fiction (which she invented) to historicals, family sagas, and romances. An Alabama native, Ms. Strother began writing at the age of ten, and initially published as a poet and short-story writer. After college in Tennessee, her occupations included radio and TV announcing and writing, a stint for a New York weekly newspaper, and a twenty-year career with a New York labor union. Ms. Strother lives with her husband, Bob, and their four cats, in New York's Greenwich Village, where she now writes full-time.

By the year 2000, 2 out of 3 Americans could be illiterate.

It's true.

Today, 75 million adults...about one American in three, can't read adequately. And by the year 2000, U.S. News & World Report envisions an America with a literacy rate of only 30%.

Before that America comes to be, you can stop it...by joining the fight against illiteracy today.

Call the Coalition for Literacy at toll-free **1-800-228-8813** and volunteer.

Volunteer Against Illiteracy. The only degree you need is a degree of caring.